HOW TO BORROW A DOG

T M Kirchner

ISBN:
978-0-9876282-1-3

The
Pleasure
Recycling
Co.
TM
Est. When you stopped using it.

Sam sits on a large rock a third of the way down the steep hill puffing heavily. Twice she's nearly turned her ankle in pursuit of Hasta and now she's given up. The early afternoon sun is strong and bears directly into her face sending a cascade of salty rivulets streaming into her eyes. She squints in an attempt to see where he's gone but the combination of sweat and sun stings, blurring her vision. The Sunday picnickers sprinkled below now appear like hundreds and thousands on a mound of green icecream and Sam has no choice but to close her eyes. When she opens them again she immediately catches Hasta's large brown bulk darting between picnic groups. He is terrorising them. Plunging his wet nose into crotches and slapping his long tongue onto exposed skin. Sam sits on her rock, the cascade of sweat now easing. She shakes her head and smiles broadly at the commotion the big dog is causing below. It hasn't occurred to her that Hasta is simply trying to sniff-out his owner.

Sam has enjoyed her time with him but he isn't her dog and despite earlier thoughts where she entertained the idea of keeping him, she now feels relieved to be returning him to his owner. She is also relieved to see him back to his usual friendly state and not agitated by the thumping, marathon party at a neighbouring block of flats. He is usually a placid dog and not easily stirred but the smashing of discarded beer bottles in the laneway next to his courtyard from the 24hr-party-people had him in a frothing state. It was then, lying in bed listening to Hasta argue with the revellers, that Sam decided that if the owner hadn't returned by morning she'd take the big dog out for the day. She'd first considered the idea at work when it occurred to her that she hadn't had a proper day-off in years. Partly her own doing she conceded, for allowing work to dominate her life but now with things changing drastically for her – and not for the better – she decided it was time. The trouble was, she hadn't known how to spend it. She'd thought about contacting friends but hadn't spoken to any of them for so long, continuously forgetting to return their calls that the problem was now compounded by a feeling of embarrassment. Then she thought about the big dog. She figured he knew her well enough having shoved his big snout and impressive pink probe through a large gap in the fence to say a slurping hello to her every day for, well, at least three years, she concluded. 'Funny', thought Sam, that she should be well–acquainted with the neighbour's dog but had never met the neighbour. Or even seen them for that matter. She then realised rather disappointedly, that she could barely recall seeing any of her neighbours over the past couple of years. Her work was demanding there was no doubt about that. The very nature of what she did required it, but she'd also let such demands entirely consume her. She arose at 5.30, was at work by 6.30 and was rarely home before 8.30 at night, plus she worked weekends more often than not. These days her social life revolved around colleagues who worked as obsessively as she did and when at home she would merely sleep. 'No wonder I never see anyone,' she thought. Finally Sam drifted off to sleep despite Hasta's relentless barking but not before pondering her unusual decision – at least for her anyway – to take an unknown neighbour's dog on an outing without their knowing. She wondered whether the idea had less to do with her not knowing how to spend her day off and more to do with the influence a particular work assignment was having on her. A project she now sensed was affecting her more deeply than she realised. Either way, she liked this spontaneous, peculiar plan and she was doing it. She'd been at a loose end as to how she might spend her day off and now at least she had someone to spend it with – even if it was the neighbour-who-she-didn't-know's monstrous dog.

~

Tarnasay looks about his empty courtyard that appears larger now his big dog is absent and not crowding it with his boundless energy. He feels a little odd. The irony of the situation isn't lost on him. He's been told many times that his ways – his antics, stunts, tricks, expertise, artistry and even his "magic" would catch up with him. Perhaps encouraging, "some kinda reverse spell for time too well spent" his close friend Franz once explained upon hearing the retelling of one of his more audacious adventures. But there's no myth about Tarnasay Evermore and this explains why simply mentioning his name to friends causes them to stop what they're doing and look at you with an expectant twinkle in their eye. Similar to a twinkle in the eye of a child watching a magic trick for the first time. That excited, pleasantly anxious twinkle, the spark of imagination, the mysterious whisper that says, *'Hey guess what... anything is possible when it's fun.'* And fun goes a long way to explaining Tarnasay's motivation for his adventures and indeed, making them possible.

Tarnasay has been described as a dare-devil but not the kind who jumps things or eats strange objects for the thrill of a crowd, short-term fame and a trailer full of cash. He's probably more akin to the faceless BASE jumpers of the world who leap off the tallest object around and, if they've got it right, land safely before hopping into a waiting cab or a mate's getaway car. Disappearing like some weird superhero who just completed a low-profile training routine. There's no fanfare or stupefied applause from people who don't fully understand why they're clapping. The only acknowledgment he receives (or many would argue, possibly warrants) is a rare smile of admiration from a mate and some scatty footage possibly destined for Foxtel Sports News. And that seems to be enough attention for guys like this, who appear motivated more by the personal thrill than any real public attention. But Tarnasay, who despite sharing a similar quest for the private thrill and adventure to that of BASE jumpers wasn't doing it to test the limits of gravity, nerve or crowd idolisation. He was more interested in the adventure aspect of his daring, in exploring lifestyles, objects and activities that were usually off limits for a simple, middle class, urban-bound boy like him. And when Tarnasay decided to fuck with the world as he understood it, "it wasn't formed around obvious anger, childhood neglect or the by-product of failed parental projections of fascist proportions" as Franz expressed it. No, Tarnasay simply decided to do things that are considered amazing to everyone except those who actually do it, things that no-one really does, things many of us dream of and plan for, but too often die never knowing.

Tarnasay kicks over his dog's water bowl littered with leaves and watches the water flow rapidly through the pavers of his courtyard.

Just a substance with no cognitive direction or destination in mind, a small testament to the cliché 'just going with the flow.' His thoughts turn to his travels. He enters a private library. A vast library cataloguing a rare collection of stories, snap shots, vivid mental postcards recounting a modern adventure that represents his own idea of just going with the flow. A private podcast, an internal audio book, all this accessible to him only, to his mind's eye and ear only. Each instalment forming part of an incredible journey. One which today sees him anointed as an underground figurehead for a mysterious organisation that has gained notoriety worldwide – an organisation he inspired, but had no direct involvement in establishing – *The Pleasure Recycling Co.*

Ubetcha

Timing matters in sailing and Tarnasay knew as much when he heard about Maxie Burgess' superyacht 'Ubetcha' moored at a Sydney yachting club. To recognise a shift from the usual conversations he had with friends, and friends of friends, like a good helmsman on a racing yacht who spies a squall on the water where others see only water. Particular opportunities taught to be identified which soon enough just presented themselves. He'd mastered the art of keen observation and practised patience like a monk, and as a result discovered that timing mattered most for realising his schemes. Schemes which, if he followed his three rules of acquisition: cognisance, composure and conception, appeared to take shape before him. Almost as though they were scripted and he was merely an actor whose task was to appear, deliver the correct lines and the rest of the act would just fall into place around him. But he knew it was also timing that made it so – timing and a bit of daring.

Maxie Burgess was a well-known, big stakes gambler who had inherited a fortune as a young man. "MB" as he was known in gambling circles spent his time travelling the world playing poker and attending whatever major sporting event took his fancy at the time. His inheritance came from his grandmother's ingenuity and passion for knitting and embroidery where she'd established a massively successful international mail-order business in the 1950s. Sadly, 'Grandma B' as she was known the world over, died along with most of her immediate family including Maxie's parents when her private jet plummeted to the ground in India on one of her purchasing trips. This left Maximillian Burgess, at the age of twelve, as the sole inheritor of her knitting and embroidery empire. By the time Maxie was eighteen he'd already planned how to maintain his Grandma's flourishing company and took the natural step of extending the mail order business to the internet. The "online onslaught" as he fondly remembers it. To this day Maxie Burgess has never truly worked a day in his life – nor has he ever held in one of his chubby hands, the famous knitting needles which made it so.

To get drunk after a night of reasonable takings is not unfamiliar in the gambling world and a short way into Maxie Burgess' visit to Sydney saw him showered in million dollar chips and shitfaced. The significance of his completely obliterated mental state was also paramount to the timing of Tarnasay's planned acquisition of Mr Burgess' pride of wealth, his spectacular yacht, *Ubetcha*. Maxie was aware of his tendency, should he win, to become inebriated beyond the ability to recall where he was staying let alone what city he was in. In this instance MB would call upon his one and only assistant earlier in the evening to arrange for him to be "deposited" at a casino suite until late the next day rather than return to his yacht as was his usual routine. It was learning of this break in routine that had caught Tarnasay's attention.

Initially, he became aware of Maxie Burgess and his spectacular yacht's arrival in town through a short piece at the end of the nightly news. Perhaps subconsciously, this was the moment he first entertained the audacious idea of liberating MB's superyacht Ubetcha. However, it was while attending a party in the Sydney beachside suburb of Bondi that Tarnasay's mind really began to lock onto the idea and the first of his three rules of acquisition, that being 'cognisance' came into play. He was listening to a petite, redheaded girl named Lily who was a head croupier at the Sydney Casino. Lily ran the 'hi-rollers' room in the casino and had become familiar enough with the oafish MB to have been given a tour onboard Ubetcha by his assistant as a means of apology for his behaviour on a particular night.

"He is an obnoxious pig really," said Lily, "I mean, he tips generously if he's winning and in the mood but if not then he's unbearable. Almost anyone else would be removed for his behaviour but because he bets so big the casino tolerates it of course."

"So what sort of stuff does he do?" asked someone. There was a small group of people listening to Lily recount her recent experience with MB. Perhaps any other time it wouldn't have interested them so much but with the local media being fixated on MB's superyacht

Ubetcha he'd become quite the topical story.

"Well he was gambling in Texas not so long ago and he's decided to take up chewing tobacco and wearing a Texan cowboy hat. Fucking ridiculous. Anyway, does MB request a special spittoon? No. He just spits it right there onto the carpet. Can you believe it? It's fucking revolting. This is the sort of shit the casino is prepared to tolerate. Anyway, I wasn't, so on that night I asked to be taken off his table and this resulted in him apologising to me the following night and offering me a tour of Ubetcha."

"Did you go?" asked another anonymous voice within Lily's captive audience in the spacious kitchen of the Bondi house.

"Yeah. But only with Michael my boyfriend at the time. I wasn't going on that creep's yacht alone. Y'know, he's propositioned me and other girls on numerous occasions as if we double as call girls too. As if for the right amount of money we'll just rip off our casino uniforms to reveal raunchy lingerie and off we'll go. To be honest, I wouldn't have bothered, but Michael who works as a sailing deckhand was keen to see it. The strange thing is that on this night he was actually quite the gracious host. He says he shouldn't drink, that he becomes aggressive and obnoxious particularly if betting isn't going so well. He explained to us that he's trashed his yacht in a drunken rage more than once and also physically assaulted a couple of staff which had cost him millions. So these days if he's over-intoxicated he stays onshore at a hotel. But no-one's allowed to reside on the yacht when he's not there, staff are relieved of duty and told to find their own accommodation and later reimbursed for costs. "Ubetcha is my baby," he says continuously but it's just a fucking boat y'know? Okay so it's a big, special, fancy boat full of tricks but it's still a boat? It's not a pet or something. I dunno, it's just weird to me. Maybe it's a guy thing, or maybe a filthy rich guy thing. Anyway, Jerome his assistant organises accommodation for staff if he can and of course MB. If he sees where things are heading. Jerome's always by his side, he's really nice. I don't know how he puts up with MB though. Must be paid a shitload."

"Full of tricks?" asked Tarnasay.

"Yeah, well things like these incredible pop up bars. Michael saw this discreet little button in a hallway and pressed it and up pops this amazing little bar right before our eyes. It was crazy. It's definitely state of the art. MB bragged how he likes to be up on the latest technology. He reckons it's neverending – updating things like his security and a malfunctioning GPS navigation system which apparently they're doing while he's here. He said it was costing him some astronomical amount to install this amazing new system made in Germany. He's also having new spas installed, lounge suites, bathrooms redone etcetera. At this point I was getting pretty bored. Anyway he's getting all this done here because Australia is one of his favourite destinations and because all the work takes time he'd rather be staying somewhere he likes. He stays for about six months each time he visits he reckons. What a lifestyle eh?" said Lily to an audience of nodding heads. Tarnasay had developed an almost intuitive ability to listen carefully when an opportunity was taking shape before he'd truly become aware exactly what that opportunity was. Before he had actually processed and understood the importance or the value of the information he was being given. For example, through a short casual conversation with Lily and others, Tarnasay could now recall specific information about MB. He not only learnt that Mr Burgess never slept on his yacht when intoxicated but that he also refused anyone to reside there in his absence. He also learnt that on his last two visits to Sydney he stayed for just under six months. However, most crucially he learnt that that apart from gambling, MB was here for an overhaul of his yacht in particular the malfunctioning GPS system onboard. To almost anyone such information would seem trivial or vaguely interesting but to Tarnasay it was like someone outlining a plan for a scheme he was yet to devise.

Later in the evening, Tarnasay engaged Lily in a private conversation which was perhaps the first mental scribblings to such a plan. He introduced himself properly to her.

"Hey Lily, I'm Tarnasay. But you can just call me T if you like. I was listening earlier when you were talking about MB and Ubetcha."

"Oh hi Tarnasay. Yeah, you asked me about Ubetcha's tricks," she said with a small laugh.

"Yeah that's right," said Tarnasay who was a little taken aback that she said his name correctly. Usually he has to repeat it at least once. "Listen, I work as a freelance journalist for a few publications and I was wondering if you'd be able to help me out," said Tarnasay.

"Sure. If I can, what is it?" said Lily.

"Well he's an interesting character this MB..."

"That's one way of putting it."

Tarnasay grinned. "Anyway, I'm writing an article about him and I have a special request I want to put to you – and I understand completely if you say no – but I was wondering if it's possible that I could give you my number and then have you call me on the nights that MB's betting big?"

"Sounds tabloidy," said Lily.

Tarnasay laughed. "Freelancing can be a tough gig sometimes," he said.

"Hey it's cool. The guy's an arse as far as I'm concerned. I'd be happy to call you when he's betting big. Usually it depends on what mood he enters the casino. So it'll be like an 'MB mood forecast' for you," said Lily smiling a little mischievously.

"Perfect," said Tarnasay.

"Hey I don't suppose you're *that* Tarnasay who used to pop up in the media a lot a while back borrowing all kinds of rich boys toys and other stuff and leaving notes behind. I remember there was one particular stunt he did which I'll never forget – he got into the National Gallery archive and took home some very famous paintings, hung them on his lounge room walls and sent pictures to the gallery and the media before returning them. He was incredible!" said Lily laughing.

"Ha! Yes, I remember," said Tarnasay. And he certainly did. He'd hung them on his walls for a good six months before he sent those photographs. "Well I hate to spoil your party Lily, but I'm not him," said Tarnasay smiling.

"Yeah. I figured as much. Mostly only posers in Bondi," said Lily with a cheeky smile.

"Mostly," said Tarnasay, "Hey thanks for doing this. It's really appreciated. Helps a lot with my research," he added.

"No worries. It'll be kinda fun actually," said Lily.

***

In the meantime, Tarnasay set about finding not only an experienced skipper but one willing to join him on his audacious adventure. He posted a small, somewhat cryptic ad on a selection of yacht club notice boards around Sydney and waited for his phone to ring. In just over two months he had compiled a long list of candidates. Initially, it wasn't difficult for Tarnasay to discern the most likely candidates from the list. Choosing from the short list however, would prove more challenging. To assist him with the process and for his personal use only, he scribbled down his selection criteria and then typed it up for the pending interviews. Although his selection criteria included just three critical factors to determine a potential candidate, it was the last two, he knew, would be the most difficult yet crucial to fulfill: *1. Highly experienced in skippering cruisers and large yachts. Preferably demonstrated experience in the skippering of superyachts (or equivalent vessels in terms of size). 2. A genuine risk taker. Daring and free spirited but calm and at ease with themselves. Non-judgmental and most likely to take part in what is fundamentally – a planned, highly orchestrated crime – or at least consider it. Previous criminal background is acceptable perhaps even beneficial but subject to reason: no assault charges, no junkies, no roughnecks. 3. Rapport. A natural affinity. The successful candidate must be engaging, interesting and fun. Articulate, a good conversationalist, relaxed. Completely open-minded. Single, nor bound by family commitments. There must be a connection, and the clear potential for a strong friendship. A good sense of humour.*

Another month passed before Tarnasay finally narrowed down his list to just a small selection of candidates. He felt quietly confident that amongst them he would find his skipper and following that, commence the final planning and preparation towards absconding with Ubetcha. At this moment thinking about it brought a tingling sensation to the nerves at the base of Tarnasay's neck; like someone had just brushed over it ever so lightly with a feather duster. A sensation he often felt when he could see the outline of a plan becoming coloured in with the richness of reality.

Col Barrington

The first time I met Tarnasay it was a scorching hot summer's day and he was wearing a suit. A fucking suit. We sat down in his beautiful courtyard oasis to have a chat over a couple of beers and I found myself staring at it in detail. I've never been a 'suit' man myself, never found them particularly comfortable. Not due to the fabric which always feels good but because they make me feel stiff and always at attention. Wearing one seems to put me on edge. As though at any moment I may be summoned by someone important to somewhere important for something important for which I may look the part but in truth are ill prepared. I remember the fabric on Tarnasay's suit seemed to be shimmering in the afternoon heat, the pin stripes behaving like streamers. Thankfully, the pop of beers opening snapped me from this almost hypnotic state. Even sitting in the shady part of his courtyard surrounded by plants my brow was heavy with sweat. It was then I noticed that Tarnasay didn't have a drop of sweat on him. The man was wearing a suit but there wasn't a bead of moisture to be seen. I wasn't sure whether to be impressed or suspicious.

"Hot isn't it," I said.

Tarnasay said nothing but handed me an ice cold beer with a warm smile. He took a sip of his beer, no doubt observing my sweatiness before him. It felt like it was raining inside my clothes.

"Love your courtyard," I said.

"Thanks," said Tarnasay, "It's my sanctuary. I'm trying to make the concrete disappear."

"You're winning."

Tarnasay smiled again. A goodlooking bloke. I could see why he smiled a lot.

"So Col, you're a boat builder?" said Tarnasay.

"Yeah. More refurbishing luxury yachts these days but when I started with my father we were building boats. Since he passed away a few years ago I've been working on my own. But I haven't taken on any major building contracts for quite some time. Mostly smaller refurbishments. I love the work y'know, but it's all consuming now as a one man show. And to be honest I've felt burnt out for a while. I need a change mate. Hence my sitting here," I said.

How I came to be sitting in Tarnasay's courtyard oasis and being interviewed as his potential skipper was simple enough really. You see, I'd been adventurous all through my twenties and then – in my mid-thirties – I began to wonder why I'd suddenly stopped. Why I'd replaced my passion for surfing with a PlayStation version of it. Why I'd knocked back nights out with the last of my single mates and instead sat at home drinking beer and watching crap TV. "What the fuck is going on?" I asked myself late one night, while drunk and flicking through TV stations and pages of porn simultaneously with little arousal forthcoming from either end. Something had to happen. So the next day I visited my yacht club to catch up with a few sailing mates which had been my only means of social interaction for a while. I remember they were gathered around a bar leaner all staring up at the TV screen perched above them as I walked past to buy a beer. Almost in unison they said a cheerful g'day, raised their beers before returning their stare to the 'feel good news report' about Maxie B's superyacht Ubetcha being in town. At this time, it'd also become routine for me to check the club noticeboard. To keep an eye out for potential job opportunities. Hoping to see something exciting in the way of sailing adventures. I was even prepared to be just a deckhand if it was the only way I could break my presently monotonous lifestyle. But nothing had appeared on the board for months until one day I spied Tarnasay's little ad fluttering alone in the sea breeze conspicuously. *Daring, highly experienced yachtsman required for South Pacific Adventure. Looking to escape the city? Got a strong sense of daring'* the ad read. "Might be a job on Ubetcha!" one of my mates called out having noticed I was paused before the note and they all laughed like stupid drunken pirates. I turned and smiled at them before moving to the bar to grab a beer. While I waited, I discreetly scribbled down the phone number from the note on a beer coaster before joining my mates perched at the table. "Bit heavy on the detail eh," I said facetiously disguising my actual interest in the peculiar note. They agreed by way of nodding and raised eyebrows. Their attention was then drawn back to the television. A tinge of interest momentarily spread across the face of each of my mates almost in sequence, as though they were passing on a collective facial spasm. Eyebrows raised and heads falling to a slight angle they looked like a pack of dogs trying to comprehend a new command. I wondered how much time they'd been spending together lately.

"You have a lot of sailing experience and the CV you emailed shows that – but I'm going to cut to the chase here because I need a skipper who can sail a superyacht. Your CV makes no mention of it – have you sailed superyachts?" asked Tarnasay as he flicked away a leaf that had landed on his expertly pressed suit pants.

"Many. Here and abroad," I lied. I surprised myself with how easily I told it.

"So why doesn't your CV mention it?" said Tarnasay.

I laughed. It was a good laugh. A natural sounding one. One that gave me a beat of time to think of a convincing response. Tarnasay didn't laugh with me. It was possibly the most important thing he needed to know, and he was looking for the right answer. Not the wrong one disguised as the right one. He watched me closely. Measuring my behaviour. He would later tell me he could usually tell whether someone was lying. He may have got it wrong on occasions, that someone was indeed telling him the truth but if he didn't believe them he wouldn't work with them, simple as that. And because he'd never been let down, as far as he was concerned, he'd always got it right.

"Do you know how often I get asked to skipper a superyacht?" I said, and although I posed the question as more of a rhetorical one, I let it hang for a moment as though it was real. Confusing us both. But it gave me a fraction more time to forge a solid answer.

"Never," I said finally, "And to be honest, I doubted the sincerity of your note." The answer I was to now give formed itself with clarity in my mind. It was as though someone had whispered it to me and I delivered it without pause or hesitation. "In all my years sailing, I can't recall ever seeing an *advertisement* for a superyacht skipper and certainly not on a noticeboard of a yacht club. But it had me intrigued. That's why I'm here. The CV I sent you was the one I sent before being awarded the job of skippering luxury private chartered yachts up and down the east coast of Australia. I figured that was enough demonstration of my sailing expertise to at least warrant an interview for something whose plausibility I doubted. All the superyachts I've skippered over the years, here and abroad have come from networking, word of mouth, friends of friends. It's quite a unique skill set, well-paid, highly coveted and therefore usually kept within a tight, relatively small international fraternity." It was a good answer but an even better lie.

Tarnasay stared at me for a moment. I stared back. I was glad it was stinking hot because I felt I was beginning to sweat for a different reason. Although the lie had come out naturally enough I wasn't sure maintaining it would be as easy.

"Fair enough," said Tarnasay after what seemed like minutes, "Makes sense."

I took a sip of my lager.

"So is that what I'll be skippering?" I said. My mouth felt immediately refreshed. Cleansed of the lie.

Tarnasay's face broke into a broad smile and he laughed.

"Well I do like a captain who is confident," he said.

~

The next two meetings saw the two of us truly warming to each other. I sensed our working lives had been quite different but there was enough overlap in interests and I liked Tarnasay's sense of humour. I'd forgotten about the suit. I could see myself working and sailing with the guy over an extended period of time. It seemed that he must have come to the same conclusion at the same time because he soon began asking me quite technical questions regarding the sailing of a superyacht. He also showed me detailed plans of the boat I was to skipper if I was the right candidate and indeed interested in taking on the journey. My interest was immediately sparked. I looked at the detailed plan before me for a moment and then at the room around me. Tarnasay had clearly done well for himself. His home was stylish with beautiful parquetry flooring and a mix of modern and antique furniture that had been well-matched, artfully combined by someone with taste. An aesthete. As a renovator for prestige boats in more recent years I've had a bit to do with aesthetically inclined clients and learnt quite a bit myself about high quality furnishings and interior decorating. He had large original artworks on the high walls of the airy, light-filled room in which we sat with a clear view to the spacious, meticulously arranged courtyard oasis. A space that was so dense in parts, it was like a defiant fortress of green; a private jungle that held steadfast against the tide of suburban concrete pushing against it. However, for all its style, comfort and well spent means, it wasn't the home of someone who owned a superyacht. As with most people, I'd been fooled more than once by an inclination to stereotype and stopped myself at that moment from asking exactly what his relationship to this superyacht was. Instead, I allowed it to provide the assumption that he must be representing someone else. A concierge of sorts, I figured. That would certainly account for his beautifully appointed home which made it clear he held a certain amount of money, but not the significant amount that would see a man such as him own a superyacht. It didn't even sit entirely right with who I'd began to ascertain this man was, his demeanour, his style. If he did indeed own a yacht it seemed to me far more likely that it would be a true sailing yacht, a luxury one perhaps, with no expense spared, tastefully renovated inside and out, but far more humble in size than the grotesque indulgence of the vessel spread on the table before me. I studied the plan more closely. I found myself getting excited at the prospect of skippering a superyacht. A good friend of mine had been doing this very thing for years, for a host of clients throughout the Mediterranean and for a time he'd pushed hard for me to do the same. On numerous occasions my mate had invited me to visit with the promise of work but I hadn't taken up the offer. My boat building business which I'd inherited from my now-deceased father had kept me busy inbetween short stints of skippering small tourist charter yachts from Sydney to Rockhampton. In more recent years though, both sides of my work had slowed. I'd grown tired of the skippering jaunts up and down the coast, visiting the same spots again and again, listening to the same tourist spiel from the charters resident spruiker over and over, and increasingly I'd begun to decline the sailing assignments. The void now left from these journeys hadn't been filled with new boat building contracts either, where the satisfaction which had come from such projects in the past had waned. Both sides of my working life had always paid well, but for the past couple of years I'd found myself unmotivated by either vocation. I wasn't taking on skippering jobs, nor was I pursuing new building contracts. The trips up and down the eastern seaboard of Australia had always been disruptive, with tours and adjoining ones lasting for up to three months at a time. It had cost me girlfriends and regular contact with good friends outside of the sailing fraternity. And if it hadn't been for the fraternity, the club of sorts, the clique where friendships were easier to maintain because there was a mutual understanding, a shared mental tethering with those who worked in the industry - those who were also somewhat ironically bound by the transient, nomadic lifestyle we led - it would've been a lonely existence. Long periods of time apart only punctuated by short reunions at the yacht club where we'd barely register a look of surprise upon our tanned faces when another of our brethren suddenly reappeared, having been away on assignment for months on end. It was this very thing that had begun to weather within me because it'd never been quite nomadic enough. I kept having to stop and turn around when I really just wanted to keep going. In more recent years, I'd done very little of anything, just enough work to pay the bills and just enough socialising to stop from going mad. And in doing so I'd allowed myself to become deeper embedded in a rut of routine I now despised, more than the one that put me there. Now on the table before me was another opportunity and perhaps my last. My last chance to shake myself free from the complacency which I'd recently come to the conclusion was not me. I was meant to be doing more. To be somewhere else. Even better, nowhere at all. I was still young and strong enough to be adventurous and spontaneous. There was nothing holding me back. Nothing. I had the skills and knowledge necessary to skipper such a vessel, and if there were matters where I felt I needed to be brought up to speed, I had access to information and a host of friends within the sailing fraternity who could assist me. It was too easy. It was also too easy to miss such an opportunity. To grow old, fat and bitter through a private lament for letting such a dream sink to the bottom of the ocean in which I knew, in order to be truly happy, I should be buoyant upon.

The Introduction

It wasn't until their fourth meeting that Col was introduced to Tarnasay's outrageous, speculative, criminal plan to "borrow" Maxie Burgess' superyacht Ubetcha. Of course, this was something that had never entered his mind. Initially, he listened with a dismissive mindset, thinking that he'd completely misread the guy and was getting close to leaping from his chair and telling him he was, "A fuckin' fruit loop and better off bagged and thrown out to sea." But the more he listened, the more impressed he became with Tarnasay's plan. It happened quickly. Tarnasay wasn't naive, he spoke eloquently and with purpose. He'd decided he wanted Col as his skipper and now he needed to draw a battle within this no-nonsense man's mind. He had to do it quickly and convincingly. He had to start a fight between commonsense and imagination. To reconnect him with his wild streak, to let it escape through the city, make its way out of the filth, the crowds, the concrete din to which he was prone to rant about, and into a vast expanse of possibilities and experiences. He had to make this mid-thirties man, young and daring again. He had to bring forth the juvenile boy that lies within, like it does within almost every man, and combine it with the knowledge and wisdom that came with the benefit of his true age. Just as Tarnasay did with himself, he had to blend his argument, he had to combine the focus, the discipline and the knowledge for this outrageous idea with the madness, the daring and the fearlessness of it. To make him say 'Fuck You.' To have the words 'Fuck you I won't do what you tell me!' resonate in his mind again, just like it had in his mid-twenties at the "unforgettably intense" Rage Against the Machine gig he'd reminisced about last time they met, where they had talked, beer after beer, wine after wine, scotch after scotch, about their interests and discovered a mutual, deep-rooted love of music. But this time it had to be for real. This time, rather than a young man's angsty chant, his rage, his disillusionment had to be harnessed and put to use. Tarnasay needed him to scream it in his mind, scream it with his actions. There was an element of the evangelist within Tarnasay or a persuasive anarchist perhaps. And it was this persuasiveness, this passion that Tarnasay was counting on to find the inner punk again in Col. To make a grown man take the greatest risk of his life, to say a grand, "Fuck You."

It was simple but thorough. Initially, Col listened still full of doubt and disbelief and humoured Tarnasay with questions but the more he probed the clearer the plan became. The more serious he knew he was. That this was going to occur with or without him. Every question he asked, a satisfactory reply was given. Satisfactory because, although Col hadn't embarked on criminal behaviour since adolescence with the exception of illicit drug taking, even he knew that when it comes to pulling off a plan like this, there are no definitively "right" answers. The are only anticipations, predictions, possibilities and chances, as much as there are unknowns, unforseens and variables. It was a crime they were going to commit. Laws were about to be broken. Things were about to happen differently to what everyone expects or hopes and there is no way anyone can completely prepare for that. That's where the thrill lies regardless of which side of the law you're on. As far as Col was concerned, Tarnasay with the help of a mysterious friend named Franz, had done his research and nothing obvious was left to chance. Col was now rooted to his seat. He wasn't going anywhere. He felt dangerous. He felt rejuvenated. He felt punk. He listened carefully to Tarnasay explaining his reconnaissance and felt that somewhere during their discussions his tone had changed. He was no longer being sounded out by him but debriefed instead, 'The clever bastard knows I'm in,' thought Col.

Tarnasay began outlining the future for Ubetcha once they had sailed her to Thailand and his intention to in fact sell her through a contact Franz would establish whilst they were at sea. Col suddenly found the words he was hearing louder and clearer. It was as though Tarnasay had somehow raised the volume of his words but not his voice, each word isolated from ambient noise travelling up through his ear canal and announcing itself in no uncertain terms to his mind. For some reason it had taken until this moment when Tarnasay spoke in a relaxed, matter-of-fact manner about the sale of the famous superyacht as if it were merely a second-hand hatchback. It was at this point his commonsense took a stand, objected in the closed court of his mind and demanded a final plea to reason.

The plea to reason gained just another week to think about "the business proposal." In that time Col's commonsense mounted the strongest case it had ever engaged in against that of his natural impulsion. Commonsense probably wasn't assisted by Col's decision to borrow a glorified scrapbook with news clippings of every exploit Tarnasay had ever committed on Australian soil. To describe it merely as a scrapbook however, is unfair to the ex-girlfriend who made it for Tarnasay one Christmas. A talented designer, she'd gone to great lengths to compile and then have bound, a beautiful, hardback leather book with a gold-leaf embossed title, *'The Art of Borrowing.'* It was sitting on the coffee table like one would see any other nicely presented coffee table book in a thoughtfully decorated apartment. No expense had been spared with its presentation. The paper on which all the articles had been reprinted was of the highest quality and the images of the various items Tarnasay had "borrowed" since the time he first began his shenanigans at the age of seventeen were sharp and detailed. Col flicked through the book compulsively while Tarnasay prepared them cheese and crackers. He was engrossed and now understood why the book resided on the coffee table. It was one of those books that you felt compelled to keep reading. It was titillating, funny and the excitement and daring of what he'd done seemed to magnify from each page. The tone of the headlines shifting over time, from mild amusement to outrage at his antics and the authorities who continued to fail in their attempt to identify and capture him. Many of Tarnasay's infamous hand written notes left behind at crime scenes, bold and mocking for their simplicity, simply stating *'Cheers! Tarnasay'* featured throughout the book, written on various types of paper and in different pens. Later, the notes appeared more uniform in style and written on what appeared to be the same stark white paper.

No longer did the notes seem an impulsive, last minute decision scribbled on whatever paper was lying around at the time. Now as Col flicked through the book towards more recent times it became clear that the notes were consistent in hand. They had become his trademark. Col could now recall some of the news reports about Tarnasay's crimes. In particular, he remembered the ageing radio shock jock's missing purple Ferrari and how delighted he was to hear about it. He remembers how he thought about his actions at the time, how he had said to himself – a tad in awe, and at this point he was rarely in awe of anything – that this guy was 'something else.' Although Tarnasay too, found the book amusing and beautifully done, Col sensed by the way he spoke about it, that it wasn't usually present on the coffee table for the world to see, that perhaps he thought it was a little silly or even embarrassing. Tarnasay then explained as though he'd read Col's mind, that he thought certain aspects of a previous 'borrowing' was relevant to this pending heist and that by simply reading it, reminiscing the old act, certain details about how he did it came back to him. But Col loved it. He loved that someone had done all this and gotten away with it. That the guy was 'a professional fucking borrower'. That he was so good at this bizarre, daring, criminal thing he did, he had whipped the Australian media into a frenzy over a long period of time. That a girlfriend had felt impressed enough to compile a secret tome to document, champion what perhaps she foolishly believed were his achievements. Eventually, Col closed the tome and lifted it up to inspect its binding, its quality more closely. Tarnasay explained that she had indeed intended to get it published as a quirky coffee table book but he'd told her there wouldn't be a big enough audience for such a book. Particularly now that he'd stopped and was no longer appearing in the media on a regular basis. The truth was Tarnasay just wasn't keen on the idea. Partly because, even though no one knew it was him, he just didn't want that kind of attention. He knew that authorities and most likely "other people" were looking for him and that a detailed chronological profile of every crime he committed was on display in that book, effectively acting as an investigator's or profiler's handbook. He was concerned that it may be possible for behavioural patterns and habits to be discerned and the less information about his past actions the better. He knew very well that there was not one piece of information in there that wasn't already publicly available, he just didn't want it so readily available, to be so conveniently accessible as this beautifully rendered coffee table book. Tarnasay told Col there was only one other copy which his ex-girlfriend had, identical. Years later, when he ran into her, she told him it had gone missing and asked if she could have his copy but she'd never come to collect it and it'd been residing on his bookshelf ever since.

"When she says 'it went missing' she probably absentmindedly put it in a garage sale," said Tarnasay half-joking. "She was always moving.

She could be very vague, it wouldn't surprise me at all if that's what happened."

Col didn't say anything. He just stared at the book on the table and then looked at Tarnasay who he now noticed was frowning a little. "Seems like that bothers you mate? That she lost it," said Col finally.

"Ahh…" said Tarnasay rubbing his forehead, "Not really."

Col didn't say anything again. He just watched Tarnasay and saw he looked clearly perplexed for the first time since he'd met him.

"It's a silly thing really. Probably nothing in it. But you see – I keep what I've done very tight. I plan things, think it through and that's why I've always gotten away with it. Although it may appear to people, particularly due to the notes I leave behind, that I'm rash and unpredictable, half-mad but I'm quite the opposite, I'm meticulous and very sane. That's why I've never been caught. I don't leave trails. Notes maybe…" he smiled, "But not trails."

"But it's just a book," said Col, "I mean, the information in there is available to anyone, authorities and the like as you said. No worries there surely or they would've been onto you by now," scoffed Col cheerily.

"No, no that's right," said Tarnasay, "It's just that…" Tarnasay paused again thinking.

"It's just that when she told me she'd lost it, she also told me for the first time that I actually had her copy and that another copy, intended for me as a gift was with her, or had been…" Tarnasay stopped, smirked and shook his head. "And…" said Col impatiently.

"And well she wrote a note in the copy intended for me, the missing copy, the note was saying Happy Birthday and all that but she wrote it using the correct spelling of my name and the date – my birth date."

"Perhaps you shouldn't be telling me this," said Col, "Are you trying to make me nervous? Are you telling me just before I join you in stealing a superyacht that you're worried there's a possibility the authorities now have this book and they've probably worked out who you are and they're watching your every move?"

"Ha!" said Tarnasay.

Col just stared at Tarnasay wondering if indeed this had changed everything. But before he could confirm it Tarnasay spoke again.

"Possibly in any other circumstance, I'd agree and we wouldn't be sitting here now but – wait on, I'll show you something." Tarnasay got up, walked over to his bookshelf, opened an old timber box and rummaged through it.

"Yes. Here we go," he said clutching what appeared to be a bunch of birthday cards in his hand. Tarnasay sat back down at the coffee table and handed the cards to Col.

"As I was saying, in any other circumstance, in any other person's handwriting. I'd be concerned."

Col opened one of the cards, attempted to read its contents and raised his eyebrows.

"Jesus," he said.

Tarnasay just smiled and nodded knowingly, returning to his default relaxed manner.

"Was she illiterate? Dyslexic? That's the worst handwriting I've ever seen. What the fuck does that say?"

"That's my name. The original spelling," said Tarnasay.

"Right," said Col shaking his head still trying to make sense of anything, to decipher something. "Yeah. I've been wondering about that, about how you leave these little indulgent notes of yours behind and your name. I mean, I figured it's a misnomer, an alias. To use your real name, a very unusual name would be pretty silly."

"Ha! Indulgent little notes," laughed Tarnasay.

"Well they are man. It's pretty fucking cheeky."

Tarnasay just smiled. "Anyway, it is my real name, just altered. The spelling is different. The spelling on the notes is phonetic. There's more than one way to pronounce my name."

"Well," he said finally after looking at it for a couple of minutes. "All I can determine is a 'T' and 'H' and an 'A,' out of what is supposedly your name and yeah, I can make out her name 'Mia.'"

"Yep. Well that's good to know. And as you can see she writes like that every time," said Tarnasay.

"Seriously mate, I'm surprised this would even raise an eyebrow of concern from you." said Col who was now looking perplexed himself. "I mean, I know you like to keep everything extremely tight but... well, it's borderline paranoid to worry about this. For starters, what are the chances of the cops or investigators ever getting their hands on that one lone book? And then if by some freakish chance they did – good luck deciphering that shit," said Col smiling.

Tarnasay smiled too.

"True," he said, "But I know a bit about freakish chance too."

Col conceded a nod of agreement to this, but with Tarnasay's well planned yacht heist proposal filling his every thought and his bound curriculum-vitae of successful subversive behaviour in his hands, Col's natural compulsion which had been missing in recent years made a sudden reappearance. It reappeared and it was looking dashing, confident and persuasive in its suit of spontaneity. Meanwhile, commonsense shuffled around nervously looking not so much as drab, dressed in its thoughtful balanced way, but certainly unexciting and definitely ordinary. This sudden miraculous reappearance in his life was the very thing his commonsense had built its argument around and was trying to draw to his attention. Natural Compulsion was rash, unthinking and potentially very dangerous, "This proposal has the potential to destroy your life," argued Commonsense. "Or make it unforgettable," countered Natural Compulsion.

In the end Natural Compulsion won the case. Commonsense never stood much of a chance against the all-empowering excitement Natural Compulsion exuded. And it had got into Col's ear early-on when Tarnasay first announced his plan, "Wow", it whispered to him excitedly, "Can you imagine?" He could, and he did. He imagined himself sailing Ubetcha out of Sydney Harbour and into the expanse of the South Pacific rolling out in heaves before him. He found his heart tingled when he thought about it, stung by the tiniest amount of adrenalin such thoughts sent when passing through it. And Col had grown tired of Commonsense. Its gentle reasoning, its innate knowledge but nonetheless beige promise in a wonderful, colourful world. And it wasn't as if it was to be ignored forever – or even could be – but neither could it hold sway against the rush of freedom and adventure and risk now running wild through his veins.

Their next meeting would be their last contact before they commandeered Ubetcha. Over the day they would discuss the finer details of the plan and go through a checklist of items for travel and sailing but also create one for potential 'unforseens' that Tarnasay may have overlooked in regard to the heist.

The Plan

Apart from learning about the rude, boorish behaviour of MB and the pending security and GPS overhaul to his superyacht while in Sydney, Tarnasay also learnt that the nights MB was most likely to win big directly correlated with the amount he was prepared to bet. And this was usually driven by the attitude with which he entered the casino. Lily happily gave Tarnasay her "mood forecast" for MB as she called them via the phone as arranged. All Tarnasay needed to do now was be patient. He just had to wait for Lily's mood forecast and then call the Casino's reception on the nights in which he was most likely to have bet big and possibly won big. Over a period of three weeks, Tarnasay called only a total of eight times and on the final call he received the reply from the receptionist which he'd been wanting to hear, "Mr Burgess, one moment please." Despite hanging up abruptly, those words were a green light to Tarnasay. He now knew Ubetcha would be uninhabited by MB that night due to him winning big and as a result too drunk to return. From here the plan was simple. Call Captain Col who had been waiting patiently, if not at least a little nervously, for him to call. Meet him at the mooring, board the famous Ubetcha and sail her out of Sydney.

Col had always imagined they'd be crawling around 'in the cloak of darkness' dressed from head-to-toe in black like something out of a Hollywood action thriller. That they'd enter the mooring at an hour most people are snoring and just slip away into the darkness. Tarnasay, had planned otherwise. He wanted to conduct the heist in broad daylight. Not only that, but to Col's initial incredulity, he wanted to do it at the busiest time of day. When the marina was bustling with drunken day-trippers returning from Christmas parties held on private yachts, and with owners and their friends who had embarked on their first outing of the year to herald the holiday season on otherwise dormant boats.

"It's the perfect time," explained Tarnasay to a yet-to-be-convinced Col who knew the convincing was about to come. "I've been observing the mooring closely and it's been getting increasingly chaotic down there at this time of year."

Col adjusted himself in his seat and crossed his legs in the same manner he did when preparing to watch a film. For a brief moment he wished he had a punnet of popcorn. Unlike other people he knew who shared a similar trait, he actually found Tarnasay at his most engaging when explaining things in minute detail. Of course, the fact that such detail was critical to his well-being no doubt helped to sharpen his attentiveness.

"Col," said Tarnasay almost sternly. "For us – the busier the better. The more people milling about, getting in the way, clogging up the decks, making a drunken nuisance of themselves – yelling, screaming, distracting the staff – the better."

Col sat quietly. He felt he should be contributing more, critiquing and suggesting more. But he needn't have worried. Tarnasay hadn't engaged him to figure out the minutiae of the heist, although he was ready to listen to any concerns Col may raise, his task was to use his expertise on the boat and the ocean he was to sail. That was all Tarnasay was asking of him, apart from of course, him agreeing to take the biggest risk of his life. Col may not have realised it but he already had Tarnasay's confidence. Tarnasay's first challenge was to give Col his.

"By being conspicuous we'll be inconspicuous. This is how it'll go. Our main challenge is getting to that yacht unseen. Once onboard it's your task to get her going. First, we slip stream behind a christmas party group to enter the mooring as discussed. Secondly, we jump in one of the yacht club's complimentary tinnies, loop around broadly before entering the yacht from the starboard side and obscuring us from the yacht club. You start her up, I don my 'MB style' jacket and hat, sit partially obscured by the boat side like he does, and wave as though I'm royalty like he does to anyone we encounter as we set off quietly. You see, MB, when not being a public oaf, is a very private, unpredictable person. No one will think twice about his yacht moving on." Once again Col felt compelled to say something, to contribute. So he did. Then wished he hadn't.

"We should look well tanned," he said. It was then that he noticed properly for the first time Tarnasay's flawless tanned-like olive complexion. Tarnasay just smiled broadly, his teeth gleaming absurdly white like a toothpaste commercial.

"I mean..." continued Col, "We should at least look a little weather worn." Tarnasay nodded politely if not a little too quickly. The type of nod one may encounter in a tense corporate boardroom discussion or an intimate dinner party where someone blurts out something unexpected, unusual or irrelevant and following 'The fast nod,' discussion is quickly recommenced to hide the person's faux pas. Tarnasay continued on briskly with further important details. Col listened intently, attempting to forget he'd said anything.

~

Col found himself back at the yacht club. Ever since he'd made the decision to engage in the most daring thing he was most likely to do, he'd been anxious. But avoiding social interaction with friends at the yacht club wasn't making matters any easier. In fact, Tarnasay had said as much last time they met, "I know it's going to be filling your head until it happens but seriously, you need to go about things as usual, and as much as possible. You need to distract yourself. We've prepared as best as we can so now it's about controlling your nerves. Run the whole scenario through your mind a thousand times, because visualisation works. I know this. But you must also switch it off. Keep to your routines or maybe do something new, but don't dwell on it incessantly. Visualisation is one thing, obsessing another." What Col found did help was visualising Tarnasay as some kind of zen guru when he ran these words through his mind again. It made him smile. Visualising him reciting these words to him from atop a misty peak, complete with long, dazzling deep purple cloak and meticulously groomed but irritating chin goatee. He didn't doubt the wisdom of his words but it was the earnestness in which Tarnasay had delivered them that manifested this image. Nonetheless, having heeded the message from Tarnasay the Guru, Col now stood at the bar ordering a round of beers for his mates. Half there, half not. The raucous banter between his mates was distracting him somewhat but not entirely until he overheard a conversation his mate Paul was having with a younger man he knew only casually. He had seen him around the yacht club the last couple of years and he was always polite and busy. A hardworking young greenhorn deckhand. He was in his early twenties and Col had noticed, a little drunk as he went about explaining to Paul how he was now on security duty at the marina where Maxie B's yacht was moored. The young man explained how he could give him clearance to get in and could do the same for his mates if he wished. At this point Col caught the young man's eye and smiled, Paul turned and seeing Col welcomed him into the conversation. The man introduced himself as Michael. His voice continuously fluctuated in volume between loud and quiet as though it was automatically adjusting to the ambient noise around him. When other conversations grew louder and more raucous Michael's voice would adjust accordingly. He was drunk but Col could tell he was a sharp young bloke, keen to share his information with them but he wasn't keen for everyone to hear it. He went on to explain that he and a few of his deckhand mates who also doubled as security had been 'joy riding' boats at night or during the day if they knew the owners were away. He explained that he'd personally been onboard Ubetcha some months earlier and MB himself had mentioned that the yacht was undergoing a GPS and security overhaul. Knowing this, and being in charge of security at the marina he'd recently been on board her again to see if this was still the situation. He then said with a nervous laugh showing his age, that he and a couple of mates were "kinda tempted to joy ride Ubetcha". "Anyway I'm in charge down there now," he went on to explain. "But I only work the gate Fridays, so if you want to get it on another day you'll have to let me know. I've got a couple of other guys in on it but I'll need a heads up for those days. Anyway, this is all you need to do to signal you want in as you approach me or one of my guys on duty," said Michael as he hand gestured a quick double pump of the surfing 'hang loose' hand sign. "Ha," said Paul, "So what do you want from me then?" he added smiling. It was smile that expressed a known understanding between the two of them. Paul was a party hound, a legacy or perhaps a perpetual hangover he maintained from his days skippering superyachts throughout the Mediterranean. These days he was content to skipper small private chartered yachts up and down the eastern seaboard of Australia and around the South Pacific and operate as a small time recreational drug dealer. Col figured Michael's 'contra deal' was with the intention of securing some kind of illicit substance.

Not long after, at their final meeting Col delivered to Tarnasay a blessing of his fleet to be. A significant development he believed would make entering the marina far easier. He explained that for the next month an acquaintance was on security duty at the marina where Maxie B's yacht was moored and he had clearance to get in. Col explained to Tarnasay that it wasn't uncommon for deckhands who doubled as security to 'joy ride' boats at night or during the day if they knew owners were away.

"They borrow them," said Tarnasay smiling.

"Ubetcha," said Col with a wink.

"Am I really going to have to put up with you making jokes like that all the time"

"Ubetcha," said Col.

"Anyway, it's cool you have a back up plan to entering."

"A back up plan?"

"Well I've said all along that I want to enter the mooring anonymously, so how do we achieve that with this development? It seems the person on duty will know you."

"Not really."

"So how do we get in then?"

Col performed the waxhead hang-loose double pump hand signal.

"What the fuck was that?"

"It's the hand signal we need to give the security guy to get in."

"What – are you sixteen? Do you think this is a game Col?"

"Don't be a patronising prick Tarnasay."

"Seriously Col. I will not be performing hip-hop style hand signs to get in."

"It's a surfing sign actually, it's the hang loo–"

"I don't give a fuck if it's your Great-Great-Grandmother's secret family code I want to be completely incognito. And crap like that is just not my style."

"'Not my style,' listen to you."

"Well you read that glorified scrapbook didn't you. You know what I've done. It's all there. And the reason I'm still here having this stupid conversation with you is because I've never engaged in what this stupid conversation is about."

"Calm down, it's just a back up plan then."

"A way, way, way back up plan Col."

"Anyway. There's something else which I know you'll definitely be happy to hear. I certainly was."

"Great. What's that?"

"Well the same young fella told me –"

"Yes," said Tarnasay cutting in, dubious of what he was about to hear.

"Look – putting aside your clear dislike of his secret hand signs, the young guy's actually switched on. Anyway, he was explaining to my mate Paul and I, that he was on Ubetcha some months back and again more recently, and that the GPS and security system overhaul hasn't been done yet. He knows this because he and some mates have been entertaining the idea of taking Ubetcha out on one of their joyrides. He said he's spoken to some of the contractors who he's given access to work on other aspects of Ubetcha's overhaul - the bathrooms and spas, etcetera – and although they'd been completed, the state of the art GPS system is apparently still on its way from Germany. It confirms what Lily told you a while back," said Col.

Tarnasay was flicking through a small notebook as Col spoke, he suddenly stopped and cast his eyes up at him sharply.

"What's this guy's name?" said Tarnasay.

"Michael," said Col.

"Well I'll be..." said Tarnasay. He remembered Lily's boyfriend at the time was named Michael and that he was a deckhand. This was where Tarnasay's attention to detail, his memory, his powerful cognisance came into its own. It was too much of a coincidence not to be the same Michael. It was also the strange serendipity Tarnasay had experienced on other occasions when he was planning a particular 'borrowing.' He wasn't superstitious so he never spoke of it openly to anyone, but it was uncanny how often it occurred to him. Franz had noticed though. He raised it with Tarnasay once but he'd dismissed it as "Superstitious nonsense." Col was right. It was very pleasing information which immediately removed what had become a nagging concern in the minds of both men. The concern was a significant one. They feared that Ubetcha may have already undergone the scheduled GPS and security overhaul before they got to her. The overhaul Lily had mentioned to Tarnasay some months earlier.

"At the time Lily was given her tour of Ubetcha her then boyfriend's name was Michael, and he was a deckhand," said Tarnasay. His eyes were sparkling.

"Good news then," said Col.

"Ubetcha," said Tarnasay.

~

On the day of their final meeting Col still needed some convincing about Tarnasay's timing for the actual heist of the yacht. Earlier meetings had seen them discuss at length what was required once on board Ubetcha to get her moving. Both Tarnasay and Col had familiarised themselves with the layout of the yacht. On separate occasions they even created a crude replica of the yacht's three levels using old furniture and other pieces of junk in Col's boat building shed. It wasn't quite to scale but close enough to allow them to practice moving about the boat quickly with limited visibility. They didn't want something as simple as the internal lights failing, to force them to literally abandon ship mid-heist. They needed to be confident enough to press ahead. Col also sought out invaluable knowledge from his mate with superyacht skippering experience. Paul briefed him on some of the intricacies most common in the mechanical operations of superyachts and any common problems and tricks he'd learnt skippering them. He also handed him a couple of mechanical plans of two of the largest superyachts in the Mediterranean he'd skippered over the years, giving Col a clearer idea of what to expect below deck and exactly where. Col's interest in learning about such matters never raised an eyebrow from his mate. Perhaps Paul was a little disappointed he was actually off to skipper such vessels now and not before, but he accepted Col's earlier explanation and was happy to share his knowledge. Despite his relatively young age, Col was a very experienced sailor and they'd often discussed the skippering of different vessels over the years. Col had also taken an interest in his mate's skippering of such yachts throughout the Mediterranean because, well, they were superyachts in the Mediterranean and not everyone experiences that. So quite quickly Col became more than familiar with the mechanical operations most common to superyachts. Whether he would ever need to draw on his learnings he had no idea, but with each morsel of information taken up by his brain his confidence grew and he found it easier to visualise the successful heist of Ubetcha.

At the end of the day the two men sipped their beers slowly. Satisfied with their final plan, their conversation gradually shifted away towards more general, everyday matters. Occasionally, something else purporting to importance regarding the heist would spring to mind and they'd discuss it. But they both felt at ease or at least as much as nerves and anticipation would allow. Even Tarnasay for all his outward composure felt the rush, the almost stinging tingle of adrenalin ripping through his body whenever he ran the plan through his mind. He liked the sensation. More significantly, he believed he needed it. It made him sharper, more alert. "Needle nerves, tighter turns," he once heard a Formula One racing driver say in a post-race interview, and although quite young at the time, Tarnasay knew exactly what he meant.

THE UNEXPECTED INFLUENCE OF UNCLE LOU

Tarnasay rights Hasta's water bowl and for a moment reflects on whether the flippant remarks made by friends about the levelling of luck over time could perhaps be true. That perhaps, if the concept of Karma exists, does it not apply both ways for everyone beyond merit? Does it not also apply to the robber who was robbed? That a wrong done to you in any manner beyond circumstance, will somehow be righted in another way beyond any logic or reason.

Tarnasay never felt remorse for stealing Maxie Burgess' yacht. In most instances, he'd always reconciled within himself that he only intended to borrow items regardless of how much a particular target disgusted him. They were on loan by him, for him, for his amusement and not for personal gain. It wasn't that his conscience stopped him from gaining from the things he stole, it simply didn't appeal to him. It wasn't about getting ahead illegally, it was about the thrill of it, the experience and he couldn't deny, part of it was about teasing, antagonising those he determined were vulgar and nasty, or greedy and obnoxious. He was also comfortable with making a judgement call. Playing a twisted god of sorts, a fucked-up Robin Hood, who didn't give to the poor but sure made them laugh. And he loved it. So did the vast majority of the public too. His targets weren't always high profile either. Many were people he'd met through work or socially, and their manner and ways grated him. If there was one thing that always worked in favour of Tarnasay in the public eye and helped trivialise his criminal behaviour, it was that all his targets were seen as obnoxious individuals – either publicly and famously, or privately and insidiously. They all had reputations. Tarnasay took delight in traumatising them. And he relished doing it to the boorish billionaire Maxie Burgess whose head must have been spinning with the unlikely, unfathomable pirating of his pride and joy. The sending of postcards back to his suite in Sydney provided many a night of drunken inspiration and laughter for Tarnasay and Col. It was easy to be cruel to a man like him.

However, while his dislike of greedy, bigoted people played a major part in his idea of fun, there were deeper underlying reasons for why he did what he did. It wasn't just disgust with a certain type of person. They just made easy targets. And while it was no doubt present in his motivations, at least privately if never openly expressed, it wasn't simply an attack on the trappings of the modern capitalist world and its imbalance of wealth. Nor was it simply a personal 'fuck you' to the capitalist dream either. Those elements were certainly there, they definitely contributed to his motivation whether he fully realised it or not – and yes, when Tarnasay said it was about him having outrageous fun, it was, but those who knew him well, knew the motivation had to go deeper than that. And they were right. For Tarnasay, the biggest single motivator was a simple thing one person said to him as a young child. That person was his Uncle Lou.

~

Uncle Lou had long grown out of his hippiedom from a fashion point of view. And by the time Tarnasay and his brothers got to know him, he wore way too much brown, carried his pants way too high and smoked a large, pungent, kid-repelling pipe. They all hated the pipe and truly believed they could smell it a day before he came and for at least a week after he left. But despite his pipe and his 'senior public servant' appearance, Uncle Lou still maintained some of his 'Age of Aquarius' views and often delighted the kids with opinions, antics and attitudes that made their Mum and Dad seem stiff and boring. He was misshapen like a semi-deflated beach ball but amazingly agile and energetic. When he visited it wasn't uncommon to see him tearing around the streets on a bike three times too small for him, hotly pursued by a trail of screaming, maniacally euphoric neighbourhood kids. They couldn't believe their luck in having their very own big brown clown to play with. So when not smoking his pipe, Uncle Lou often had the kids' undivided attention and they listened attentively to whatever he had to say. And it was here that Tarnasay discovered the true value of things. Not the monetary value but the purpose of things, what they offered and why they existed in the first place. If he'd been a little older and wiser, he may have also realised why so many of the neglected toys which usually formed part of their front garden landscape always seemed to disappear around the time Uncle Lou came to stay. A rusting, metal tank thrust between fence palings, forgotten and left to rot like a casualty in a miniature war scene would suddenly become conspicuous in its absence. Sometimes a robust family discussion of sobbing and tantrums would ensue regarding the disappearance of certain toys, and then a day or two later they'd miraculously reappear in exactly the same spot.

It would be some years later before Tarnasay discovered that it was actually Uncle Lou who made the toys disappear. And it was at this point that Tarnasay believes he made a life changing decision about the modern world he lived in and how he could appease himself with its nagging shortcomings and enjoy it. He can still recall with clarity the lazy sunny afternoon when the sun got too hot for games and mad circus-like cycling antics, his Uncle Lou explaining to a throng of neighbourhood kids seated neatly before him on the front lawn, legs crossed like they were at school, why it was important to look after the things they had. Uncle Lou wasn't a storyteller nor did he harbour a hidden yearning to be a school teacher or feel obligated to instil certain values in the young. He just didn't like to see things go to waste. Whatever form they took – whether practical, digestible or just ornately majestical – he didn't like to see them become waste. And so he said to them as they sat together on the lawn with an attentiveness that would've been the envy of their 3rd grade school teachers, "If you're not going to use something or have fun with it, think about giving it away or sharing it with someone who will." He said it plainly. He wasn't attempting to be profound or guide them, or necessarily teach them a lesson, he just wanted to say it to a group of little people because he believed it. He thought it was important and since he had their attention, he figured that – just like anyone else - they should at least consider it. He said it like he would say it to his own mother. Tarnasay doesn't know how this simple tip or hint was understood by the other kids or his younger siblings. All he knew was that this simple unadorned suggestion affected him – and that's all he saw it as – 'a suggestion' not a command, rule or warning as it seemed the way every other adult deemed it necessary to impart information. No, it was just a simple suggestion to consider sharing things that would end up impacting on him and guiding his life in a far greater way than his great ol' Uncle Lou would ever know or Tarnasay himself had ever foreseen.

Today it brings a smile to his face whenever he remembers why some of his and his siblings' toys had suddenly disappeared from their various points of abandonment around their house. The fact that Uncle Lou took it upon himself to become a kind of 'toy monitor' whenever he stayed with his family. How he'd take note of what toys appeared to be abandoned or disregarded and then, one by one, take them and store them in his bedroom cupboard. He would then simply wait a day or so to see if their absence was missed and if not, give them away. No-one knows exactly how many toys Uncle Lou gave away because – and this would probably be the point he'd make were he alive today – they were never missed. Not like quirky, fun Uncle Lou who one sad day finally ran out of his abundant energy and passed away. On the day he died, Tarnasay imagined him puffing away on his pipe contentedly while he cycled towards oblivion on one of their rickety little bikes.

So Tarnasay believed his motive for temporarily obtaining some of the more desirable material possessions in the Western world transcended the obvious "Hate the rich!", "Greedy capitalists must die!" modern day, heavy left-winger's daily mantra and moved towards what he liked to call "personalised materialistic waste control" or the more catchy "pleasure recycling." Much like his beloved Uncle Lou but on a significantly grander scale, Tarnasay found himself disillusioned with waste that he saw piling up like an international mega-meal of refuse. He was over the waste of wealth, the indifference and the idle. In the words of his Uncle, "What's the point in having a fantastic new road bike if it never hits the road? Or putting in a spectacular winning bid for a painting only to hide it away in your holocaust-proof vault?" When others accused him of being "an outright criminal" for stealing their bike or car or boat (ironically, only after they discovered its absence once he returned the object), Tarnasay found private comfort in the knowledge that he was merely enjoying the neglected object for its purpose and its pleasure. He knew that his dear old Uncle Lou would have approved. But no-one, with the exception of his close friends and sections of the general public would ever accept this motivation as an acceptable explanation. It would afford him a kind of "reasonableness" his victims would say, "a flimsy justification," appearing to lessen his crime through popularising his antics. "Just having a bit of a lark" and "A likeable scoundrel" were two descriptions that were often used as sound-bites for the evening news when it became apparent that Tarnasay had struck again. But the fact is, none of Tarnasay's "victims" would've known he even existed had it not been for his penchant for leaving notes for the possessions he borrowed. Sometimes he'd leave a short note offering an explanation for the item's disappearance and when they could expect to see it again. On other occasions he simply wrote, 'Cheers. Tarnasay.' Despite signing off such notes with his unusual name, police and private investigators employed by victims to identify him had no information and none had been forthcoming from the community at large either. Interpreting names or shaping them into an accessible English form can sometimes be a whimsical, imaginative practice for new immigrants. Tarnasay's parents had clearly enjoyed blending his father's Welsh heritage with that of their imagination. The result being, that at many places he'd worked during his youth and later as a young adult it had proven easier to tell almost everyone that his name was simply "T." And those who may have guessed or known who he was such as his old school teachers, shopkeepers and past landlords never came forward with information for the only reason one can conclude – they liked him.

~

Tarnasay slowly unwinds the courtyard hose and fills Hasta's water bowl with fresh water. He watches as a small leaf falls into the dish and jostles about in the burbling water like a tiny boat caught in rough seas.

THE HEIST

"Ready?" said Tarnasay. He was smiling. Like usual.

However the fact that he was smiling at this critical moment also made me smile.

"Ubetcha," I said. Tarnasay shook his head but I could tell he was glad to see I was relaxed.

"Well that's our group Col," he said as he gestured towards a large excited group that was milling outside the yacht club entry to the moorings.

I now kept apace of Tarnasay as he strode with purpose towards them. After our earlier discussion I'd agreed to Tarnasay's approach of entering the mooring. His idea was to simply join a large group entering the mooring, to pretend we were part of that group. All that would be required was for us to engage in some excited friendly banter with those on the tail end of the group as we entered.

I watched as Tarnasay immediately delivered a compliment to a woman in a colourful summer dress as we joined the back of the group. He smiled his best smile as he said it. The woman was delighted and friendly banter carried on between them. My first attempt to engage with a member of the group failed when a man merely grunted at my friendly introduction. Fortunately, a woman next to him was in high spirits and introduced herself.

"Hi I'm Gale," said the woman cheerfully as she offered her hand to me, "I'm from the regional office."

"Hi I'm Col," I said. "Beautiful day for it, been a while since I've been out on the water," I added avoiding the need to disclose where I was from. I hoped broaching the topic of going sailing would steer the conversation in a different direction.

"Well it's my first time!" said the woman, "I'm like an excited little girl. Just hope I don't get sea sick," she added laughing.

"Me too Gale," said the woman in the floral dress who had been speaking to Tarnasay and overheard us. She moved closer and introduced herself to me.

"Hi I'm Megan," said the woman. I was relieved she didn't qualify where she was from.

"Well ladies, my good friend Col here knows a trick or two about how to ward off sea sickness," said Tarnasay who proceeded to introduce himself to Gale. I felt relieved that there was now a four way conversation. I was even more relieved when I realised we were already passing through the mooring gate as I began listing a few supposed ways to avoid sea-sickness. It was just as another bustling, day-cruising group giddy from sun and champagne were exiting. It was perfect. It was loud and busy. At a glance I noticed that the young security guard on duty was far more interested in the attractive women passing through than anyone else.

"And perhaps my favourite way to avoid sea-sickness is to simply look up and out to sea. Don't be fiddling with your phone, just look at the sea and the swell and your brain will adjust to the rhythm," I said.

"Or you can just take one of these," said Tarnasay as he popped a sea-sickness pill into his mouth. The two women laughed as we excused ourselves explaining that we wanted to grab a couple of things at the club's cafeteria before setting sail.

Tarnasay's observations regarding the busyness of the yacht marina providing a distraction had proven true. Entering had been easy. There had been no need for the wax-head hang-loose double pump hand signal and I knew Tarnasay was relieved. Not only did the idea of performing the hand signal irk him, he simply didn't want to acknowledge or interact with anyone outside of those within an anonymous group while entering the mooring. "This isn't a teenage prank we're conducting," he felt the need to remind me.

We proceeded quickly to one of the yacht club's complimentary runabout tinnies. We boarded Ubetcha on the starboard side just as planned. I began running through all the checks, ensuring that the GPS system was indeed absent or a least completely disengaged as envisaged. Once my checks were done, it was time to get her going. It was a sweet sound to hear Ubetcha's twin engines start up immediately, their heavy, powerful drone burbling beneath the surface of the calm water. Raring to go.

We'd been cruising for no more than five minutes when we heard the arresting, *Thoompf! Thoompf! Thoompf!* of a helicopter's propellor overhead. Tarnasay froze in front of the floor-to-ceiling mirror that adorned the lavish lounge room on the top deck where he'd been adjusting his MB impersonating jacket and tie. He caught my startled reflection glaring back at him.

"Security?" I queried incredulous but in a calm manner.

"Nup," replied Tarnasay firmly without a hint of doubt. He then continued to smarten his MB tie, straighten his MB jacket and adorn his MB hat which he pulled down hard at an angle to hide his face, "We've made the News."

***

The real MB grunted and rolled over in his palatial penthouse suite bed disturbed by the TV blaring at him and fumbled for the remote on the bedside table. His sweaty, heavy hand shaking uncontrollably, still wreaked by the previous night's copious intake of alcohol. Finally, he grasped it and hit the off button just as the network announced a live cross to the chopper filming Ubetcha raising anchor.

"Well Larry, we've been cruising all about the city today and on a beautiful summer day like this it comes as no surprise that everyone is on the move and guess what – we've discovered that even 'Ubet- " the reporter began to yell from inside the chopper as the TV went dead. MB sighed heavily in relief as he too headed off somewhere in his drunken slumber.

***

Although I was keeping my composure with this unexpected development, I felt more reassured when Tarnasay finally turned away from the mirror, smiled, winked and walked past me onto the deck. That was until I realised how pale he looked. He looked sickly. His rich, smooth chocolate coloured skin suddenly looked pasty, even a tad translucent. 'Jesus he's really taking this hard, he's completely fucken shaken up.' I felt negative thoughts creeping in. My previously controlled fear was increasing in strength as I watched Tarnasay sit down ever so slowly. He sat partially obscured by the starboard side of the boat just as he said he would. He then called to me in a relaxed manner. "Mate would you mind putting the cap back on that tube of zinc sitting on top of my bag. That stuff's a nightmare when it gets on clothes, and grab me a scotch please. I noticed there's some nice stuff on the shelf inside. Grab me the newspaper on the bench too. Cheers." I quickly looked back inside to the lounge and saw Tarnasay's bag was open and a large tube of white zinc sitting on top of his clothes. I saw the source of Tarnasay's sudden and emphatic whiteness. "Also inside one of the cupboards next to the mirror there's a white waiter's coat and a hat, put them on before you come back out," continued Tarnasay. I set about the tasks stumped as to how in such a short time he'd observed so much.

The sound of the chopper continued to thump above us as it manoeuvred to give the cameraman the best shot. We were careful to keep our heads low and shadowed by our broad-rimmed hats. I delivered Tarnasay his scotch and newspaper and went back inside to change my jacket before continuing to skipper the yacht and familiarise myself with the real thing, the real Ubetcha; no longer just an abstract shape stretched out upon my kitchen table in the form of a plan, nor a wilful sailing dream, but the hallowed famous amazing boat itself. And although we weren't out of trouble yet I couldn't help but think to myself, 'This is my vessel now.' I felt goosebumps rise and tingle upon my forearms for the first time in many years. I watched as Tarnasay sipped his single malt scotch and patted his lips together rapidly for a moment, perhaps attempting to relieve the dryness that tension had brought to his mouth. Or maybe just attempting to guess its age. He then raised his arm and waved his pasty white hand quickly and dismissively at the chopper hovering above, just as he'd seen MB do on occasions when he was being harassed by the media on his yacht. Probably by the same crew. The network News chopper hovered almost motionless before suddenly swooping down and around the yacht a couple of times stalking like a sea eagle. Tarnasay continued to enjoy his scotch but I noticed he was careful to subtly adjust himself in his seat when they swooped in ensuring that they never got a clear, intimate view of him.

Finally, the News crew captured the images they wanted and arced away from the yacht gracefully, heading back towards the city that appeared haloed in a summer haze but was just as likely light smog. I then released the full might of Ubetcha, I booted the 148ft of gambler's grandeur into high speed and sliced through the calm sea. And for the moment, I relaxed. I was as cool under pressure as I had hoped. I understood that time was now more crucial than ever. That we had to knock up fast nautical miles to put the safety of distance and the great South Pacific Ocean between us and those who'd soon be chasing Ubetcha's wake. I looked out to the horizon beyond the Sydney heads and smiled. I watched as Tarnasay raised his glass in a private tribute to the world adventure ahead and drained the last of his scotch.

Sam's Neverending Day Off (Part 1)

Hasta chose the spot for them. He'd run ahead up the hill and he was lying down panting heavily in a grassy clearing atop of the reserve lookout far enough away from tourists who alighted tour buses, squinting at the sun and appearing disorientated. When Sam finally arrives she is impressed too, "Nice spot fella."

On the way to the top she'd been conscious of not letting him off the leash partly because she wasn't entirely sure he wouldn't just bolt away and partly because they were in a nature reserve. But he was a powerful dog and he had let her know it. Perhaps that's his plan thought Sam, 'Wear her down and you're free lad!' So Sam had hardened-up and reined him in a little, asserting her hierarchal privilege. For a while Hasta had complied, then, as Sam had speculated, he wore her down. She was carrying her picnic basket and rug and Hasta seemed to be gaining more and more energy as they moved up the hill just as she was losing hers. Finally she'd released him and sure enough he'd bolted out of sight. "Shit," spat Sam who continued to plod slowly up the hill. Then Hasta suddenly reappeared bolting from behind some bushes and Sam was relieved. Until she saw how fast he was moving, and that he was doing a bee line for her. "Jesus fella slow down, slow down...Hey! Slow – AAAHHH!" screamed Sam as she braced herself for the collision. But Hasta just pulled up sharp, skidding a little and then dropped in by her side like the world's most obedient dog. "Idiot," muttered Sam who wondered what the hell she'd got herself into.

But Hasta was fine. She realised this was just something he did, to burn off pent up energy perhaps. Running ahead and then looping back down towards her at speed before coming to an abrupt halt and rejoining her at human speed, walking by her side for a while before shooting off again. This pattern continued until Sam finally reached the top of the reserve lookout where Hasta now lay panting happily in the sunny clearing waiting for her.

~

As Sam pitches her large tartan blanket over the lush patch of grass she can't help but smile. A life changing decision is being punctuated by a picnic. After more than a decade of intensive work as a high level investigator contracted by the Australian Government to work alongside the Australian Federal Police to uncover hidden identities, the masterminds behind notorious, highly organised crime syndicates, she is leaving it behind. Her most recent case, by far the most challenging that she'd been assigned, had ended badly. Badly, as in it had been closed. Against her wishes, against her professional opinion. She'd always worked hard on cases which in turn brought successful outcomes for the private investigation firm for which she worked and she'd enjoyed an enviable reputation for "cracking the uncrackable." This case had been one of them. But on this occasion, the success that usually followed hours of dedication and self-sacrifice had failed. She hadn't succeeded. Well, she had. She was just one click away from solving it, when they closed it. Her seniors closed it and filed it: Unresolved. It was over.

Mental furnishings

Light pours through the broad floor to ceiling apartment windows, illuminating an eclectic mix of objet-d'art upon his large bookshelf. Although many of the items were delicate and beautiful and actually quite valuable, their worth was unassuming to the untrained eye. Over the years his apartment had been broken into twice and on both occasions they had taken all his 'home entertainment' goods and other mod-cons such as his DVD, stereo equipment, microwave, even his washing machine, but never any of his valuable pieces. Some of which individually, were worth more than the total sum of the other items stolen. But Tarnasay understood that the average burglar pillaging a house wouldn't suddenly stop mid-raid and exclaim "By George! That's a Henry Moore wood carving!" or upon seeing a Chinese vase within a cabinet wonder, "Hmm...could that be Ming Dynasty?" So he'd always been content with a kind of mental insurance rather than home insurance. Perhaps due to his own collection of art lacking such things as a Ming Dynasty vase, but nonetheless, he still felt the chances of his valuable items being stolen were slim. Sure, he recognised the possibility a burglar may decide to bag something on the off-chance it may be worth something but through experience he'd observed that the main focus always seemed to be on fast moving consumer goods. The replacement of which always annoyed him but only for the inconvenience and immediate expense – they were not unique or crafted or sentimental – they were replicated, manufactured and replaceable.

Tarnasay knew he would always overcome the disappearance of a TV set far sooner than he would a unique item of sentimental value.

And for most people too, he believed this would be true. Many times he'd heard bushfire victims on News reports lament and grieve the loss of family heirlooms almost as though they were family but he was yet to see someone sobbing over the loss of their beloved flat screen TV. Not publicly anyway. But despite this, it seemed to Tarnasay that unless someone actually faced the devastation of losing everything in a bushfire, the mod-cons and new technology temptings that surround us tended to occupy a greater part of our lives and minds. These items demanded our attention through the persuasive argument of advertising and the convenience they promise. Tarnasay couldn't help but think that modern society as a whole had somehow devalued the time honoured heirloom, perhaps an item that on the surface lacks the attraction of modern items. He wondered how many of us today are inclined to nurture what we believe will one day be a precious family heirloom for our grandchildren. Something special. A beautiful piece of hand-made furniture painstakingly realised by a master craftsman or a delicate piece of pottery. Perhaps the original Xbox, provided it hangs around in the garage long enough, may one day have some value to collectors, but how many people these days bought something of true quality he wondered. Something rare and unique and beautifully hand crafted, something of patience and skill, something of talent, something special to touch, to smell, to puzzle over, to marvel at.

Tarnasay knows he's not alone with these thoughts. It's not as though he believes there's next to no-one left in society who appreciates things of great skill and craftsmanship. But personally he feels that he was – along with almost everyone else in modern, Western society – party to an ever-increasing throw-away mentality. It isn't as if he pines for simpler times or shuns new technology like a disgruntled luddite, it's just that he feels that society as a whole, in particular Western society is too inclined to discard things under the spell of immediate gratification. "Things don't last like they used to," he often hears people lament. And they're mostly right. Many manufacturers and their marketers realised something long before anyone else and compounded this lament accordingly – no-one expects anything to last as long as it used to, so why make it that way. Planned obsolescence. They can churn out products more quickly and we just buy a new one when it fails sooner than expected, resigned to the simple fact that, these days, it's just the way it is.

But Tarnasay wonders why this is "just the way it is." Why had a friend purchased three new fridges over the last twelve years while his 60 year old Kelvinator continues to hum away ever so reliably, as though in perpetual meditation of food preservation. Of course it's in the interest of companies to move more and more products, more and more quickly, but is it worth doing so at the expense of quality? If a fridge lasts a lifetime or longer does this work for the company that built it or against them? If, because they last so long, does that mean they sell less or does the fact that they do last so long and the resulting reputation it brings mean that they will sell more? Tarnasay catches himself before he entertains the idea of writing a PhD on Modern Consumerism or a lonely, unread blog about the subject and takes a sip of his beer.

He notices the sun has now stopped illuminating his collection of beautifully turned timber bowls, delicately carved figurines from South East Asia and a beautiful ukelele he discovered one night at the famous Moonlight Markets in Chiang Mai. He watches intently as the sun leaves them, and their very existence, their visceral vigour appears to fade in time right before his eyes.

THE DISPENSARY

Despite possessing almost every conceivable technological gadget of convenience such as touch pad door openers, sensor lighting and hidden pop-up plasma screens in all three spas, Ubetcha also represented by way of its décor, everything one may expect from someone blessed with an abundance of money but poverty stricken in taste. Had Ubetcha not been absconded by the two brazen thieves, MB would have done well to overhaul the interior decorating of his ship at the same time as he'd intended to update its antiquated GPS navigational system. A colour scheme of faded mandarin interior walls combined with deep purple lounges carried through the two entertaining levels only to be offset by Edwardian style bathrooms and bedrooms ornately detailed with stunning Mahogany timber, marble basins and large brass fittings. It was where 1980's corporate interior decorating met early 1900's Edwardian sensibilities and it almost made the two men wince when they first encountered it. There would be no easing of their judgement either regarding these decorating decisions even as they became accustomed to everything else the floating boat of bourgeois boasted.

On occasions either man could be seen shaking his head when leaving the warmth of his Edwardian style room where the deep hues of mahogany timber insisted they relax. They would be shaking their heads because they remained puzzled by the polarity of the decorating decisions; confused that someone had made a conscious decision to combine the pastels colours and furnishing style of the 1980's immediately outside a room that appeared as an Edwardian time capsule. Col believed it was, "Enough to change a man's mood."

When time allowed, Tarnasay and Col set about discovering Ubetcha's hidden tricks and treasures. It was while anchored in calm seas on the West Norfolk Ridge, in-between monitoring for news reports of their heist, that a brief game of decadent one-up-man-ship ensued between them as they scoured the majestic vessel like excited fourteen year old boys. The challenge was to find the most indulgent, extravagant modern mechanism or function onboard Ubetcha. Over the years Col had been onboard many fine yachts, some with a great deal of customised refinement but never had he encountered indulgence such as this. MB was 'larger than life' as they say and wouldn't have appeared out of place had he been written into a James Bond script as a pugnacious, eccentric villain and his vessel, for all its absurdity of riches and grotesque indulgence, would have played a starring part too. They discovered one of Ubetcha's more indulgent, bizarre customisations were the series of small pop-up drinking cabinets that Lily, the croupier had spoken of to Tarnasay some months back. They were hidden throughout the vessel, neatly nestled either within walls or beneath the floor; where upon pressing a very small discreet button, a smooth, graceful mechanical process would take place. A secret panel door would be released followed by the appearance of an instant miniature bar showcasing a fine selection of single malt scotch, cognac, muscat and port. Alongside the selection of drinks sat a small beautifully crafted timber box which soon revealed itself to be in fact a refrigerated chest where upon opening you were suddenly presented with – like an absurd magic trick for the bourgeois – an elaborate cheese board. With a delicate yellow silk ribbon a fine selection of mature cheddars, blue veins, bries and camemberts were strapped to the board like captives, untouched within their original packaging. Elsewhere, neatly tucked away within the night-cap treasure chest were olives, dried fruits, nuts and small sealed parcels of smoked trout, salmon, assorted punnets of pate and water crackers. Perhaps one or two of these strategically placed, pop-up bars may not have come as such a surprise but to discover no less than six sprinkled throughout the yacht had them spinning. It was as though someone (perhaps MB) had decided that there was simply no way one could move through the yacht without having the sudden impulsion to stop, have a scotch and a selection of fine cheese before moving on. They even discovered one of the secret cabinets in the hallway to their rooms but this one was particularly special as it also featured small fold out chairs. The chairs presented themselves ever so smoothly and in perfect synchronicity with the drinks cabinet that they appeared to be performing a pretty little mechanical dance. Silently, the two men took numerous turns opening and closing the secret cabinet with its twin chairs. Neither of them said a word. It was as though they weren't sure what to make of it, confused as to whether they should be disgusted by something so unnecessarily decadent or charmed by it. They were watching what seemed to be the result of some mad but gifted engineering craftsman who'd built something so precise with its delicate action and gentle mechanical sighs that it was simply impossible not to admire it. It wasn't long either before Tarnasay heard the distinct crunch of someone eating water crackers outside his room at a ridiculous hour. Opening the door, he peered out to see Col in the opaque light of night and day crossing paths. He held a scotch in one hand and somewhat daintily in the other, a water cracker loaded generously with smoked trout, a large dollop of very ripe blue vein cheese which oozed awkwardly over the side and topped with a plump dried apricot. "What?" he had said to Tarnasay, a tad sheepishly.

Finding Maxie Burgess' stash in the orlop of Ubetcha however, was a little more than Tarnasay and Col had expected. It wasn't that they thought for a moment there wouldn't be drugs on board or perhaps some of the weirdest pornaphelia available to man, in fact Franz's reconnaissance on MB had revealed that there was a certain amount of cocaine to be found on Ubetcha, "I couldn't find out exactly how much is onboard but I thought you should know. Anyway I doubt it's anything more than for personal use," said Franz. But the amount of cocaine they were to find went from being exciting to incredulous to downright worrying. Franz had come across the information at the latest stage possible – on the morning of the heist. Both men had been informed but neither of them paid it much attention. They were stealing a superyacht after all, what difference will a little cocaine make. And neither of them had even mentioned it to the other. This was despite Col learning from Franz that it was in fact Tarnasay who was supposed to relay the information to him. Although they didn't let the revelation that the yacht would now be missed by far more dangerous people than the sluggish bully MB dampen their hedonistic spirit, they knew it was a course changing discovery.

The discovery involved moving away from the Australian eastern seaboard as quickly as possible and remaining closer to the North Island of New Zealand than anywhere else. From there they headed north into the Coral Sea towards Papua New Guinea. The idea was then to take their time, carefully skirting the coast line of Papua New Guinea through the Torres Strait and into the Arafura Sea and Timor Sea in order to make their way to Thailand. Looping around the top of Australia was the part that most worried Col. Being so close to the Australian coastline put them at the greatest risk of being located. Initially, Col had proposed that they simple hunker down at sea near the West Norfolk Ridge nearer New Zealand while attempting to discover where the Coast Guard were dispersing in the hunt for Ubetcha. Col had switched the B-Sat transmitting box off shortly after boarding, they were untrackable. They began monitoring news reports on TV, online and the radio awaiting stories about the heist of Ubetcha and her most likely whereabouts. But when they heard nothing, they actually heard a great deal. They comprehended the silence smartly. They immediately changed tack heading towards Thailand as quickly as Ubetcha could ferry them. The two cavaliers had realised, in a cruel twist of irony for MB, that the amount of contraband onboard Ubetcha had silenced the otherwise noisy man. MB simply had no choice but to attempt to hide the fact that his vessel had been stolen and for as long as possible. Col stood at the helm of Ubetcha, already pumped high on adrenalin, snorted two fat lines of cocaine, took a swig of scotch and screamed like a demented pirate as the boat smashed its way through the heavy coastal swell before him.

~

Before long they fondly began referring to the orlop as 'The Dispensary.' Although the main contraband onboard was cocaine, there was also an odd mix of amphetamines within a small wooden chest and initially they indulged rather heavily. During this time great speculation was spent on why the likes of MB, with his apparent wealth, would have such a significant haul of cocaine on onboard. It now appeared that whatever else he was doing visiting Sydney, trafficking drugs was a part of it. This puzzled them no end. Realising they may never know, Tarnasay concluded that it probably came down to little more than greed and opportunity. His theory was that perhaps initially, it had been about "Personal use and large parties, etc," but somehow, somewhere, someone along the line has brought his attention to how easy it would be for him to arrange the despatch of vast amounts of drugs. Perhaps one of his crew got in his ear Tarnasay suggested, "And being a risk taker of sorts, a gambler - and a greedy one at that, he just figured it was 'Money for jam' as they say." Col listened to a pissed, and very high Tarnasay espouse his theory but it seemed too straight forward. It still didn't quite make sense for him but perhaps Tarnasay was right, because they don't think like him it's difficult to comprehend behaving like him. Tarnasay's theory went some way towards the reason MB was trafficking drugs. His risk taking and greedy nature indeed played a role but Col's hunch was right, it wasn't as simple as that. It wasn't as simple as him just wanting more and someone close to him suggesting an easy way to do it.

The truth was Maxie Burgess, for all his abundant wealth, had got himself into a bit of trouble. No longer content on visiting the Hi-Roller rooms around the world, he had got himself and his mad gambler's mentality embroiled in what could only be described as a kind of extreme gambling. Extreme versions of just about everything exist in modern times and it seems gambling is no exception. Initially, the game was played privately amongst Russian billionaires before attracting the attention of the Chinese and shortly after the rest of the world's wealthy elite. The game itself is not unique and it would be exactly the same as any other poker game if it weren't for the billions upon billions at stake for every hand - and therefore rich men's dreams and their empires. With very little recourse to "buy time" in order to settle debts it is rumoured that entire fortunes have been reduced to nothing in less than 24 hours. MB wasn't as insane as those rumoured to have lost everything in a fervour to regain a dwindling empire but he'd gone close and had asked for whatever little time was given to settle his debts. If over the years, he hadn't indulged in so much and invested his fortunes so broadly and into myriad complex deals (many of them under-performing) he could've settled things quickly. But MB, as was his want and nature, had over-stretched. Selling out was proving difficult - and sometimes expensive. So MB's fortune which was built upon his grandmother's ingenuity was now at stake and the best plan he'd devised to resolve the situation quickly was to traffick drugs from port to port. A celebrity of sorts known in many parts of the world for his penchant to go from country to country to gamble, he could often avoid maritime scrutiny and government red tape. It had proven easy for him to conduct his new business affairs and had been working perfectly for him. Until now.

Col and Tarnasay took advantage of substances that allowed them to remain focussed for long periods of sailing, provided they kept alcohol consumption to a limit and didn't take too much MDMA. Concerned that there may already be search vessels employed privately by MB to hunt for them, Col and Tarnasay crept along all through the night. They knocked up nocturnal nautical mile after mile, completely wired, blatheringly alert, discussing anything and everything. Tarnasay's screening process prior to choosing a captain for his sailing adventure included more than a couple of questions regarding the candidate's attitude to recreational drug-taking and he was glad he had done so. He simply wasn't interested in being stuck on a yacht for potentially months on end with a teetotaller or someone strongly anti-drugs. Nor was he interested in having a drunk or a junkie as a Captain, but it was important that he had someone open-minded towards the matter of mind altering substances. It wasn't enough that they "don't mind" if he indulges but chose to not partake themselves as some of his candidates expressed. He wanted a shipmate that was happy to get shitfaced on occasions or blow a mast-sized joint on the high seas when he had the desire to do so. Drug taking for Tarnasay was an essential presence in his life but not a necessity. It was about mood, and he applied as much thought to the decision of whether he'd indulge on any one occasion, as he did when deciding to have a coffee. He was a self-confessed hedonist after all and it was an overwhelming hedonistic streak that was a major factor in him embarking on his adventures in the first place. Fun was of the utmost importance and fun came in many forms for Tarnasay – some of them illegal. So he ruled out anyone but the free spirited and open-minded when it came to choosing his captain. And he was prepared to wait even at the risk of Ubetcha leaving until he found the right person. Someone with the proven skills to sail a yacht the size of Ubetcha and someone with a thrill-seeking side to match. Fortunately, he found Col. It wasn't too far into the interview with Tarnasay that Col revealed his penchant for a good time and that "should drugs be a part of that, then all the better mate," explained Col in his no-nonsense manner. A manner which Tarnasay had liked immediately but one which he couldn't help but think sat rather oddly alongside his "deadset fondness for pingers and trips" and other recreational drugs Tarnasay had only vaguely heard of. He found Col spoke about drugs and bands and partying with an earnestness and sincerity that was reminiscent of his Uncles standing around a BBQ discussing the merits of their favourite Holdens or secret fishing spots. In fact, he decided, as he listened to Col waffle on about his various partying exploits, if certain words were replaced there was very little difference. Many people would be alarmed by this but Tarnasay felt reassured. It was like having a favourite Uncle come along for the ride. Tarnasay momentarily found himself thinking about his Uncle Lou and how he would have loved the idea of taking part in his adventure. Instead he had the handy Col, a man who was Uncle-like in manner, even shaped like an Uncle, he thought, but most definitely not typically Uncle-like in outlook.

Tarnasay was pleased that he'd made the right decision by employing Col as his Captain and Shipmate; someone he could easily spend time with when he knew there'd be little or no other human contact. And when their conversations became shorter and good moods swung in and out like warm currents, he needed to be with a person who could handle the isolation. He wasn't worried for himself; he enjoyed his own company and could easily amuse himself but he needed to feel as confident for the mental well-being of his shipmate. Fortunately, Col had sailed solo on many occasions and he too knew how to amuse himself when the days drew longer. He played guitar, was a keen reader and liked to whittle weird things out of small pieces of timber. So when they ran out of things to say to each other for the time being, it wasn't difficult or awkward, they'd just go about their own tasks and hobbies for a time. Col whittled away the hours.

However, due to the unusual circumstance of navigating a floating pharmacy, the two of them had gotten to know each other at an accelerated rate. Tarnasay found himself in the unusual predicament of talking about his immediate family in far more detail than he'd ever done. He revealed to Col that for many years from the age of seventeen he'd lived with his father's brother, his beloved Uncle Lou. His father, a history professor had accepted an academic posting to Wales and the family with his younger siblings were to relocate. Except for him. He was seventeen at the time and it was thought best that he remain "settled" in Australia to live with his Uncle Lou as he prepared for university. Col could see in Tarnasay's eyes he'd clearly thought otherwise.

"I've seen my family twice since then" he said, "Dad sends me birthday and Christmas cards of course. *Cheers, Dad* they say. Nothing else."

For a while they shared a comfortable silence that only good friends, which they now truly were, can let stretch as far as the horizon. And on this calm day at sea the horizon stretched and bent forever. Col broke the silence. He told Tarnasay the pain he felt the day before they left, when he said what may well be a last goodbye to his mother. He explained how she'd become increasingly cocooned in the isolating world of dementia, and he spoke almost choking on each swollen word, of his devoted father's death which came way too soon. Again they let the silence that followed attempt to process and lighten the heaviness of words just said.

There's only so much cocaine you can continuously enjoy with the one person even if you like them. And this revelation becomes ever truer if there's also an absence of sexual attraction. It wasn't too long after leaving Australian territorial waters that both Tarnasay and Col realised that their two-man party ship had to lessen its drug haul. But this wasn't until they had sampled everything on offer and had passionate discussions about almost everything that may enter a man's mind as he floats about the sea. One evening, following a three day marathon of drugs, when the upper became a downer and the downer became an insult, Col decided to question Tarnasay's motivation for his adventures. He wasn't in a particularly good mood that afternoon either. At least once in the morning and once in the afternoon, they had made a habit of watching News reports to see if the story of the heist had broken. It had; and the level of attention they were receiving back home was high. Experts on superyacht heists were everywhere it seemed. It was also revealed that Tarnasay had left behind one of his infamous notes. *'Cheers. Captain Swift! (And Tarnasay)'* the note had read. At first he couldn't believe Tarnasay had even found the time and presence of mind to do such a thing. But then he remembered who he was with. Col listened to Tarnasay explain in his nonchalant, matter-of-fact manner when he discussed such things, how he'd simply placed the note inside a sealed clear plastic envelope and attached it to a small buoy and hoicked it overboard as they left. "I'm stoked they found it. I thought it might be missed," he said smiling. It was then Col had the sudden urge to hit him. His nerves had been on edge lately and something about Tarnasay's cloaked cocksure manner, his unreal, incomprehensible confidence suddenly aggravated him. Heightened by the amount of drugs he'd consumed recently but the irritation had been there on other occasions too. Maybe it was based on a kind of jealousy because the man always appeared so calm about everything and unaffected. Whatever it was, it was particularly annoying Col this evening. And although he was playing the devil's advocate when he began challenging Tarnasay's actions – because after all, he partnered him in the commandeering of Ubetcha – there was more than a tinge of antagonism towards Tarnasay's trait for "supposedly" borrowing things. A hobby of sorts which had then became an unorthodox, borderline criminal career. This was what Col was still struggling with. He had allowed himself, a grown man, independent and confident, to be influenced, persuaded, charmed into committing a serious crime like a teenager succumbing to peer group pressure. But the truth was, there had been no pressure. It was always his decision. But what was troubling Col now that his excessive drug taking over the past month saw his mood slump to a worrying low, like it was tied to an anchor sinking well beyond self-doubt and confusion, past disappointment and anger, and deep into the depths of despair; was whether he had rather quickly, fucked up his life. Now that the thrill had worn off leaving him numb like the last line of cocaine, he found himself increasingly worried that he was in some serious shit and there was no way back.

"You know, in truth, you're just a thief Tarnasay," blurted Col suddenly while they both sat staring at a sea so smooth it appeared coated in black rubber with giant rollers running gently beneath it. Earlier, they'd both enjoyed the spectacle of watching a massive school of dolphins cruising beside them in a lazy celebration of summer; their arched backs pushing fins rhythmically through the black rubber with the precision synchronised swimmers can only dream of.

Tarnasay was silent for a moment before answering. Perhaps disappointed that their perfect day at sea now headed towards a possible storm front building in his shipmate's mind. "Of a kind I suppose, Col," he said.

"Of a kind! Ha! Fuck. You really are somethin' Tarnasay. Of a kind eh? In my book mate you're either a fucking thief or you're not. You either take something that's not yours or you don't."

"Well I suppose I'm a thief then," conceded Tarnasay.

"I know you justify it to yourself by saying that you only *borrow* these things and never keep them but you're still stealing them."

"I say borrow Col, because I return them. Mostly."

"Mostly! Have you ever thought that some people truly appreciate their luxurious possessions, appreciate the painstaking detail of effort and creativity that went into the creation of these items, these objects?" continued Col.

"Of course. But sometimes they're not appreciated."

"How do you know they're not appreciated?"

"Because they're neglected."

"How do you know?"

"They're unused and idle."

"How do you know that?!" asked Col, incredulous.

"Because they're rarely missed."

"Ah rarely missed hey? So they are in fact missed?"

"Well everyone will miss their Ferrari Testarossa..." explained Tarnasay.
"Of course," said Col, almost patronising in tone.
He was staring intensely at Tarnasay. Tarnasay held the stare. Their stares stopped everything. The water's gentle lapping against the boat was gone. The spying sea gulls which only moments ago flew gracefully next to them had disappeared. Dolphins departed. It could have been a government ad for drug abuse - *'If you abuse drugs... relationships quickly breakdown... crimes are committed'* – at this point a spear gun would be produced and fired into someone's stomach.
"Unless they own eight of them," said Tarnasay finally pressing play again. Releasing the tension like a valve.
Col scoffed. But it wasn't the disapproving scoff he would have preferred. It was an affable, agreeable scoff.
"So that makes it okay to steal them?" he then queried.
"To borrow one of them?..." said Tarnasay, "Yes, I think so."

He then released his pan-faced stare and smiled at Col who struggled to maintain his stoic expression, but he too gave in and smiled back. Smiles mostly come in pairs otherwise spear guns and the like would be far more prevalent in society. Col slowly raised his glass to cheers Tarnasay.
"But I still think you're a dirty thieving cunt," added Col grinning happily for the first time in two weeks.

~

Col continued to worry as they edged their way closer to Thailand but now he made his worry, his encroaching, tormenting concerns tack in a different direction. He used his sailing knowledge and skills as a metaphor for redirecting his mental state, tactically steering his mind across the prevailing wind of worry attempting to push him back. He used this worry in a way which, rather than attempting to correct or rewind the situation, was employed to better it. To make it safe, to ensure that they succeeded, that they didn't get caught. He switched from worrying about getting caught to worrying about ways not to. He allowed himself to fantasise more and more about the possibilities that the proceeds from the organised sale of the contraband and later, possibly Ubetcha, would bring forth, just as he had done prior to them completing the heist. He reminded himself that this was the reason he joined Tarnasay in the first place. That, and the need for excitement and daring which had all but disappeared from his life in recent years. Fortunately, it worked. Because foolishly he'd decided against raising his continuing negative, depressing thoughts with Tarnasay believing there was nothing he could have said to change it. 'Sure he's got magic of a kind but he can't change thought patterns and he's not a psychologist,' he'd reasoned, ignoring the simple fact that sharing your feelings about anything with anybody is always better than sharing nothing with nobody.

Prior to the stealing of Ubetcha and later, while they briefly hid floating in the South Pacific on the edge of West Norfolk Ridge some 800 nautical miles off the East Coast of Australia, Tarnasay had discussed at length the scenario for the yacht's sale with Col. For all Tarnasay's forthrightness with him regarding all aspects of their heist, he never mentioned that a crucial element to their success and the reward for Col's bravery in committing to it actually hinged on the delivery of a drunkard. It was possibly the only thing that made Tarnasay uncomfortable. But he felt it was simply too dangerous to reveal. That such information, even for Col, for all his measuredness and broadmindedness – may have trouble understanding. Particularly when he stood to either benefit from it greatly or be buried by it completely.

The call was a welcome distraction for Col who was keen to hear the development regarding the despatch of drugs and the sale of Ubetcha. Anything that helped sharpen his mind towards evading detection kept negative thoughts in check. He'd remained focussed on charting a course through the Torres Strait that offered as little visible contact with other vessels as possible and was pleased that his course skirting around Norfolk Island via the South Norfolk Basin and up along Three Kings Ridge before heading across to the Coral Sea had resulted in minimal encounters. And despite the fact that Ubetcha's profile would still remain distinguishable to those familiar with the vessel, Tarnasay had, just as they'd discussed prior to the heist, still gone to the effort of carefully removing the word Ubetcha from its sides and aft and applied a striking new motif. It was this kind of attention to detail and the seeing-through of planned actions, one of which Col had all but forgotten, that helped to alleviate those moments when his doubting concerns returned. One thing he knew about Tarnasay was that nothing was done half-arsed.

It had been an eerie moment for Col when late one afternoon he discovered Tarnasay dangling from the side of the boat. He'd been looking for him for some time having last seen him reading on the upper deck when he finally walked out on to the lower deck calling for him. There was no response. He stood there on the deck staring into the expanse of the ocean. There were no birds and the silence suddenly felt suffocating to him. Too still. He began calling for him again slowly getting louder and louder until he felt he was on the verge of yelling. "Yes mate!" he suddenly heard Tarnasay reply but Col couldn't see him. He called to him again and Tarnasay replied again "Yes mate!" "Right. Stop fucking around where are ya?" "Here!" he replied, "Where?!" "Here!" Col then saw a long squeegee type object waving from the starboard side of the boat. "Fuck man," he said walking over to the starboard-side and peering down to see Tarnasay's handy work revealed. "Ah right. Nice work. Man, don't freak me out like that. I've been looking for you for about half an hour eh." Tarnasay pointed to the headphones he was wearing, "Just listening to some tunes while I've been doing this," he said smiling, resting back into his harness and gesturing towards the newly adhered motif. "Looks great. Fuck I was starting to think you'd fallen overboard!" Col scoffed. It then occurred to him that gone are the days where he privately rejoiced in the isolation of solo sailing adventures; solitary trips where you had nothing other than your own thoughts and a scratchy radio signal for company. Back then it didn't bother him; it was a comfortable loneliness, one that he welcomed, sought out. He was happy just to float upon the fringe of a world that, for the most part, only revealed some of its secrets; the vast bulk of its busy life mysteriously hidden beneath a surface that was just as often volatile and dismissive as it was endearing and embracing. He'd always likened the ocean and its certain unpredictability, its moods to that of man. He thought of it as a 'certain unpredictability' because mostly, through satellite information, forecasts and to a much lesser degree, personal observation, it could be read, understood. Not unlike man, who could also be read, predicted, understood through the shifts of political currents, storms of war and sunny economic prosperity. But too often, just as with man he thought, it would surprise you, rise up and slap you in the face just when you thought you understood its behaviour. At least the ocean would never offer a pathetic rationalisation for its barbaric actions, thought Col, it's perfectly happy slapping you in the face for no apparent reason.

A short time after they anchored just off the Thai coastal town of Takua Pa, having avoided contact with almost any other vessels, Tarnasay received the much awaited call from his contact at home regarding the sale of Ubetcha. The call came from Franz who had made a connection with a buyer in Hong Kong. The buyer had a representative in Thailand and Franz explained that he would be their point of contact and told them exactly where they were to meet. Prior to the heist Tarnasay had met with Franz and briefed him on his requirement to find a buyer for a stolen superyacht – but no ordinary superyacht, a high profile one. Franz simply chuckled when Tarnasay put forward his request. Tarnasay had called on Franz over the years with peculiar requests but never had he asked for a request such as this. Franz never probed as to the reasons for his unusual requests, whether it was to gather the names and backgrounds of certain people, he would just carry out the task for a set fee. He never asked questions that were not relevant to the task. He'd simply do what was asked of him. However on this occasion, Tarnasay had expected perhaps a question or two, as this request was in a different league to those that had gone before. He had anticipated a little gentle probing from Franz. But Franz just chuckled and shook his head slowly, then said something that fell awkwardly between earnestness and melodrama, "Good luck brother. Your life is like no other I know."

Tarnasay had no reservations or doubts about the soundness of the contact Franz had established. It was true that Franz drank too much. An alcoholic by anyone's standards. But Tarnasay had known him a long time and he was one of the only people he had ever truly confided in, he was more than a vault, he was a labyrinth made of keyless locks. Every room in his mind that harboured confidential information was built like a bunker, mentally reinforced to withstand the heaviest of verbal bombardment. And although Tarnasay had concern for the toll such drinking may be taking on Franz's body, he had never observed it affecting his judgement or his ability to work. There had been more than one occasion where he had drawn on Franz's considerable general knowledge and the many contacts he had. And Franz knew a lot of people. He was also well liked and on the occasions when only his close friends such as Tarnasay would know he was well-oiled enough to do so, he would burst forward into verse and deliver an impromptu performance to the amazement of those around him. His born shyness and modesty cast adrift by the bravado of word smithery. But he had to be shitfaced to do so.

~

Col felt a gentle slapping of his face from the squeegee and saw Tarnasay's large eyes blinking up at him mockingly, "Hello in there..." Col returned from his thoughts and spoke abruptly, "Yep. It's best we sell her as you said." Tarnasay looked at Col a little confused as though somehow he'd missed part of a conversation they'd apparently just had. "Nah, I mean... sorry mate," Col continued as he helped Tarnasay back onboard, "But I was just thinking about it and I reckon you're right, she's too hot a property to hold onto. It'd be crazy even trying." Col thought about what he'd just said and felt privately stupid. Although it was definitely a major factor, he knew it was really because he no longer liked the idea of sailing alone. But why didn't he just say it? Why was he hiding how he felt? Why did he have this in-built, macho notion about not expressing exactly how he felt about something? "Fuckin' bullshit man," he suddenly blurted out causing Tarnasay to again wonder if he was dozing off between words. "Nah bro. You know, the truth is I just couldn't bear to sail alone anymore. I like company."

"Good for you. I can understand that, I don't know how you ever did it really. I'd have been terrified," said Tarnasay, completely oblivious to the mental milestone Col had just reached in regard to his perception of masculinity.

"Yeah. But you're a pussy," said Col. And he felt good saying it.

~

Tarnasay would never have let Col continue on with Ubetcha. He had decided long ago, that should Franz fail in finding the extremely rare, safe buyer for Ubetcha and her illicit haul – which had been a strong possibility – someone who through their wealth and power was confident enough to disappear and somehow rebirth Ubetcha into another sailing incarnation, he'd simply dump her. He'd abandon the majestic vessel; the floating capital pride of MB. There was no way he would allow Col, now the closest of friends, to get caught with her. Not after they'd succeeded in doing something incredible. Not after he'd made the big bloke find his inner punk again and in the most outrageous, insane way. 'That would just suck,' thought Tarnasay, who had a tendency to use teenage-like language when thinking about serious scenarios he didn't like. The simplicity of the language, the ultimate understatement of saying that something of such life changing devastation merely "sucked" somehow put him at ease. As though it lessened the weight of the serious adult issue being considered. 'Yes, if that happened, it would put an end to any of the future fun my juvenile man-mind had planned,' thought Tarnasay, 'And that'd "totally suck balls," he said again attempting to shake the weight of the adult issue from his temporarily fragile, juvenile mind.

A YELLOW SMILEY FACE

Not long before I was to carry out the most serious business in which I had ever engaged in, to sell a famous stolen superyacht laden with contraband – something possessed me while conducting a final check of the vessel and gathering my things. I visited 'The Dispensary' a final time. More out of curiosity and fascination than anything else. It had always been a surreal sight to me and Tarnasay every time we ventured beneath the lowest deck on Ubetcha and into the orlop where the most drugs either of us had ever seen resided in one place. Meticulously organised and packaged, it had seemed only natural to refer to it as The Dispensary. I lifted the heavy timber hatch door that lead down to the orlop and looked at the neatly stacked collection of drugs. Ordered in classification of substance – cocaine, ecstasy, morphine, and sheet upon sheet of LSD tabs contained within a spring-bind art folder. I flicked the portfolio pages of LSD casually, each sheet featuring a colourful signature motif. We'd only indulged in some of them earlier in the voyage but each of the symbols were now familiar to me, having looked through the folder many times. There was something about its arrangement within the A3 art portfolio, with each of the colourful illustrations in the individual perforated boxes repeated the length of each sheet that made it fun to look at. A tripper's portfolio, their 'Tab de resistance.' It was at this moment while admiring the effort, the ingenuity even of someone who'd bothered to present them in such a way, that one of the sheets caught my eye. Although the image on each tab dizzyingly repeated again and again was familiar to me, and almost universally to everyone on the planet, I couldn't recall seeing this particular sheet before. The illustration was the classic yellow smiley face. Then I noticed that one tab within the plastic sleeve was loose. The rest of the sheet was whole and untampered but there was one, lone smiley face. One smiley face too many. For reasons to this day I'm still unsure, perhaps nerves, perhaps the inner punk within me, I reached inside, picked up the tab and before giving myself time to consider the serious possible consequences of the action, I swallowed it.

'Mr Bank' as he was to be called met me close to Koh Phayam Island just off the coast of Ranong Province, Thailand. The destination was of his choosing and fortunately, in the anticipation of a clean exchange of Ubetcha, I had already familiarised myself with the exact coordinates and how I was to make my way to Ranong and onto the mainland of Thailand. Koh Phayam Island, the country's northernmost island on the Andaman sea near to the border of Myanmar still remained a stunning, relatively undiscovered tourist destination and from my brief reconnaissance of the area I would've happily enjoyed a few days respite there in any other circumstance. But I knew that wasn't possible and following the delivery of Ubetcha I planned to leave as soon as possible.

Mr Bank arrived in a vessel which although it rivalled Ubetcha for size, clearly lacked her grandeur and modernity. Her expense. 'Perhaps they're just up-scaling,' I thought as I approached the vessel resting on the calm sea, 'And they'll just gather all their shit here and now, pile it onboard Ubetcha and just head off. Just like that. Leave the other vessel just floating here like a ghost ship.' It helped me to think of such a thing at this moment. To make me smile and forget about the seriousness of the business I was about to conduct on the strength of a relatively new-found criminal friend's word. If I had allowed myself to think too much about that – to allow commonsense to creep back in right at this crucial moment, right when I was about to conclude an amazing feat, having fought off commonsense long ago when its nagging voice of reason was inadvertently dragging me into doubt – I may well have just given up, jumped ship and fed myself to the sharks.

It was at this point I decided the idea of them suddenly boarding and taking off with Ubetcha was the funniest thing I'd ever thought of. I was no longer thinking rationally. Now, as I approached the vessel for the riskiest business exchange I could ever conjure up so very far away from the comfort of my lounge room in the Eastern Suburbs of Sydney, Australia, I was pissing myself laughing.

"Ahh Captain Swift," said Mr Bank from the small craft now roped to Ubetcha, "Pleased to meet you." I had regained composure and forgotten about the funniest joke in the world. However, with the hearing of 'Captain Swift' my mind shifted and I offered a terse smile and found myself shaking my head in disapproval. "Well my name's actually C-" but I caught myself. 'Your real name! You were going to use your real fucking name! A simple everyday name like 'Col' with no exotic, pretentious fucking spelling to hide its real identity! You fucking idiot.' I thought. My mind raced as I beat myself up mentally for a moment. I then blamed Tarnasay for causing me to almost make what I believed would've been the world's most stupid mistake. 'That cunt!' I thought, 'He told them my name is Captain Swift... that motherfucker.' But I was overthinking the whole thing. The acid was really starting to kick in, coming on strong. It was getting the better of me. Meanwhile, the rotund Mr Bank, who indeed looked as though he'd just stepped out of a board meeting for one with his attire completely unsuited to sailing, made his way awkwardly on board Ubetcha from the shuttle craft.

"Captain Swift!" he said again but this time more triumphantly now that he was on-board and directly facing me. He offered his chubby hand to shake. This time, however, the absurdity of being called Captain Swift with such earnestness from the friendly, smiling man with the equally absurd name, Mr Bank, made me almost laugh out loud. But I managed not to. Instead I just beamed a smile that the laughter inside forced out. At first I imagined it was a beautiful smile. A smile that I believed Mr Bank would also acknowledge privately and think to himself "I've just met the man with the world's most beautiful smile." But gradually I felt the smile was taking over my face. That my face was now appearing before Mr Bank as just a big smile and nothing else. No eyes, no nose. Indeed, it was a weird smile I held. Ironically, whatever nerves I had prior to the most important meeting of my life, the same nerves that made me drop acid, were now completely gone because of it. But while my nerves may have gone, the seriousness of the business that was about to take place was now usurped by a level of LSD absurdity. Surrealness in an already surreal situation. I was spinning a little. Within minutes I'd gone from rising panic and anger to now straining to fight off a maniacal laughing fit. For there I stood, 'Captain Swift' no less, onboard one of the most famous, now hunted, superyachts in the world just off the West Coast of Thailand tripping off my head and smiling like a maniac at 'Mr

Bank' who was smiling back at me just as crazily, himself probably spinning from the amount of cash he was about to pay this weird smiling man.

Tarnasay had arranged via Franz for a quarter of the total money agreed on for both Ubetcha and the contraband to be given to me in cash at the physical point of handing over of Ubetcha. One half was then to be deposited in an account set up for me and the remaining quarter into Tarnasay's. I was to become instantly, a very wealthy man.

It took until the handing over of the money before I finally lost it. I opened up the large multi-tiered case, picked out a handful of thick, perfectly bound US hundred dollar bill wads and began to laugh along loudly with the millions upon millions of Benjamin Franklins laughing before me. Oh, how we laughed. Mr Bank joined in too. Initially. For a time. Then his faced had a look of disapproval as he watched for too long, the idiotic laughing Captain Swift, who now had also begun to dance. Finally Mr Bank had seen enough. "Ha-ha! Ho-ho! Captain Swift. Shut up! Stop it! Time for you to leave," he yelled at me.

I sort of cowered as though attempting to take cover from the booming voice of Mr Bank. It'd taken this outburst to snap me from my private laughing club. I then realised that I'd fully gone into a trance of sorts. I didn't remember previous tabs being this strong and now I fought to maintain my composure for the conclusion of the business exchange. Fortunately, there remained little for me to do apart from leading Mr Bank and his assistant, who I now realised for the first time was also on board, to our private 'Dispensary.' Mr Bank was satisfied and, as he stood rocking back and forth gently upon the other end of the colossal deal, it was done.

We returned to the lower deck and like a magnet I was drawn back to the large case that appeared custom made for carrying absurd amounts of cash. I was standing before the case that was expertly stacked and the four tiers that previously formed the one tower were now exposed like clothes drawers. Mr Bank approached me and smiled again. I smiled back, more normally now but a tad sheepishly. He then leaned in towards me as my eyes kept finding their way back to the money where I could still see millions of Benjamin Franklins laughing and asked me in a polite, almost hushed voice, "Have you Captain Swift by any chance, taken something, something on board that is to be part of the agreement?" Feeling uneasy and disoriented, I reached into one of the draws and produced a one hundred dollar bill.

"Yes. I have," I said as though answering a school headmaster, "I took a tab of acid sir," I continued, smiling, waving the bill before Mr Bank. "But I can pay!"

"*LSD!*" roared Mr Bank with laughter and so too did Benjamin Franklin, I noticed.

I was delivered by Mr Bank and his assistant to Ranong. Mr Bank had returned to his warm, affable nature now that he realised I was under the influence of LSD. "*LSD!*" he continued to roar periodically with laughter whenever he looked at my increasingly frazzled self. He seemed to be fascinated by it or knew very well its effects and was enjoying his efforts to freak me out. But apart from this irritating habit which continued to startle me, putting my nerves excruciatingly on edge, Mr Bank had also taken to rubbing my back in a fatherly manner. He was telling me to get some rest the moment I was booked in. Although it was in truth a genuine gesture of goodwill on behalf of Mr Bank, the back rubbing behaviour was making me more anxious than his yelling. So too, was the speed in which we powered towards the shoreline which I couldn't see.

At Ranong, Mr Bank bid me a last fatherly farewell and stressed that I stay put in the hotel and not go anywhere until morning. He then produced a sheet of paper that held the contacts for a private superyacht charter group in Thailand, where it had been arranged, if I so wished and at a date of my choosing, I could skipper a superyacht back to Sydney or somewhere else I wished. Mr Bank then folded the sheet and tucked it into my pocket. He then directed his assistant to accompany me to a nearby hotel to ensure I was safely booked in and not left to wander the streets in a deranged state while wheeling millions upon millions of giggling Benjamin Franklins. But shorty after I'd checked in and Mr Bank's assistant had departed, I checked out. The LSD's intensity had began to subside but I was beginning to feel more anxious and paranoid. Although there was no reason to doubt Mr Bank, and I now realised that if at any stage they'd entertained the idea of shafting me, reneging on the deal with Tarnasay, they would've done so when I was a laughing, dancing idiot. Nonetheless, I knew well enough that 'mood' often effects the path an LSD trip takes you down and right now it was telling me to move. To go somewhere else. So I did. I got a tuk-tuk, squeezed in awkwardly with my wheeled rack of millions gripped in my hand like a child in danger and went somewhere I felt safe, somewhere where no-one knew I was. Not a soul. Not even Tarnasay. I began to giggle.

To the tune of Chiang Mai

The camaraderie of hedonism that certain parts of Thailand celebrates is intoxicating. So much so that it wasn't long before arriving in Bangkok that Tarnasay found himself headed for the Northern Thailand city of Chiang Mai. It would offer him the rest he was looking for. The large northern destination was still busy and popular with backpackers from almost everywhere, but he found it was more than a step and a half off the pace that was Bangkok. There was much to see in Chiang Mai with its many festivals and thriving markets, rich in its own brand of Thai energy, but he didn't find it as relentless and as unstoppable as Bangkok. It was its relaxed country cousin, prepared and willing to have a good time but not at the possible expense of its sanity.

It'd been some time since his last visit and on that occasion it felt more like a large overgrown town, now it seemed to genuinely fit its northern 'city' title. It had sprawled as was to be expected but he was delighted to see that not only did the friendly, comfortable hostel where he last stayed remained, but so too did many of his favourite restaurants and bars. His last visit where he stayed for nearly two months saw him exploring the city and its region thoroughly, this time he was happy to spend his days doing very little. He wasn't interested in visiting crowded markets having just spent two and a half months with only one other human for company. Although many people would assume social contact would be high on the list of things to do after being stuck on a boat in an almost solo situation, Tarnasay felt the opposite. He needed to ease into it a little, spend some time reflecting on what he and Col had just done and now, more importantly, what he may do next. He was also still concerned for Col. It would be some time until he'd know the result of Ubetcha's transaction. He never once doubted Franz when told the deal was "sound" – he believed him without asking another question. When Franz said something was "sound," it was. It always had been. The word acting as the full stop for any discussion between the two men regarding the accuracy of information. Nonetheless, you can't steer your thoughts when emotion is driving your mind.

During the day Tarnasay was content to wander around the less busy parts of the city or spend much of it reading on the grassy banks of the canal running through the heart of the city. He would read his book while sipping longnecks of beer and eating the many varied delights that came his way. Delicious street food ferried by vendors on their way to busier places who often crossed the path where his shadow stretched out beneath the gentle trundle of their carts. He found it uncanny too, that nearly every time he felt peckish, he'd hear the distinct sound of a heavily laden cart approaching followed by its broadly smiling vendor. He wondered if they took notes: 'Foreign guy. Sits on grassy bank near canal reading everyday. Eats way more than he should. Doesn't count his change. Prime visiting times: Almost any. Worth diversion to main town centre.' At night though, Tarnasay would venture out for a meal at one of his favourite restaurants and then more often than not he'd visit a couple of small blues bars he knew had live music.

Over the next couple of months that Tarnasay remained in the large northern city he became a regular at many of the live music bars. One bar in particular quickly became his favourite haunt and this was due to the freakish talent of a local man who often performed there. It was at a venue called 'The Hug' that Tarnasay met an amazingly talented guitarist called, Jimmy Thattiyacorn, who impersonated the legendary Jimi Hendrix with incredible precision. It was a tiny little bar which, like many throughout Chiang Mai, offered great food and a relaxing atmosphere. But after watching Jimmy play and being so impressed with his performance which went beyond impersonating Hendrix and included some great blues and general jamming, Tarnasay had become a regular at The Hug. It wasn't long before he'd struck up an easy friendship with the affable, free smiling Jimmy who enjoyed riffing his way around the crowded bar tables.

One night following a particularly steamy gig that included more of Jimmy's own material and saw the little bar spilling a mixture of enthralled locals and western ex-pats onto the street, Tarnasay decided to quiz Jimmy about his musical ambition or if there was any. It wasn't the first time that Tarnasay wondered if anyone had approached him regarding his raw talent, perhaps accompanied by promises of the world. It wasn't the first time either, that he wondered if Jimmy wasn't simply content with his regular little jaunt playing to a cosy, appreciative crowd. Maybe he enjoyed it this way, underground, uncomplicated, unharassed by fame and propelled along only by modest means and awe-struck faces. It turned out that Jimmy was simply terrified of flying. Tarnasay listened as Jimmy listed the numerous international bands and performers who'd asked him to join them on tours and festivals around the world as their guest. And although he'd considered travelling by boat, timings had never been right. Tarnasay watched as he slowly reached into his well-worn leather jacket and solemnly placed on the table before him a valid return ticket to New York and a large box of valium.

"You heard of The Venkmann Equation?" he asked Tarnasay.

"Ohh yeah," answered Tarnasay knowingly. He'd seen the amazing German experimental techno rock fusion act not long before he'd commandeered Maxie B's yacht and cruised out of Sydney Harbour as a way of relieving pre-heist tension.

"Well this ticket is an invitation for me join them for a gig in New York," muttered Jimmy who really should've been smiling his beaming smile when he said it.

"Wow," said Tarnasay who stared at the ticket for a moment before asking, "And the valium?"

"To put me to sleep if I decide to go," said Jimmy smiling but at the same time almost sighing at the thought.

"The Venkmann Equation are cool y'know, real cool. They know I'm scared to fly but they gave me the ticket anyway. Just in case," this time Jimmy sighs outright. Tarnasay could see the frustration of a man with a rare talent who clearly wishes to buckle up without a worry, to venture out and share his talent with the world but is instead fastened by a phobia to a chair on a stage in Chiang Mai.

"Well," said Tarnasay, who suddenly had that twinkle in his eye which may have not been familiar to Jimmy yet but to anyone who knew him well, meant he had a plan. "You're going to do this."

But Jimmy didn't raise his head to see the twinkle. He just stared at the ticket on the table.

"No good Tarnasay. I've tried everything; therapy, medication, herbal treatment, even fucking voodoo sex man...I'm not meant to fly," said Jimmy. "But it's ok, my music flies here instead," he added with his trademark smile returning for a moment but not enough to convince Tarnasay.

"Did you just say voodoo sex?" asked Tarnasay momentarily distracted.

"Uh huh," answered Jimmy matter-of-factly. Tarnasay stared at Jimmy for a moment and found himself speculating about voodoo sex and the assortment of fascinating things and objects and rituals it may involve as a treatment to cure the fear of flying.

"No man you're going," said Tarnasay firmly snapping out of his sordid ponderings, "I'm taking you by boat."

Jimmy released his eyes from the torment of the ticket he'd been staring at, looked at Tarnasay and saw the twinkle in his eye for the first time.

"Tarnasay you're a good man. I know you're trying to help but it's too late. I've checked all the boats and cruisers and again the timings not right, no-one is leaving when I need to go or they're all booked," explained Jimmy.

Tarnasay suddenly felt anxious with excitement. At this instant he made a spontaneous decision which he knew could change Jimmy's life. He felt like he was about to hand someone a winning lottery ticket. But it was better than that. Realising a dream trumps cold hard cash anytime. Being given the chance to achieve a life goal is far greater than being given the means to simply buy one, he figured. He'd read once that the problem some people have after winning a large lottery prize is that they're not quite sure what to do with themselves when they do. One minute they're slugging away at life, working, working, working to pay the bills, and not necessarily bitterly because for almost everyone that's just the way it is. And deep down, whether they realise it or not - or want to, it gives their lives purpose, focus and helps colour it in. Whether they like it or not, it's the medium for which they paint their life picture. But for some, when they win, suddenly that picture they were working so hard on is miraculously coloured and complete, they become flummoxed. Of course there's the initial relief, the holidays, the handouts and the hangar full of sports cars; but for some also comes the boredom, confusion and loss of direction that one without a sense of purpose, a definitive goal, a very demanding hobby, or a pet philanthropic project may endure. Nonetheless, there was a good chance Jimmy, like most people, would still be more than happy to see how they'd go handling a multi-million dollar lottery ticket. Tarnasay on the other hand, was glad he was simply offering him the opportunity to realise a dream. To give his talent a leg up to a bigger stage he thought it deserved.

"Not on my boat they're not," said Tarnasay.

Jimmy looked at Tarnasay. Before him sat a man dressed in traditional Thai backpacker fashion. He saw darkly tanned wrists adorned with various bracelets and multicoloured leather bands and a neck hosting large, beaded necklaces which most likely found their way onto him whether he liked them or not. He also saw faded boardshorts, a holey singlet and world-weary thongs.

"Ah really Captain Tarnasay, not on your boat?" surmised Jimmy sarcastically.

It was a fantastic, indomitable surprise that appeared before Tarnasay one night at The Hug a couple of weeks earlier that now brought forth the spontaneous decision he'd just made. A large, familiar presence he saw leaning against the bar surrounded by a group of raucous Irish travellers. The unmistakable shape of someone who, over a relatively short time he'd grown to love like a brother, a shape he now recognised as easily as his own hand, a shape that was none other than that of Col Barrington. That night it had truly felt like he was reuniting with a missing family member. Someone who now felt as close to his heart as had been his Uncle Lou. It may have only been weeks since they'd last seen each other but it felt like years. It felt like years because barely a day had passed in Chiang Mai where he hadn't found himself speculating about how the events of the transaction of Ubetcha had transpired. Whether everything had gone to plan, whether Franz had, once again, delivered a "sound" resolve to what had seemed at one time an almost impossible request. Col's bulk embraced within his arms that evening told him he had. Franz had delivered. He gave the big bloke another hearty squeeze at that moment and imagined he was Franz. On this night the two men partied together like ancient kings, like long lost brothers reunited, like the successful criminals they now were. He told Col he was stealing a chimpanzee. Col trumped him and said he'd bought a superyacht. In the weeks that followed, Tarnasay had been wondering where their next adventure may roll out in heaves before them, now he could see the swell building clearly.

"Yep, my beautiful 120 foot Grand Banks yacht," said Tarnasay plainly.

"What? You're telling me you have a 120 foot yacht!" laughed Jimmy in disbelief.

"Well, technically it's not mine but let's just say I have access to one," said Tarnasay.

"Are you serious?"

"Voodoo sex serious Jimmy," answered Tarnasay smiling.

Col

I couldn't go back to Sydney. I made my way over from Ranong and was now on Koh Pha Ngan which was known as a bit of a party island. Much had changed on the island since my last visit, progress had got stuck into it like everything else, but it still had the fun and openness I'd enjoyed in the past. Everyone was keen to mingle, share stories and party together. The idea of returning home with a bank account full of money but a head empty on ideas what to do with it scared me. Besides, I'd fallen back in love with Thailand's food.

I found myself thinking about how I'd stepped away from things I adored. Thai food was one of them. There are Thai restaurants everywhere in Sydney too, I'm sure I walked past one every day. What the fuck have I been doing? I found myself revisiting that pressing question again. Do you blackout in your thirties or something? Does part of your brain suddenly erase memories of anything you really loved in your twenties, deciding that from your thirties onward they're irrelevant? Which was partly why I now found myself on Koh Pha Ngan with a mongrel hangover from the previous night's Full Moon party. I had indeed gone there for some crazy fun, to really let go after all I'd been through. I'd enjoyed the place so much in my mid-twenties I was keen to return for a short break while deciding my next move. Now I was nursing my head and trying to decide whether I should try to reunite with Tarnasay. It had been in the back of my mind the whole time I'd been on the island and after last night's shenanigans I felt the need to make a firm decision. My thoughts were then interrupted by a smiling Thai girl wandering past with a cart full of freshly cooked fish cakes. They were good fish cakes too. Decision-making fish cakes. I decided that it was time to reconvene with Tarnasay. I had no way of knowing whether Tarnasay would still be in Bangkok but I was going to find out either way. Besides, I'd had enough of partying for the moment and I found myself thinking about the last couple of night's weirdness involving stray dogs.

The lead-up to the main mind-bender experience for me while spending a week on the small island happened early on the morning before the Full Moon party. I never really understood why they bothered with the Full Moon parties – because in truth, it seemed every night was like a Full Moon party on the island. And I felt this was confirmed when I awoke one morning with my face planted in the sand of Haad Rin Beach. A friendly Queenslander, Mick who I'd befriended earlier in the week woke me by throwing a bucket of water over me.

"Freak," he said with a laugh before wandering off.

Rudely awoken, I sat up spitting sand from my lips and realised I was surrounded by a large ring of sleeping stray dogs. And although I felt at once reassured and spooked by this strange sight, it was nothing compared to the next morning's experience.

I'd been sitting around a large bonfire on the beach in the early morning hours of the Full Moon party getting messy with a bunch of backpackers from around the world. It was while sitting around the roaring fire that I found myself becoming irritated by the crazy barking of a dog some way down the beach. I decided to go for a walk and investigate. Perhaps now believing, following yesterday's events, I had a kind of special kinship with dogs. I walked for a way down the beach before I saw the silhouette of a man and a very large black dog digging in the sand. I headed towards them as they continued to dig. As I walked up to them I noticed there seemed to be bouts of digging followed by long periods of the dog's crazy, non-stop barking. Soon I was with them and watched them digging. The man didn't seem to notice me standing there and I listened to him muttering something over and over again while he dug. Finally curiousity got the better of me and I spoke to the digging man.

"G'day. What are you doing?" I said.

"Oh hey man," said the man looking up from the large hole he was digging. I noticed that the man smiled at me with wide excited eyes as though we were long lost friends. "I didn't see you there. Well, I'm just digging with this dog."

I stood silently watching the man and dog as they kept digging. The man then stopped digging, sweat was pouring off him. He looked exhausted. The large black dog stood right in front of the man barking loudly and every now and then the big thing would lunge aggressively at him. I wasn't sure whether the dog was actually aggressive or just playing. I then watched as the man hunched over again and recommenced digging. The big dog then stopped barking and joined him.

"You see. He only stops barking when you dig," said the man.

I just stood there quietly again for a bit watching the man and dog as they continued digging.

"What? You're joking," I said.

"No," said the man.

To demonstrate the man then stopped digging and stood up straight. Immediately the dog began to bark aggressively again and lunge ferociously towards him.

"No joke man. Do it. Just start digging and you'll see."

I laughed. But I got down on my knees and started digging in the sand and sure enough the dog stopped his relentless barking and joined me digging. Laughing, I started to get right into it and began to dig furiously and the big dog matched my tempo and enthusiasm. Together we got into a digging frenzy. After a while I was laughing almost uncontrollably at the absurdity of what I was doing.

"Haha! Fuck man that's insane! He really gets into it doesn't he!" I said excitedly. The man didn't reply but I continued to dig playfully with the dog until my arms finally couldn't take any more and I stopped.

"Whoa!... man... ok. Well that's me!" I said, my chest heaving. "Thanks for the dig big fella but I'm all dug out hey...haha," I added while still on my knees and facing the big dog who'd already struck an aggressive pose and was barking directly into my face. "Yeah, anyway thanks for that mate," I continued speaking to the man as I rose to my feet and patted my sandy knees clean. "But I think I'll leave you two to it." But the man was gone. There was no one there. Just me and the aggressive, barking dog. I began to look around urgently for the man. I began calling out.

"Hey mate! Where are you?" I called. "Hey mate your dog!"

The man was nowhere to be seen and there was nothing to be heard except the vicious, intimidating bark of the big black dog in front of me. A dog who was clearly becoming more impatient and irritated by the minute. I stared in somewhat disbelief at the dog barking crazily in front of me for a long time. I tried soothing him.

"Shhh...come on fella, it's ok. Stop now. Shhh, shhh come on now," I cooed. I called loudly again for the man. I tried throwing sticks to see if he'd chase them but the dog just ignored them. He just stood staunchly in front of me barking, barking. Whether it was out of panic I also stupidly tried to run away but this only made the dog even more frenzied, chasing me and herding me like a stray sheep. His barking and his snarling lunges towards me becoming more aggressive.

"Shit," I said.

I then slumped to my knees and began to dig. I would dig and dig and dig and then I would stop, and the dog would bark and snarl and bark and snarl, and then I would dig and dig and dig some more. I wasn't wearing a watch, but figured I'd been digging for near on two hours with no sign of the mad dog tiring when I spied someone approaching in the distance. Beyond the person I could see the bonfire I'd left still burning but not so brightly anymore. Meanwhile, as I awaited the stranger's approach, I dug and dug and dug. I'd even developed a digging mantra to help with the monotony and strain, and although it wasn't at all poetic or inspiring, it worked.

"Stupid fuckin' mongrel bred bastard... stupid fuckin' mongrel bred bastard... stupid fuckin' mongrel bred bastard... stupid fuckin' mongrel bred bastard," I said over and over again. It worked so well that I didn't even notice the stranger was now here and watching me and the dog.

"Hi. I've been watching you and wondering what you're doing?"

"Oh hi mate," I said looking up from the large hole I was digging. I smiled at him with wide excited eyes as though he was a long lost friend. "I didn't see you there. Well, I'm just digging with this dog."

I sat up, sweat was pouring off me, I was exhausted. The large black dog was standing directly in front of me barking loudly and relentlessly again. Once or twice he lunged quite aggressively at me and began to snarl a little. I then hunched back over and recommenced my digging. The big dog then stopped barking and joined me.

"You see. He only stops barking when you dig," I said.

"Ha ha! What? You're joking?" said the man.

To demonstrate I stopped digging and stood up straight. Immediately the dog began to bark aggressively again and lunge ferociously towards me.

"No joke man. Do it. Just start digging and you'll see," I said.

The man chuckled. But he got down on his knees and started digging in the sand and sure enough the dog stopped his relentless barking and joined him digging. Laughing, the man started to get right into it and began to dig furiously and the big dog matched his tempo and enthusiasm. Together they got into a digging frenzy. After a while the man was laughing almost uncontrollably at the absurdity of what he was doing

"Ha ha ha! He really likes to dig hey!" said the man.

I didn't reply but the man continued to dig playfully with the dog until his arms finally couldn't take any more and he stopped.

"Whoa!...ok. Well I'm done! Thanks for the fun dog but I cannot dig with you anymore," said the man puffing while still on his knees and looking at the big dog who'd already struck an aggressive pose and began barking directly into his face. "Thanks too man, that was fun but I've gotta go now," said the man to me as he rose to his feet and patted his sandy knees clean. But I was gone. I was not there. It was just the man and the now aggressive, relentless barking dog. The man began looking around urgently for me. He began calling out.

"Hey man! Where are you?" he called. "Hey man your dog!"

But I was nowhere to be seen. There was nothing to be heard except the vicious, intimidating bark of the big black dog in front of him. A dog who was clearly becoming more impatient and irritated by the minute. The man stared in somewhat disbelief at the dog barking crazily in front of him for a long time. He tried soothing him. "Shhh...come on pal, it's ok. Stop now. Shhh, shhh come on now," he cooed. He called again for me. He tried throwing sticks to see if he'd chase them but the dog just ignored them, he just stood staunchly in front of him barking, barking. Whether it was out of panic the man also stupidly tried to run away but this only made the dog even more frenzied, chasing him and herding him like stray sheep. His barking and his snarling lunges towards him even more aggressive.

"Shit," said the man.

~

Luckily, Tarnasay had told me where he'd be staying in Bangkok if I changed my mind about returning home. Tarnasay had already moved on to Chiang Mai at this stage but left a note with the hostel reception addressed to me should I come looking for him. The note simply read, 'Chiang Mai! Cheers Tarnasay.' I was as happy as a face full of fish cakes.

Soon I made plans to head to Chiang Mai but not before visiting the

Yacht Haven Marina in Phuket. At first I planned to travel by train and then by bus to Chiang Mai but this was before I remembered the amount of money I was lugging about in my backpack. I soon learnt that it was best if I just forgot the money was there because every time I thought about it I got nervous and light headed. I felt stupid for not having deposited it all when I split my new found wealth into two separate accounts. My head was still cloudy from the LSD on the day I visited the bank and although I had the good sense to deposit most of it; I was annoyed that somehow I'd decided that an absurd amount should still be at hand. Just short of 20kg in US 100 dollar bills I later discovered upon weighing my bag at a chemist. I felt particularly light headed when I realised I had enough US dollars strapped to my back to buy a luxury motor yacht. I was feeling the weight of having serious money in more ways than one. Just under 2M of it. At least with this latest dizzy spell came a solution. I knew the Yacht Haven Marina in Phuket well from previous sailing trips to Thailand while working as a young deckhand. I also knew that many a wealthy American would sell their yachts to brokers here. I would go boat shopping.

Visiting the Phuket Marina as a buyer for the kind of yacht I'd worked on as a twenty three-year-old greenhorn deckhand was not something I imagined I'd ever be doing. And certainly not in the way I was doing it. I'd decided it was best to contact Franz back home to do the ground work for the purchase of the type of motor yacht I had in mind. As a boat builder, my knowledge of motor yachts was broad, but the majority of boats that my father and I had built over the years were smaller sailing yachts and fishing trawlers. After my dad's passing, business had slowed for a time and instead of chasing large boat building commissions, I'd taken up smaller but still demanding and well-paid work refurbishing luxury motor yachts such as Grand Banks. I repaired and customised these motor yachts which came to me in various states of disrepair. This was when I'd fallen in love with them. I even had one of my own but it was a beaten, sea-shocked old thing that I saw as a retirement project. The Grand Banks are beautifully built motor yachts which mirror the same kind of detail and craftsmanship that my dad and I had been renowned for, although on a smaller scale. And now, I was in a position to buy one outright in near mint condition. I'd asked Franz to look for brokers with Grand Banks yachts within their listings and it hadn't taken him long to find one at the Yacht Haven Marina much to my delight.

My excitement soon peaked when at the marina I discovered that this particular Grand Banks motor yacht was actually grander than any I'd seen before. It was everything I loved about the Grand Banks 76 Aleutian RP, but it was a one-off custom built boat re- sized on a special commission at 120ft. I quickly removed my absurd backpack wallet which contained 2M US Benjamin Franklins stacked in a remarkably neat manner considering what I was carrying them in. I'd gone to great effort to rebundle the entire amount one night following my call back home to Franz. I'd also counted out what seemed like the entire amount over the phone to him in a Texan accent while he listened and got quietly pissed at the other end. Franz had convinced me it'd be a good idea to pretend that I was an eccentric Texan billionaire to assist with "the oddity" he explained, that I'll be handing over an incredible amount of cash for the luxury yacht. He believed it added a degree of caution to the whole transaction. Numerous times I lost it. Screaming down the phone from the privacy of my luxurious Thai villa, I told Franz that the whole idea was "Fucking ridiculous! – It's just not neeeded!" But when my last outburst was delivered in character and the accent sounded convincing to Franz, I calmed down and agreed to go with it. "Don't worry I'm not asking you to wear a ten gallon Texan hat or anything, that'd just be clichéd and silly." "Well why the fuck not donkey boy!?" I asked him loudly down the phone in my now honed Texan accent causing Franz to laugh and painfully expel beer from his nose.

I didn't wear a ten gallon hat but I did find being in character for the entire transaction helped calm my nerves and lessen the craziness I'd initially felt about rocking up to buy a yacht in this manner. I still wasn't sure whether this was by Franz's design, who I'd long ago realised was a very clever and shrewd operator, or just Franz being Franz and taking the piss a little. Either way, it worked for me.

The actual transaction for me felt as though it was being conducted in a church. I've never actually been to a church but the broker's manner of almost tip-toeing around the office, the barely audible way he spoke and the almost deathly silence of the place is what I figured it must be like. It was as though a ritual and not a sale was taking place. I always imagined that when I was spoke to the broker I'd go into the somewhat ballsy, forthright Texan accent I'd practiced so keenly with Franz, instead I found myself speaking with a whisper in a polite Texan drawl to match the quietness of the broker. I placed my backpack on the broker's desk and carefully removed the cash as though at any moment it could shatter into a million pieces. I was at pains to be quiet, to mirror the broker's gentle actions. Once the money was removed and counted in an almost zen state by the him, I was handed a bound leather wallet with the legal papers for the yacht. I took a quick glance to check that it was indeed my name on the papers before being completely startled by the smiling broker ringing a cowbell madly in my face while yelling crazily, *"Yeeeee harwww!"*

"Fucking Franz," I thought ever so quietly.

Now it goes without saying, that I knew Franz had spoken to the broker in detail about the proposed exchange of finance and that his client, me of course, was a rather eccentric Texan billionaire who preferred to make cash payments via a backpack regardless of the amount. The thing was, I didn't know the exact details of what was said, until later when I queried Franz about the fucking cow bell.

This was possibly the most I'd ever heard Franz laugh as he attempted to tell me how it came to be. "Seriously, this wasn't my first intention. I mean, initially the whole Texan thing came about as a means to sound out the broker's attitude towards receiving 2M in cold, hard US cash. Many wouldn't think twice, but others would talk. I didn't want a talker," said Franz.

"So I told them –" at this point Franz lost it for a bit and went into uncontrollable laughter. I could see he was chuffed, if not a little surprised that the broker had stuck so earnestly to his joke. I also knew hearing his recollection of events was going to be torture for me. Kinda like being laughed at twice for the same practical joke that you were way too nervous to find funny the first time. Anyway, I'd allowed the freak Franz to continue on his merry way telling me his tale.

"Sorry, Col" said Franz. He then took a moment to compose himself. "Ok. Ok. So I told them – " And the fucker lost it again. This time totally cacking himself stupid until I told him to stop it. Franz composed himself again. "Ok, so I told them, he likes to dress down, so don't be alarmed if he arrives wearing boardshorts and a holey singlet. He's not one to bring attention to himself and he likes to be discreet about his purchases. Listen, there's just a couple of other things he likes if you'd be so kind as to indulge him. Afterall, it is quite a transaction that's taking place here isn't it? Yes, well he likes absolute quietness when conducting the business until it is settled and then, well this is where his eccentricity kinda kicks in a little, he likes someone to ring a cowbell loudly and yell *"Yeeeeee Hawww!"* Can you do this? It doesn't have to be a cowbell per se but something like it would be great. I really appreciate you accommodating this for the transaction."

There was little else Franz needed to say to the politely spoken Thai broker whose educated English had more than a tinge of an American accent. Whether the broker completely believed him or not didn't concern Franz too much, initially it was more about sounding out the broker's attitude towards receiving 2M in cold, hard US cash. Many wouldn't think twice, but others would talk. Franz didn't want a talker. He wanted someone who respected his client's request for discretion and their eccentricity. And he would often go into character himself when arranging transactions such as this. He'd simply imagine that he was indeed representing an eccentric Texan billionaire and then think about how he'd go about doing that. Nonetheless, Franz had been satisfied, he knew it was "sound" as he liked to say. He believed the broker accepted his client as real, and if he was mistaken, it didn't matter. This broker wasn't a talker. He would simply take the cash and I, the Texan billionaire would take the yacht and they'd both have happy clients. Albeit, one with a fucking cowbell rung loudly in his face while a man screams, *"Yeeeeee Hawww!"*

~

I arrived in Chiang Mai and set myself up in a guesthouse that would be considered luxury by backpacker standards. I'd backpacked around Thailand when I was a twenty year-old greenhorn deckhand and had stayed in some very basic guesthouses. They were always clean but featured little more than a bed to sleep on and basin to wash your face. This time I treated myself to a more upmarket guesthouse pretending to be a resort. While I was keen to reconvene with Tarnasay and see what adventure the man had in mind next, I still felt in need of space. The two of us had just spent over two and a half months together in close quarters, grown as close as brothers through experiencing something extraordinary and rare in the successful heist and sale of a famous superyacht, and right now I wanted to catch my breath. And in hindsight, Koh Pha Ngan hadn't really been the right place to do it. Early on, and more recently lugging around 2M in US dollars on my back, I realised I could never be, nor would I ever want to be, the likes of Tarnasay. The intensity of being him I couldn't bear. I'd had a taste of it. The risk-taking, the thrill-seeking, the craving daring. The planning, the watching, the absolute meticulousness of it all. The blanketing of fear, of being watched, of being followed and finally, the horror, of one day maybe being caught. I felt nauseous just thinking about it. But on the other hand I hadn't felt this alive in years. I now felt there was no doubt that we should push ourselves every now and then; both mentally and physically. Perhaps take a holiday, freak yourself out and come back feeling brand new.

Defy what I call the "society age," the age at which society seems to begin defining what activities are most appropriate for you. Rather than simply letting the individual decide whether they're up to it, mentally or physically. It seemed to me that there was a strong implication in society to always "act your age." What act and at what age? I wondered. Even if it meant finding out the hard way what I was, or was not capable of, I was now going to keep pushing at it as though ten years younger. I wasn't going back to dormant, fragile Col. Perhaps I'd chosen to ignore it, but now I recognised that many of my friends within the sailing fraternity had been defying their "society age" for a long time. Their level of fitness, strength, ability and most crucially, their mind-set, belied their age and delivered them the goals, the life spark, they sought.

My breather would involve exploring Chiang Mai and my soul a little more too. It had been many years since I'd last visited Chiang Mai and the large Northern city had grown significantly since my last visit. I bought a map, hired a small motorbike and spent the day relaxing by the river eating a range of delicious finger foods and plotting a tourist trail in and around the city. I would head out over the next week exploring a part of Thailand which from previous visits I had fond memories, and later I would look for Tarnasay. Perhaps after a week or two alone, I'd know for certain whether I truly wanted to reconvene with Tarnasay and take part in whatever he had planned next. I knew Tarnasay wasn't about to stop right now.

In his own weird way the man was pushing himself too. I found myself revisiting a particular conversation we had one calm day on Ubetcha as we made our way to Thailand. The two of us peaking on a smorgasbord of stimulants; Tarnasay had revealed a deeper, underlying reason for why he did what he did. "I've see my family twice since then" he said, "Dad sends me birthday and Christmas cards of course. *Cheers, Dad* they say. Nothing else." Although it was at this moment I confirmed something I'd always suspected, that there was more than one factor at play for why Tarnasay did what he did, it just hadn't occurred to me until now how much of a factor it most likely was. That it wasn't purely – as it appears to many, or even as he himself presents it with his cheeky, antagonising notes – just a crazy, radical kind of fun.

That it did in fact go well beyond stealing and enjoying someone's expensive, neglected item of pleasure just for fun, just for the hell of it, just to fuck with the over-indulgent and the privileged. That the influence of his beloved Uncle Lou and how he later interpreted it, wasn't the only motivator. They were clear factors. But now I realised, that although Tarnasay was far from a tortured soul, someone whose actions manifested from a dark, troubled past, his past had nonetheless, played a significant role in the catalyst for his "borrowings." Certainly more than it appeared on the surface. The gleaming, fun-loving, magnetic Tarnasay surface. It also occurred to me, that perhaps as much as his behaviour was a public statement on capitalist trappings, it was also a personal one. It's not just expensive items that can be neglected, taken for granted, major priorities can be too. Priorities like people. And whether one comes from a background of means or otherwise, has nothing to do with it. Tarnasay was proof. Proof that Tarnasay believed that his father had placed a university degree above that of his being with immediate family. Of Tarnasay's own desires. And right when he was on the brink of manhood. Right before he could legally choose to make life altering decisions of his own; decisions he believed were more important in the bigger scheme of things.

My thoughts turned to that of my own Dad as we had made our way to Thailand. I'd been flicking through a small notebook I'd bought before we took Ubetcha which I ended up using as much as a diary as I did for marking lists and taking notes. In it I remember reading of a place near Chiang Mai which I'd jotted down. It was a place that my deceased father had travelled to some years earlier and had spoken of very fondly. "Beautiful relaxing place, lovely people," I remembered him saying. When my mother's dementia had become too much for dad to handle and we reluctantly had to move her to a nursing home, I began urging him to take a trip. "Maybe to South East Asia?" I suggested. The last couple of years had taken their toll on dad and I could see it. Now I wanted the man to do something for himself. As sad as it sounds, I found myself wanting dad to get as far away from mum as soon as possible – to forget her for a time, instead of watching her completely forget him. I'd sailed and travelled to Papua New Guinea and South Pacific islands, such as Tonga and Samoa too, but as I'd spent far more time in South East Asia, I felt I could pick some places that, if I could just convince him to go, he would love. With dad retired, and me having taken over his boat building business which continued to flourish, I decided to push the idea hard. To my surprise he agreed. But now in hindsight, I know the driving force was my dad's underlying, secret illness. Which in the end, took him out well before his beloved wife, my dear mum, who is still at the nursing home and healthy if not lost in a maze of past and present. Not long before I left with Tarnasay, I visited my mother for which I knew may well be the last time whether we were successful or not. I sat with her watching the ABC News just as she'd always done and I listened and watched as she dropped in and out of lucidity. It was hard for me now. She had practically left everything she'd ever known behind. Even my dad and I. And it's a rare thing for her to recognise me these days. She's just a mould of my mother now. Her shape, her mannerisms and movements are the same, tells me that she is my mother; but the contents, my mum's rich mental contents that had served her so well, are all but gone.

***

She did recognise him one last time though. Some days after he'd left. *"Captain Swift!"* she suddenly screamed at the TV completely out of character and terrifying the nursing staff. *"Haa! Haa! Captain Swift! That's my boy!"* she yelled excitedly as the breaking TV News report spoke of the taking of Ubetcha and the note Tarnasay had left behind. 'Cheers. Captain Swift. (And Tarnasay!)" the note had said. Col's mother would've been horrified at his actions had she been of sound mind and understood the implication, but she wasn't, so it was fantastic. It was fantastic that she'd remembered him. Remembered him whispering to her before he left with tears streaming down his fleshy cheeks, "Captain Swift is going sailing again mum. He's not sure when he'll be back. But he wants you to know he loves you more than anything."

Island in the Rice Fields

It was Col's father who'd called him Captain Swift. He was eleven and the NSW State Junior Keelboat Champion and his proud father liked to call him that and his mother loved to scream it when he crossed the line in first place, much to his embarrassment. His father even managed to have it etched in brackets on one of the many trophies he won. At some stage during their planning meetings when the beer and scotch flowed as the two men got to know each other, and they talked and talked, Col had told Tarnasay of this and he'd clearly not forgotten.

***

Mae Rim was the place just north of Chiang Mai that my dad had visited some years earlier. There was a guesthouse there which he loved but apparently it didn't have a name. I had explored Chiang Mai city a little, visiting the Night Bazaar and eating at some good restaurants along the canal but I was keen to escape the crowds. It was February now, having sailed in MB's yacht all through January, and the tourists from Australia and New Zealand were out in force. So I upgraded from my small rented motorbike, bought a second hand trail bike in good condition, packed my bag and headed off to Mae Rim. When I got back, I'd attempt to track Tarnasay down, that much was certain. I just hadn't fully made up my mind whether I'd join him in whatever he had in mind. And I knew the guy would have something in mind. But I wasn't concerned if I missed him. If Tarnasay simply slipped away, disappearing like the magic trick he is. All it would mean was that our story together ended here. And I'd be happy with that ending, but I wasn't knocking back the possibility of an epic sequel either. My stunning Grand Banks yacht now named 'Mai Pen Rai' waiting for me at Pattaya Marina, was testament to that.

Doi Pui with its Hmong hill tribes, slow pace and lush landscape was the environment I felt I needed to be in. I'd wound my way well into Doi Suthep National Park and before I knew it, I was being led by three young Thai men on trail bikes towards a beautiful guesthouse I'd been told about called Indie House at Mae Rim. Before this I was heading to Mae Rim on my own but I was having trouble correlating the map to my surroundings where trails seemed to be leading everywhere. I then got talking to a couple of Aussie backpackers also on trail bikes at a lookout near Bhu Bing Palace in the National park. They told me they were heading back down to Chiang Mai having just returned from the guesthouse I was now ripping through the National park with three young Thai guys to get to. They'd told me about their ride to the guesthouse excitedly and as a result I got excited about the idea too. It was then I noticed they were decked out in far more serious trail bike riding gear than me. I had second thoughts. It'd been a while since I'd ridden a trail bike seriously, over tricky terrain. I'd learnt to ride as a young kid at my Uncle's property at the peculiarly named, Captain's Flat near Canberra. And although my Uncle's property was anything but flat and I'd learnt to ride quite well over steep, slippery hillsides – I was still feeling hesitant. I looked at the map they'd given me with directions to the guesthouse. It seemed no clearer than the one I was using.

"Hey man," said one of the guys who I now noticed was about ten years my junior, "Not sure how good you are on the bike and headin' up there on your own," he said. I must have been looking worriedly at the map. "But I've got the number of a local Thai crew who work as trail bike guides. Great blokes. They just brought us back down and they're heading back up, if I can catch them now they can take you up. It's worth it eh. Great place to chill man, fuckin' sick of Full Moon, Half Moon, Smidge of a fuckin Moon parties y'know," he added smiling. For a moment the big black dog appeared in my mind and barked at me. I watched as the guy, his face covered in tiny flecks of mud that looked like freckles flicked through his phone to find the number. 'Fuck me,' I thought. 'Never had a mobile when I was backpacking, that's awesome.' But that was all I needed and I thanked the guys for hooking me up. I was in. Afterall, I said I was going to continue to push myself from now on, so what better way to do it than screaming up a mountain in Northern Thailand behind some half-mad Thai trail bikeriders.

I took a couple of heavy slides much to the amusement of my Thai guides but made it to Indie House safely. 'If Australians are known for their laid-back attitude in the West,' I thought, 'then surely the Thais are known for it in the East.' My guides stayed for a beer or two and told me some places to check out whilst in Mae Rim. I then paid them generously and asked if they'd return in a week's time to take me back down to Chiang Mai. In the meantime, already feeling relaxed, I cracked open another Singha. From the large, shady deck, I sat looking around at the beautiful 'island in the rice fields' that was Indie House, and couldn't help but think that this was indeed the place my dad had meant.

I explored Mae Rim and surrounding areas thoroughly through the day and in the afternoon I'd relax on the broad deck overlooking the beautiful rice fields. I played the guesthouse's complimentary guitar and just watched the unique environment; to my eyes anyway, while sipping Singha after Singha. I visited hill tribes who were welcoming and bought a horde of bracelets and bands I'd never wear. I ate like a king, read, walked, sat, talked, played hacky sack with local kids, did nothing. It was perfect.

I also thought a bit too. Thought about where my head was at back in Sydney and where it was now after stealing and sailing one of the world's most famous superyachts. And although it would seem absurd to many people, my mind was clearer now. No longer in a funk. I also thought about how both my parents would've been shocked if they'd ever known I'd done such a thing. A thirty three year-old man blowing a solid boat building business for committing a crime that could send him to gaol for many years. It would be indefensible to them. Strange. But to me, so was the idea of being safe all the time. It's not like I felt the need to steal something such as a superyacht to colour what I saw as the becoming of a bland life, but I knew I needed risk and challenges of some sort. And even if I got back into chasing and surfing big waves as I did with mates through my twenties, it still wouldn't be enough. I wanted to live excitement of a kind everyday. It didn't mean being a criminal, or risking my life physically, it meant not being bound by any one thing. And I could do it. I was responsible for no-one but myself. Like almost every person on Earth, I wasn't alone with the idea of desiring to have outright freedom. Physical, financial and mental freedom. To do and go as you pleased, but how do you get that? I understood Tarnasay's attraction to do what he did. Most people work hard, tow-the-line, but ultimately only a few either through talent, old money or luck get the chance to experience absolute freedom. And I know, whether people like it or not, to find that freedom through criminal activity also takes talent. But risks such as the criminal kind are not seen as a viable passage for most to that freedom. I didn't see myself or Tarnasay as representative of a typical criminal mind-set but simply two risk takers prepared to expose themselves to the consequences of committing one. A very big one. One we would never have the need, or the desire to commit again. Tarnasay never borrowed the same thing twice and Ubetcha was apparently one of only a handful of things he'd ever stolen. I didn't feel ashamed. And I didn't feel sorry for Maxie Burgess. I knew there was still a possibility of being caught but I know the odds are somewhat in my favour. They know more about Tarnasay than they do me. And they know fuck all about Tarnasay, I reassured myself. It was the craziest, flukiest thing I'd ever done and short of Tarnasay wanting to steal anything else, I was now certain I wanted to continue the adventure with him. For a time at least.

It wasn't until my last day at Indie House when asked if I had carved my signature into a huge timber board for visitors that I confirmed that this was indeed where my father had stayed a few years back. I wasn't sure if it was sentiment but the whole time I was staying there, despite being in another part of the world, a foreign place was made familiar because I'd felt close to my dad - and if I wasn't in the actual place he'd stayed, just being in Mae Rim felt close enough. But it was the place. The exact place. My dad's signature proved it. Visiting Mae Rim had been great for me. It felt good to visit a place that felt special to my dad. The last place he visited before he died. Cancer had taken him way too quickly and by visiting that final place, a place I knew my dad had enjoyed and made him happy, I felt relieved. When I looked at his signature and the carefully carved smiley face next to it, the same one he used to draw for me as a kid; and much more sound than the one I recently swallowed, I felt that somehow I'd managed to pinch back a little time.

***

Col's mother meanwhile back in her Sydney nursing home, would continue yelling excitedly every time the TV mentioned, "Captain Swift." *"Captain Swift! That's my boy!"* she'd yell and beam proudly at the smiling nursing staff oblivious to the fact that in this instance, her mind was as clear as day. And Col would've been happy to know that every time she did it – she was pinching back a little of her own time too.

THE COURTYARD PLAQUE

An eye-piercing spark of light fires from the surface of a World Animal Protection plaque hanging somewhat absurdly on the courtyard wall wounds Tarnasay, momentarily blinding him. He adjusts his chair away from the light, tops up his beer, looks at the gate where he hopes to see a four-legged bundle of fun pushing his way through the weathered wrought iron and charging towards him. But the heavy gate is still. His attention turns back to the plaque that was blinding him. He stares at it with a bemused smile. He'd never known what to do with it so he'd hung it on the courtyard wall where it'd become partially obscured by a rambling star-jasmine vine now in full bloom. It was sent to him as recognition for his "incredibly generous" donations to the fund. From the tone of the letter that accompanied the plaque Tarnasay surmised that, either it was extremely rare for the organisation to give out such things or, this was indeed the first time it'd ever been done. However, the strangest thing for Tarnasay regarding this gleaming recognition of goodwill was that he'd never once donated to the World Animal Protection organisation. He was well aware of their work and had always admired them but he'd never been a contributor. He'd helped save a chimpanzee in Thailand with a bunch of backpackers he remembers vividly, but that was all he'd done personally in contributing to animal welfare, apart from looking after Hasta of course. It was shortly after receiving his commemorative plaque that another mysterious item first appeared in his letterbox – a plain brown recycled envelope which sat conspicuously amongst a thatch of glossy retail brochures.

CRUELLA, THE MISTREATED CIRCUS MONKEY

Col waited until early afternoon before heading out to see if he could track down Tarnasay. His reasoning was that Tarnasay was more likely to venture out at night and hit some of the bars around Chiang Mai. Cruising from bar to bar Col hoped he'd find him before he got too shitfaced. At the sixth bar he visited, Col found Tarnasay. At the first bar he visited he'd asked some Irish backpackers if they knew of any bars where live music is played. Col's reasoning was Tarnasay's love of music and particularly live acts. They said the only place they knew of was 'The Hug.' Col decided to have one more drink with them before heading there but instead found himself on a bar crawl that eventually ended up at The Hug. His attention was immediately drawn to a Thai reincarnation of Jimi Hendrix rocking out the place.

Col was buying a round of drinks at the bar and had almost forgotten he was meant to be looking for Tarnasay when the man himself came up to the bar and added another beer to Col's order. Col immediately recognised his voice. He turned around, wrapped his big arms around Tarnasay and gave him a drunken bear hug. "You just couldn't leave me could you Col," teased Tarnasay. "Nothing to do with you mate," Col said slurring a little, "It's the food that's kept me here. Ahhh the food." He was studying the meal of a man seated next to him at the bar when he said it and looking at it too closely causing the man to frown and shift his plate from Col's leering eyes. Tarnasay helped Col with his order and invited him and his new Irish drinking buddies to join him and his friends at their table. Drunken revelry and the endless banter of every stranger's travel tales seeped into the hours, blurring time. It was one of those nights where every minute is full, so packed full of life and energy, empathy and laughter; that it's as though time itself feels the weight of it, concedes to the moment, tips it's hat, buys you a drink and slows down too.

At some point during the evening, Col had heard talk of a 'monkey heist.' He immediately shot a look at Tarnasay who just smiled and nodded. Col had been listening to Marieke – a very attractive, verbose Dutch girl with more than a hint of an American accent in her voice – passionately discussing the conditions and treatment of a chimpanzee they saw recently at a travelling Circus. For the first time that evening, Col felt the sudden surge of his natural cynicism flow through his brain. 'Here we go,' he thought, 'Some bleeding heart, politically correct Gen Y'er attempting to correct the ways of her narcissistic generation by championing the one-off rescue of a flea-ridden fuckin' monkey.' But Col listened politely, even nodding at times, as if in agreement with the gorgeous Marieke who cast her impassioned stare at all those listening. Which he was in truth, at the crux of it. He hated seeing any animal mistreated, but he was simply wondering, 'why it'd taken this girl a backpacking trip to Thailand to actually give a fuck.' 'Are there not mistreated animals back in your country?' he found himself questioning her under the veil of his mind. 'When you donned your backpack did you also stuff in there every kind of 'Save the world' issue as well? Are you just as passionate about this stuff back home or is it just on holidays when the Singha and Sang Thip kicks in - when you talk big with your spoilt Western comrades while wielding mummy and daddy's credit card like a sword that slices through third world currencies as though silken tofu?' Col was getting himself rather worked up and had begun subconsciously swiping at the lemon peeking over the top of his Corona with a straw. One of his Irish bar hopping buddies then brought Col to the attention of what he was doing, "On guard!" he announced, giggling drunk, and the two of them proceeded to engage in a miniature sword fight with their straws. The battle took Col's attention away from Marieke whose voice now became more like ambient noise. Tarnasay came over and sat next to Col.

"Man I'm stoked you're here, that you decided to stay," he said. "So what are your plans after Thailand? Want to go on another adventure bro?" said Tarnasay who Col realised was now completely pissed. Tarnasay only said "bro" when he was completely pissed or really high. Tonight chances were he was both.

"For sure man, that's why I'm here in Chiang Mai. I want to see what you get up to next," said Col who then raised a shot of something that had just been placed in front of them by Marieke and the two of them offered salutations. The two cavaliers then decided they'd move to a smaller table away from the raucous shenanigans now taking place around them. Tarnasay was fascinated to know how the "despatch" went with Ubetcha. Col had no idea where to begin with that particular episode so he dodged the delirious details for the moment. "Yes but first of all Tarnasay, I've got to ask you about this... monkey business?" said Col. Tarnasay laughed in a manner which showed he knew this was coming.

"I mean..." started Col before pausing. Tarnasay realised Col was completely pissed or really high. Probably both. Col always started his probing, sometimes long winded, drunken rants with lengthy pauses. "Drants" as Col self-deprecatingly called them.

"I know it may seem as though sometimes we are (lengthy pause)...and that you no doubt wish we were (lengthy pause) ..." Tarnasay hoped Col wasn't going to take too long with this particular drant because his concentration was waning and he found himself being drawn towards Marieke who was continually glancing over at him smiling, no doubt thinking about monkey business too but not the kind now running through Col's mind.

"But... (lengthy pause) I can assure you my good friend" continued Col excruciatingly, "That we are indeed (lengthy pause)...not (lengthy pause) ....in the fanciful movie (lengthy pause)....The Cannonball Run."

Tarnasay chuckled then sighed, hoping for closure.

"Therefore this brings me to the following question...(lengthy pause)."

'Yes closure!' thought Tarnasay.

"A chimp? (lengthy pause)..." Col asked him incredulous. "You're going to take a fuckin' chimpanzee?..."

But once again Col found himself rooted to his seat, although this time in a Chiang Mai bar as Tarnasay convinced him why. His reason was simple. He'd been sleeping with Marieke. But he also explained that he'd seen first-hand how the animal was being treated and that it really was hard to ignore when stealing her was so easy. And yes, Marieke had asked for his help and he had agreed. That night just before he was going to sleep and running through his pickled mind the items he needed to purchase for tomorrow's heist, it suddenly dawned on Col that despite his misgivings about the rescue, he was in, 'How does he do it?' wondered Col.

The next morning Col told Tarnasay of his superyacht. His grand purchase. "It hasn't got as many tricks as Ubetcha and it's a little smaller – 120ft customised, one-off Grand Banks. But she's gorgeous. I'm having a few extras added to her fit-out now. She's everything I've always loved about Grand Banks yachts but just on a slightly larger scale – a superyacht scale I suppose. The previous owner had her commissioned for Christ knows how much but I got her for a good price. Amazing what a backpack of cold, hard cash can do. And just in fuckin' time too, look at what it was doing to my shoulders," said Col showing Tarnasay his shoulders that were rubbed raw, scorched red like severe sunburn. Tarnasay didn't look at his shoulders or properly process the absurdity that Col had been lugging around Thailand over 2M in a backpack. He just stared at Col's face in disbelief, then his eyes twinkled and his smile broadened but he said nothing. He just sat there smiling almost idiotically. Col smiled too and chuckled quietly. He could see that Tarnasay's mind was now flooding with all the possibilities this brought. Finally Tarnasay spoke.

"You bought a superyacht – you now own a superyacht?" he asked still somewhat incredulous.

"Yep. I own a superyacht," confirmed Col who couldn't deny that it felt good to say it aloud.

"Completely legally, no catches – you have papers, et cetera?" asked Tarnasay.

"What are you my fuckin' dad? Yes, I have papers. It's legally registered and it's mine."

"Awesome," said Tarnasay somewhat sternly, as though he just received the most important fact.

"Ubetcha," replied Col.

Tarnasay grinned at Col, his eyes still twinkling from the news, the possibilities, the freedom.

"You love saying that don't ya," said Tarnasay.

"When it's appropriate, yes," Col confessed smiling like an excited child.

"So where would you like me to take you Mr Tarnasay, you have a superyacht chartered mate and a Captain at your disposal – ah wait, that reminds me – there's one condition to you boarding my vessel..."

Tarnasay looked at Col his eyebrows raised in interest.

"If you ever refer to me again in those indulgent little notes that you're so fond of leaving behind as 'Captain Swift' I'll have you walk the fucking plank."

~

The simple fact that all those involved in Cruella's rescue and their impassioned reasons why she was, in their belief, "an utter bitch of a chimpanzee" went some way to supporting Tarnasay's claim that his "temporary loans" were never for personal gain. And despite his patience and him having witnessed first hand Cruella's sinister mistreatment, he too found himself wondering whether she had by some strange karmic twist actually brought it upon herself. Wisely, he decided no. But more wisely he also realised that the myriad flaws we see amongst ourselves, the selfishness, the vindictiveness, the violence and the greed, is not unique to mankind. That Cruella had certainly made the most of her 98% shared DNA with humans and that the untameable, uncoachable, inexplicably wild 2% which remained, she wielded to fantastic, man-sobbing, mercy-blubbering effect. Of course today, in the comfort of his home with a wee dram of scotch and some put-your feet-up retrospect, he can't help but admire a lone female chimpanzee whom managed to embed such an everlasting, almost perpetually haunting memory on a group of humans. But he didn't feel such admiration at the time.

"She's an absolute fucking bitch of a chimpanzee – a really, really nasty, piece of mother nature's work. To be honest and this may sound a little over the top but that's only because you weren't there when it happened. But I was actually embarrassed that although we're a different species we still share a *'female'* sexual identity y'know. We both belong to a *common planetary sisterhood* if you like. But despite this – I just found myself wanting to slap the bitch," explained Marieke late one night to a bunch of fellow backpackers who had recently arrived at the hostel she shared with Tarnasay and Col and the rest of the rescue crew.

"It was supposed to be symbolic, but more importantly, a pro-active event. Not just rhetoric. The actual rescue of a suffering animal, the liberation of a defenceless, mistreated creature from one of man's many exploitative, self-serving, self-defeating missions y'know? So why is it now that I find myself thinking that if the species was completely wiped out tomorrow I just wouldn't give a fuck."

The new arrivals had heard about the recent rescue effort and were keen to hear the details and perhaps why Marieke had a series of bald patches amongst what was otherwise a lush, fullbodied head of hair.

Tarnasay and Col were also listening and were surprised to learn that the compassionate reasons which motivated her to organise Cruella's rescue in the first place were now long forgotten.

"I suppose my feelings towards the whole rescue thing began to change when I saw her punch Ben in the gut and steal his new retro Ray Bans," explained Marieke.

"We'd just rescued her and Ben was given the task of holding the chain leash while the rest of the rescue crew readied the cage trailer for her transportation. So y'know, I'm just watching the guys when Cruella casually wanders in front of Ben and lets out what we soon learnt was her signature terror scream, 'Eeeaaaa! Eeeaaaa! EEEAAAAO!' Then rips a really hard right into his gut and completely winds him. The poor guy just doubled over and then she casually stole his sunglasses. Then – and fuck man I'll never forget this – the bitch grabbed his chin and slowly raised his face until he could see her dilated primeval pupils and slapped him hard across the face!"

Hearing this, a number of her listeners had burst into laughter. Including Col and Tarnasay. But Marieke was not smiling and her manner did not change.

"Of course, yes at the time everybody thought this was hilarious too," Col was smiling and nodding his head vigorously. "And yeah ok, Ben freaked out a little and had a bit of – what do the English call it - a hissy fit. Anyway, this chimp who pinched his new Ray Bans was now wearing them in the back of the trailer with this strange kind of detached animal coolness. Little did we know that this was just the beginning of the torment to come and although she'd broken three of his ribs there was much worse ahead. And not just for me either. The strange thing is, I can kind of forgive her for that one now because I have since learnt that a company that once owned Ray Bans supplied Rhesus monkeys for laboratory testing. So in a way it ended up being a weird kind of karmic recompense I suppose – which Ben just happened to be a part of. I don't think it was personal."

With the help of Gavin Mills, a one-legged ex-pat Englishman who worked for the circus, Tarnasay, Col and Marieke led the team who would rescue Cruella. Gavin Mills was a very quietly spoken man in his late fifties who when approached by the passionate, very persuasive Marieke didn't take much convincing to assist them in the rescue. For a long time he'd felt ashamed of her treatment in which he played no direct part but still felt that he should do something. He explained to Marieke that "releasing a chimp like her is one thing, looking after her another." He couldn't do so himself nor could he find anyone else. In fact, many people laughed openly at him when he suggested it. Cruella did have a volatile reputation and he was surprised at just how far it reached. It seemed everyone in surrounding districts was aware of her having hospitalised the circus's previous Ringmaster. The current Ringmaster however, was far more domineering and brutal towards her and she was never given an opportunity to exact revenge. His treatment of Cruella was what had snared Marieke's attention in the beginning. She had slipped out briefly during the final act to get a drink and on her return witnessed the Ringmaster lasso Cruella, pulling a slip-knotted rope violently against her throat. Even now when Marieke recalls to others what she saw she finds herself getting upset and angry. It remains vivid in her mind. The way the rope closed tightly around her neck. Shrinking it to an impossibly small size like it was some kind of hideous torture corset. She also remembers the horrible shrieking, gasping sound Cruella made as she struggled for breath; and the nonchalant gait of the Ringmaster as he dragged her through the dirt towards her cage. She remembers spinning around to see if anyone else was witnessing it, listening to Cruella's terrified gasps and shrieks. But she remembers no-one was there except for the person she now knows as Gavin Mills. He too stood watching with a blank face before disappearing hurriedly into the darkness the moment Marieke laid her eyes on him. She remembers the drums. The drums building relentlessly towards the climax of the final act that continued inside the main tent, drowning out her shrieks. She remembers Cruella's mouth cast wide, agape in pain but chillingly mute as the Ringmaster dragged her away beneath the rolling, thundering drums.

Even Col for all his initial cynicism regarding Marieke's motivation to rescue her, can't help but become riled up whenever he listens to her recount that event. Marieke was too shocked and upset that night to approach the Ringmaster immediately. She decided she would wait until the next night when she would go again to the circus but this time accompanied by Tarnasay. Tarnasay was disturbed by what Marieke had seen but reluctant to take Cruella for the sake of taking her without some kind of plan for her welfare post-rescue. Marieke stressed to him that she'd ensure Cruella would be found a safe home. The next night when Marieke, now accompanied by Tarnasay, witnessed the cruelty again it became too much for her. This time against Tarnasay's protest she confronted the Ringmaster directly. He simply told her to "Fuck off" twice. Once in Thai and once in English.

That was enough for Tarnasay, that and witnessing the cruelty first hand was enough for him to agree to free Cruella.

No one is entirely sure how Cruella managed to trap Gavin Mills in the same trailer cage he'd driven to transport her to freedom. Perhaps she wanted him to know what it was like to be caged. He was bruised about the face and had several long scratches down the length of his arms which indicated she had also attacked him. But Gavin's only concern was the whereabouts of Cruella, "Not for her safety either," he said solemnly, "But for ours." He was the only one who had some inkling into the nasty behavioural traits of Cruella. But he obviously realised the make-up of her personality was not the reason for her rescue. It was simply the importance of rescuing a mistreated animal. The rescue team scoured the guesthouse where they were staying looking for her. She was nowhere to be found. Mr Mills stressed to Tarnasay and Col that it was crucial that they find her and that they had to be careful when they did as she was highly agitated. He was in no state to help them but he asked to be informed how their search went. "I want to know if I need to shut the windows of my room or not." When they later visited Mr Mills in his room and informed him that they hadn't found her. He was silent for a moment then said, "God help us." Col couldn't help himself and scoffed, "Bloody hell mate you're being a bit dramatic aren't ya, she's not the *Alien*." "No. She is not the alien," agreed Gavin who looked straight and hard at Col, who now noticed the full extent of Gavin's injuries; his left eye was badly swollen, and the gashes upon his arms seemed deeper despite being treated by Angela, an Irish nurse in the rescue team. "She is Cruella," said Gavin plainly.

Later that night when everyone but Col, Tarnasay and a couple of the Irish lads had gone to bed the men heard the distinct, primeval scream of Cruella's *"EEEAAA! EEEAAA!"*. This was followed by an equally distinct primeval scream from a female human. Shortly after an hysterical Marieke came running towards them. Her head now featured a collection of near bald patches where a reddened, traumatised scalp could be seen in place of where there had once been luscious brown hair. Cruella had attacked again and this time it had been a case of ferocious, savage hair pulling. 'Ouch,' thought Col. "Told you so," said Gavin Mills quietly to himself in the comfort of his room. Tarnasay took Marieke back to her room and comforted her while Angela treated the badly traumatised scalp. Col and the Irish lads went looking for Cruella around the guesthouse and clumsily explained the commotion and screaming to the owner but managed to avoid revealing they were harbouring, or at least attempting to harbour, a stolen, rampaging adolescent female chimpanzee. That night despite closing their windows and locking their doors, harrowing screams were heard at random times until early morning. Cruella's sudden aggressive signature screech always the precursor to yelling, screaming and swearing. She may have been free but she had a strange way of expressing her gratitude.

The next morning Tarnasay, Col and Marieke, who was still sulking over her attack, watched as a parade of people slowly emerged from the rooms and made their way to the al fresco-style restaurant like casualties of war. Some of the victims were not part of the rescue team and they spoke in hurried, haunted voices about the deranged chimp that had attacked them. With each recounting of their story, Cruella gained an inch on King Kong. But none of Cruella's victims required serious medical attention. The most common injuries were scratches, facial bruising and welts from being heavily slapped while slumbering. Angela, the very patient, gentle natured Irish nurse had been busy throughout the long night looking after those who believed they needed medical attention, but in truth most just required comforting. And although she crossed paths with Cruella once through the night, watching her leave the room of a screaming victim with the surreptitious air of a seasoned killer, she wasn't attacked. Cruella just stared at her from the corridor partially obscured by the shadows of night while Angela's hand nervously gripped the handle of her first aid bag. But Cruella just walked past. She paused ever so briefly, looked up into Angela's eyes as she went past then kept walking. Col had been fortunate too. He sat enjoying one last beer on his own after the Irish boys called it a night and Tarnasay had escorted a distraught Marieke back to her room, when he felt the uneasy sensation of someone watching him. As he took a sip of his beer he slowly turned his head sideways. He then spookily saw Cruella mirroring his exact actions. She too had a bottle of beer to her mouth, she too turned her head slowly, she too, looked at him wide eyed. Col couldn't help but laugh into his beer causing it to explode from his mouth. Cruella then appeared to laugh herself in a mocking way before she suddenly shrieked aggressively and pitched the bottle at speed towards Col's head. It narrowly missed and smashed into a timber post beside him. She then disappeared into the night. Col a tad shaken, finished his lager, cleaned up and went to bed.

It soon became apparent to Tarnasay and Col that their involvement with the rescue of Cruella wasn't about to end there. The original plan for Marieke, Ben and the rest of the rescue team to take care of her whilst they found her a new home was lost when they flatly refused to have anything more to do with her. The forceful arguments put forth by both Tarnasay and Col which involved reciting to them their much espoused credo of "animal liberation" simply fell on deaf ears. And although initially Col had taken some convincing to rescue Cruella, he now made it clear to Tarnasay that he wasn't about to abandon the animal like those "spoilt little pricks." Tarnasay wasn't in favour of abandoning her either but he sure as hell wanted to get rid of her. However, when their efforts to find her a caring home failed, Col put an end to that idea too. One morning over breakfast he simply announced to Tarnasay that there was no other choice, Cruella would sail with them and Jimmy to the States and if he didn't like that scenario he'd "Better get another Captain. And a boat."

Sam's Neverending Day Off (Part 2)

Sam has brought some of her personal notes on the case to read. Oddly though, she hasn't brought them along because she's still smarting over an abrupt end to an assignment that has dominated her life for so long. To pour over the details as a kind of personal assessment, a mourning of lost opportunity which would have been completely justified. It was quite the opposite. She feels entirely at ease with the sudden development which has surprised her. She isn't numb or shocked, in a state of denial or smouldering beneath her exterior. She feels free. Released from something that's had a crippling hold on her. Liberated.

Sam knows through experience that regardless of how tightly an organisation has bound its operation in privacy, covering it in a cloak of confidentiality; details and information tend to fray at the edges over time and unravel. Sam's job within the Criminal Assets Confiscation Taskforce (CACT) at the Australian Federal Police had been to identify where it was beginning to fray and then pick at it. Pick at the loose threads of an organisation's heavy cloak like a cat pawing at a ball of string. On this occasion Sam had been picking at the company for quite some time. But it had proven to be more elusive, more heavily cloaked than most. There was very little fraying. No loose threads. Pressure for Sam to demonstrate progress towards unravelling this secretive, supposedly criminal organisation, to identify a link, or at the very least an association with organised crime or international fugitives had been mounting. But she had nothing, which Sam could scarcely admit to herself let alone her superiors. After nearly four years working on the most stubborn case she ever encountered, she had barely more information than a hack writing about the same subject for a national tabloid. Mostly conjecture, definitely speculative and too often wrong.

Hasta finally settles down for a rest and snuggles up close to Sam. He playfully nudges her leg with his wet nose and rolls onto his side urging her to scratch his belly. 'I really could keep him' she thought, 'Now that I'm moving, I could just take him with me.' "Would you like to come with me?" she asks him. Hasta seems to let out a whine of indecision which makes her laugh. Along with her decision to leave her job, Sam has also decided that she will leave the area she is living in too. Change everything for a while, she's decided. She looks at Hasta again. He really is a good-looking, happy dog. A bit unpredictable but smart and fun, and gentle natured. He would make a good companion. It's then she realises that although she didn't like the fact that he'd been left on his own for three days, he isn't a mistreated pet. Just looking at him and seeing his healthy spirit was proof of that. Sam feels ashamed that for a split second she wishes he had been. That she would then be justified in taking him because he was filthy and malnourished. Uncared for and entirely neglected. Then she wouldn't even think twice. She would be his. Not him hers. Because she would be entirely dedicated to him. Her devotion and care for him as reciprocal love because he would always be there for her. 'Panting' she suddenly thought. 'Yes, he'll always be there, panting, because he's a dog, and whether I'm laughing or crying he'll be there and the chances are he'll be panting.' When was the last time I got laid?' Sam suddenly queried herself. It had been awhile. She now realises how much she's missed genuine companionship, not just a couple of social drinks after work with some of the more fun, like-minded colleagues, but a night out for dinner or at the movies with a good friend. She looks at Hasta for a moment and he looks at her with his big eyes. He is panting. She smiles at him. As much fun and indeed genuine companionship a good dog like him would be, they could never just sit down and yarn away the hours listening to music and get stupidly, happily pissed together. Just for the hell of it. Like she did with friends in the past. She knew too, that her friends had suggested as much, their needing to get away from it all as much as she did, whatever 'it all' may be. But she'd continually postponed such nights. She liked the idea, she really did "But work is just so full on at the moment," she'd say, "let's try next month." And they'd agree, and they'd call again and again and again until eventually they stopped. Sam can't even remember now when they eventually stopped. They just stopped. She has to stop now too she realises. She has to stop thinking about it because it's starting to bring her picnic high down. As though on cue Hasta suddenly sits up and licks her ear causing Sam to yelp and he yelps back. "Crazy dog," she says.

Planet shed

The collection of empty beer bottles and a freshly opened bottle of red on the table signals that Tarnasay is growing more anxious on the whereabouts of Hasta. The gradual increase of his intoxication is also lubricating his reflection into the past. Like a well-oiled drill his thoughts are now digging deeper into his mind, driving into a hardened mass of old memories, loosening them and casting them up at speed. He watches as they pile up on top of each other forming a bank. He stops drilling for a moment. Something in the mound catches his eye. He goes over to it, picks through the rubble and finds Uncle Lou.

~

It was Uncle Lou who had given Hasta his name. From the beginning he'd observed the stubborn determination of the dog to obtain everything within its vicinity. Regardless of what it was the dog would gather it up. "He just hasta have it," said Uncle Lou. And so 'Hasta' was his name. Friends of Tarnasay soon became familiar with the ritual of sorting through a pile of miscellaneous items for their keys, thongs, jackets, handbags and shoes before heading home. But Hasta never destroyed anything. Even as a pup, he never sat there gnawing away on thongs, shoes or jackets. He just wanted them. He was simply a hunter-gatherer of things. Tarnasay remembers how Uncle Lou was completely fascinated by the dog. Unlike everyone else who would shoo him away if they found him pilfering something, Uncle Lou would just watch, enthralled. He loved the dog. He loved the way he slept soundly beside his bounty of things and never once protested or growled when someone approached in a huff searching for their lost item. But what fascinated him most about the peculiar creature, which Tarnasay believes he'd never have noticed had Uncle Lou not brought it to his attention, was that Hasta always knew which item belonged to which person. When an often frantic person approached Hasta's pile in search of their keys or jacket, Hasta would, if snoozing, immediately awake and quickly, almost methodically nudge his nose through the pile of things until he found their item. He would then pick it up gently between his teeth or nudge it out into the open with his nose. The hurried person never had to search for their missing thing because without fail, Hasta would have their item in clear view by the time they reached him and his hoard. This fascinated Tarnasay too. It also explained why, despite being stirred about his "Weirdo dog" or his "Half-breed hoarder" no-one had ever complained about having lost anything. Today, knowing more about his Uncle Lou and the man's own penchant for hoarding things, Tarnasay can see how his affection for Hasta went well beyond a fascination with the unusual behaviour, and most likely had more to do with identifying him as a kindred spirit. The fact he may have had a kindred spirit in the form of a dog rather than another human being wouldn't have even entered Uncle Lou's mind.

~

Tarnasay looks down at the pile of memories at his feet and sees Uncle Lou again. He picks up the memory and studies it, looking at its form and texture. Uncle Lou had no time for religion. And although he wasn't afraid to express strongly held views about its supposed worth and its origins, he never begrudged or dared ridicule another man's personal belief or his right to have it. He understood how through the harrowed path of history it had given people a sense of hope and strength, a focal point, a purpose. But it was in modern times, and the ever presence of "organised religion" in particular, that he felt it to be antiquated, redundant, a dangerous way of thinking. Selfish even. He failed to see its worth. "The moral code and ethics," he would argue, "was not born of the religious as they'd have us think, but the by-product of necessity. Long before the first scribblings of the bible, man was thrust into situations that, although in far cruder, primeval terms, were not terribly removed from those we may face today. I'm talking about negotiation. From the time man could communicate, deals and favours would've been struck. – *Damn. I missed spearing that bloody mammoth today by a sabertooth's whisker and now I have nothing to feed the family. Hmm...but look over there. Big Glak has nailed two of the hairy buggers. Maybe I could try to kill Big Glak and take them; or maybe I could do something different. Ask a favour. Negotiate. I could ask him to share his kill with my family today and fiery balls of lava above! – should tomorrow he fail to make a kill, I'll share mine with him."* Uncle Lou believed that 'means of survival' saw the beginnings of a moral code. And the caring notion of sharing and cooperating we know today were, in their infancy, a means of strategy and survival in prehistoric times. Something which then became more refined and more sophisticated just like the tools we held in our hands. Something that evolved with us towards civilisation and left behind the strategic, cruder form of sharing as a means of survival. This was at the core of how Uncle Lou passed through the world. He believed we should be closer to the pinnacle of human compassion and empathy by now. More inclined to share our lot with those less fortunate and less possessive of things that fall short of bearing sentimental value. And for him, religions of all persuasions had fallen well short of this, their compassion and generosity too closely entwined with the growth of their belief and resulting influence on power. Rarely, he felt, was it ever done in truly altruistic terms. It had lost its way. He would never deny or argue that there weren't those within any given religion who demonstrated extraordinary compassion for fellow man, but he would argue that those men and women would have done so anyway without any brand of belief should that have been the situation. That they were naturally inclined to care and share, perhaps due to a combination of genetics and upbringing but certainly not simply because they chose to follow a set of religious beliefs. "Compassion and selflessness are not exclusive virtues of the religious," he would say, "To receive compassion one shouldn't have to read the fine print in the form of a religious doctrine and those offering it shouldn't be delivering it that way either – *Oh by the way, this compassion was proudly brought to you by...*"

Uncle Lou could never share his own compassion in monetary terms. But through patience, presence and an infectious positivity he was the richest of philanthropists. He found time. He listened, he acted, he shared. It was difficult to go anywhere with Uncle Lou because he was always cornered by someone saying hello or thanking him for something. Tarnasay remembers that as a young boy he once asked his Uncle why people were always thanking him, "It's because I have one of those faces," he said, "It just makes people feel better about theirs." He stared at Tarnasay blankly for a moment before smiling broadly, Tarnasay pushed him playfully. But he knew better than to ask him the real reason. Uncle Lou would only ever tell you what he believed you needed to know, the rest you had to find out for yourself. Which one day Tarnasay did. During the summer holidays Tarnasay's family would always visit Uncle Lou and stay for a few days. They were the summer days that people love to reminisce about. How they seemed longer, more vivid, and stretched out forever like the over-sized postcard of the beach they'd send home to friends, stirring envy. Tarnasay felt that way too. These were easy memories, forefront memories. Never far from the surface of his mind. Many things would bring them back; the smell of a particular suntan lotion, the loud and intense throb of cicadas where their pitch and beat seems to dictate the heat, a song, an old car, or just something said. These are the memories we cherish like possessions. Tarnasay can still see Uncle Lou's shed in so much detail he can almost smell it. Rusting fruit tins aligned neatly on flimsy shelves made of old, grey fence palings sprouting splinters as nasty as cactus. Ancient number plates that seem to be ordered in hues of sepia, tyres that looked like they just rolled in off the street, paint tins, nuts and bolts of every kind, stacks of timber, piles of plastic, a circus, tools and tools and tools and tools. In that shed there was order and there was chaos. "You just gotta know how to look at it," explained Uncle Lou earnestly. Tarnasay and his brothers knew how to look at it. They looked at it like it was another world. A shed planet, a planet of everything shed, a shed full of everything every other shed ever had. And more. It was 'the more' that really had Tarnasay and his brothers fascinated.

Tarnasay has never forgotten the clown that he met in the depth of Uncle Lou's shed. Its maniacal smile, crazy hair and loose, chaotic clothing that appeared to be the patchwork effort of a Grandma on LSD. He remembers its stiff hand coming down and resting on his shoulder as he floundered around in the dark with only a small candle for guidance. He remembers screaming. He remembers no-one hearing him. He remembers it all now with a smile but he can't deny how that encounter affected him and well into adulthood. Clowns in shopping malls or anywhere else were avoided for years because he found himself with an irrational but overwhelming compulsion to scream at them. And he wasn't entirely sure whether it was a scream motivated by fear or anger. He even considered getting therapy for it at one point but figured that seeing he didn't encounter clowns all that often it wasn't really justified. Eventually in a crazy twist of irony, it was watching the film 'It' (based on a novel by Stephen King about a psychopathic killer clown no less) that forced him to confront his fear. He was well into his twenties at the time when his new girlfriend had brought home the movie to watch. He figured he couldn't scream all the way through the film or it would be over. And he really liked the girl. She complained he squeezed her hand too tightly at times but he managed to control the urge to scream madly at the TV. That night he finally overcame his fear of people dressed up in bad make-up, wild wigs and mismatched clothing. The touch of the clown's hand on his shoulder now runs through Tarnasay's mind again. How real it seemed. But it was just a life-sized mannequin clown that his Uncle Lou had refashioned with a crudely robotic arm. He explained with great disappointment that it had only ever worked "Now and then" and that apparently no one had seen it move for years. Tarnasay still feels a little uneasy that its only movement in years just happened to be when he was fossicking around 'Planet Shed' late one night on his own.

Tarnasay and his brothers spent hours exploring the shed and its contents. Apart from what appeared to be an historic collection of every tool known to man and a dizzying assortment of strange-shaped objects, some steel, some timber and others plastic, the purpose of which even his dear old Uncle Lou had trouble identifying, there resided an amazing collection of toys. Toys that could almost form a periodic table for playtime. His younger brothers once attempted to count the number of painted tin toys, their colours faded and chipped from years of child abuse but gave up when the number went beyond their counting ability. Plastic Star Wars figurines would pop up in front of you like magic leprechauns from the future, watching you from the most unlikely places as you explored Planet Shed. There were balls for every kind of ball game, billy carts, pots of plasticine, shelves of board games to rival department stores at Christmas, bikes of every size, skateboards, dolls, puppets, frisbees, tennis rackets, pogo sticks, yo-yos, buckets of marbles, buckets of bouncing balls, buckets of Lego and miles and miles of Scalextric track. And that was just as far as Tarnasay and his brothers could see. Tarnasay joked to his little brothers that to go any further into Planet Shed they'd need a "Special space-like survival suit." The concerned look on their faces told Tarnasay they missed his joke and that such a suit might indeed be required. And that was the affect that Uncle Lou's shed had on them – as much as it was awesome, fun and exciting, it was also a little overwhelming and scary.

In time of course, as they got older they came to realise there was nothing to be scared of. But not for Tarnasay. And this time it had nothing to do with the clown. This time it was the gyre of materialist refuse that one man, his Uncle Lou, had accumulated in his shed in a relatively short amount of time. By now all the whispers, secrets and endless childhood speculations about why Uncle Lou had Planet Shed had been revealed. They learnt that the shed was actually his workshop and that many of the toys and other things were being repaired in order to be given away. Tarnasay now knew the real reason so many people stopped to say hello or to thank his Uncle Lou. At some stage he'd probably given them something or repaired an item for them. He'd shared his time, his skill and his patience and they were thanking him. It was patience that worked for Uncle Lou. He'd never learnt a trade nor was he a particularly great handyman, but over time he gained the skill and knowledge to fix most things and this came down to patience. It wasn't always that way. Tarnasay distinctly remembers his mum and dad were never too keen on his brothers and him hanging around the shed when the large timber doors were closed. It meant Uncle Lou was working. It also meant they were likely to hear every profanity currently in use in every foul combination possible.

The gyre of material refuse fascinated Tarnasay as much as it repulsed him. It wasn't until he saw it before his eyes gathered in one large space that he realised just how much "crap" there is in the modern world. Today of course he need only visit the local 'Two dollar' shop to experience the same feeling. A space almost entirely dedicated to useless trinkets, throw-away pieces of pointless plastic of the kind that are found in Christmas bonbons. Items so bereft of imagination and appeal they'd struggle to raise a smile from a toy-less toddler.

Captain Swift visits the Gulf of Aden

The wisdom behind Col's decision to take Cruella with them to New York had been questioned many times. And by none more so than himself. It wasn't only the crash course in basic animal care that Col found he had to undertake prior to their sailing but the added responsibility of Tarnasay appointing him as her main "guardian." Tarnasay had agreed, against what he believed to be his better judgement, that Cruella would sail with them. Col was undoubtedly Captain of his own boat but he knew that neither Tarnasay nor Jimmy would sail with him unless he agreed to take charge of her. And Col had no reason to sail to New York otherwise. Jimmy hadn't actually witnessed Cruella's legendary bad behaviour but had learnt of it when hearing of her rescue. He too doubted the wisdom of Col's decision.

What came as a surprise to everyone was how Cruella behaved around Jimmy. She became serene. But, in keeping with her odd personality there was of course a catch to this serenity, her new found calmness. The catch was that she only entered this endearing state when Jimmy had his guitar slung over his slender shoulders. It wasn't essential that he played it, which she adored when he did, it just had to be there. On his person. If it wasn't, even if it was seated next to him on a chair or placed on the floor, Cruella's behaviour would return to her default state of violent unpredictability.

It had taken some time and more than a few "man slaps" from Cruella (as Col had coined them) across Jimmy's face before they came to a rather stunning realisation. And it was a relief to all. But none more so than Jimmy whose previously smooth, light olive complexion had been replaced by a disturbing, permanent looking ruddiness. He also looked as though he was developing a nervous tick. Neither Col or Tarnasay had said anything to Jimmy but they noticed he'd begun flinching and jolting back and forth hastily whenever the yacht creaked loudly, or when another sound such as water lapping hard against the boat became more audible than usual, startling him. It was as though he was protecting himself from some unseen danger and exactly the same kind of protective behaviour he'd engage when under attack by Cruella. They weren't sure whether Jimmy was aware of this fast developing tick or whether due to his extraordinarily patient manner, he'd just decided to deal with it. Or perhaps, he was just so relieved to be finally heading abroad to places previously denied that a few hard slaps across the face every so often from a deranged chimp was nothing to complain about. Either way, Tarnasay and Col knew something had to be done about it. They also knew that they couldn't just keep her locked up continuously as she had been back at the circus when she wasn't performing.

It was the - not performing - that Tarnasay finally realised was the key. As long as Jimmy had the guitar slung over his shoulder, in much the same manner as her brutal trainer had worn his circus sash when performing, she'd be okay. Fun and entertaining even. But the moment the guitar – the sash to her – was removed, she became agitated, hyperactive and unpredictable again. It meant the performance was over. It meant that she'd be returned to the boredom and filth of her cage. Cruella was simply associating Jimmy's guitar with that of her previous owner's circus sash and she despised the routine it symbolised. Although this discovery now meant that they could better manage Cruella's behaviour, there were still days when Cruella was on deck and when Jimmy, having grown tired of a guitar constantly hanging from his body would remove it and these were the days that Jimmy got a good slapping.

Of course this wasn't how Jimmy had hoped his voyage from Thailand to New York for his first international gig would transpire. Although he wasn't entirely surprised either. That isn't to say that he somehow half expected to be living in fear of a face slapping chimpanzee, it was just that he was familiar with things not turning out perfectly. Jimmy had become almost philosophical about it. "It was never this way before," he told Tarnasay and Col one night when Cruella sat opposite them. She was as calm as the sea they lolled upon and contentedly eating a fruit salad heavily ladened with banana. "So why would it be this way now?" Jimmy was referring to the fact that nothing had ever really gone smoothly for him. That although he'd always eventually managed to achieve his aims they'd never happened, "Without some kind of... I dunno, some kind of cosmic compromise, y'know." Col didn't know but he nodded along with Tarnasay nonetheless. He didn't know about "cosmic compromises" that is, but he knew about the struggle. He knew how things don't always go to plan. He also knew it was this way for most people too and he said as much to Jimmy, "Mate you're not alone there. Although they'll pretend otherwise, for most people things don't turn out exactly as they hope. There's always a pay off, sometimes the pay off is the struggle, the almighty life sapping struggle just to get there – to get what you want. Then more often than not, it's just a part of it. Part of what you want. Not all of it. But then, and here's the weird bit Jimmy – if we ever finally do get what we want – it's never enough! No! We want more! But that's a whole 'nother story right there mate." Col's words brought a smile to Jimmy's face. "Of course," added Col, "There are always exceptions to the fucking rule, exceptions to the struggle," he then darted his eyes quickly towards Tarnasay who was listening but gazing absentmindedly out to sea. Jimmy smiled.

It had taken Col some time to work out why he wanted to reconvene with Tarnasay. To hang out with him again. To see what happens next. And the realisation had come to him while making his way from Phuket to Chiang Mai. It was the reason he now had his own special yacht. It was because things go to plan for Tarnasay. They happen just the way he expects them to. He gets what he wants. He doesn't struggle. Col had gone from initially being intrigued by this, to fascinated and now bewitched, because when he thought about the beautiful, customised 120ft Aleutian RP Grand Banks motor yacht awaiting his return at the Ocean Marina yacht club in Pattaya, he couldn't help but think that somehow some of this bloke's magic had rubbed-off on him. He didn't feel the struggle when he was with him. He didn't feel he was losing time or missing opportunities; that there was something more important he should be doing. He felt the opposite – that for once he had control, that he controlled time, that this is what's important, that this is where he'd create opportunities and not simply chance by them. One such opportunity was to sail Mai Pen Rai, his own glorious superyacht all the way from Thailand to New York.

~

There were days as they sailed deep into the Atlantic ocean which seemed to be as broad as the ocean itself. Hours were anchored, minutes tethered. They were the days that unless you occupied your mind with certain tasks that required a certain amount of concentration it would wither and warp. The fascination of the sea and all its inhabitants replaced by frustration and a foreboding sense of tedium. And each of the four seafarers dealt with it their own way. Jimmy occupied himself with learning new songs and writing his own music. Tarnasay also jammed with Jimmy, sketched a little and read a lot. Col whittled interesting things out of timber, also jammed with Jimmy and Tarnasay and began filming parts of the voyage. Cruella screamed, slapped and eventually to everyone's relief or perhaps disbelief, began to more often than not just sit still and observe the ocean. Of course this didn't happen until they were well into their voyage to the United States of America. Up until that point Jimmy had to be diligent about maintaining the presence of his guitar upon his person should he not wish to be slapped about the face by Cruella. But ever so gradually she was being weaned from the guitar's presence. Jimmy had begun, at the risk of a slapping, not wearing the guitar but always having it seated next to him. Bit by bit, slap by slap, this eventually began to work for Jimmy. Col and Tarnasay were impressed. Although this meant an end to what had become for Col a filmic journal of 'man-slapping' where he'd been secretly filming Cruella's attacks on Jimmy and posting them on YouTube, he was happy that her reign of terror was almost over. To Tarnasay's delight Col had taken to posting the video footage of Cruella's attacks upon Jimmy under the monicker 'Captain Swift.'

Initially, Col felt trepidation about showing Jimmy the YouTube postings. It wasn't that Jimmy was the only victim in the 'man-slapping' series but there was something about seeing the same guy again and again getting ambushed by the same deranged chimpanzee again and again that was very funny. So Col had grouped them together on his postings. He never really believed they'd become as popular as they did. He thought it was just something funny to share with a few mates back home. Some violent slapstick he knew they'd appreciate, good old fashioned 'schadenfreude' as the Germans would say. Soon though, once they got moved on beyond his friends and people realised that the postings were by none other than 'Captain Swift' everything changed. They became one of the highest viewed

YouTube videos listed. They even made the News in certain countries where they discussed the possible whereabouts and dangerous antics of 'Tarnasay and Captain Swift.' Some even went as far as to venture that "the malnourished Asian man" in the attacks was a possible hostage being tortured for their sick amusement. Col's poor attempts not to giggle stupidly like a naughty schoolboy while filming the vicious attacks on Jimmy no doubt convinced some of "the callousness of the two wayward cavaliers." At this point, Col became concerned that he'd violated Jimmy in a way far worse than Cruella. Violated his privacy, ignored getting his permission. He asked Tarnasay for his thoughts and quickly wished he hadn't. "Bit late to be worrying about that isn't it Captain Swift?" said Tarnasay smirking. Col had a sudden urge to punch Tarnasay.

Neither of them had ever heard Jimmy laugh so hard. He couldn't stop watching them. He thought they were brilliant. Only once did he playfully (but not without a touch of venom) punch Col in the leg when his giggling became clearly audible over Jimmy's frightened yelps. The only thing he found offensive in the whole thing was when he learnt of the media referring to him as "a malnourished Asian man." "Fuckin' mother fuckers," he said. "Fucking malnourished. Fuck them. I'm slim. Not just slim either, sexy slim man. Look at me," he said asking Col and Tarnasay for affirmation. They both nodded. "Fucking mother fuckers," said Jimmy sternly before he clicked on another video and began laughing again.

Distractions such as this, on what was to be more than forty days at sea were welcomed. Distractions that took their mind away from the potential peril of piracy as they sailed into the Arabian Sea before entering the Gulf of Aden and onwards through the Red Sea towards the Suez Canal. It'd been some years since Col had sailed in this part of the world and he'd been in regular contact with friends back home regarding the dangers of piracy. He also queried other sailors he'd befriended after purchasing his yacht earlier at the Phuket Marina, where he, Tarnasay and Jimmy spent a week readying themselves with supplies. He was told the dangers were very real and that much of it came down to simply a matter of chance. They were out there and there was no real way of minimising the chance of contact on a voyage such as theirs. "Just a matter of luck really," said one of his mates familiar with sailing in this part of the world in a tone that acknowledged what he said was unhelpful. Col had considered charting alternative, supposedly safer routes, but each one added at least two weeks to an already long voyage. Even then there was still no guarantee of safety. So through the Arabian Sea then onto the Suez Canal and up through the Mediterranean it was to be.

Col couldn't help but think that if they got to the Mediterranean without incident they'd be okay. He didn't want to alarm the others unnecessarily or overstate the risks but he was also not one for holding back what he believed others should know, particularly when it concerned their safety. Col had both Tarnasay and Jimmy accompany him on at least two occasions when he met with his sailing friends in Phuket to discuss the charting of the voyage. But nothing that either Tarnasay or Jimmy heard gave them serious pause for thought. Col wasn't particularly concerned with Tarnasay, the man was in many ways all about risk and chance. Jimmy on the other hand was an artist who had a simple desire to realise a dream, to accept an invitation to perform with world renowned rock musicians on their stage - but was he prepared to take a potentially dangerous voyage to realise it? "Safer than flying, in my mind," he told Col. The worrying concern for encounters with pirates however, was soon overshadowed by a greater one when they fully grasped just how much attention Tarnasay had now gained internationally. There would be people on the lookout for them on the high seas regardless of how they perceived Tarnasay's actions. And although no-one outside the acquaintances they made briefly in Thailand knew who they were, Tarnasay and Col's previous sailing adventure was still making world headlines.

~

The gun wasn't loaded of course, and the fact that they planned the whole thing didn't change the sense of urgency the three men felt to get below deck and away from Cruella. It was something about seeing Cruella stomping upon the roof of the yacht shaking a shotgun like an enraged warlord again that made them nervous. Now they just had to hope the pirates barely a hundred metres away would feel slightly perturbed too or at least a little more cautious than usual if they decided to come in for a closer look.

Whatever it was it worked. They didn't really think that the pirates who came in for a closer look at the strange shenanigans upon the top of Col's yacht were actually frightened. Nonetheless, it did seem that the highly unusual circumstance before them, that of a highly excited chimpanzee brandishing a shotgun which only moments earlier they heard fired into the darkness of night had been enough to forgo boarding Col's yacht. Tarnasay, Col and Jimmy watched silently, hidden below in the depth of the yacht. They watched as the pirate vessel cruised past stealthily. They remained below deck for some time, concerned that the pirates may return but they never did. Perhaps they figured there were easier targets than one containing a mad chimp wielding a shot gun. Maybe it was just too weird even for the pirates. Either way, they were relieved that the first encounter and hopefully their last didn't escalate into a life threatening situation.

It had been Col and Jimmy's ingenious idea. The moment they identified that it was most likely a pirate ship in their midst, Col killed the lights of the yacht. They accessed the three shotguns stored in the basement. They knew they were being watched by the silhouetted pirated ship barely a hundred metres away. Jimmy suggested releasing Cruella and sending her above deck for no other reason than a strange distraction. Col joked that they should give her one of the shotguns. They all nervously laughed at the idea until Tarnasay said "Y'know. It's not as stupid as it sounds." Col ran with the idea. "That's it! Jimmy and I and Cruella will go to the upper decks on the starboard side where they can't see us and fire off a couple of shots to let them know we're armed. It'll also stir up dear Cruella, then we empty the gun, give it to her and get her to climb onto the flybridge roof, y'know how she loves it up there. Hopefully she'll jump around manically with the gun...*like that other time.*"

Tarnasay thought back to *'that other time'* when Cruella appeared on deck brandishing one of the shotguns screaming and pumping it in the air like a spear. She'd accessed the orlop of the yacht and discovered the chest containing the shotguns before venturing unseen to the upper deck and climbing onto the yacht's roof with one of the guns grasped awkwardly in her hand. This wasn't the first time Cruella had ever seen a shotgun but it was the first time she'd ever held one.

The first time Cruella saw a shotgun was one lazy, deadly still afternoon when the three men had gotten spontaneously drunk. Col had all but killed the motor as they putted along. The water had been mirror-like all day so he decided they should just idle along and enjoy it. At some stage after hitting the whiskey they somewhat dangerously decided that it would be fun to launch a few coconuts into the air to fire at as targets. Coconuts that Jimmy had brought along for cooking. Aware that the sound of the shotgun may agitate Cruella, Col fired a test shot into the air. She loved it. She danced up and down and did her excited little flips which they learnt long ago meant she was in good cheer. It was game on. Tarnasay clambered onto the flybridge roof and proceeded to hoist a coconut as high into the air as possible before Col took aim as though it were a fat, hairy pigeon and fired. First shot he hit it. The hard, hairy brown casing exploded into a million fragments and they all cheered like the stupid drunk men they were. Cruella was beside herself. They'd rarely seen her so excited. Tarnasay remarked that maybe in her monkey imaginings she saw the exploding coconut as representative of her former brutal ringmaster's head. They continued blasting coconuts out of the sky that afternoon until Jimmy did a quick stock take and announced rather solemnly that his "Coconut count is low," which was met with laughter and the agreement that the game was over.

The next time they saw one of the guns was in Cruella's nimble hands. Logic told them it wasn't loaded but when Tarnasay and Jimmy saw Cruella brandishing the gun in the air it still terrified them. Particularly when she spun around and pointed it at them playfully. Both of them subconsciously leaned out of her line of sight. Then Tarnasay heard Jimmy giggle a little nervously and announce that he had an idea. Col was below deck doing his routine maintenance check of the yacht and was unaware of the monkey business going on above. Jimmy decided it was payback time for all those monkey slappings he'd recorded. He called down to Col suggesting that he take a break as he was making some afternoon cocktails and if he could bring a coconut with him when he came up. Col thought that was a plan and wrapped up his maintenance check. Tarnasay and Jimmy then made their way to the bow of the yacht, crouched down behind the deckchairs and waited for Col. Cruella followed them around with the gun still pointed which kept them uneasy. Until Col arrived. "Alrighty then!" announced Col cheerfully as he strolled out onto the upper deck clutching a coconut to his chest like a rugby ball. "Where are these cocktails then Jimmy ol' mate," he said as he turned around looking for him and Tarnasay. Instead he found Cruella who was now screaming excitedly at him from the flybridge roof and pumping the gun in the air as though on cue, as though she understood the joke. "Jesus fucking Christ!" gasped Col terrified, quickly shifting around on his chunky legs for somewhere to take cover. It all happened too quickly for him to reason, as the other two had, that the gun wouldn't be loaded. They were missing, nowhere to be seen and he was startled, all he saw now was a screaming chimp with a gun. He felt the presence of the coconut again now that he hugged it tightly to his chest.

"No," he said to himself in disbelief.

'She watched us blasting coconuts from the sky,' he remembered with horror. He stood there open and exposed on the deck and ever so gradually lifted his stunned gaze to Cruella. He watched her raise the shotgun slowly to her eye and take aim at the coconut like a veteran sniper. The coconut now felt big and heavy in his arms like a medicine ball.

"*NOOO!*" bellowed Col from the very core of his being.

Tarnasay remembers it was the loudest scream he had ever heard from another man. He could've sworn the boat shifted. It was primeval. A man who saw death coming.

He also remembers the silence afterwards and that he and Jimmy remained cowering behind the deck chair at the bow for some time. It hadn't really occurred to either of them at the time that this was a very dark joke they were playing. That's not to say, that they no longer thought it was funny, they thought it was hilarious, but they wouldn't dare laugh at this dark joke yet. And as much as it would always be dark, they both knew while cowering behind the chairs, that it was only going to get funnier with each retelling of it and the loosening of time. In the meantime, Col refused to speak to them for days, which would've been difficult for him. Tarnasay remembers that Jimmy cheekily named the delicious cocktail he made just the two of them that night with the decimated coconut left behind by a fuming Col and the butt of the shotgun. 'Hold the coconut, Col,' Jimmy called it.

"And hopefully, because of the shots we fire before sending up Cruella, the pirates will think the gun's loaded. It may just be enough. You can almost hear them muttering amongst themselves now, *Hmmm. I dunno Harold. It could be some special forces trained monkey killer,*" Col's voice was getting quieter now drawing Tarnasay back to the urgency of the situation they faced but neither he nor Jimmy could stop their outburst of laughter at Col's special forces monkey killer scenario.

"Look it may be just weird enough for them to have second thoughts about boarding us."

"Trippy," said Tarnasay smiling but not in his usually broad, relaxed way. Jimmy tried to suppress nervous laughter at the whole idea of seeing Cruella with a shotgun again.

"Worth a try eh?" said Col. "Yep," agreed Tarnasay.

"But hold the coconut hey Col," said Jimmy who then began gurgling and popping in a determined effort to smother a full-throated laugh. Tarnasay shot a startled look to Jimmy as if hoping to see some kind of acknowledgement that yes, he had just been reading his mind.

"Very fucking funny," said Col before heading to the chest below holding the guns.

Fortunately, this proved to be their only encounter with pirates during the voyage. Their fears that the pirates may return for another look, purely from a curiosity point of view or for more sinister reasons did not happen. Mai Pen Rai surged ahead into the Gulf of Aden towards their next port of call at Aden, Yemen where they would stop to refuel and purchase supplies. Prior to leaving Col had consulted both with Franz back in Australia and his sailing friends in Thailand regarding the best possible itinerary for low-key refuelling. Ports that offered the least scrutiny for visiting foreign vessels. If entering a port was to be envisaged as risky Col would contact Franz in order for him to arrange 'at-sea' refuelling options in various countries as they made their way towards the United States of America. It'd already come at some expense for Franz to organise such matters and it would come at far more if they had to engage such services but as the alternative was getting caught, it was money well spent. Besides Col and Tarnasay weren't counting their pennies, that would've been absurd. It didn't need to be said that if they played it smart they'd probably never have to again. This was about extending their adventure, having fun and not getting caught for pulling off a heist that had the world spinning. And they were prepared to spend every last cent of their new found wealth to ensure that didn't happen. It was fortunate that the two men saw it the same way, that this whole thing was still about the experience and the daring of it more than anything else.

The days leading up to ports were always filled with endless banter about food. All three men loved to cook and eat and this made for quite an intense culinary battle.

An on-going one-up-manship involving pots and pans and tantalised taste buds. It was an easy contest to concede defeat too, because no one really lost, the contents of their plump bellies always won. Since their first port of call, where they'd gathered an amazing range of food supplies, their dishes became increasingly more elaborate and sophisticated. On occasions, other tasks and hobbies that would usually engage them for hours, distracting them from what was sometimes the conundrum of the sea, would be put aside to allow for a day long dinner preparation. Five course meals were not out of the ordinary at the height of their culinary contests. Nor was the photographic record of the more grand achievements. Col's cakes were coveted. The big man happier than a country lady winning a cake competition when Jimmy and Tarnasay went silent and rolled their eyes at the flavour filling their mouths. Tarnasay was considered a master of Italian and French dishes and his Indian cuisine (which had got off to a rough start due to the complications of a particularly feisty attempt at a Vindaloo compounded by heavy seas the following day) was also marked for commendation. But overall, it was accepted by both Col and Tarnasay that despite their efforts and the modest denials of Jimmy to the contrary, he was indeed the Master Chef. His Thai feasts were a sight to behold. Colourful, delectable, works of art. His balance of flavours, which teetered this way, and teetered that way, made their taste buds gasp before standing up to applaud vigorously. The pungent, mouth-watering scents that ensconced the yacht when he cooked distracted the other men to such a point that if they were doing something that required a degree of concentration they'd simply have to stop, put on some music, read a book or just stare out to sea until Jimmy presented them with his gastronomic magic.

Eventually Jimmy confessed he'd worked for a time in his grandmother's kitchen of some renown in the heart of Bangkok. It made perfect sense to them. There was something about his cooking, even when cooking traditional, popular western dishes that set them apart. Little twists of Asian flair to the meals that never overshadowed the original recipe and its flavours but embraced it, livened it up, just made it better they thought.

~

Working in his grandmother's kitchen was just one of the many interesting things that had taken place in Jimmy's life. Born in Mai Sai his family moved shortly afterwards to Chiang Mai. His early years were spent at the relaxed pace of the large northern city before he was sent to live with his grandmother in Bangkok in order to attend International School Bangkok (ISB). From an early age Jimmy's exceptional musical ability was apparent and he had proven a good student throughout his primary education. In Bangkok, it was felt Jimmy was better placed to thrive. He was fortunate enough that his parents were in a position to give him this opportunity and to this day he feels indebted to them. And for a time Jimmy did thrive. He excelled at language studies and his musical ability flourished. He became enchanted by the sound of the guitar where his early performances gained attention immediately. But he also excelled "At just fucking about" as he puts it. And rather than going on to study music further or going on to University after graduating High School, or continuing to maintain his reputation as a formidable Muay Thai fighter; or simply continuing to work at his grandmother's busy kitchen whose reputation and business appeared to be expanding with the placement of every meal, he simply drifted into the party scene. He found himself hanging out down south, playing a little guitar here and there and working in bars, but generally just getting endlessly high at 'Full Moon parties' on Koh Pha Ngan and Koh Samui. Apart from the little money he gained playing guitar and working in bars on the islands, he siphoned his father's commercial pilot salary to pay for his existence and his pleasure. Before long Jimmy's youthful opportunities had just passed him by. He was a borderline drug addict and alcoholic who had squandered his talent and potential for the simple pursuit of getting pissed and popping pills. For more than three years he barely plucked the strings of any one of his three guitars. He began to get tangled in the sticky tentacles of methamphetamine, lost good friends and punched girlfriends. His father, having realised that he was freeloading, cut him off completely, contact included. When he reappeared one day before his grandmother looking dishevelled and disorientated, she, who was secretly proud she could never admit to him that his 'Gaeng Keowan' was better than hers, would not reemploy him. She could scarcely bring herself to look him in the eye. She just said in a markedly measured tone "Tụ̈n k̄hụ̂n mā khn deīy" (wake up alone) and quietly shut the door of her kitchen. It was the quiet disappointment of his grandmother, more than anyone – even his mother or father that impacted most on Jimmy and sent him scampering back to Chiang Mai with a fledgling drug habit. There, avoiding contact with his parents, drugs and alcohol he set about reestablishing contact with the only friend that didn't possess the power to judge him, his guitar. For more than a year Jimmy reeled himself back from the temptations of substance abuse. Avoiding the lure of long nights, he played at bars and markets through the day and through word of mouth on the back of his talent, he was invited and paid handsomely to play at private weddings, corporate functions and occasionally tourists events throughout the city. Gig by gig he was slowly getting back to where he should always have been, when the girl he was seeing at the time and growing fond of very quickly was killed in an accident while riding her moped. A short time later all three of his guitars were stolen. For a time he lapsed again but somehow managed to reel himself back. Before spending all that he'd saved, he had the good sense to buy himself another guitar. To start again, to write aching love songs, to keep going. To play at day and sleep by night. Although he isn't sure, and it's the very thing that keeps him in check – Jimmy was lucky he pulled up just where he did. That he made it harder for himself to be exposed to what was drawing him in. All the temptations remained as obvious as the drugs that still surround him at the bars where he plays today. And maybe because he's still inclined to drink and party, sometimes too much, or because it's a way of keeping himself in check – he doesn't quite believe it when others say that it's as clear as the beautiful sounds his slender fingers draw from his guitar to their ear – that he caught himself just in time.

Meeting Tarnasay came at the right time for Jimmy. The loss of his girlfriend, the continuing estrangement from his family despite his year long effort to 'wake up' was weakening his ability to remain focussed. He allowed himself to work nights again. To hang around too long after gigs. Good-looking, open natured and talented he was constantly approached by Western travellers keen to talk and share a drink with him. It was how he'd met The Venkmann Equation and other high profile bands enjoying a break in Thailand before heading for the long summer tour of Australia and New Zealand. They immediately recognised he had something. He wasn't just a dude with a guitar and a couple of cover songs. He was fresh, experimental, captivating. He had flair. He rocked.

Jimmy warmed quickly to Tarnasay. He drank but not like it was a competition. He would enjoy his lagers and scotch over a long period of time but never got too loud or too drunk or became obnoxious in conversation. He was glad when he saw him rock up to one of his gigs at The Hug. It meant he could sit down after performing and have a drink with someone who was like a pacemaker. He used Tarnasay's pace of consumption as a measure. It slowed him down and he found it easier to resist the endless flow of shots that came his way and would usually see him staggering home feeling sorry for himself. Jimmy hated it when he felt sorry himself. He didn't believe it was justified.

~

It was inevitable on an adventure such as theirs, three men, two of them wanted by authorities, the third making up for lost time and a psychologically damaged chimpanzee, that piece by piece their personal history and most private thoughts on almost everything would float to the surface like emotional flotsam and jetsam. And for Tarnasay, although an open, engaging and animated personality for the most part, he did have a tendency to keep his personal background and motivations private. Col however, through force of his own personality and frankness had already extracted enough information from Tarnasay to form an idea of who exactly the man was. Partly before they embarked on the taking of Ubetcha but also on their maiden voyage to Thailand where any natural resistance to reveal personal information was eventually compromised by not only the continuous ingestion of MDMA capsules, but also the fact that there was only ever one other person with whom to babble to. Tarnasay and Col had grown close in a very short amount of time. It was of course, due in part to the very nature of what they had planned and then realised together. The honesty about the risk revealed when discussing the practicalities of carrying out such a plan. The naked trust that simply had to be there for both of them, to ensure they gave themselves the best possible chance of making their way briskly to the Southern port of Rangong in Thailand and succeeding. For Jimmy on the other hand, Tarnasay had remained largely a mystery. Unlike Col, who was forever forthcoming with information about himself, his family, his background and his thoughts, Tarnasay mostly only revealed who he was in the present. Jimmy noticed that he would only ever reveal as much as he thought necessary, he wasn't one to elaborate acutely on personal matters. This realisation, which Jimmy knew was highlighted by the fact that Col was almost the complete opposite, never concerned him. In fact, in many ways, he preferred it that way. For Jimmy it seemed to fit with who and what he saw as this man, Tarnasay. He was in many ways truly deserving and the essence of the 'Man of mystery' monicker. He also understood, more simply, that it was also the by-product of what he did. To borrow, to steal, meant to be hunted, which in turn meant secrecy. Jimmy had also made his own judgement about him and his actions too, and he never would've joined them if he saw Tarnasay as nothing more than a common thief.

~

It took the lead up to one of their final ports and an encounter with a disturbingly surreal spectacle, that being an ocean gyre of human rubbish the size of at least ten Olympic swimming pools floating before them, as the catalyst for Tarnasay to open in a truly uninhibited way. It stirred something within him, drew forth deep emotions related to his beloved Uncle Lou and the disappointment he would've felt at such a sight. He couldn't help but imagine that if the big man was with them he would've insisted on attempting to scoop up the waste with the biggest fishing net he could find. Puffing away on his foul pipe, dressed in unflattering beige pants and shirt, he would heave on board as much of the junk as his strength would allow. Then he would sit before it and patiently sift through the assortment of crap looking for items that could be salvaged and re-used. All the time shaking his head and muttering about the selfishness and shortsightedness of modern man. Staring at the bizarre smorgasbord of human discards – from chip packets to pegs, car tyres to plastic toilet seats made him wonder what other sea-goers thought when passing. Do they shake their head in disgust and ignore the fact that many of them may have contributed to it throughout their life. Perhaps they're the same people who admire the sunset from aboard their cruise ship whispering the words, "Absolutely beautiful" in a reverent manner while simultaneously flicking a cigarette butt into the ocean below. The thought of which reminded Tarnasay of a clever cartoon he once saw stuck to his Uncle's fridge by a cartoonist named Jim Baker. He'd always remember the cartoonists' name, in fact, he made a point of remembering by writing it down because he thought it was such an acute observation of modern man and his growing habits. The cartoon depicted a man with his young family abreast standing outside his car with caravan in-tow, "Gee that's slack!" says the man pointing towards some bushes a little way off, "The rubbish we left down there last year hasn't been cleared away yet!" With such strong thoughts of his Uncle Lou and how frustrated and saddened the sight of this waste made him feel, Tarnasay's mood had shifted drastically from the good spirits he'd been in before encountering it. He went quiet. They all did. Although Tarnasay was well aware of gyres and had read about them and how they effectively saw us increasingly at risk of eating our own refuse; because plastic never completely breaks down and the fish eat it thinking it's plankton and then we eat the fish - a neverending plastic cycle of life; he was incredulous at the sight before him. There's a difference between reading about a horror of sorts and experiencing it. Col too, was well aware of gyres having seen them growing before his eyes over the years as he sailed past, but even he was shocked at the size of this one having not sailed into the middle of the Indian Ocean for some time. Jimmy was completely dumbfounded. He had no idea such a thing existed, "Really?" he asked rhetorically, staring at it amazed. They were all quiet now, contemplating the mess we'd all made. For a while no one spoke. They just stared at it, their eyes flicking randomly from one piece of crap within the floating collage of refuse to another. The only sounds breaking the silence was the ocean lapping gently against the side of the boat and an argument of seagulls pecking away at something which they'd at least decided was of some value. Finally Jimmy broke the silence. "It's as though a giant representing all mankind has just vomited everything he's ever made into the ocean." That comment and its disturbing, poetic accuracy caused Tarnasay to shoot a look at Jimmy who he saw staring at it, transfixed. He then looked back into the giant's partially digested plastic vomit. He saw a handful of large green balls bobbing up and down amongst the floating mass of material mucus, 'Peas,' he thought, 'They're fucking giant plastic peas.'

~

Arriving at their second last port in Aden, Yemen meant much more to the three men than just stocking up on more food supplies, however passionately they had discussed the subject at sea. It meant everything to them, other people, other things, other objects, other routines for a few days. While being at sea undoubtedly gave one an exhilarating feeling of freedom emotionally, it was somewhat cruelly reversed physically. The are only so many places you can go and so many things you can look at on a boat no matter how big it is. And this would be the last time they set foot on solid ground for the next two weeks, so open spaces, crowds of people, strangers, potential friends, hopeful sexual encounters, none of this was being taken for granted. Faro, Spain would be their final port but only to refuel before heading straight into the North Atlantic towards the United States of America, so they were excited about visiting this ancient middle eastern city.

The beautiful ancient Arab port city of Aden represented life far removed from their own and the three men took to exploring the city not only as procurists for supplies but as tourists. They were to stay three days returning to the yacht each night moored in the safety of the broad bay. On the first day they found most of what they needed by way of food staples and were also delighted to find a broad selection of spices and fresh fish available. It was decided that they would wait until their final day before purchasing fish from the local market. Meanwhile, they decided to take a brief guided tour of Aden. It was the first time they had indulged such a thing at any of the ports they visited. Past moorings had been strictly for collecting supplies but this time rather than choosing to ignore the inviting beauty of a particular port, and nearly all of them had their charms, they allowed the uniqueness of this ancient port to draw them in. No one raised concerns or protested about the possible dangers of doing so. Tarnasay had suggested it and Col and Jimmy were excited by the idea. It was obvious everyone needed some firm footed relief and outside stimulation. What better way to do it, than at a stunning harbour city in a Middle Eastern country they knew very little about. At the same time, they weren't completely oblivious to the country's international political troubles either, nonetheless the attraction to set foot on dry land before another solid two weeks of sailing proved a strong enough incentive. The decision to stay on was also helped when they were approached by a very affable local tour operator whose English they informed him was better than their own. He was an engaging character who, although his charm and natural warmth went some way to hiding it, they couldn't help but detect a hint of desperation from his invitation. Jimmy stated he was going regardless of what Col and Tarnasay decided. This was his first time abroad, his first ever tour offer, his first proper time off the boat in three weeks, and lastly he felt – as they all did – that this was the first time in quite a while this friendly, slightly dishevelled man before them had met people who may be interested in a tour of his city. A city which he clearly loved.

Jimmy wasn't alone in his desire to take the tour and all three of them agreed to go. Murad, their guide turned out to be as much an historian regarding the city and his country as he was an accommodating tour guide. The ever so slight air of desperation he'd carried with him when they met had been let go. He probably put it down in one of the many streets he drove them through. Or he may have placed it at the Sira Fort where his voice had gone higher, more excited, more energetic as he discussed its history. Maybe that was when the weight of desperation lifted from his old frame and for the moment he felt lightened from its burden. Despite knowing only too well that he'll have to lift it again sometime in the future, go back and pick the heavy, dark, sodden thing up. He always did. Meanwhile, he was back doing what he loved and through the attentive, fascinated faces of the foreign seafarers he had as his audience - his valued   customers – he knew he did it well.

The three foreign seafarers enjoyed a two day tour of Aden and happily paid Murad for three. He took them through the ancient seaside city whose streets today, after its many incarnations and occupations, reflects a fascinating mix of Yemenite, Indian and Victorian architecture. They also ventured in the canals and lastly, they visited his home where they enjoyed a delicious meal made by his ageing, equally charming wife, Heba. They had all discussed it privately while on tour and had made a unanimous decision to leave behind a substantial amount of money for Murad. There was only one barrier to doing this and they knew it was a big one with the likes of Murad. Pride. So to his delight, it was Jimmy that was given the task of secretly stashing enough rial that Murad would never have to carry the weight of desperation they had all sensed ever again. And they were right. There was still enough rial for Murad and Heba to live comfortably after the hip operation when he tripped over the loose paver Jimmy had stashed it under.

At their last two ports, the management of Cruella had proved a challenge. Mostly for Col. Each time they arrived at their destination Tarnasay made a point of reminding him that he was the one responsible for her behaviour if she was to come on land. Although everyday she spent at sea saw an improvement with her behaviour and that she'd realised long ago that she was not going back to the horrible jail house in her memory, she still possessed an unpredictable streak. It was this unpredictable streak that still had them all a little on edge when it came to Cruella.

It was also the reason that, although they left it open more often than not, and made it comfortable with a pile of cushions and toys and gadgets she liked, they still made her sleep and reside in her cage when need be. It was on the final day while browsing throughout the markets where they finally learnt that it was best practice to leave Cruella safely caged back onboard Mai Pen Rai. It wasn't that she was constantly attempting to flee, but on this one occasion where her actions suddenly made their presence conspicuous they had to scurry back to the yacht and set sail immediately.

Col, Tarnasay and Jimmy had been enjoying a stroll through the lively fish markets as planned. However, Cruella who was leashed and happy to walk alongside Col suddenly got excited at the sound of a monkey shrieking loudly from a nearby stall. Before Col had a chance to tighten his grip she had sprung free and taken off at speed towards the monkey. All three men went in pursuit of her and soon encountered a bizarre scene which quickly brought home not only the reality but the gravity of the situation they'd embarked on. A screaming reminder with both Cruella and the monkey causing a horrible aural ruckus. Prior to this it was clear that they'd been ensconced in their own world, of feasting, drinking, making music and shooting coconuts from the yacht's deck. They'd been living large while at large on the high seas. Isolated from daily news or at least allowing themselves to increasingly ignore it, Tarnasay and Col had become somewhat complacent. For the past three weeks they'd almost forgotten they were wanted, hunted fugitives. That outside their water tight cocoon the rest of the world was still waiting and watching. Waiting to see when they'd reemerge, watching to see what would happen next.

They arrived at the stall puffing and found not two, but three impossibly excited primates shrieking crazily. Two of them, Cruella and the small caged monkey were present before them, but the third, to their disbelief and screeching away in footage broadcast from a TV positioned precariously on a stack of crates outside the makeshift stall was also Cruella. For a moment all three men stared at the TV dumbfounded. They watched Cruella screech and bare her teeth, rolling her lips back high in aggression. It was footage of Cruella they'd never seen before and it wasn't Col's. They knew immediately it hadn't been cut from his infamous 'Man slapping' series starring a terrified Jimmy. It had been shot by someone else. The footage was rough and jumpy having most likely been filmed on someone's phone. It was poor footage too by anyone's standards, in and out of focus as though the cameraman couldn't decide at which depth to film.

They continued to watch the scatty footage of people with large blankets attempting to shepherd an angry Cruella into a cage located on the back of a trailer, the camera spun around briefly and showed a battered Gavin Mills sitting on the ground nearby. It was then Col and Tarnasay came to the same realisation simultaneously. "It's fuckin footage of Cruella's rescue" said Col incredulous.

Then he spoke again but this time it came loudly from the screen, "Eh! Turn that fuckin' thing off you idiot!" said Col whose paw-like hand then smothered the camera ending the footage as a sheepish sounding Irish man was heard to apologise. "Fucking Andy," said Col shaking his head and looking away from the screen. He recognised the owner of the sheepish Irish voice to be Andy, one of the Irish boys who had helped with the rescue of Cruella. A reporter then appeared on screen standing next to a yacht and began to speak, Tarnasay casually reached out and turned the TV off. He then looked to Col who either hadn't noticed that a rather large group of local men now began to crowd around him or he felt more comfortable pretending they hadn't. "We'd better go," said Tarnasay underneath the protest and abuse now coming from the store owner whose TV he'd switched off. Cruella had stopped screeching as had the caged monkey and Col calmly picked up her leash trailing down from the shelf next to the TV where she sat. "Show's over boys!" said Col firmly as he turned and confirmed that he did indeed know there were about twenty or so men crowding around them. The men simply parted, chatting amongst themselves animatedly as he moved through them, Col appearing like a giant to most, and Cruella, Tarnasay and Jimmy fell in behind him like humble, silent deputies.

They reached the safety of Mai Pen Rai relieved that no-one had attempted to stop them and equally relieved that they'd done their shopping for supplies a couple of days earlier. There was nothing to stop them from pulling up anchor. A smaller crowd of sullen more threatening looking men had broken away from the larger crowd and continued to follow them down to the wharf where the port master of sorts minded the shuttle boats for yachts such as theirs. The men attempted to follow them onto the pier but the port master spoke quickly to a couple of hefty men standing by his side who set about herding them back. There was a brief yelling exchange between the man and the mob and he simply waved his hand dismissively at them as he took payment from Col who tipped him generously and thanked him. The man smiled, "Ubetcha," he said with a wink to Col's disbelief.

~

That night all three men studiously went about performing reconnaissance. They discussed the possibility that either Tarnasay or Col could've appeared earlier in the footage they'd watched at the market. Realising that they'd come in at what appeared to be halfway through the report they now speculated about what may have been shown before. As it stood, the only glimpse of either of them in that footage was Col's grizzly bear like paw and Tarnasay's thonged foot which briefly came into view when Col discovered the surreptitious recording of Cruella's rescue. Talk then turned to the need of finding out just how extensive the footage had been. Col remembered telling Andy to delete it at the time and he'd agreed but Col failed to follow up and now it was clear that the man hadn't.

"I thought you told him to delete it?" asked Taransay as the three men sat around a table on the lower deck. It was a calm night with a warm, westerly breeze blowing.

"I did," said Col.

"But did you check?"

"No,"

"Pretty big fuck up Col," said Tarnasay.

"Is this where you're going to lecture me like a child Tarnasay?"

"Fuck Col. That kinda oversight will get us caught. Sorry if you think I'm anal about details and the following through of really important fucking shit that will keep your arse out of jail - but, y'know, it just so happens that *attention to detail* is the reason I'm still fucking here."

"I'll grab us some drinks," said Jimmy whose eyes shot back and forth between Tarnasay and Col as he stood up from the table. It was the first time he'd seen the two men argue and the tension was as taught as an anchor line.

"Don't be an arse about it Tarnasay. I'm well aware I fucked up," said Col.

"You sure did."

"Oh fuck off Tarnasay! Seriously – don't be a cunt about this, let's just try and work out what the implication is now," said Col.

"So when did you realise you'd forgotten to check? Why didn't you say something earlier, I could've got Franz on to it," said Tarnasay.

Jimmy returned with three elaborately dressed cocktail drinks. Each featured a seagull's feather tucked artfully amongst green herbal foliage of some kind and in the centre a delicate curl of orange peel hung down the tall tumblers like a slightly over stretched spring. The two men looked at him simultaneously with blank expressions. Jimmy shrugged, took a sip of his expertly made drink and sat down.

"Alright then golden boy - why the fuck didn't you tell me that you knew Ubetcha had coke onboard from the beginning?"

"What?" said Tarnasay quietly. He wasn't expecting to hear that.

"Oh I see - so I'll admit to my mistakes but you won't yours. I thought you despised hypocrisy," said Col.

Now Tarnasay was quiet. On the morning of the heist Franz had discovered that Ubetcha was apparently harbouring cocaine and had immediately informed Tarnasay. "I couldn't find out the exact amount onboard but I thought you should know. Anyway, I doubt it's anything more than for personal use," said Franz. It was agreed that he would inform Col but he hadn't. Now it was clear that Franz had.

"You're lucky that I didn't care at that stage. Because I was stealing a fucking superyacht afterall, what's it matter if there's some cocaine thrown into the mix. Otherwise you would've needed to find another captain," said Col.

"Well my reasoning for *not* telling you is exactly the same reason you chose to ignore it. I assumed Franz was right, the amount would be insignificant. Anyway, if I had to get another Captain I'd have made sure it was someone who had actually sailed a superyacht."

Now it was Col's turn to fall quiet again. All that was heard for a moment was a soft burbling noise coming from Jimmy's straw as he drained the last of his cocktail. The two men looked at him again blankly. It now occurred to both of them that at least Franz had both their interests at heart. Although Col had convinced Tarnasay that he'd sailed superyachts, Franz' reconnaisance on behalf of Tarnasay had revealed otherwise.

"So you're both filthy liars then," said Jimmy, "Awesome."

Tarnasay and Col couldn't help but smile. Albeit, a tad sheepishly.

"Mai pen rai," said Jimmy, "Now drink up and I'll make some more while you two work out whether we're in more trouble than you think."

It didn't take Tarnasay long to decide the easiest way to find out was to contact Franz back in Australia.

'That footage!" laughed Franz, "No, nothing to worry about there. That was it. Mostly Cruella screeching horrendously for three minutes. I don't know why they even bothered fucking airing it. I think they're getting desperate because there's been no 'News' from you guys," laughed Franz. "Anyway I'm pretty sure it only appeared a few times on one network because people complained about Cruella's crazed screaming," hecontinued.

'So how'd they get it?" asked Tarnasay.

"Well that young Irish fella got bailed up in Thailand for trafficking. Nothing huge apparently but enough that he'll be in the Bangkok Hilton for a bit, or for a bit of mummy and daddy's money anyway," he laughed again. Tarnasay could tell Franz was a little pissed. "The Thai Authorities released it. And yes before you ask – I've already dug around a bit and there's been no computer composite of either of your twisted heads and flukey arses forthcoming from the AFP or otherwise. Apparently this chap explained that he was just passing by when he saw the commotion and decided to film it for a "bit of crack." He said he knew nothing about stealing a chimp or either of you two. They bought it. Besides, apparently his eyes are a bit shit - he has quite chronic myopia and can only see really close-up – hence the shitty footage. I assume you two weren't really that close to this fella, Mr Evermore?" said Franz in a way that hid nothing of his love for this kind of thing. The low level but no less risky espionage he often engaged in on behalf of Tarnasay. He didn't provide it for free but just as well could have, such was the thrill he drew from it. It was the only thing he found slowed his drinking. To speak to his many contacts, some of them well entrenched in the establishment but corrupt, dangerous and rotten to the core, required him to be sharp. For his mind to be clear and hands still. "They don't suffer fools," he once told Tarnasay, "They fuckin' suffocate them."

"No, Col knew him better. He did blink a lot though," said Tarnasay not intending to be funny but recalling his brief association with Andy and linking the information Franz had just given him.

'Well even if they have a comp of anyone from what his name – Andy! yes, eagle-eye-Andy, it wouldn't be much good and I doubt they'd have much faith in its accuracy."

It so happened that the AFP did have one. One for every person who Andy apparently saw, but Franz was right, they were completely useless and nondescript, whether Andy intended them to be or not.

"But I must say Tarnasay," said Franz finally at the end of their conversation, "Your foot does have a lovely tan."

Tarnasay knew how lucky he was to have someone like Franz on his side. If it was reversed, he'd have been caught by now.

Sam's Neverending Day Off (Part 3)

The day has been still and balmy. The only breath of air she's felt the whole time she's been reflecting on her career and nibbling at her antipasto is when Hasta has brushed past her at speed chasing terrified birds. Sam has been thinking about how five years of intense research and investigation, two years longer than any case she's ever worked on, has failed to deliver the result to which she and her superiors have come to expect. Sadly for Sam, the devastation hadn't ended there. Although it was never officially indicated or formalised, she found herself demoted. Some people, whether delusional or otherwise satisfied, call it "shifting sideways," but to her, when receiving her next case appointment it was clear, she'd been pulled down. By her own standards too, Sam was disappointed. Nonetheless, she still felt hard done by and she was furious. She'd worked over-time to the point of madness and lost good friends in the process. All her previous assignments had been successful and her one failure, her one "unresolved" brief saw her effectively demoted. And just when she knew she had the answer. 'That's loyalty for you,' she thought.

Sam looks over and sees Hasta battling to drag something from a bush a few metres away. He is pulling at it heavily, hurling his bulk backwards and shaking his large head vigorously. It looks like an old boat rope that in retirement may have become a kid's tree swing before it's fallen back down to earth. She listens to him growling as he yanks at it, as if warning it, but he isn't winning. He takes a rest every few minutes and then resumes his tug-of-war. But the old rope is defiant, it won't budge.

Sam thinks about her own recent tug-of-war. How she attempted to pull favour with her seniors within the AFP taskforce to gain an extension. But her pleas were denied. She stressed to them the strength of the lead she had, that she believed it was the breakthrough they'd been looking for but she didn't receive a response. Then somewhat desperately, she had championed her record; 'I'd like to refresh your memory of my record' stated the subject matter of her group email and she attached a file that was a comprehensive overview of all previous assignments within the Criminal Assets Confiscation Taskforce (CACT). It was impressive. Every brief had been met. Every case a success. She was clearly the best investigator they had. But again her request was met with silence. And the longer the silence went on, and the longer her email inbox remained empty, she knew, the longer the odds were that she'd be granted her request. Sam found herself becoming increasingly frustrated by the situation. It wasn't just the silence that she felt went beyond being condescending and was now in the realm of rudeness. It was the way her whole workplace now operated. People cooperated because they had to, not because they enjoyed working together to resolve something. Everyone was in competition, and everyone was conniving on some level, constantly attempting to position themselves for advancement. She knew this was not unique to her workplace and that no doubt this kind of behaviour played out in offices everywhere on a daily basis. But she liked to think, perhaps naively, that when it involved solving something significant like criminal activity which had the potential to affect and hurt many people, they may have put that issue first. That their own agenda would cease to be the priority in the interest of others. There may have been a time when this was the situation, thought Sam, but not so much anymore. These days she also had to fight the doubt that crept in regarding some of her colleagues. So fine tuned had her investigative instinct become, and when coupled with intuition, she often found herself honing in on something from an almost subconscious level. She was a woman afterall, and her mother had always stressed to her that "a woman's intuition should never be ignored when it comes because it's just uncanny how often it's right." Sam agreed it was indeed uncanny. She worked hard in investigation, harder than most, but she also felt the intuition her mother had spoken of. She'd heard her loud and clear on that matter unlike many others where she didn't. But throughout her career Sam followed her intuition like a mental sniffer dog and it had worked. Nonetheless, like many women she didn't see her intuition as some kind of psychic gift. But if it wasn't that, then what was it? Whatever it was, Sam figured that the chances are it was a woman who decided that it'd be best for all women folk of the world if they simply referred to the phenomenon as "women's intuition" lest they all be burned at the stake as heathen witches. Men of the world had enough trouble dealing with everything that a strong woman represented, if she was psychic as well that would just do their head in. And it was terrifying to think what such a revelation would mean for many women in certain places throughout the world. No, it was much more acceptable and gently, magically Nanna-ish if it was always simply referred to in a vague, unthreatening way as nothing more than "women's intuition," Sam figured.

But it was this intuition she felt the need to turn-off, or at least ignore when sharing a work space with some colleagues. It was as though some smelt of corruption like body odour. And as sad as the situation was, investigating an assigned case is one thing, investigating what one suspects is a corrupt colleague is something else altogether. So Sam would fight the urge to peruse the desks of those whose motives she doubted. And it wasn't as if the feeling was rife. Just as there were good cops, lazy cops, solely-career-advancement-in-mind cops, there were also corrupt cops. And they were the dangerous ones. The clumsy re-ordering of her own notes on her desk when sharing a double cubicle always concerned her. That someone was obviously rummaging through her work with no explanation. Not even her immediate boss Clayton would do that. But this very thing had happened to her recently during an office re-shuffle where she briefly shared a space with one of the AFP's leading investigators, Colvin Manning. The always smartly dressed, always aloof Colvin wasn't working on her case so it was unusual he'd require any information that Sam had. At the same time, she had no real proof that it was him. They worked in an open-plan office after all, it could be any number of people, any number of those whose bodies simply smelt of corruption when standing next to her desk. But she did have her intuition. And it was her intuition that drew her attention to the practically bare desk of Colvin Manning. She wasn't about to begin rummaging through his stuff even had it been overloaded with files and notes, but she couldn't help but take a cursory glance. Intuition told her to. But there was nothing. Nothing but the signs of someone a tad slovenly which did strike her as rather odd considering the meticulousness of his dress sense. Not that she expected there to be something ridiculously, obviously, condemningly corrupt but when intuition is aroused it's hard to ignore. So in a nonchalant, playful manner Sam pushed hard with her legs and rolled over at speed in her office chair to his side of the large space they shared. There were three half finished cups of coffee, one with mould, a half eaten muesli bar partially undressed from its wrapper and three very thin coffee stained manilla folders. Next to the folders was an A4 note pad with various scribblings including the name 'Franz' repeated a couple of times with dates and times. The desk was silent. Of course, she had no idea what it was supposed to tell her. Intuition may point you in a direction but she'd learnt long ago that it was rarely any more specific than an excited, barking dog trying to tell you something. And in this situation, even if intuition did bring forth something dubious about a colleague, where was she to begin? Yes, there were those who she could approach regarding such a matter, such as her boss Clayton, but such accusations required a strength of evidence on a whole nother level and that takes time and effort, not to mention risk. Those matters get messy. So for better or worse, and against a purity of conscience, Sam largely ignored her intuition unless it applied directly to the case at hand, such as the tricky one she was pursuing now. She justified it in her mind that it was simply her job to solve that conundrum and not those of the police force as a whole. So she told herself, but not very convincingly. Ultimately though, in this situation and working on the Tarnasay case where she had been struggling to gain anything solid, someone rummaging through her notes didn't really concern her. In fact, it kind of excited her, because if they're clumsy they might just reveal something they never intended too. Sam glanced at Colvin's pad again and looked at his various messy scribblings, the name Franz stood out clearly but for no other reason than it was legible. There was nothing of any relevance to her case there, well not that she could see anyway.

Eventually, Clayton visited Sam one day in her office and explained that the case had already been extended twice without her ever needing to request it. No, he said, they'd given her the benefit of their doubt on these occasions but now the case was officially closed. "Sorry Sam, but it's time to move on. Face up to a new challenge and crack that one," he said in a manner she couldn't deny seemed earnest. She'd always seen him as one of the good guys. He was approachable and encouraging and she knew that the only reason the previous extensions he'd spoken of were granted was because of him. He had always believed in her talent but now even he was saying that it was time to move on. 'Time to move on,' Sam had found herself honing in on those words as she began clearing away her desk. Cleansing it of her failed assignment. Filing away notes and documents and shredding others. Removing the evidence. Was she being too hard on herself? she wondered. Probably. But there was more to it than that. She found that she wasn't repeating those words as a private lament to her failure or as a way of encouraging herself to forget it and indeed move on to the next task; but as something more significant, more profound. She needed to move on from here. From work. From her work life. Her life work. Her life. 'Fuck,' thought Sam, 'I need to move on from my life! Because this is my life!' Sam felt a sudden sense of urgency, like she was running out of time, like the grim reaper just appeared next to her desk with a stop watch and a clipboard and whispered "Ready?" There was so much she'd been putting off that she'd been putting off time. Time with herself. Time with family and friends. Time at the beach. Time to go bush walking. Time to see bands. To go to festivals. To go sailing. Travelling. Sitting on a big rock in the middle of fucking nowhere. Or just go on a picnic with an unknown neighbour's quirky dog. "Time to move on," she said aloud, "It's definitely time to move on." The following day Sam put in for one 'Day off' only, but she knew she'd never go back. And when they emailed her, rang her phone and knocked on her door, she just met them with silence, silence to which she knew they understood.

Hasta forfeits his fight with the old rope. Instead, he busies himself around the picnic area fossicking for what seems a new challenge, completely unperturbed by his recent loss in a game of tug-of-war. Sam thinks that she would do well herself to follow his dogmatic example. To busy herself with something entirely new, reveal and revel in fresh opportunities. But not until she's soaked up some more sun, she thinks. Sam raises her face towards it and closes her eyes, feeling its warmth masking her, running from her face down through her body. She imagines the heat melting away all the stress she's recently endured and almost feels ashamed. That enjoying something as simple as the sensation of the sunshine on her skin again feels so new, that it's been so long since she's just sat still and enjoyed such a simple pleasure. Meanwhile, Hasta makes a discovery of discarded items and sets about collecting them with vigour.

Sam allows herself to remain in a meditative state until the sun grows too strong. Allows, because usually a part of her brain would be nagging at her to do other things. Pressing her to do more research on a case, to follow up potential leads, to simply get more done. Now she feels relieved of that anxiousness. There is nothing. There is just the moment. She is in the 'moment' and she feels more alive, and she could swear her senses seem heightened as a result; scents of the surrounding bushland stronger, sounds around her – distant and close, more acute. 'Everyone should sit still for at least five minutes a day,' she decides. Regardless of where they are, just stop, sit still and take in their surroundings for a moment. Do absolutely nothing for five minutes. Barely think. It suddenly occurs to her that this is probably what Buddhist monks are aiming for when they meditate. She knows little about meditation but if this was getting close to what it's about, then she understands the attraction. She remembers a year or so ago that her work had offered an introductory course in meditation but she'd decided not to participate because, well, it seemed a waste of time. To sit in a room, eyes closed with a bunch of colleagues who, for the most part, she already believed had their eyes closed.

'WRROOF!' Hasta suddenly barks right into Sam's face which until a second ago reflected momentary serenity. "FUCK!" Sam barks back startled. Her eyes now open wide and wild. That certainly isn't the way a Buddhist monk would exit a session of meditation, she thinks. Sam looks around to see if anyone heard her outburst. But only Hasta is there panting away happily. "You idiot," says Sam, "Couldn't you just gently lick my hand or something?" Hasta just groans a little.

Sam notices that while she's been in a meditative state or at least deep in thought, Hasta has piled an impressive collection of abandoned items on the picnic rug. A broad smile suddenly cuts across Sam's face for the first time in many weeks as she looks at Hasta's hoard. She shakes her head in amazement. "Why on earth did you gather all that stuff mate, hey? Aren't you a funny fella," she says to him as she ruffles his head and peruses his bounty. It's then that she notices, although it is an eclectic mix of items, there is nothing useless in there. A couple of tennis balls have seen better days on court but apart from that the items are good. There is a beach towel, a jumper, a bike pump, a kids sun hat, a large beach ball ('How on earth did he manage that?' Sam wonders) a frisbee and three plastic hiking drink bottles. Now it seems Hasta is keen to go for a walk, for further exploration into the surrounding bushland. Sam agrees encouraged by Hasta's playful nudges to move. He certainly wouldn't last long at a buddhist monastery or ashram, thought Sam. As she stands up and stretches, she feels refreshed, her mind clearer and uncluttered. She walks along slowly behind Hasta who has begun his looping antics again, running ahead, disappearing into the bush for a bit before suddenly reappearing and rejoining her. Sometimes it seems he performs a magic trick. Exiting the path into the dense bush on the right only to magically reappear a short while after from the left. Sam watches his looping activity again and again as she follows behind slowly, the sound of the sandstone gravel on the well-trodden track crunching pleasantly beneath each step.

The sound of loud, deep base beats a couple of houses away breaks the calm of the afternoon and Tarnasay could swear that his beer is now producing more bubbles as a result. They're good beats though, resonant, hypnotic, a solid groove. He listens for a moment to see if he recognises the artist. The base is clear enough but the music is slightly muffled overall and he is unable to identify it. He takes a sip of his beer, an ice cold Lowenbrau left behind by Col who'd been house-sitting for him and looking after Hasta while he'd gone away for a few days. A few days that had caused this day. This very long day. He allows the taste of the Lowenbrau and the music travelling down the laneway to bring back memories of hanging out in New York with an exciting, new electronic–rock–pop outfit from Germany. He allows it to distract him from worrying about his missing companion. His mate. It was in New York that Tarnasay became a rockstar for a night.

Port of New York

Our epic sailing adventure had come to an end. I eased us into Gravesend Bay finally seeking respite from the vast expanse of the North Atlantic Ocean before motoring gently into Upper Bay and the Port of New York. We all fell silent as we entered the bay to the famous city of cities. Franz' clandestine, underground networking skills had once again provided us with the means to move about without fear of detection; the visas for each of us sound and passing the scrutiny of the US Port Authority. Tarnsay and Jimmy leaned over the Mai Pen Rai's starboard side looking at the visual cacophony before them. I was feeling a little anxious and tingling from the energy the colossal city seemed to exude even from the tranquillity of the boat. No doubt natural excitement and anticipation played its part but also the combination of the city's reputation, not to mention all the American movies and TV shows I'd seen over the years where it all but starred. It was the first time any of us had visited New York, well, maybe not Tarnasay, who explained that apparently he'd been there before partying with Franz for a couple of days when they travelled to the states after Uni, but sadly, or more so embarrassingly, he had only a vague recollection. Such was the nature of time spent with the formidable party machine that was Franz back then. "Piss weak," I said unimpressed, "Even if I wake up naked next to a donkey I always know what fuckin' city I'm in." Jimmy seemed to be nodding too earnestly at my comment, and when he caught Tarnasay staring at him with a bemused smile he quickly looked back towards the shoreline and the parade of structures streaming before him. We had arrived in New York having sailed for more than two months from Thailand only to discover there was yet one more barrier for Jimmy to overcome before he could unleash his talent to the biggest audience he had ever known.

The Venkmann Equation had fallen ill. Too ill to perform and the upcoming gig was all but cancelled. But it hadn't been cancelled which was the crucial factor for Tarnasay and his ever-present optimism. Lana, the band's bass player and Si their percussionist and multi-instrumentalist were the only two who hadn't been struck down by a virus that had ravaged the band shortly after arriving in New York a month ago. Lana explained that Si, in an effort to isolate himself or at least use it as an excuse, had subsequently disappeared into the New York party scene and embarked on a classic rock'n'roll style marathon bender. The last time she saw him was a week ago when he looked wrecked, "He was totally drug fucked and giggling stupidly and pointing at things here on the wall." We all followed Lana's pointed finger to the broad, entirely bare, off-white wall before us. Listening to Lana, Jimmy maintained his smiling charm but Tarnasay and I knew he must have been hugely disappointed. After all the speculation and what seemed the impossibility of getting to New York, it had happened. He had sailed from Thailand and he was ready to do his thing but now, just as before, destiny appeared to be messing with his riff. And had it not been for his fear of flying, Jimmy probably would have jumped on the next plane back to Thailand, put his guitar away forever and become a Thai monk.

Luckily, Jimmy was with Tarnasay who had an uncanny knack for seeing opportunities where others see only missed ones. That night after rendezvousing with Lana, the three of us returned to the yacht moored at Shipyard Marina and Tarnasay revealed his idea to Jimmy. Although he didn't know it, I had instilled the confidence in Tarnasay (on the one occasion he may have needed it) to now put forward a radical idea that may still see Jimmy hit the stage. I had purchased a quality mixing deck for my new yacht having listened to Tarnasay mixing with his inferior portable one on our maiden journey together on Ubetcha. I was stunned at the time, that he had the gall to even think of bringing such a thing on a heist. It wasn't that it was cumbersome or awkward having been clearly designed to travel, but it became more apparent to me, as Tarnasay revealed book after book and game after game, that it was as though the man had packed for a fucking holiday not a heist. We'd agreed to carry on one bag each, a large waterproof hiking sack, but I had filled mine with items more likely to see me through a holocaust than a miserable day at sea. It had proven to be the optimist's miserable day at sea which saw Tarnasay's unusual survival kit coming to the rescue. Foremost among the items in his rescue kit for boat bound tedium were portable mixing decks. Both keen on music, the two of us spent many hours in heavy rolling seas mixing beats when horizontal rain on any of the decks risked spearing our eyeballs. Tarnasay was already quite familiar with the decks and I had noticed (more so than was obvious with his guitar playing), that he'd a natural feel for mixing. So later when it came to the enviable task of fitting out my very own superyacht in Thailand and customising it as much as time would allow, a top line mixing deck was something that came to mind quickly. Naturally, its inclusion proved a hit with the others. Jimmy's gift for rhythm became obvious almost the first time he began experimenting on the decks. Meanwhile, Tarnasay and I mixed up a range of material from new music we'd been listening to, but also heavily bolstering driving beats from old favourites, bringing the likes of Fleetwood Mac's hypnotic, embracing anthem 'Tusk' and Devo's classic 'Freedom of Choice' stomping like a doof loving giant onto the modern dance floor. And the new stuff for Tarnasay just happened to be The Venkmann Equation a band inspired in part by the likes of Devo, Talkingheads and more recently Daft Punk, Pnau, The Presets, Groove Armada and the many and varied offerings from Mike Patton. I had been listening to him mix their stuff from when we first headed to Thailand and since then, on the long haul to the States where he'd benefited greatly from the input and creativity of Jimmy who'd begun layering his impromptu, improvised riffs over the top. I knew they had something. "Pretty damn good. I'd paid for it," I told them.

Jimmy listened to Tarnasay explain his idea and his eyes widened. They would propose to The Venkmann Equation that alongside Lana and Si they would like to perform their first ever DJ set. Lana had explained that the band were disappointed about missing the opportunity to perform their first New York gig but there was a greater concern. They were concerned that failing to fulfil the gig, they jeopardised their growing popularity in the states. They were huge in Europe and despite a strong cult following in the US they were yet to secure a solid following to ensure and fund future tours.

"This is a real opportunity for you Jimmy," said Tarnasay, "For you to perform, to really be seen - more so than being a special guest – you get to star and for me...well for me, I finally get to be a rockstar too...for a day." Tarnasay struck a rockstar pose. I scoffed.

'If some people have a bucket list of things they wish to do before they die …', I thought as I listened to Tarnasay putting forward yet another of his fantastical ideas, 'then this guy has a shipping container.' I sat there wondering for a moment where he got the audacity, this unfettered, unyielding confidence from. A type of self-belief that would be nauseating if it didn't come wrapped in such beguiling charm. He seemed to possess a naivety of failure. Perhaps he has a new, undiagnosed psychiatric condition. 'Maybe he's an *Impossiopath* – one who fails to comprehend the meaning of impossible regardless of risk. Or a *Magiopath* - one deluded by, but at the same time unaccountably gifted by a sense of magic.' Whatever it was, looking at the smile now enveloping Jimmy's pleasant oval face, it was easy and infectious to be around. He had a way of making things seem far less dangerous, far less ridiculous and far more possible than commonsense would otherwise have you think they were.

There was little time to waste now that Tarnasay had Jimmy excited about his proposal. The next day, they headed to downtown Manhattan while I stayed aboard Mai Pen Rai and kept Cruella company. We had left her alone the day before having locked her in her cage and it was quickly acknowledged by the slap across my fleshy cheek on her release that it wasn't appreciated. Cruella was tame now by anyone's standards and as a result had spent the vast amount of time on Mai Pen Rai free to roam, returning to her large, comfortable cage when she pleased; but being in a new environment with new sounds, voices and more than the burbling utterances of the ocean which she had grown used to for the past six weeks, there was a concern she'd become agitated and frightened and unpredictable again. So I stayed behind to look after her. There was also another task for me too, and a surprisingly emotional one, because not too long ago I would've happily carried out the same task without a sniff of sadness – and that task was finding Cruella a new home. I couldn't continue on through life with a monkey literally on my back. I had already shifted the metaphorical one when I hooked up with Tarnasay, and as much as I'd grown to love the little beast that was Cruella, she needed to be found a proper home. The difficulty of the task had already been lessened with my contacting Franz back in Australia. I asked if he could find a contact with the aim of releasing Cruella to a suitable zoo. I'd engaged Franz because some way before reaching the states we realised that we'd need to find her a home quickly. Too much attention would be brought upon us if it became known we were harbouring a chimpanzee at the Shipyard Marina. I was also wary of remaining moored for too long in the one location seeing that our voyage had gained worldwide attention since releasing my sensational 'Cruella - Man slapping Series' on YouTube. However, while everyone knew we were out there; the infamous Tarnasay and Captain Swift with an apparently unidentified, tortured, malnourished Asian man as our captive, and a violent man-slapping chimp, no one knew where we were or where we were headed. And those who were attempting to track us via satellite would only enjoy a small window of time before we ceased transmitting and powered at speed towards a distant location. We had chosen the times to upload the videos carefully, usually whilst moored at a busy location using a free wifi signal and always just before briskly heading back out again to the oceanic wilderness.

It soon became apparent that most New Yorkers were way too self-focussed to pay much attention to anyone but themselves. Whether in truth they were or not, they certainly seemed to embody the idea of 'busy people.' Busy talking, busy eating, busy walking, busy yelling, busy doing stuff. So it'd proven relatively easy for us to wheel a cloaked cage containing an excited Cruella through the streets of New York. Some passersby would busy themselves with intrigue but never for too long. Their questions would be spat out at speed but always in a good-natured way and never too nosy. And for those younger, worldly, outward looking New Yorkers who may have finally clicked as to who we were after running a replay of our funny Australian accents through their mind; laughing about the fact that we were wheeling along a chimpanzee, their busy New Yorker legs would've already taken them too far, too far to make a commotion. Otherwise the situation could have been quite different.

"Hey! HEY-HEY! You're those crazy fuckin' Ossies who stole a superyacht! Yeah - I know you! You took a fuckin hostage and had him beaten by a fucking mad chimp and posted it on YouTube! Fuck yeah man - I loved that shit! That's was some seriously funny shit! Hey, so where the fuck is he? Is that you bro - BULLSHIT! IT'S THE FUCKING MALNOURISHED ASIAN MAN! Hey bro – reckon I can get a pic of me just pretendin' like to slap you or somethin' yo?" Fortunately, especially for Jimmy, we were spared any of that.

Tarnasay wasted little time introducing the idea for Jimmy and him to perform with the only two standing members of The Venkmann Equation. In their large penthouse suite the rest of the band were now lined up bizarrely before him on individual beds like overgrown orphans in the world's most privileged orphanage. There was no doubting their sickness with each of them sharing the common pallor of zombies. They took turns blowing stuffed noses and spitting into small buckets having hacked out mouthfuls of phlegm. Each had a heavy cough that resonated deep from within their chests. It wasn't pretty. Lana had issued everyone masks before entering the room and I isolated myself in the kitchen, and I was glad I'd done so. It genuinely look liked the flu to me and not a common cold which I believe people too often mistakenly refer to as the flu.

Tarnasay accompanied by Jimmy and Lana sat before the band and he began to put forward his proposal muffling it out loudly through his mask. He'd already asked Lana whether she'd considered the idea of still performing with Si and Jimmy, a kind of condensed version of The Venkmann Equation. He put it to her that because the band was so esoteric in many ways this afforded them such an option. They often had far more people on stage than the original band due to guest performers and additional musicians for certain tracks, so it would barely raise an eyebrow if the band suddenly appeared with less – provided it still sounded good. But Lana's face held an expression that wasn't so sure. She wasn't worried about Jimmy, she was one of the first to hear him and suggested the idea of bringing him over to perform on tour as their mystery guest. And no doubt she had reservations about Tarnasay, who although Jimmy had spoken of flatteringly, she'd never actually met or had the slightest inkling of his ability. But there was more to it than that. She'd been worried that with crucial members of the band missing there simply wasn't enough time to fill the gap with musicians familiar enough to play their music convincingly, or more importantly with the harmony which comes from playing together. She explained to them that it wasn't that the band was so precious that they'd never consider allowing a talented session guitarist or the like to don one of the signature masks for a gig and replace one or two of them if need be. Talents like Jimmy of course, and perhaps the likes of Tarnasay too, once she identified what he had to offer. No, for Lana, her greatest concern was about it sounding right and this was why she had reservations about Tarnasay's proposal when he first put it to her. But this was the very thing that put the idea in Tarnasay's head, the idea that he and Jimmy would join The Venkmann Equation for a night and play their first DJ set. It had been while listening to Lana explain earlier that she and the rest of the band felt that there simply wasn't enough time to find good enough replacements, musicians who could not only play their music but were fans of it as well. Musicians who felt certain chords almost to touch, and sung choruses with such passion it was as if they'd written the song themselves or at least wished they had.

I've observed that Tarnasay allows little time for self doubt. He is decisive. And I believe this is what has allowed him to do what he's done for so long and that is to bring his ideas and dreams to life. Perhaps it's the very nature of what he does that allows such self-confidence, the fleetingness of it, its ultimate triviality; it wasn't as though he was studying to be a surgeon or overseeing the launch of a space shuttle, he simply identifies something he likes and regardless of what it is, sets about borrowing it. In this instance he was borrowing the experience of being a 'Rockstar' for a night. To do what he's done isn't as some would have you believe, that it's based on something burgeoning on magic; it's about focus, paying real attention. In his own peculiar way Tarnasay is a master of discipline and a student of patience. Discipline sets like concrete in a man's mind when he sees the benefit of unrelenting practice and dedication. If it makes things easier. Patience on the other hand is something that can only be studied and never mastered because it is at the whim of too many changeable factors, one's mood, one's circumstance, one's environment. Patience is ruled by emotion and only emotion decides whether you've been patient enough. The two are often seen hand in hand, but patience for better or worse, will always release its grasp when emotion tells it so. And a man like Tarnasay, along with perhaps Buddhist Monks were probably closer than most to understanding this. It was this blend of discipline and patience that has allowed him to get away with his mischief for so long. He practised for what he wanted, he prepared, and he was very, very, patient – not only with everything around him but most importantly, himself. He told me that he attempts to measure his emotions - his fears, his eagerness. This is how he managed to commandeer one of the world's most famous superyachts, this is how he learnt to mix The Venkmann Equation, this is where his confidence comes from, this was the source of his so-called magic.

The Venkmann Equation went very quiet when Tarnasay finished putting forward his proposal with just intermittent sniffing and what sounded like forced farts breaking the theatre-like silence. I thought to myself as I remained isolated in the kitchen, that had I been Tarnasay and Jimmy's manager I would've suggested we leave. Politely remove our masks and just head out the door. I would've been wrong though. After staring at Tarnasay and Jimmy for what seemed like minutes, The Venkmann Equation began muttering amongst themselves in German. Lana then turned to Tarnasay and Jimmy looking at them almost scrutinisingly and said, "Play for us now," her accent and neutral expression made the request sound close to a command. Jimmy's blazing smile though, was almost enough to heal the room.

I had heard it all before but something about hearing it there in a large room and seeing the two guys perform; Jimmy in full flight, strutting around, flailing, being the rock god he perhaps thought he was meant to be, had me and Lana bustin' a move on the floor. Pingers taught me to dance, I've often explained to people. I've always loved music and thought I was content just to listen to it until the first time I took ecstasy, then I really wanted to dance. It was like an awakening or really a re-awakening. As a kid I was into it. But as an adult I thought big chunky blokes like me weren't meant to dance. Then I took that thing and went, "Fuck it! – Watch this mother fuckers!" Then it all came back to me I explain to them. The moves. How my days in high school, when even then I was big and heavy, I'd become a body-popper of some renown. Younger 'Year seven' students would approach me, asking how they too might learn the subtle art of making your body look as though it was electrified. I could also moonwalk in a way that didn't look like you were simply walking backwards, achieving the same floating effect as Prince or 'Turbo' from Breakdance, a hit movie at the time. But my biggest coup et tat, my biggest move with my big body in my hip-hop, break dancing repertoire involved somehow getting my body elevated enough to perform the 'Helicopter' perfectly. I can swing my chunky legs and trunk-like torso as though I'm a human propellor and have them remain elevated, pushing up on my arms enough to twist and then drop my shoulders to the floor with each spinning rotation of my body. Initially, the two young African American exchange students who taught me how to do it had stirred me, "Man if we get you in motion yo'll tilt the fuckin' planet!" "Yeah brother yo'll never stop – yo'll spin *FO-EVER!*" they said laughing and high fiving each other. But amongst the chuckles and the disbelieving shakes of the head they agreed to teach or at least show me how it was done. And they shook their heads again when less than a week later I demonstrated I could do it. But they were right about me getting in motion and causing havoc, and I soon realised that if I was ever to do it I needed a lot of room.

It must have been the excitement of hearing The Venkmann Equation DJ set rehearsal that had turned into a performance of a sort, with Jimmy and Tarnasay not holding back, and perhaps a couple of lines of coke I'd discovered behind a box of opened Cornflakes that put me 'in the zone' as they say. The music was intoxicating. Intoxicating enough for me to dip to the floor onto my arms drop my shoulder and swing my heavy legs into a spin for the helicopter. It had been sometime since I'd last performed it but I managed to get the speed of rotation fast enough to complete full rotations with my lethal, heavy legs continuously suspended in mid-air. Lana clearly had no idea this was my intention and had remained dancing close to me, grooving down, getting low down to the deep, thumping beats Tarnasay was now producing. Cruella screamed with excitement, Jimmy's guitar wailed relentlessly, perfectly between and over the top of the intense beats, and Lana suddenly found herself amidst a human tornado. A ball of me, "An Uncle shaped comet" as Tarnssay was to later refer to it, that was hurtling around at speed upon the polished parquetry floor of the penthouse. She attempted to dance and duck her way out of danger but upon my fifth or sixth rotation where I had really gathered speed, the petite Lana was caught by my legs which swung around like out of control boom gates. I sent her flying with just enough height to clear the island bench in the kitchen and crash heavily into the cupboards. This brought an abrupt finish to the audition and the room went dead silent as everyone looked to the kitchen where Lana was last seen plummeting. The only sound for a couple of moments was the swooshing sounds of my body which was still in high rotation. Apparently I could be heard saying "Yep" upon the completion of every loop of my legs. I must have been in the zone too because I was completely oblivious to cleaning up Lana during my break dance performance. I knew I'd hit something but because it didn't feel human-like I kept going. They all stared at the kitchen and watched as they heard a delicate cough and Lana slowly rise from behind the marble bench. *"Fuck yeah!"* she yelled excitedly.

Jimi Hendrix's 1968 Stratocaster

Si had been tracked down. He was the only member of the band who hadn't been present for Jimmy and Tarnasay's audition. He returned with rock'n'roll style tales of debauchery that failed to impress or excite the other band members. Whether such tales always failed to impress them or it was due to their illness wasn't clear. Apart from his bounding, hyper-energy, Si appeared in no better shape than the rest of them. He hadn't been outside for weeks. His skin wore a sickly, translucent nightclub tan. He was excited about Jimmy's arrival which had been a long time coming. He was also excited by the news of Jimmy and Tarnasay joining him and Lana for The Venkmann Equations first ever DJ set. It was this apparent lack of ego that transcended the path many of their peers take, a willingness to experiment, to be creative, and not possessive of their band. Si's excited reaction to the news was testament to this. It was also most likely why their music always sounded fresh and dynamic. Maybe that's what their namesake alluded to (notwithstanding also, a possible reference to Dr Venkman a character from the hit 1980's movie *Ghostbusters*) – that it was an equation of creativity, the sum parts of the musical whole. Si explained with rolling thumbs and darting eyes that he'd been clubbing like a maniac recently and was pumped for it. Everyone nodded knowingly. He also said he had a rush of ideas and was keen to begin rehearsing, "To see where you fuckers are at," he said with his strong German accent.

Si was right about his recent inspiration having been exposed to some of New York's hottest DJs and fusion acts. Along with his infectious energy, his openness, he brought fresh ideas to what was an already tight set which Lana, Jimmy and Tarnasay had already been refining in his absence. They rest of the band called him 'The Sponge.' Not only for his capacity to soak up illicit substances but also ideas and sounds. And when he arrived and heard the deep, bowels of the earth beats from Tarnasay and the clever riffs that Jimmy artfully worked in and around them and what was his obvious, spontaneous improvisation, Si's mind was set alight. He then added his own formidable talent and the set was again taken to another level. At the rehearsal Tarnasay found himself thinking about why he loved this band; he had an inkling this was it. This very thing he was now privileged to experience - pure creativity, a willingness to experiment, to add and subtract, to not be so formulaic and predictable. Of course, the band had their signature tracks but they'd be weaved within a broader musical tapestry. Particularly when playing live, they wrote a new musical story every single time. In a rare moment of self-consciousness, Tarnasay suddenly felt a tad dizzy. He felt dizzy because, incredibly, he was now playing in the band of which he was sure he was one of their greatest fans. "Tarnasay," said Si quietly, "Are you with us man?" Jimmy was looking at him too, and Lana. He'd been taken away by his thoughts, he'd lost it, lost the chugging rhythm they'd just had. Lost concentration. Left the zone. He had to stop thinking about it. Yes, it was incredible, incredibly unlikely to be in such a situation but then, so was much of what he'd done. This was just another one of those things. 'You wanted it and you made it happen,' he told himself, Then it occurred to him that he now knew their secret. One that was likely the secret of any successful artist he figured, provided they maintain it. And that was to always be a fan. Don't leave it. Don't attempt to rise above it, always remain a fan. 'Tomorrow night, I'll be like the other members of this band - both a fan of The Venkmann Equation and The Venkmann Equation - one and the same,' he told himself.

Everyone was excited. They'd even managed to drag a couple of the other bedridden band members from their sweaty sheets down to the hotel's auditorium where beats from the rehearsal all but shook the building to its foundations. "That is shit hot," muttered Ralph to the others before he and Torstan made the effort to drag themselves from bed and gingerly towards the auditorium.

Later that night, following the excitement of the rehearsal, they sat down for drinks.

Si continued to recount some of his recent nightclubbing adventures and gigs of other high profile bands he'd seen. It was while visiting the green room for Groove Armada, one of The Venkmann Equations earliest inspirations where he met a young fan of theirs named Will. He was a musician himself and equally inclined to party, so the two of them had teamed up and gone on a marathon bender together, which he explained, had only ended when Lana finally tracked him down. His still translucent skin and bloodshot eyes confirmed it. Si went on to explain how he and Will, who was a very talented guitarist it turns out, had gone to his father's property in Upstate New York where locked away in a cabinet in a hidden room, it was revealed to him, was Jimi Hendrix's 1968 Stratocaster. After much discussion and too many lines of cocaine he managed to convince Will to let him see it, "But man no matter how much I begged him he wouldn't let me plug that baby in and play it. I could only look at it." He went on to explain that as far as Will knew no-one had played it since his father had bought it. Not him and certainly not his father who couldn't play. "I mean really man," said Si shaking his head, "Yes-yes, so it's Jimi Hendrix's guitar and must be worth well over a million dollars by now, but still. It's an instrument y'know, it's meant to be played, not sitting in some fucking untalented rich bastard's cabinet like a stupid trophy. And the worst part is - if you're going to have it as a trophy and not an instrument - then at least display it like one! It's just lying down in this cabinet in its case."

At this point Col shut his eyes. He could almost hear Tarnasay's mind outlining what was surely to come next. "Is that right?" he heard Tarnasay say. 'Here we go', thought Col. By now he knew Tarnasay well enough to understand that "Is that right?" was probably personal code for 'We'll see about that.' Even Jimmy found himself staring at Tarnasay with a bemused smile. He too knew the man well enough by now to surmise what he was most likely thinking. 'Sitting in some fucking untalented rich bastard's cabinet like a stupid trophy,' Si's words rang through Tarnasay's mind again as he snorted a fat line of coke and then announced, smiling his broad smile, "Let's... borrow it." Col grinned and shook his head, there was nothing to say. While he was content to have left their adventures where they were now, safe, completed, and no longer so keen to push their luck around watching it tetter on the edge like an overloaded wheel barrow, Tarnasay wasn't. Col looked at him disbelievingly and saw his eyes, he could've sworn they were twinkling, twinkling like the brightest stars on the darkest night. Twinkling more than anyone's eyes had the right to. He looked away, 'The guy's a freak,' he thought. Jimmy saw them too, and Col wasn't seeing things, Tarnasay's eyes were definitely twinkling like the brightest stars. He'd seen it before.

Si, once convinced that they were indeed only intending to "borrow it," agreed to introduce them to Will. He was well aware of Tarnasay's history, he knew he didn't need the money, he knew he wasn't the criminal as he was most commonly portrayed. Tarnasay was emphatic. They were only borrowing it for their upcoming gig and it was to be played by none other than their very own Thai reincarnation of Jimi Hendrix – Jimmy Tatthiyacorn. Jimmy couldn't believe his luck. His first musical idol, the man who inspired him as a kid to take up the guitar and now he was going to play his guitar. All the 'Man slappings' from Cruella to get here were now distant bruises. Will was reluctant at first to show Tarnasay and the others the famed Stratocaster but on the strength of Si's word, his assurance and friendship, he agreed. It was decided that part of the trip to his father's place was to also jam together, however, this was by design. The idea was to simply perform a switch and in order to do that, they needed to have a guitar case and a similar colour and shaped Stratocaster.

Will obviously trusted Si enough to allow the viewing of Jimi Hendrix's famed guitar to his friends but he wasn't about to leave the room. They asked to see the guitar when they'd arrived and Will had escorted them all to the hidden room. The cabinet was rectangular and not unlike a long buffet with a glass top, and inside just as Si had said, rested the hallowed guitar hidden in its case. Will opened it and they all marvelled at it.

They discussed it for a while. It was then as Col, Tarnasay and Si continued the discussion that Jimmy was to back away to the end of the room and surreptitiously plug in his portable amp. Then they were to wait until Tarnasay suggested they start their jam, at this point Jimmy was to move quickly back to his guitar. Then as he and Col watched Will begin to shut the case, Jimmy was given a signal to blast his guitar, almost at full and let loose with one of his insane riffs startling everyone, especially young Will. At this point it was hoped that a startled Will would be distracted long enough that Tarnasay could make the switch with the cases.

Everything went to plan. Will was fully startled, distracted and then found the whole thing hilarious. Tarnasay deftly made the switch as Col's bulk partially obscured Will should he suddenly turn back. Eventually he did.

"Fuck me! That scared the shit out of me! The crazy fucker!" he said to

Col and Tarnasay laughing.

They were leaning against the cabinet and laughed along with him. Col didn't know about Tarnasay but he suddenly felt bad for tricking this young, good natured kid. They weren't stealing it of course, but the whole process of duping him like this made him feel uncomfortable. Col decided this was the last time he'd take part in one of Tarnasay's borrowings. Everything else had been fun and he'd happily taken part, but for some reason this made him feel uneasy. It just felt shitty to him. Too sleazy, too sly, too criminal. Which seemed weird, considering not long ago he'd stolen and then sold for a ridiculous sum, another man's yacht. But then again, he thought clearing his conscience right out, 'that guy was a prick.' Little did he know, Tarnasay felt the same. Fooling this generous, easy-going kid didn't feel like fun at all. Tarnasay thwarted his plan. Jimmy stopped wailing.

"Fuck man. I have to confess," said Tarnasay, "I was gunna borrow your old man's guitar for tomorrow night's gig. Borrow being the operative word. Serious. Borrow not steal. Big difference. The idea was for this Jimmy there, that extremely talented man you just heard put this instrument back to its use, its purpose, just as the original extremely gifted owner had done."

Tarnasay knew the young guy didn't know who he was. His history of borrowing. He was just a friend of a new friend. Si and the rest of the band knew they had to keep everything tight regarding them – the famous trio, Tarnasay, Captain Swift and Jimmy, particularly if they one day wanted to play with the now famous 'Malnourished Asian Man'.

"Here Will," Tarnasay offered him the case. "I just switched it with another when Jimmy blasted his amp. That was to distract you while I swapped my case with this one - your dad's."

"Ha ha. Very funny," said Will, "What are you guys the practical joke party? What the fuck's with that? How about we just go play some tunes now," said Will not buying a word of it as he flip-locked the case containing the fake stratocaster and closed the cabinet.

"Before you lock it mate..." said Tarnasay. He placed the case containing one of the world's most valuable guitars on the cabinet and opened it.

"Holy fuckin' shit!" said Will incredulous.

The Venkmann Equation [DJ Set] 11.45pm Live, Barclays Center, 620 Atlantic Ave, Brooklyn, NY

Will watched from deep within the throbbing crowd at The Venkmann Equation and didn't care. At that moment, he didn't care what happened later. At that moment, in the buzzing, hyped crowd, when Jimmy appeared on stage with his father's Jimi Hendrix two million dollar stratocaster hanging from his body as though it was part of him, he didn't care. And when Jimmy set it alight – metaphorically of course – and truly put it to purpose, he totally didn't care. He listened in awe as Jimmy brought it back to life playing the classic signature riffs of Jimi Hendrix with such precision that the guitar must of felt that it was back in the hands of its true owner. Will felt higher than at any stage in the past two weeks of drug abuse.

The Venkmann Equation were now ready for their first ever DJ set. Si had designed their stage set which was inspired by the likes of Talkinghead's 'Stop Making Sense' tour back in the mid 1980's. He'd watched it recently when coming down from his marathon bender and had fallen in love again with the stage show masterminded by David Byrne. He loved the big shadows, giant silhouettes created by clever lighting and the elevated stage tiers at different heights which each performer stood upon. He wanted it more stripped back and bare than their usual gigs with artfully managed white light emphasising shadows and creating a powerful black and white contrast. He also had striking new black & white helmets made that were quite ominous looking and even more futuristic than the slick polished steel ones the band usually wore as their trademark. The Venkmann Equation made no secret of their fondness for the dark motorcycle-like helmets Daft

Punk wore in the video clip for their hit song 'Around the world.' And where Daft Punk had left that image behind, the Venkmann Equation went on to embrace it as theirs. They not only enjoyed the 'look' it gave the band, but also the anonymity that came with it. It was particularly convenient for Ralph, who in any other circumstance – in any other 'look' – probably wouldn't have been in the band. His father simply wouldn't have allowed it. But Ralph's predicament was never the reason for them donning the signature futuristic helmets. It was simply a tip-of-the-helmet to Daft Punk, one of the bands they'd admired from the beginning, and the fact they thought it suited their futuristic fusion of music. They rarely did live interviews which rather than diminish their profile, simply added to their enigma. And if someone ever asked them, what their style of music was, what category it fitted into, their answer came in the form of an unnerving type of silence. The type of silence that can only be created by five people staring at you in jet black helmets.

Shortly before taking position on his own elevated private tier upon the broad stage, Tarnasay had felt like he was almost taking part in a spiritual ritual. He'd looked at Si and Lana and they smiled at him and Jimmy excitedly before, practically in unison, they raised their helmets like crowns and slowly lowered them over their heads. He'd been nervous until that moment and he could see Jimmy was too. Jimmy was a seasoned performer on a stage in Chiang Mai but he'd never seen or felt the buzz generated from a crowd the size of the one he was about to face. But watching their crazy, beaming smiles which disappeared a second later within the expressionless black and white helmets made the two new Venkmann members laugh and relax. They didn't need to say anything, their smiling faces said it all – "Don't think too hard - this is going to be fun." Jimmy copied them. He slowly turned to face Tarnasay beaming his broad, beautiful smile and raised his helmet ceremoniously before he too disappeared into his helmet. Now it was Tarnasay's turn. He was already smiling effortlessly when the other three band members' took what seemed like small robotic steps towards him. Helmeted, expressionless, they now waited for him to don his Venkmann veil. Tarnasay was close to laughing again. But he didn't. He honoured the impromptu ritual. He simply smiled back at them gleefully, and wondered whether The Venkmann Equation actually did this before each performance. He too donned his helmet. He disappeared smiling, now content with whatever The Venkmann Equation that night was to become.

That quirky ritual helped calm Tarnasay's nerves, but so too had the sight of Col in the stage wings rocking out to the pre-gig music, already high on something other than adrenalin. They were all on stage now, in position and hidden in the shadows, but he could make out Col's shape dancing like a maniac to a cracking 'Presets' track. They hadn't even begun to play and it seemed Col was already standing in a pool of his own sweat. Tarnasay laughed almost like a sneeze and quickly learnt that this isn't the most comfortable thing to do inside a helmet. The helmet was comfortable overall though, and they'd already worn them a couple of times in rehearsal. They looked heavy and foreboding but the Venkmann Equation had gone to great lengths to have them manufactured extremely light and the breathing was easy. The band had been refining their helmets for some time now and had practically removed any sense of a confined awkwardness – real or perceived. And although they were invisible from the outside looking in, faces hidden, it was the reverse from within the Venkmann cocoon, they could see everything.

A light at the back of the auditorium began to swirl around and shot across the sell-out crowd. The sea of bodies let out a thundering roar over the music that was now fading. Then there was silence. And anticipation. And Tarnasay wondered if it's possible to squirt adrenalin from your eyes. This was it. If he was looking for a bigger thrill than stealing Ubetcha he'd found it. Any moment now Si would hit the beginning notes from his synthesiser heralding the opening track and within a moment, Tarnasay would be part of the sum of the Venkmann Equation.

The music exploded. It exploded into the crowd and sent bodies heaving in every direction. It was as though, despite being fans and having heard this famous track a thousand times over, they'd all suddenly forgotten how to dance to it. As if it was simply too much. Too overwhelming. Too exciting. Their bodies swilled, clashing in directions like they were caught in wild surf, like they were human soup in a pot stirred by a crazed giant. If such energy can be entrancing as a fan, it can be mind-numbingly so for a musician, as Tarnasay was soon to learn. He'd been in the 'zone' making music before, but this was on another level. He was well and truly there, with every beat and every loop and every single person in the audience, but he was somewhere else too. When he looked at Si, Lana and Jimmy they appeared in slow motion, when they danced and jumped around it seemed as though time had slowed – but yet somehow they moved ahead of the music they were making. They were the music before the music had happened. It was mind blowing for Tarnasay, the four of them were in a bubble made entirely of their own magic.

Si and Lana had told Tarnasay earlier in the day that if things feel "Tight and right midway through, don't be afraid to improvise with your mixes, just go with it – with what you feel, ride it. Take us off track from what we've rehearsed and we'll work off it," Si said. "That's where the real magic happens," added Lana, "And we love it." As confident as he was to perform, that he could mix their music extremely well, well enough that The Venkmann fell in love with the idea of Jimmy and himself helping to create their first ever DJ set, this suggestion seemed too much for Tarnasay. He wasn't Jimmy. But it proved to be true. That "Tight and right" sets the agenda more than you. The collective sound and energy of a group of musicians clicking together sets you free.

Tarnasay remembered how when he first rehearsed for The Venkmann Equation he found a deep harder beat and rhythm to what he played before when remixing their hit track, 'Smithtown Nebula.' He remembers Jimmy's rocking nods of approval at the base and beat to which he could wield his guitar magic upon. He remembered that this is what caused Col in excitement to drop onto his broad shoulders and go into a spin that had cleaned up a stomping, grooving Lana.

This time he was to do it again. But go even further. To take the beats somehow even deeper. He'd recorded Si's thumping drums and percussion earlier in the gig. Now he brought them back, layering Si's hammering beat and drum rhythms over each other and then boosted them over the already pounding, chugging rhythm he'd created. It was so deep and pulsating some people seemed to go into a trance. They stopped moving and were simply nodding their heads and smiling ecstatically and wide eyed as he built the colossal beast of a beat before them. Jimmy looked over at Tarnasay and shook his head. He knew though, that it wasn't a shake of disapproval. He knew he was smiling his arse off under that helmet. And when Lana shot a look at him and Si pointed at him almost ferociously, and the white light hit him and cast his shadow on the wall behind him like a monster, he felt as though he was shifting Earth's tectonic plates.

At this moment everything seemed hyper-real as he looked at faces in the crowd. Everything felt more acute, each face he looked at became magnified. The beads of sweat on the tips of their noses looked like bubbles. The audience was euphoric. The Venkmann were creating the spontaneous magic that Si and Lana longed for as musicians not prepared to simply go through the motions. There was no doubting they'd found "Tight and right" and now they were in a musical fantasy land.

Tarnasay continued to enjoy his heightened senses while in the zone. The wall of sound they'd created now chugged along like something otherworldly, and just as Si had said, it was taking him with it. He looked again at the gleaming faces at the front of the heaving mosh pit as he rocked with them in perfect synchronicity. At that moment he caught the ecstatic face of Will, whose father's Jimi Hendrix Stratocaster guitar was now on stage in their own Jimmy's amazing hands. His face was electrified, it was wild, and singing its own tune of youth and freedom and vitality. Tarnasay had seen that expression before, he'd seen it throughout his life in the aurally intoxicated faces of those beside him at unforgettable gigs. Gigs and concerts that bookmark a period of life, that provide a backstage pass to memories never forgotten. He knows because, he's held that expression too, so many times. That of the fan. The face of someone completely lost in the moment that music makes. Apart from right now, it's about as Zen as he's ever felt. Even when he could taste the sweat of strangers on his lips, and felt kicks to the head from dumb-arse drunken, drug-fucked crowd surfers. It's real, it's raw, it's the primeval tribal drum reincarnated again and again for the craziness of the time it represents. It's the soundtrack to lives unseen. To the battles they may face, and to those they win. It conjures the good, the bad, the past, the present, the future hope. At that moment it's everything and everything else is nothing. It's magic, it's music, it's life. It's you.

~

The following day featured on the front page of the New York Times website was a close-up photo of a masked Jimmy flaring the stratocaster. Even from the depth of a mosh pit it hadn't taken long for those in the know to recognise the guitar. And at the same time as The Venkmann Equation gathered together as a messy rabble in the kitchen of the penthouse suite, still partying, still buzzing from the success of the band's first ever DJ set and attempted to read the front page article, Will's father almost choked on his morning bagel at a cafe. It wasn't top billing on the front page of the site but the headline still shouted, *'Back from the Dead: Jimi Hendrix 1968 Stratocaster in Action for The*

Venkmann Equation.' It was a short article which to the delight of The Venkmann Equation was as much about their "Incredible, thumping, intoxicating musical journey," as it was about the mysterious appearance of the two million dollar stratocaster. While Will kipped peacefully on the penthouse lounge, his father raced home in his Bentley, scrambled up the stairs, entered his hidden room and unlocked the cabinet. Expelling air heavily, he took a fresh breath and opened the guitar case. But there she was, the Jimi Hendrix 1968 stratocaster. As usual. Just as she always was, just as she had been for the past ten years. Lying there. Dormant.

Captain Swift drops anchor

The post-Venkmann Equation gig party seemed never ending. I hadn't indulged like that since Koh Pha Ngan. It was wild fun but now it hurt. I had disappeared back to the tranquility of Mai Pen Rai and discovered Jimmy had done the same. He was lounging on a pile of cushions on the lower deck sharing a bananna with Cruella. It was sad to think that just when Cruella had become relaxed enough to just hang out with us on deck, we were in the process of finding her a new home.

"Hey Jimmy. You had enough too eh?" I said.

"Gotta keep it cool Col," said Jimmy who appeared to look quite fresh.

"Me too mate. In fact, I may as well tell you now, but look I'm gunna bail home to Australia very shortly."

"Oh," said Jimmy. He wasn't expecting me to say that.

"I haven't told Tarnasay yet so if you see him before I do, I'd rather you don't say anything until I've spoken to him."

"Yeah, yeah sure," said Jimmy.

"I've been speaking to Franz. He's been to visit my mother recently and she's not really not well. She's had a major stroke."

"Shit. Sorry to hear that Col," said Jimmy.

"Yep. Anyway listen mate, seeing that I've have to nick off pretty quick and fly home, I was wondering if you could do me a favour and look after Mai Pen Rai while I'm gone. She can be your home here for as long as you like. And Tarnasay's if he's sticking around," I said.

"Wow. Who's doing who a favour here Col? Thanks man."

"No worries. We'll discuss rent later," I said as I turned to head up to the upper deck. I then stopped on the stairs and poked my head back out to look at Jimmy. He had a rather blank expression, or maybe it was a "Whoa. Suddenly I'm in a serious fucking rent situation" face. I smiled and winked at him. I'll miss fucking with Jimmy.

It had come time for me to return home. To part ways with Tarnasay, to leave him to fulfill his next twisted adventure. And to farewell my new found rockstar friend Jimmy Thatthiyacorn. It had been an incredible experience but there were now other factors that had drawn me to this decision. Before we'd embarked on our voyage to the US, I'd asked Franz if he could visit my mother periodically while we sailed across the Atlantic. I had grown homesick for her. And although she was barely aware of my presence these days, I still felt the need to be with my mum as she nears her final days. And sadly that day may now be approaching fast Franz has informed me. She was not recovering well from the stroke. It's hard to be a self-serving anarchist of sorts and care about people you love deeply at the same time. But it hadn't been my mum's failing health that acted as the catalyst for this decision, it certainly sealed it, but the initial reason was that I'd simply lost my nerve for the daring which I had embarked on. I couldn't keep up with Tarnasay anymore, and I could no longer contain my worry, my fear of being caught. He's one of a kind but ultimately a loner on an unusual quest. And although I truly found his mild mannered, measured form of craziness intoxicating and exhilarating to be around, and that our views and thoughts on the world we live in crossed paths at many junctions, I also realised some time ago that we are very different creatures. He is a man who, although by no means on an inevitable path to self destruction, is nonetheless a risk taker and an utterly fearless one at that. And to ride with someone like that, while it may seem rebelliously romantic at first, let me tell you, it's completely fucking exhaustive in the end. It seems to me, there's a limit to all but a few. And he is one of them. I've encountered it before. My past big wave surfing days put me amongst those who were just that bit more daring than me, prepared to push it when they knew the odds were against them. When the drop was considered unmakeable and to try, insane. But they'd go anyway. And sure, part of it is ego and fame but at some point it goes well beyond that. It becomes personal. An innate desire to push themselves further each time, to discover their own measurement for what one calls a 'limit.' And just as with my surfing days, and my long adventures sailing solo, I have now found mine with a risk taker of a completely different kind in Tarnasay. So I have decided it's best for both of us if we part ways now. 'End on a high note' as they say.

We'll be friends for life, as will Jimmy and I, but in the mean time I need to return home and be with my mother. I'm not sure when I'll see Tarnasay next, I have heard talk of him heading to Germany, but who really knows. I doubt even he does. But I'll be keeping in touch with the rogue bastard no matter where he is, and listening to his antics like I'm eaves dropping on a Hollywood thriller on acid. I'll look forward to hearing his tales and later his inevitable return to the Australian shoreline. Meanwhile, I will fly home very soon. Franz will be there waiting for me. I'm glad he'll be there. I'll be coming down from an incredible, surreal high at break neck speed, so it'll be good to yarn to someone who has been a close part of everything. Because well, to be honest, I've been crying a lot lately. And no-one feels comfortable when a big bloke weeps. Which is silly and wrong but it's true. It makes them uneasy. Seeing an apparent robust, strong looking specimen suddenly appear vulnerable and fragile. It confuses them. Maybe they feel cheated or something. Anyway, it's big-blokeist and it's a real thing. I've been on both sides of it. Needless to say, being in such an emotionally frazzled state, I think it'll be good to spend some time with Franz. And backing off recreational drugs for a period may help too. Apparently Franz's presence lately has seen my mum enter the present more frequently, when he has visited her as my friend, she actually remembers him. She says his name, "Franzzzz" apparently she holds onto the z for way too long, which kind of freaks him out. But they've had conversations in the present and she's very warm to him. I've spoken to a couple of nurses about this when I called recently and they said they're amazed at how at ease she is with him. They say he talks about me of course and my pending arrival, but rarely have they seen her so at ease when re-entering the present, particularly with a stranger. Hearing this has put me at ease too somewhat until I return. Well I've stopped crying as much anyway.

Mai Pen Rai who I shall sail again soon enough will remain at Shipyard Marina in the good hands of Jimmy. It'll be an opportunity to catch up with him on my return, I sense he'll be sticking around these parts for a bit. Although the idea to return home has been on my mind for some time, the actual decision to do so has come quickly with news of my mother. I'm hoping for one more break from her private dream time, a moment of clarity, a moment in the now. I'll tell her I've been sailing again (not in the exact manner in which I did it of course) but

I'll tell her Captain Swift has been catching the currrent again. She'll love that. She always loved hearing of my sailing adventures. I'll tell her about my beloved Mai Pen Rai and how I sailed her across the Atlantic with a man who became the brother I never had. I'm looking forward to this. I really am. I saw a poster ad on a bus shelter here the other day with two young women cruising in a convertible, one of them, the passenger had her ams outstretched in euphoria and the headline asked, *'When does a minute become a moment?'* Well, I can tell you when. And it has nothing to do with cruising along in a convertible sports car on a hot summers day. It's a bit better than that. It's when you lock eyes with a loved one, one last time. It's when my mother will lock eyes with mine in the now, in that moment. When she sees the love she's given me reflected in swollen tears. When I tell her that I love her and she says, "I know." That is, my friend – when a minute becomes a moment.

The Pleasure Recycling Co.

If it hadn't been for the company's statement that its beginnings were inspired by one of the world's most – for a time at least – notorious criminals, 'Tarnasay,' the organisation would've been one of the darling success stories of international business. They had established operations in six of the world's major capital cities and continued to post a profit margin that was the envy of many companies far greater their size. Their professional reputation, whether business to business, or with individuals was, as they say, "beyond reproach." And although they weren't a charity - in many ways that matter - they acted like one. Their reputation for the quality of their recycled items, whether it was a bicycle or a biplane, was impeccable. They made things work again. And customers the world over knew if they bought something from The Pleasure Recycling Co. (TPR Co) it would work, and if for some reason it didn't, they'd come to you and fix it again, no question.

Nonetheless, no amount of goodwill, good ethics and good business practice could save them from being raided in various countries as though crystal meth labs. In Germany, France and the United States, at the height of the Tarnasay phenomenon they were raided under the presumption of harbouring and reselling stolen goods. "Copycat crimes" as they were called, were evident across the globe. Police were inundated with reports of stolen luxury cars, motorbikes, paintings and yachts at the highest, most expensive end of items stolen, moving down the scale to a broad range of still prized possessions such as high-end mountain and racing bikes, jet skis, golf clubs, collectible guitars and so on. The targets for these items were for the most part – the rich. At the beginning, wealthy, elite suburbs in all countries were being scoured for the easy pilfering of expensive leisure items. Gangs of youths in econovans falsely detailed as trade vehicles or courier companies – with their attire complementing the charade – brazenly entered unoccupied open garages in broad daylight and stole expensive items of leisure and pleasure. As time went on the groups became more organised and sophisticated. They learnt to identify unoccupied luxury homes or estates, override security systems, or corrupt the individuals working within security firms in order to steal items of incredible value. Authorities the world over had become increasingly alarmed, even paranoid, at the rise of what they believed to be criminal organisations disguised as legitimate businesses who cited Tarnasay (as TPR Co had done previously) as their guiding inspiration. Many of them presented themselves in a similar manner as TPR Co, as businesses merely in the interest of recycling and re-selling what was by most commercial standards considered defunct. Others were simply groups interested in mimicking what they interpreted as his anti-establishment behaviour, his supposed anger and disappointment at the ever growing gap between rich and poor. In most cases too, the authorities vested with the power to investigate these miraculously appearing cashed-up start up businesses were right. They were indeed opportunistic highly-organised criminal operations using the popularity of Tarnasay – albeit irreverent and controversial – to leverage their market presence and re-sell stolen goods.

The TPR Co however, much to their disappointment, wasn't one of them. And it's been suggested by more than one media commentator on the subject, that "Perhaps it's no exaggeration to suggest that the company's rapid growth in wealth was substantially assisted by successful litigations against the heavy hand of certain governments." Those governments being Germany, France and the on-going, but increasingly burgeoning case against the United States government. There was no denying these high profile cases had proved lucrative for TPR Co. Crime authorities who had acted rashly and aggressively on behalf of these governments in their efforts to scrutinise and expose TPR Co now, ironically, found themselves not only the subject of scrutiny in the Court of Law but also by the very government which had until only recently, readily empowered them. No doubt crime authorities acting on behalf of a government but operating autonomously and independently of it, sometimes provide no greater service to that government than putting distance between them and their shortcomings. "Yes, they were empowered by us but they were by no means controlled by us" was a typical, palm-to-the-mike response from government spokespersons, quick to draw attention to the distance between them and the authority in question. Meanwhile, the reputation of TPR Co continued to grow and so did its wealth. Even the media whose interest initially focussed so acutely on the apparent association with Tarnasay had begun to wane. Some of the more outspoken social commentators on popular networks had gone so far as to suggest that certain governments were "Bullying" the organisation unjustly. To this day, although the scrutiny has significantly lessened, The Pleasure Recycling Co remains under the watchful eye of many international authorities, and to this day they have found nothing.

~

Nicolas Muller and Rudy Einhaus in an unorthodox, round-a-bout way, came good on their parents vision of them becoming highly successful young men of society. It just didn't happen the way they expected. Nor had it for Nicolas or Rudy for that matter. It wasn't that they weren't ambitious of which their parents accused them, it was simply that they weren't excited or stimulated by the idea of a typical professional life. Instead they'd just ambled along doing manual work in vineyards scattered throughout the Rhineland-Palatinate in Germany. The relevance and value of their university degrees becoming less significant with every bucket of ripened grapes they collected. And although they may not have realised it, they were in truth biding time. Neither of them, despite being content with the work they did around the various vineyards, saw themselves doing so indefinitely. But at the same time, they didn't know what it was they ought to be doing. This concerned neither of them which went a long way to explaining why their friendship had remained close after university. Most of their mutual friends, with the exception of those who became artists and musicians, had gone on to corporate careers and although they kept in touch, their lives were heading in different directions. Those friends were climbing the solid, polished steel ladder of the modern corporate world for future prosperity while they were treading lightly upon a rickety, wooden one simply for existence. It was a choice they made. One being a specified place within stylised concrete, the other an ever shifting location amongst the elements. Both Nicolas and Rudy often talked about different ideas for setting up businesses or speculating about certain careers but neither of them had hit upon an idea that would suddenly cause them to up and leave and pursue it. And it wasn't as if one was waiting for the other, waiting for inspiration or motivation, something sudden and unpredicted but nonetheless anticipated, "Well I'm off. I've thought of something I should do. And I think it's time you did too." No, both of them were content to wait, not that they had expressed it to each other. They were just content to wait patiently and privately. For exactly what, neither of them knew.

It was while on a break from fruit picking when Nicolas Muller was handed a mobile phone from a laughing English backpacker who was showing fellow workers YouTube footage of a vicious female chimpanzee doing a bit of 'man slapping.' Ever since it had been revealed during the Tarnasay phenomenon that he'd also stolen a chimp and she was possibly now sailing with him onboard Ubetcha, Cruella had become something of a celebrity and was noted for her 'man slapping' as it was called (at this point authorities the world over still believed Ubetcha was out there somewhere). There was a series of videos showing her various man-slapping attacks on hapless, unexpecting humans and they were a hit. Jimmy featured in many of them. People found the sight of a small chimpanzee slapping people mercilessly, hilarious. And Nicolas Muller whose hearty laugh belied his small stature, agreed. When the young Englishman explained to him that this was indeed the very same chimp that was sailing with the infamous international fugitive 'Tarnasay,' Nicolas immediately found himself unnervingly excited. Somehow it hinted at the spark of excitement he'd been waiting for. There was something about the grainy, amateur footage of Cruella slapping people about the face that suddenly made the whole 'Tarnasay' hype very real. In a minute it seemed to go from something outrageous, almost fanciful and unbelievable which he'd followed closely on news reports and in various newspapers and magazines; something he discussed, joked and marvelled at with friends – as though at any moment it would all be revealed to be some kind of hoax, a beat up – to something absolutely, undoubtedly, real. And it didn't matter that there was no actual footage of Tarnasay or Captain Swift, just hearing their voices, their flat Australian accents in stark contrast to the European accents in the background of the jumpy, crudely shot footage was enough to convince him that they really did exist; that they really had stolen a superyacht from Sydney harbour in Australia and embarked on a crazy adventure regardless how much larger than life the whole idea seemed.

This realisation changed everything for Nicolas Muller. It suddenly gave him a sense of urgency that he'd been lacking, subconsciously longing for. Now he felt the impetus to do something. That if he didn't, he'd miss out. It was time to embark on his own adventure and it wasn't to involve commandeering yachts, or screaming away in someone else's Ferrari – but it did have something to do with the freedom it represented. This is the moment that a morsel of an idea wedged itself somewhere in the brain of Nicolas Muller like a small seed between teeth. Something nagging, demanding attention, that will not go away until it's dealt with.

The nagging thought which became an idea that in turn became TPR Co began to take shape while Nicolas was still filling buckets with grapes at the vineyard. Ever since the jovial English backpacker had shown him the YouTube footage of a terrified Jimmy fleeing a beating from Cruella supposedly onboard 'Ubetcha', Nicolas's interest in Tarnasay had magnified significantly. It had always been there but now he spent hours doing internet searches on him to gather as much information about the man as possible. And as he expected there wasn't much, but eventually in the depths of ethernet abyss he uncovered a fledgling underground magazine that had posted an interview with Tarnasay. The interview had apparently taken place in Chiang Mai by an aspiring young journalist who was curious about his motivation for taking 'Ubetcha.' It was here that Nicolas discovered the story of Tarnasay's Uncle Lou. He learnt of 'Planet Shed' and his eccentric Uncle's unfailing generosity. Here, he got a glimpse of who the notorious Tarnasay actually was, what made him 'tick' as they say. And although it was, in truth, dear old Uncle Lou who was the real inspiration for Nicolas and his founding of TPR Co, it was Tarnasay's charisma, passion and the obvious affection for his Uncle that gave him the spark and initiative. He'd always assumed such a thing would come to him one day, and draw him away from the dead-end vineyard work. Some intangible 'thing' that would get him excited, get him thinking about what is was he wanted, what is was that would one day become TPR Co.

The international success of the conglomerate was built upon the unusual. Something that has become increasingly rare by most modern business standards – philanthropy. The generosity of many who offered their skills and time to the company in its infancy for nothing more than a nice lunch and a few lagers after closing time. In the earliest stages Nicolas and Rudy drew heavily on the contacts of friends who were happy to offer their time and particular skills towards making something new again. To simply fix something broken and give it away. The two young men without any specific experience in fixing items themselves did what they could through trial and error and education. Initially, it was items like bikes and furniture and various damaged or broken toys, but over time when it became known that they were asking for items considered broken and useless, they found the front of their compound became a dumping ground for a broad range of items. Suddenly pool tables that looked as though they'd been hauled from a bombed bunker appeared alongside motorbikes, mopeds, TV's and radios. Before long, they realised they needed to engage qualified technicians and trades people to help. And to their amazement people did. Rarely did people accept the token payment they offered them. Nicolas and Rudy had simply asked through a network of friends for people willing to give up as little as three hours of their time whenever it suited them towards fixing something, whether they were skilled or unskilled. Following this, the items being repaired became more and more sophisticated, and Nicolas and Rudy set about finding re-sellers interested in buying the more technical or expensive items in order to pay for a technician or trade person's services. The quality of the technicians and trades people they attracted went a long way towards establishing the reputation of the refurbished or repaired products as exemplary. In time, they were in a situation to assist tradesman and technicians in the employment of apprentices and contribute towards their wages. At the time all this was taking place, Tarnasay's international profile had peaked. This was the beginning of the period that saw copycat behaviour of Tarnasay worldwide. The sudden en-masse stealing of products of pleasure from anywhere they lay idle or unattended. And soon, TPR Co found its compound a depository for many of these expensive, perfectly functioning stolen items. Most likely abandoned by frightened youths. Teenagers on the brink of adulthood who let the hysteria and excitement surrounding Tarnasay's rebelliousness get the better of them and judgement. Judgement that saw them brazenly stealing all kinds of pleasure products, from golf clubs, windsurfers, jet skis, to even pool tables from wealthy suburban garages and backyards before coming to the realisation that once they had them, they had no idea what to do with them. The Pleasure Recycling Co on the other hand, did. And Nicolas and Rudy were savvy enough to make the most of the situation before the might of the authorities came down hard following pressure from the wealthy, power wielding and highly vocal part of public communities who were being targeted. The absurdity of the situation wasn't lost on Nicolas and Rudy either, who later discovered that many of the stolen items were taken by young gangs who actually lived in the very suburbs they were robbing. They were in effect, robbing their neighbours. Nicolas learnt this from his father who told him that their next door neighbour Klaus had lost his small fishing boat, which Nicolas at that instant, could recall reselling back a month or so. "It's the furthest it's moved in years!" his father laughed loudly down the phone before stopping abruptly when Nicolas heard his mother in the background scolding him for laughing at such a thing, "Well it took him two weeks to notice it was missing!" his father added yelling the defensive comment intended for his wife down the phone. Nicolas winced and held the phone away from his ear and wondered whether Klaus the neighbour had heard it too. He was often pottering around in his garden which was right outside the window where his parents had the landline. He then had a strong feeling of deja vu. It was something his father said, something to do with Klaus taking two weeks to notice it missing. He didn't ask his Father how he knew it'd taken him two weeks to notice it missing but he knew his Father was right. He remembered discovering the boat outside the compound early one morning, its dirty aluminium structure covered in spider webs and filled with old plastic plant containers. He had no way of knowing it was Klaus's boat and doubted it would've mattered anyway. At this stage things were frantic, business was moving very quickly and they were taking advantage of these neglected but otherwise perfectly working items of pleasure turning up on their doorstep. Nicolas and Rudy moved them quickly and efficiently with the help of friends more au fait with the criminal skills and knowledge required for the re-birthing and reselling of stolen goods. They realised that this window of criminal opportunity was closing fast and soon, having cleared their warehouse of any stolen property, they would alert authorities to the dumping of stolen goods outside their compound. Bringing in the authorities this close was risky they knew, but it had to be done and if it was done correctly, they'd look all the better for it. Nicolas thought about the "two weeks" comment from his father again and then it came to him, the reason it was familiar. It was something Tarnasay had spoken of in the interview with the underground magazine. It was about how his Uncle Lou would often confiscate their abandoned, neglected toys in the yard, stashing them in a cupboard for up to two weeks, awaiting a crying complaint from one of them about the missing toy's whereabouts before he'd decide to give it away. It had taken Klaus two weeks to notice his boat was missing. For a moment, Nicholas wished the boat was still at the compound. That he'd return it. He thought about finding him another boat and surreptitiously replacing it. But then it'd probably take another two weeks for him to even notice it was there, he surmised. Besides, he knew old Klaus well enough to know that it would've been his wife who noticed it was missing and she hated fishing even more than him. It then occurred to Nicolas that this was at the very essence of what he was doing. This was the very thing that he instantly liked about Tarnasay's Uncle Lou when he spoke of him in the interview, the idea that registered with him, inspired him, the matter at the very core of why he was doing what he was doing. The recycling of something good, something neglected, ignored, taken for granted by one but which is admired, coveted, dreamt of by another. And nothing changes as we get older, the toys, they simply get bigger. But Klaus's boat served as a mental catalyst for Nicolas. That and the appearance of an eight man jacuzzi on a trailer outside the compound one morning. He decided he'd no longer take in stolen items and resell them. Not only were the items being dumped getting increasingly absurd and difficult to move quickly, it was also becoming too risky. It wasn't what he believed TPR Co was about either. He wasn't interested in running a cloaked criminal organisation, he only wanted the abandoned, the broken and the genuinely donated.

~

Everyone is subject to the somewhat unnerving, fatalist, magical world of serendipity at some point in their life. And whether you like it or not, serendipity loves to dance. Serendipity loves to spin you around, around and around, and then suddenly release you with a grand flourish towards the unexpected. For some, the unexpected may be a bland occurrence of no esteemed relevance, meaning or significance "Oh wow I've been saying that I need some tree stumps and look over there! A bunch of tree stumps!." For others the experience can be far more dynamic and exciting. The dance, the spin, is incredible, perhaps faith reinforcing or life changing. For Nicolas Muller, his twirl in the dance with serendipity spun him towards a life changing encounter. An encounter with someone whom he was never foolish enough to see as a hero, but someone nonetheless who'd inspired him, and in the most unexpected way, someone with whom it would seem serendipity most loves to dance – Tarnasay.

Ralph Lehmann of The Venkmann Equation was to be the serendipitous link between Nicolas and Tarnasay. For not long after Nicolas had made the decision to leave the vineyard work in pursuit of life more fulfilling he was contacted by Ralph. Ralph told him of his plans for a friend to take over his castle minding duties so he could remain touring in the States for at least a few more months. He was asking for a favour. He wanted Nicolas to keep an eye on the well-being of his friend and to offer his company should his friend seek it. Ralph said that he'd also contacted Rudy with the same request. He then explained to Nicolas that due to his high-profile friend being in an "unusual predicament" he'd prefer to email him information rather than discuss details over the phone. Ralph ever diligent and conscious of keeping information he believed should be secret, truly secret, told Nicolas to look out for an email with the subject 'Tickets.' It'd be coming from an anonymous hotmail address that would only be used once to send the information and that he'd need to check his junk mail. He was then to read it once, then delete it. If he didn't wish to help he was to simply text, 'Good luck!" and that would be the end of their correspondence regarding the matter.

A couple of days later Nicolas found the email buried in his junk mail, read it once and deleted it as advised. He then sat staring out the window of his flat at nothing for the next hour. Tarnasay was coming to St Goarshausen. The very man who was the inspiration behind his fledgling business.

Lord Evermore and The Burg Katz, St.Goarshausen, Rhineland-Palatinate, Germany

Tarnasay arrived in Frankfurt after a long flight and felt drained, not only physically but somewhat emotionally too. A fun and exciting chapter to his adventuring had ended and he said goodbye to people who'd become strong friends. The situations they'd found themselves in provided experiences more than a step and a half from the ordinary. There were many people sailing the seas but not while harbouring a temperamental female chimpanzee and wanted by authorities almost everywhere. He and Col found a good home for Cruella, who must have sensed Col was leaving her because she slapped him hard across the face after he embraced her one last time. There was no denying that she'd been an unpredictable menace who often tried their patience, but the two men knew they'd be lying if they said they wouldn't miss the excitement she always managed to create. And Tarnasay was all about excitement. He'd also farewelled The Venkmann Equation, unsure when he would see them again despite his arrangement to be regularly in contact with Ralph Lehmann via email. Email was to play a major part in the smooth running of Tarnasay's new appointment as a castle minder. Jimmy who was to stay on and continue touring with the Venkmann crew vowed to catch up with Tarnasay soon enough but meanwhile they too parted ways. And finally, he farewelled Captain Col, the man who had the courage to join him on his most outrageous heist ever and sail him to both Thailand and the US undetected. Col flew with Tarnasay to London before they took alternate routes with Col heading home and Tarnasay heading to the next chapter of his adventure in 'Pleasure recycling.'

Ralph had no concerns sending Tarnasay as a replacement for his castle minding duties. It's not particularly easy being a radical young German rockstar in one of the hottest electronica acts on the planet when your father is an extremely domineering man of significant wealth and standing in German society. To the point that he'll rein you in wherever you are, not through persuasion but through force and put you in your place and back on the path he believes is best for you. At least until you're eighteen. His father was aware of his association with the group but had no idea that his son was actually in the band. And seeing that they wore helmets and suits and rarely spoke to the media, fans or anyone at all for that matter, it'd been easy for Ralph to appear far enough from the band that his father and his drones' scrutiny never confirmed anything other than a casual association.

An idea had come to Tarnasay while he and Jimmy were partying with the Venkmann crew following the success of their DJ set. After beers and shots of schnapps had been flowing freely for some time, Ralph who was more heavily intoxicated than the rest of them (except for Cruella who'd secretly stolen a bottle of schnapps and knocked herself out) began ranting angrily in German. Sensing that they may appear rude carrying on a conversation in their native tongue, Joseph explained that Ralph was lamenting the situation with his father. He was frustrated that their attempts to allude his domineering father had failed again and that his future with the band was "Fucking futile! Mother fucking futile!" With that expletive explosion Ralph switched back to English and continued to explain his dilemma. Tarnasay, Jimmy and Col sat sipping their beers and listened. It became clear that regardless of where he went he was soon tracked down by his father's "Drones" as he called them and issued with what was effectively a family affidavit. He explained how he'd managed to get to New York and remain undetected for more than a month before his father once again hunted him down. Ordered to call home by his father's diligent drones, Ralph pleaded with his father to allow him to stay for another month, explaining that he had only travelled to New York to see The Venkmann Equation perform. To Ralph's disbelief he agreed but when he thought about it he soon realised that it was merely his father's way of cutting costs which was always of utmost importance to him. It was simply a cheaper option for him to delay Ralph's castle minding appointment for a month and be assured that he'll return home rather than send his drones flying around the world after him. Because he knew this is what his father would do. It was this thought that caused

Ralph's angry outburst. He felt trapped, watched and part of a game in which only his father knew the rules. And although Ralph was merely months away from being an adult and then lawfully free to do as he pleased, he knew that until that moment, his father was determined to control him.

It didn't take Tarnasay long to suggest a solution that he knew would appeal to Ralph and also satisfy his own adventure fetish. And castle minding on the Rhine River in the heart of Germany's wine region blended the two perfectly. The idea was simple, Tarnasay would fly to St. Goarshausen instead of Ralph and undertake the ultimate in house sitting – minding the historic Burg Katz. Ralph was to send emails to Tarnasay containing information that Ralph's father would expect to receive from him in regard to his duties looking after the castle. Which in truth amounted to nothing and saw Ralph blowing joints from the castle's turret before heading out for a day fishing or visiting one of the taverns with old friends and guzzling steins in the sun. Nonetheless, Ralph stressed to Tarnasay how important it was that he cut and paste the content of his emails and forward them on to his father. Although his father would be abroad for much of Tarnasay's castle minding tenure ("Somewhere else in the States as it happens," he said laughing but a tad nervously), if just one weekly email update failed to appear in his father's inbox their cover could be compromised. He explained how incredibly insistent his father was about maintaining "order and consistency" and he soon learnt that by simply maintaining that order and consistency, he was free to do as he pleased, which was quite the opposite. So it was agreed Tarnasay would receive Ralph's weekly emails at a hotmail address, cut and paste the contents into another email account set up under Ralph's name on the castle's administration computer and send them on to Ralph's father. Apart from that one menial task, Tarnasay had nothing else to do and a stunning medieval castle to do it all in.

Somehow amongst all the carnage of its three hundred years nestled neatly if not conspicuously above the Rhine River, where it suffered numerous attacks from the French, the Spanish and a bombing in World War II, the Burg Katz' magnificent she-oak timber doors had survived. Tarnasay stood awestruck before them. He ran his fingers gingerly over the gnarled pieces of dented timber that stretched almost the length of the 12ft high doors and considered the history that may have caused them. Attempted infiltrations from a host of invaders whose failed efforts at forcing them open are now forever recorded as a haunting, historic patina. Tarnasay knocked on the door and listened for a moment. "Hello!" he then bellowed, "I am the invader! Open up! You are mine!" he chuckled to himself, listened to his voice echo about the ancient sandstone walls before proceeding towards one that had been introduced to the 21st century via a sleek, polished steel security key pad. Tarnasay punched in the lengthy security code and waited patiently for the colossal walls of timber to slowly fold out towards him and reveal the medieval wonder within.

Throughout life there can be many things we excitedly visualise only to discover that they fail to meet imagined expectations. A dud firework whose fantastic packaging promises so much but fails to fire. Or a delicious menu description that is far more inspired than the Chef preparing it. The Burg Katz, however, for all Tarnasay's imaginings from childhood to adulthood, about what a medieval castle may actually be, did not represent one of those moments. The second he entered the foyer of the castle Tarnasay felt almost nauseous, overwhelmed by the weight of history this one building contained. Sandstone blocks the size of modern kitchen tables formed the walls of the circular foyer decorated with historic German artefacts and strikingly vivid portraits of men and women. Tarnasay approached the Victorian portraits and his shoes made a loud 'clock, clock, clock' sound as he came in for a closer look. The sound of each footstep was clear and crisp upon spotless glassed tiles, exaggerated by the foreboding walls and made Tarnasay feel somewhat officious and important as he moved about. Which is probably how the castle's earlier inhabitants felt too he thought. He inspected the subjects of the portraits keenly and figured they were probably the castle's custodians at various points in time. They all stared back at him scrutinisingly, their self-importance and somewhat arrogant postures captured by the artist as neatly as the light upon their clothes. Their expressions were eternally patronising, as if to say to the viewer 'You're not good enough to admire me.' Tarnasay pretended to poke one of them in the eye and moved deeper into the castle. His castle.

Ralph told Tarnasay that he must not bring anyone to the castle or let locals know he was residing there. But on his first night there Tarnasay was too tired to venture out for dinner and the four fridges he inspected offered only champagne and wine. Besides he couldn't resist the idea of answering those colossal doors to receive his pizza delivery dressed in a magnificent red dressing gown he'd found in one of the castle's many vacant rooms. Tarnasay was quite fond of the red gown and it soon became his standard attire when returning from daily explorations upon the Rhine River. He'd don it shortly after arriving home and then commence further exploration of his amazing new home. To his delight he'd discovered that the castle's turret featured a large sauna, spa and a well stocked private bar and lounge that would rival any commercial outfit. After a days outing the turret soon became his favourite place to relax within the monolith. Yes, Tarnasay was now Lord Evermore of the Burg Katz and loving it.

From experience Ralph knew the potential for loneliness to set in when minding a property as significant as the castle Burg with not so much as an aloof cat for company. Although he'd rightly identified Tarnasay as the kind who enjoys his own company and not prone to boredom, every man needs some social interaction at some point. And Burg Katz with its towering halls and empty room after empty room, each of which appeared stuck in a rut of German history, had a strange alienating affect on one's psyche. Ralph knew it all too well which is why he'd given Tarnasay the contacts to a couple of close friends who lived in St Goarshausen and could be trusted to remain quiet about their castle minding arrangement. Fun, easy-going people who he knew would enjoy his company and vice versa. Tarnasay welcomed the suggestion as he always enjoyed meeting new people but told Ralph he needn't have worried, he never had any trouble amusing himself he said with a broad smile.

Tarnasay was more that just a little impressed with Ralph's intuition when a little over a month into his stay at the Burg Katz, he found himself calling up Ralph's mates. He then discovered upon meeting his friends that Ralph was a very sharp operator indeed when it came to planning a ruse and keeping things tight. Almost immediately he recognised Ralph's mate Rudy as the pizza delivery guy and later to his amusement, he discovered that Nicolas had even made the pizza. A very good one Tarnasay informed him with a laugh. He remembered how the pizza number was the only thing stuck on any of the four fridges. A note which simply had a number and the word 'Pizza' scrawled upon it. He remembered being somewhat bemused when the pizza guy winked at him as he handed over the pizza, but he figured it was just the extravagant gown he was wearing and that perhaps he fancied him in it.

Tarnasay was delighted to find that Nicolas and Rudy were as amicable as Ralph. He spent most weekdays with them during his third month of castle minding, where having ventured along the Rhine River during the day they would often end it by sipping beers in the spa upon the turret. As was Ralph Lehmann, Nicolas and Rudy were both from wealthy families but they were older than him and having recently completed their university were content to drift somewhat aimlessly. Neither of them felt compelled by the idea of high powered corporate careers their parents envisaged. They were simply content to take odd jobs which drew nothing from their education, working in vineyards and construction sites. Jobs they knew were disappointing to their parents but still managed to appease them enough to retain a monthly allowance. At least they weren't taking drugs, they figured.

The more they talked the more apparent it became that Nicolas and Rudy shared a similar life view to Tarnasay despite their privileged upbringing. They explained that although they enjoyed many of the spoils their parents afforded them as kids they weren't oblivious to the waste. The expensive, luxury items their parents bought felt at odds with how they came to view the materialism of the West. They told him how they'd heard of his commandeering a yacht from Sydney Harbour and how somewhere along the way he'd apparently stolen a chimpanzee and also taken a malnourished Asian man as hostage. They were dubious about the chimp stealing and hostage scenario but they were in awe of his audacity to steal a superyacht. They envied his daring and wished for this kind of excitement. Tarnasay saw how wide-eyed and energised they were when they recited some of his adventures back to him. Tarnasay was taken aback. He was well aware that his antics were now documented through the world media but this was the first time he'd seen directly how his antics affected some people. How excited they became exploring the idea and fantasising about some of the things he'd done. But what left Tarnasay speechless was when Nicolas explained that his 'Pleasure recycling' antics had now formed a major underground, anti mass-consumption movement throughout Europe. He listened as Nicolas rattled off a list of organisations driven by the idea of pleasure recycling, the most prominent carried the name intimately familiar to Tarnasay, The Pleasure Recycling Co. Tarnasay's tongue lolled around his mouth searching for words to express his incredulity but none came. Nicolas continued to explain passionately how these groups believed they could change, or at least assist, in changing the behaviour of mass consumerism, materialistic waste and greed. Tarnasay was flabbergasted. To him it had always been simply a private revolt, an idea that had grown from his childhood and manifested itself into what was for him, in truth, just an audacious form of adventure and risk taking. The idea that a simple term such as 'Pleasure recycling' which he created one day at a whim and in jest for one of his infamous handwritten notes to explain the disappearance of someone's neglected or forgotten possession, would one day become a catalyst for a movement, astounded him.

Was there really a collective of people who were dedicated and driven by the idea of 'Pleasure recycling'? Were they truly disillusioned with the imbalance of wealth in the world and a throwaway mentality that they wanted to cheekily lampoon it; or was it simply a guise for a more basic criminal motivation – to satisfy their own greed and materialistic desires through theft? Either way, Tarnasay began to think that his own adventure and socially subversive behaviour may soon be coming to an end.

In the meantime, Tarnasay ignored Ralph's advice to remain anonymous amongst the local community and exploited the status of his temporary title and means, that of Lord Evermore of Burg Katz. And he did it in such a way that it's already become modern folklore and the events of Tarnasay's doing are now discussed and debated throughout Rhineland–Palatinate. His first action was to open up the previously inaccessible ancient castle for 'Public Open Days' and charge a moderate fee. With the proceeds and some of his own money, he then set about establishing the turret as a slick underground nightspot called *Archie Spears*, and on the day he was to leave Lichtenstein and fly out of Germany, he put on a spectacular, world headline making art exhibition featuring missing masterpieces from no less than Pablo Picasso and Piet Mondrian.

Tarnasay had discovered the precious works during one of his many castle explorations that not only took him into the small hours of the morning but deep into the bowels of the sandstone monolith. Poking into what had certainly been dungeons at some point in its history he encountered an odd assortment of refuse that appeared to be the accumulation of materials not so much from decade after decade but century after century. In a hallway that lead to each cell, small cannons bearing the battle scars of wars long passed rested absurdly alongside dusty, high-tech treadmills one sees lining the walls of busy city gyms. Creased sepia photographs lay strewn across the cracked floor like the aftermath of an old lover's quarrel. A discoloured baseball mitt rested against the wall next to an opened but untouched timber box of mouldy Cuban cigars. Tarnasay walked slowly down the hallway past the bizarre collection of objects, each step sounding louder than the last upon the wet floor, unnerving him a little. For novelties sake he liked to fossick around the darker parts of the castle with nothing more than an old kerosene doused straw lamp stick like one sees in b-grade horror flicks. Usually he enjoyed the slightly anxious mood and nervous excitement it created as he wandered around in the shadows. It made him feel more alive, his senses heightened. The hairs on his arms acting like tiny antennae attempting to feel the way ahead. But on this occasion, as he ventured further and further into the castle's darkest veins, he began to feel genuinely scared. Things had happened down here and not good things he found himself thinking.

Tarnasay felt relieved to be distracted. A tiny beam of light had somehow found its way deep into the gallows before resting on the corner of a partially exposed painting. The light brought the colours alive, making them almost iridescent in the suffocating darkness of the cell block. He peered into the room tentatively as though at any moment something unexpected and unwanted may appear before him. But nothing revealed itself except the striking colours of the painting where its blanket veil slid from one of its shoulders somewhat evocatively. With delicate fingers Tarnasay slowly pulled away the damp blanket that'd become infused with the smell of mildew. He stared at the artwork now revealed in its entirety with disbelief. The coldness of the cell left him momentarily and was replaced with the warmth of someone discovering a long lost treasure. He now stood before the much documented missing Picasso painting, 'Head of a Woman' and hidden behind it was 'Landscape with a Mill' by Piet Mondrian. He was far from an art expert but he had always had a keen interest and had purchased more than one original artwork from upcoming Australian artists over the years and he recognised both paintings instantly. He was familiar with much of Mondrian's work but the one piece he had always admired was 'Landscape with a Mill' and now here it was, the real thing right before him. It was rare for someone such as Tarnasay, who did the things he did, to ever feel dizzy but right at this moment he did. He sat down on the damp, ancient cell floor deep within a famous German castle and stared at two equally famous paintings in marvelment.

~

The exhibition Tarnasay held prior to his departure and rescinding of the title 'Lord Evermore of The Burg Katz' was an outstanding success. He'd arranged for the exhibition to continue for a week after his departure, and as word quickly spread about the mysterious reappearance of the missing Picasso and Mondrian, it wasn't long before a stream of high profile art critics from Germany and Europe hurried to see the works on display. Perhaps it was due in part to novelty, curiosity or scepticism but the speed in which public attention and the art world responded to the showing of these lost treasures caught everyone by surprise. Nicolas and Rudy who'd dressed in vaudeville costumes to add to the bizarreness of an impromptu exhibition, and to hide their identities from locals attending the show, initially ran the exhibition on Tarnasay's behalf. But after the third week of the exhibition, when the international media had gone into a frenzy following a renowned German art critic's appearance on national television where he confirmed that the works on display at The Burg Katz were indeed "The genuine articles," they too removed themselves from the scene and found replacements. Tarnasay had expected a frenzy at some point but not so quickly and he was relieved that he'd made the decision to leave after the second week of showing. He had dipped into the generous funds, "Travel expenses" that Col had deposited into his account and funded Nicolas and Rudy to establish a small professional team to run the exhibition including security, catering and a friend who held an Honours degree in Art History. In the meantime, he set about finding a buyer for the lost Picasso and Mondrian. He introduced himself as a curator and he drew on his recent research on the works and life of Pablo Picasso whilst ensuring that the vibrant young Art History graduate Felix Vanderow was never far away. Felix revelled in the opportunity to put his education and suave, natural charm to use. He also rescued Tarnasay from an awkward, potentially cover blowing conversation.

On the second week of the exhibition when attendance was at its highest, Tarnasay had been standing before the monstrous portraits in the foyer of the castle greeting new visitors when he was approached by a portly, well dressed middle-aged man. From the moment Tarnasay laid eyes on the man who looked him up and down as though an insubordinate child he felt uneasy. "Do I know you?" said the man, but before Tarnasay could reply he continued, "I don't know you. Where's Frederich Magnussen?" Tarnasay glanced around quickly as if looking for Frederich Magnussen but was actually looking for

Felix. Tarnasay returned his eyes to the small stout man before him and stared for what seemed a long time. The man stared back for what seemed even longer. "Oh Frederich Magnussen!" Tarnasay finally said almost too loudly when he caught a glimpse of Felix's scarlet red dinner jacket in the corner of his eye entering the foyer. Felix practically froze mid-step when he heard Tarnasay say the name. He'd been heading somewhere in his usual brisk, fastidious manner but he stopped immediately and turned slowly to look at Tarnasay. Felix made his way quickly towards Tarnasay and called out loud and enthusiastically to the stout man before him. The man immediately recognised Felix and Tarnasay relaxed. Felix explained to Tarnasay that he'd been at university with the man's son and then proceeded to engage in conversation with him in German ignoring Tarnasay. In any other situation it may have seemed rude but Tarnasay realised Felix was giving him an out. When Tarnasay saw the man's face light up and laugh at something Felix said, he used the moment to politely excuse himself and drifted away to mill with the crowd. Before long the combination of Felix's outstanding knowledge of art, his natural charm and the ease of which he could deliver stimulating, energetic conversation whether it be in German, English, Spanish, Italian or French saw him introduce Tarnasay to potential buyers. He knew he had to be selective about attracting the right buyer. A buyer short on questions, but big on money. One who wasn't particularly interested in its recent history but fascinated, mesmerised by the idea of it soon having one with them. Tarnasay had observed over three days, the recurring presence of a small group of people who were often engaged in animated, friendly discussions with Felix before the masterful Picasso. They were Chinese – two men and a woman, and it appeared to Tarnasay, by way of the body language and the manner in which they spoke to her, that she was the one in charge. However, to his surprise he soon learnt that it was a young Russian man who had secured the Picasso. He wasted little time in making his offer to Felix once informed that it was indeed for sale. He simply raised his eyebrows as though he was genuinely surprised to hear of this news, smiled slyly and then quietly stated the figure he was prepared to pay. The number was right and the speed in which Felix anticipated or at least hoped the transaction would take place was proven right too - in fact, it was dumbfoundingly fast. To both Felix and Tarnasay's disbelief, the sale and collection of the missing Picasso was completed within fours hours of Felix's conversation with the Russian man. Tarnasay always anticipated a fast transaction. The missing Picasso's past was shadier than his own but to have a deal such as this, with an amount such as this, completed in the amount of time such as this, left him speechless. And when Felix called telling him to check his account "Right now" and he saw staring at him from the computer screen an obscene, abstract figure, "Wow," was all he could say. "I know," said Felix.

Felix had disappeared underground along with the rest of them. He'd done as Tarnasay had asked and arranged for the meticulous clean up of the castle and the exhibition following its closure. The Burg Katz was returned exactly as Tarnasay had found it. Empty and idle. Any trace of the thumping underground *Archie Spears* nightspot was gone and the reality that it ever actually existed now only resided in the memories of those who had been there. Otherwise, it was a myth. There wasn't even a stray Weihenstephaner beer cap to be found. Nor was the true owner of the Burg Katz either as it happened. Tarnasay had calculated correctly when he made the decision to hold *The Lost Picasso Exhibition*, that the owner of the historic structure wouldn't be so quick to make an appearance. There would be some explaining to do. He had always counted on at least a couple of weeks grace before the authorities would come asking questions. And when they finally did come, the show was over. As magically as the exhibition had appeared, it had also disappeared. And so too had Ralph Lehmann apparently, the castle's appointed caretaker, noted the authorities.

Not long after Tarnasay's departure, Nicolas and Rudy made an incredible discovery of their own. Despite their protests he'd insisted that they be paid for being, of a sort, his "Carers" and had asked for their banking details. It felt great for him to send a final message from the balcony of his hotel suite as he sipped his scotch in the comfort of the warm, afternoon sun.

They stared at the bank accounts alone in flats that were suburbs and vineyards apart, but the two young Germans shook their heads in disbelief simultaneously. Their bank accounts now bulged grotesquely, disturbingly. The figure beneath their names on the account so enlarged, so surreal it was as though it struggled to fit their names. It seemed too big for them, like a man trying to squeeze into old jeans with an even older body. They'd never seen their account dressed like this, at that moment it looked ill-fitted. Tarnasay had sold the Picasso and the Mondrian.

SAM'S NEVERENDING DAY OFF (PART 4)

Sam looks at Hasta's pile before her and wonders what she is going to do with it. It really does seem wasteful to just dump it in the bin. And she soon learns that her idea of stacking the things neatly beside it is also unsatisfactory to Hasta who barks at her a couple of times before he energetically sets about reestablishing his collection. Sam realises she has no choice but to placate the eccentric dog. She gathers up his precious things in the middle of the picnic rug, ties a couple of hefty knots and hoists the makeshift bag over her shoulder. Hasta appears to be smiling at her ingenuity.

~

Tarnasay's friends never believed him when he explained that Hasta had been hoarding stuff since he was a pup. They all figured he'd trained him to do it. But Tarnasay insists he'd done no such thing as old Uncle Lou would have attested. Tarnasay lived with his Uncle Lou, first as a young man at the age of seventeen where he'd come to stay, a tad reluctantly, while studying for his HSC exams, and again much later as an adult when Uncle Lou was ill. It wasn't long after recovering from a pancreatic operation, where he began to regain his strength, that Uncle Lou began urging Tarnasay, now a twenty-seven year old man to leave again, to "get on with your own life, travel some more, experience the world – eat it up." It was also the time in which Uncle Lou brought home a little pup that was to become Hasta, as if to say, "See. Look here, look at him, look how adorable he is, look how he adores me. There's no need for you now, the two of us will do just fine."

Tarnasay had no problem with his Uncle's attempt to replace him with a dog. Nonetheless, it would be another two years before Tarnasay did as his Uncle wished. With his immediate family having remained in the United Kingdom, moving again, this time from Wales to England, propelled again by his father's ever advancing academic career, Uncle Lou and little Hasta became his closest family. He wasn't about to leave either, not while he could still see his Uncle's health ebbing and flowing unpredictably. It was not only as a young man but also during these years that Uncle Lou became more of a father figure to Tarnasay than his own father. He simply couldn't bring himself to leave when he remained fragile. In the meantime, Tarnasay worked with Franz at his growing underground DJ management agency, took on dead-end part-time jobs, and continued studying having completed his impotent Arts Degree some years back. He was killing time really, killing time and borrowing things. Making headlines to the amusement of his closest friends and planning something big. He didn't know what it was, but he knew it was brewing and he was waiting and watching for when it would appear. When the opportunity for his biggest ever 'borrow' would appear. During this time young Hasta became infatuated with him and quickly learnt that as long as he obeyed his every word he could practically go everywhere with him. As much as the big dog loved Uncle Lou, who was technically his owner, and just as obedient and affectionate towards him as he was Tarnasay, he must have been drawn by the energy of the younger man. And later, when Tarnasay was to leave, satisfied with his Uncle's good health, Uncle Lou observed Hasta's behaviour. He expected him to pine. But he never did. Instead, he simply souvenired one of Tarnasay's old jerseys and slept on it soundly as if content to wait for his undoubtable return. He was lucky enough to have two devoted owners and it was clear that the attention of Uncle Lou was still more than enough.

As a young man Tarnasay's reluctance to live with his Uncle Lou had nothing to do with the man himself. It had to do with a major decision he'd made as a seventeen year old. He had been given an option and had made a decision – a personal decision, an important one – only to see it withdrawn, reneged upon by his parents. Tarnasay's father Henry and his brother Uncle Lou, although very close, were also very different. The two brothers parted ways on many issues, lifestyle and often politics but their genuine fondness for each other always rose above the raucous, sometimes antagonistic banter between them. In many ways, that was probably what they liked about each other. That they could thrash out something so heavily, where it seemed at any moment someone's head might explode due to frustration and anger, yet later be seen sitting together, sipping a scotch on the patio and giggling stupidly about something. Schizophrenic for many observers perhaps, but for them it was just two parts of the explosive mental whole they formed.

Tarnasay's father Henry Evermore, a history professor and a career academic had been offered a senior posting at Cardiff University in Wales where they had extended family. He'd discussed the offer at length with Tarnasay's mother Bronwen and they decided it was too good to refuse. The family was to relocate for his four year tenure and Tarnasay's two younger siblings, Mathius and Angus would complete their high schooling there. It was a difficult time for his younger siblings who felt conflicted about the excitement of heading to Wales to be with their Welsh cousins and the leaving behind of close primary school friends, not to mention their older brother. But with their dear old Uncle Lou ever-present for all family discussions regarding the pending relocation, and his ability to nurture the part about the big move which did excite them; that of attending high school with their cousins who'd visited them regularly from Wales with their Aunty Joyce over the years, he managed as only he could, to lighten the heaviness their little hearts felt about leaving everything they'd ever known. For Tarnasay, on the otherhand, he was given an option. Initially. He could either relocate with his family or stay on and live with Uncle Lou. He was given the option because at the age of seventeen as he was beginning preparation for university and had already established strong friendships through school - which either rightly or wrongly – his parents had decided were more difficult or dangerous to sever than those of his siblings. But, that which many parents whether of comfortable means or not fail to see, was what their son as a young man had become or was in the process of becoming. They failed to see what truly mattered to him, seeing instead, only what they thought should matter. Tarnasay was torn. It was true he had made strong friendships which are with him to this day, but he adored his younger siblings and when their big, round eyes welled up before him as they listened to the adult discussion of whether their big brother would come with them, he found himself having to scurry from the room. It wasn't as if he'd never see them again but even at this age, for Tarnasay, he placed greater value on seeing those around him happy than he did on having his own plans or goals realised. Whatever they were. At this stage, he had no plans and family came easily before friends. But just as he reached his decision, it was his mother and father who, although believing they had his best interests at heart, made a life changing, cataclysmic one for him. One that would later affect him in a far greater way than he or they were to know. A decision that saw his father and him arguing in a manner out of character for both of them with Tarnasay screaming into his face, "What happened to the option?!" "Where's the fucking option dad?!" he screamed making his mum wince, swearing at him in a way he'd never done, in a way he'd never felt he needed to. They told him he was to stay with Uncle Lou. "It's the best for your future," his father argued, "You're off to university soon enough and that's what matters," his mother had added. This wasn't what mattered to Tarnasay. Family mattered. His brothers mattered. Uncle Lou could see that too. But when it came to the final decision, and the discussion became extremely heated between Tarnasay and his parents, it was Henry who had asked his brother to leave the room. Uncle Lou left shaking his head but said no more. He didn't agree with his brother and sister-in-law and although he was asked to be present when discussing the move, there was obviously an agreement between the two brothers. That if at any stage, Henry felt that it had come to an immediate family issue that fell outside of whatever input his beloved brother may offer, that whatever he had to say on the matter suddenly felt irrelevant and not inherently "his business," he was to leave. This was one of those moments. Uncle Lou accepted it. Despite Tarnasay's father having observed their closeness over the years, the natural affinity his son and brother Lou shared; one which he never felt for jealously but rather great comfort, it was still he who was Tarnasay's father. He only. There was only one person who could ever overrule him on matters such as this and Tarnasay's mother had often done so throughout their marriage, but on this occasion to Tarnasay's aching disbelief, his mother agreed with his father emphatically.

Hasta had always gathered things, and perhaps the only thing that Tarnasay would concede may be perceived as training was when he rummaged through a day's collection and threw much of it in the bin. As a young dog Hasta wasn't nearly as picky with his collection and grabbed all sorts of useless things. Hasta would watch as Tarnasay filtered his things, fretting as he witnessed his daily collection being discarded so callously. These days, three years since Uncle Lou's passing where Hasta had naturally been bequeathed to him, he found himself throwing out less and less of his findings and instead kept them inside a large cardboard box next to Hasta's sleeping mat. It seemed as though the dog had worked out what was likely to be discarded. As though his taste had become more refined. Later, when the box was full they would go for a walk and Tarnasay would deposit the items in a clothing collection bin or visit the local charity store. He'd lost count of how many times they thanked him for his generosity and he would always say, smiling at his big dog "You can thank Hasta the Hoarder here, it's his work, he finds it." But he noticed they'd never even cast an eye at Hasta panting away proudly beside him. They just smiled back at him. Nodding politely if not a tad sympathetically.

~

Finding herself in the odd situation of carrying an eclectic mix of items home at the barking bequest of Hasta, some still useful, some not so much, got Sam thinking about a short speech she heard whilst attending an impromptu press conference held by the very company she'd been investigating. At the time she'd been relocated to London and had already been on the company's trail for more than two years. The same company that was to eventually defeat her substantial powers of investigation. The company that never frayed. Never unravelled. The Pleasure Recycling Co.

Sam remembers the event was held at the height of the global 'Tarnasay' phenomenon. The young man delivered a short, very concise statement about the company's operations before enduring half an hour of questions from the media. The Pleasure Recycling Co had come under serious international scrutiny ever since they revealed that the mysterious, elusive 'Tarnasay' was the inspiration behind their organisation. But there was very little known about the European based enterprise and press conferences were rare. The young, eloquently spoken German man by the name of Rudy Einhaus was the only face of the organisation and authorities the world over who, like Sam, had been picking at the edges of its privacy cloak had found nothing. The company's operations were completely legitimate. Its financial records were detailed, taxation reports were clean and its business reputation throughout the world was sound, if not the envy of others. They couldn't even find disgruntled ex-employees to pick at, to unravel. Likewise, the young Rudy Einhaus, the only visible member of the organisation was, as they say, "Squeaky clean." He didn't even have a drink–driving charge to his name. Although there was nothing to be gained from an investigative point of view, for some reason Sam had listened to a recording of the press conference many times. It had intrigued her. Impressed her even. The young man's words were delivered with passion and meaning and they'd come across to her as oddly poetic. She remembered them clearly.

"We take it. The discarded, the forgotten, the neglected and the broken. Then we put it back together. Sometimes we re-sell it, sometimes we give it away and sometimes we let people borrow it. Exactly what is it? Well it is something of pleasure or something of purpose. It is what people bring to us, it is what they no longer want, it is what they no longer use, it is what they cannot fix, it is what they have left behind. It is many things, massive or minute, extraordinarily expensive or ridiculously cheap, extremely important or titillatingly trivial, but if it is something that can be enjoyed again – for either purpose or for pleasure – then things like it will never go to waste...at the Pleasure Recycling Co. Thank you."

In retrospect, Sam was probably lucky the case had remained open as long as it did. Although she'd spent the most part of her time investigating the company, it was not in truth the main focus of the investigation. The main focus was always the fugitive, Tarnasay. However, information about him was scant and in lieu of intelligence on his possible whereabouts and his ultimate motivations for his actions – political or otherwise, Sam had been advised to probe into the Pleasure Recycling Co. Over time, Sam had come to the conclusion that the character 'Tarnasay' was not as her seniors, and her senior's seniors – crime authority commissioners; and their seniors, the senior's senior's seniors – cabinet ministers liked to envisage, that of his being a "Dangerous anarchistic political threat." That he was, in truth, far more likely to be just as he had been originally described when he first came to media attention, "A thrill-seeking larrikin." Even with the eventuation of groups who were indeed dangerous, loosely veiling their crimes in anarchistic political rhetoric and citing Tarnasay as some kind of mentor, Sam doubted his involvement. It was true, that information she had on him was light but she had gathered enough intelligence to form a loose, speculative personality profile from his past antics and for her it just didn't seem a match for some radical, neo-political troublemaker, some kind of "Anarchistic criminal revolutionary provocateur." A description she once heard a so-called 'expert criminal profiler' use on a Sky News discussion panel when Tarnasay fervour had escalated worldwide; its equivalent in sensationalist terms to that of a high pitched scream. That particular professional opinion had caused Sam to laugh and cringe at the same time. It just wasn't his style she decided.

Apart from the personality profile Sam had formed about Tarnasay, the notes of which she'd been reading through earlier in the day as the neighbour's bizarre dog collected discarded objects around their picnic site, was other revealing information she'd uncovered. She'd also made a small but nonetheless significant finding which she hadn't exposed to her superiors. She always intended to, but at the time she felt such information needed to be supported by more intelligence, to carry more weight before she presented it. Sam had never been in the habit or felt obliged to impart every morsel of information to her superiors as she progressed a case, and they preferred it that way too. When she held a debriefing they expected to see a full spectrum of revelations, rays of insight and leads, not just one lone beam of light focusing on one lone development. Unfortunately for Sam, at this point, as revealing as she believed the information to be, she knew it was just one lone beam of insight.

The insight Sam had gained was in regard to a particular trait that the man Tarnasay demonstrated when carrying out one of his antics (oddly, Sam had noticed, as had her superiors, that she rarely referred to his actions as "crimes" or "incidents" but more often called them "antics" or "shenanigans"). This trait, Sam observed, had manifested itself as a pattern. Tarnasay's little neatly folded notes had a pattern. Over the years of investigation, Sam had discovered the notes left behind by Tarnasay, including those prior to the sensational heist of 'Ubetcha', were always accompanied by a sign off using an exclamation mark if the item was to be returned. *'Cheers! Tarnasay,'* they read. And likewise, she identified that if the exclamation mark was absent from the note, *'Cheers. Tarnasay,'* then so too was the item. Full stop. Gone. You'll never see this again.

Sam believed this particular trait was deliberate. A conscious decision and quite revealing as to his mental make-up, his psychological profile. She didn't think he did it to tease or to challenge an investigator such as herself attempting to track him down, but simply as a spontaneous decision at the time of absconding with the item. The moment he took the item, and at that moment only, she believed he would decide whether or not he was to return it, with the exception of 'Ubetcha' she conceded. This revelation had taken quite some time for her to realise as Tarnasay had always returned far more things than he'd ever taken.

Often in better condition with the exception of the high-profile shock jock's purple Ferrari, its gleaming chassis re-detailed to feature the word Bigot in large, beautifully spray–painted script.

Cruelly, Sam's eventual breakthrough came at the exact time her superiors called a halt to the investigation "For the time being" which she knew really meant "Never." The critical intelligence Sam gained only recently had come to her in the most unexpected manner. The vital information she discovered was in respect to the correct, indigenous spelling of 'Tarnasay' and it came from a greatly disliked ex-boyfriend.

Sam felt a sudden urge to run somewhere fast when she bumped into her long ago, ex-boyfriend Tom Stoltz at the showing of a mutual friend's short film at a festival. But the fact that he was the one who proceeded to impart the valuable information, albeit inadvertently during their conversation, quickly appeased her decision not to. Sam had now taken what was for her, an unorthodox decision to talk openly about the investigation she was conducting. With previous investigations she always kept matters to herself but with this particularly high-profile matter, where she was struggling to find any information, she'd decided to speak freely to anyone about it. At least until she had something that mattered. What mattered was what Tom Stoltz said.

Sam had to concentrate hard when he spoke to her less she be haunted by images of her past with him and feel the sudden compulsion to run away again. 'Focus on his top lip, focus on his top lip,' she thought to herself repeatedly to encourage concentration. Then she saw his top lip glistening with tiny freckles of sweat and curling up ever so slowly, rolling back on itself just like it used to until it formed an arrogant, condescending sneer pretending to be a smile. 'Don't focus on his top lip, don't focus on his top lip,' she then began repeating to herself. Fortunately for her, what Tom had to say carried enough weight that it held back the memories she wished to forget.

"Oh right, so you're working on tracking down that parasite called 'Tarnasay' hey. Wow. Y'know, it's a very unusual name, Tarnasay, I can honestly say I've only ever heard that name once before. It was someone I knew briefly through a team mate on my Uni basketball team. They lived together for a while," said Tom.

Sam found her eyes being drawn back to his sweaty top lip which now appeared to be stuck in a permanent sneer even when he spoke. Sam quickly shifted her eyes away from him altogether for a moment and stared into the milling festival crowd.

"Yeah, Tarnasay was his name for sure," continued Tom. "But I remember he didn't spell it like that, it's the same name though, it's pronounced the same. But his spelling was like some weird, Welsh–gypsy–shit type combination."

Sam could no longer hold back her memories of being with Tom. His nosiness. His tactlessness. His condescension. Still, on this occasion, she didn't doubt he was telling the truth and felt compelled to ask how he knew this about the spelling of this Tarnasay's name.

"I saw a letter addressed to him one day on their kitchen table."

'Ahh still the nosiness eh Tom,' thought Sam. She suddenly found her mind filling with memories of her time with him. The shit she put up with. It annoyed her to think about it, made *her* top lip sweaty. 'The turd made me wait so many times,' she remembered, waiting to be picked up for an apology dinner for forgetting to pick her up for the previous dinner. 'And how many times did that happen? How many times did I allow him to get away with that crap just because he was good looking and charming and confident? The fucker,' she thought. The worst, she remembered was when a limousine approached one night as she waited outside her apartment and she found herself getting all excited thinking he'd done something incredibly romantic by way of apology only to be let down yet again when the chauffeur explained he was unable to make it. Sam wonders whether it was the look of disappointment on her face that allowed the chauffeur driver to convince her to have dinner with him as consolation or the fact that he was even better looking than Tom. She was so disappointed at the time it was easy to say yes. 'He was funny too' she remembered, and in funny, Sam believed, you find the greatest charm of all. Not the mildly amusing, flattery-factory appeal of a simple everyday charmer like sweaty Tom here. 'That guy was hot,' Sam now remembers clearly. 'And what the fuck happened there? I remember we were playing phone tag for a while after that and trying to line up a time that suited both of us. Then nothing. Oh that's right, now I remember, I'd just started my job at CACT as a consultant and he was preparing to go abroad. We couldn't line up and then he just disappeared. Like a vanishing trick.' If she didn't know better and didn't recall their night together and the way he impacted on her, she would've sworn he was just an illusion dreamt up by the disappointment that was Tom.

"Hey I didn't fuckin' open it!" Tom said defensively as if he'd been reading her thoughts which startled Sam, drawing her back from her memories and to Tom's sweaty top lip. She looked at Tom and then quickly away to the crowd again.

"Um, do you have a pen by any chance?" she asked him.

"Why, do you want to hook up again?" replied Tom sneering harder than ever, his top lip now looking as though it was about to turn inside out.

Sam just stared at Tom blankly. He produced a pen from his jacket pocket. Sam fished an unused napkin from her bag and she asked him to write down the spelling of Tarnasay's name. Tom snorted a laugh through his nose.

"I can tell you now it wouldn't be this guy. No fuckin' way. He was just a joker. A party dude. A dumb-arse dreamer with a weird-arse-gypsy-wog name whose only motivation in life was to get fucked up. His mate, who I played basketball with, said they were *journey agents.* Idiot. I was trying to save his sorry arse from the pains of poetry through playin' some ball," Tom explained as he scribbled down the weird-arse-gypsy-wog version of Tarnasay's name.

'Sounds like my man,' thought Sam. The one thing they truly get right on TV cop shows, she believed, is that good investigators always follow a hunch. And she was definitely following this one. Earlier in the week, Sam had received an official directive that the case was now under review and that closure was imminent. The media frenzy that had once accompanied the antics of Tarnasay had dwindled both at home and abroad since he'd disappeared. Since his silhouette vanished from the front pages of tabloids, gossip magazines and even alternative media publications who had always championed his actions. At the height of the sensationalism that swept the world for a time, even Time Magazine ran a feature article on the man of mystery under the headline 'International Hedonistic Anti-hero or Outright Criminal?' But now, depending on which side of the story you'd decided to indulge, his "Shenanigans" or his "Crimes" were nowhere to be seen. His antics were no longer top of mind either in the general public or the upper echelons of bureaucracy. "Gone underground" they said. And everyone except Sam and her close international contacts whose task it had been to identify the man, had moved on. The final proof that this was indeed the case came that very night when, following the end of the film festival, Sam had rushed into work to access the Department of Foreign Affairs database. A database she knew would reveal Tarnasay's true identity and finally solve the mystery. This time the front page of newspapers the world over would herald the image of Tarnasay, every hair, every freckle, every nuance of his face would be revealed. The world would now finally know him.

~

Sam can see Hasta bounding down the hill at speed towards the picnic parties dotted out on the lush grass below. He's already put some distance between the two of them and she decides with each near twisting of her ankle on the loose gravel trail heading down, that it was pointless trying to keep up. She lunges the makeshift sack from her shoulder and sits down on a rock to rest and watch and contemplate. She observes the arrival of another round of tour buses as they weave their way towards the top where she and Hasta recently enjoyed lunch. She can see the tourist's faces staring out the windows, some appearing excited and stimulated by new surroundings, others not so much.

THAIRNEARZIE EVERMORE, DIRECTOR OF BETTERMENT, THE PLEASURE RECYCLING CO.

The sound of a small motorbike idling outside the courtyard and the clunk of the metal letterbox flap opening and closing announces the arrival of Tarnasay's mail. He opens the mailbox and sees a familiar brown envelope atop of the more common, irritating window variety usually containing bills.

For the past five years, roughly every six months, Tarnasay has received a plain brown recycled envelope addressed to him with a peculiar title, *Director of Betterment* beneath his name. Inside it is a plain white invoice receipt titled, 'For services rendered as Director of Betterment' with a handsome figure printed below and the acknowledgement that this amount has been deposited into his account. Nothing else is stated. There is no address, no company title or logo and nothing to identify its place of origin. Tarnasay was shocked when he received the first letter and spent a good amount of time studying the invoice receipt which was otherwise plain and insignificant were it not for the high quality of the paper on which it was printed. He was looking for anything that may reveal its sender. It was recycled paper but it was good stock and presented a pleasant texture to touch. But there was nothing revealing, no hidden branding or motif tucked away in the corner of the receipt. It wasn't until the next morning when Tarnasay picked up the invoice to inspect it again and held it in a position where it caught the strong mid-morning light beaming through his kitchen window that he saw it. A watermarked logo in the paper that was only visible if he held it up to light, it was a circular design which read, The Pleasure Recycling Co.

Tarnasay takes a sip of his Lowenbrau and recalls how this mystery began to unravel for him. For a time intrigue overshadowed incredulity as he speculated who was behind The Pleasure Recycling Co. A simple throw-away line that he sometimes used to describe his adventure antics and one which he'd cheekily used in a note left behind on the tyre marks of the Ferrari Testarossa he once "borrowed." But now, when recalling all that Rudy and Nicolas had told him of the company whilst residing as Lord Evermore at the Burg Katz – in particular, the startling revelation that the now powerful multinational was in fact, inspired by his beloved Uncle Lou, he had ever so gradually come to the conclusion that – if they weren't simply avid admirers of The Pleasure Recycling Co. as they proposed – they were indeed, it.

Archie Spears

It was during his short reign as the ambassador of Burg Katz and as the ebullient raconteur of the exciting, underground night spot *Archie Spears* that Tarnasay spent many an intoxicated morning discussing the current machinations of the world with passionate young Germans, disillusioned middle-aged Germans and a hybrid of other young people from around the world. Many of them young backpackers who, having completed university degrees, had set upon discovering the world before most likely heading home to establish solid corporate careers and later rearing families. But as with many a young traveller roaming through cultures whose daily lives are far removed from those of their own, there is often an awakening. They become aware of the differences between their world and their idea of comforts, and those of which they're exploring. And while there are many affected by the lack of parity between the first world and third world cultures they visit, many are equally indifferent. The indifferent moving about these places with a passive non-reaction, unwittingly performing a dismissive shoulder shrug of the privileged ignoramus. But it's those who watched the feet of their Nepalese porter – with their own feet artfully incased in five hundred dollar hiking boots – take sure-footed steps with their 60kg pack on his back and flimsy rubber thongs on his feet who glimpsed the truth about 'necessity.' Who learn about what's essential and what's not. And that's not to say that the porter himself wouldn't welcome wearing those same boots and enjoy the benefits they offer; or that the modern design, material and manufacturing process that creates them isn't worth the feet they aim to protect, but it does demonstrate what's possible without them. It may also occur to these young travellers that those who'd benefit most from such boots will most likely only ever admire them on someone else's feet. That the right shoe can often end up on the wrong foot. And so during his brief tenure as Lord Evermore of the Burg Katz, Tarnasay often found himself surrounded by the young idealistic, hedonists who through their world travel experiences had more often than not changed their view of the world. Many now expressed a strong reluctance to embark on previously envisaged corporate careers and instead intended to replace it with more travel and more hedonism or become an international care worker. But in reality, most of them would return home and take on solid, well-paid careers as previously planned. That's not to say that they didn't still harbour their idealistic dreams or wish to travel more, it was just that they found, in the meantime, they had to work. Family expectations were present for some and for others travelling through India on the back of shelf-stacker wages was possible but that's where it would end. So they'd take well-paid, demanding jobs and as time passed find themselves having to be content with reminiscing past adventures. It didn't matter who Tarnasay spoke to from around the Western world, many of them felt the same, that despite all that they were privileged to, they still felt trapped.

But then there were the others, a melting pot of people who couldn't let go of their idealism or more simply their hedonism. They didn't want to be part of "The plan" or "The machine" as some of them saw it. They just wanted to exist, unaffected, unhindered by what they perceived as society's futile expectations and restraints. And as much as was possible, many of them went to great efforts to live outside of it. They wanted out. Of course, all this "Rebelliousness" would be nothing new were it not for the fact that these people, as much as was possible, actually did it. They lived in society but not with it. They used its conveniences but didn't respect it. Some did it easily, almost hypercritically by the standards of some of their peers, absconding with family wealth and living large and free. Others were artists, writers, musicians, nouveau drug peddling hippies, anarchists, DJ nomads, gypsies, wanderers, cypherpunks, 24-hour-fucked-up-party-people and of course to the chagrin of all, criminals. They all needed money, relied on it like everyone else, but none of them respected it. It was just another guideline to better living. These were the people that Tarnasay found himself amongst in the early hours of the morning at Archie Spears, where the beats would dig lower into the floor and slow the steps of those upon it. Where many of them after solid hours of partying would gather together wearing ancient armoured masks for a ritual firing of arrows from the turret top, their targets being large prints of despised international figureheads pinned to trees in the distance. It was during these morning rituals that Tarnasay remembers sitting down for a quiet lager and a chat with Nicolas and Rudy. He remembers that despite all of those who he'd met since he arrived at St Goarhausen and began running Archie Spears, it was these two people with whom he'd felt the greatest connection.

His adventures and antics had introduced him to many people from around the world. Some were aware of who he was when introduced and those that were like-minded or kindred spirits would often share a drink and the conversations that followed would reveal much. On occasions Tarnasay would meet those who were disapproving of his antics but it was rare that he would be alone at those times. Luckily, most social situations were enjoyed with people either envious and admiring of his adventures or fascinated by them and curious as to why he took such risks. It was during such times following an afternoon exploring the Rhine River that Tarnasay probed Nicolas and Rudy for anything they knew about The Pleasure Recycling Co. They happily expanded on what they'd initially told him shortly after they'd first met. How there were now many groups and growing organisations dedicated to following his example. They explained how quickly things had escalated when news of his brazen heist travelled around the globe. As Tarnasay listened to them he thought back to exactly where he was at this time.

They told him that while he and Col had made their way to Thailand, and remained undetected, the more the world became enthralled by their story. From all sides – those who condemned it, those indifferent to it and those who celebrated it. Of course, it was those who celebrated it who caused all the problems for authorities, they explained. And as they spoke about this, it became clear to Tarnasay that by the time he and Col had re-united in Chiang Mai and set sail for New York on Mai Pen Rai with a stolen chimpanzee and a Thai reincarnation of Jimmy Hendrix in the form of Jimmy Thattiyacorn, authorities everywhere were suddenly dealing with Tarnasays' of their own. In retrospect, Tarnasay now realises that this phenomenon, this zeitgeist he'd created by accident became his greatest diversion to being caught. They weren't just after him, they were after thousands of him. He remembered seeing the occasional news report about his heist while in Thailand and could see that the hunt for him was well and truly on, but - as had been the case back in Australia - they simply had no idea who they were hunting for. He was invisible. And although in Chiang Mai, where they were indeed a little loose about their identities initially, letting it be known to a small band of like-minded people who they were, they were effectively, underground. However, it was when Tarnasay was approached by a friend of Marieke's in Chiang Mai to do an interview for a popular underground literary magazine in Europe that he sensed something was up. She didn't speak of the growing phenomenon of copycat crimes being committed the world over at that time, but the fact that he was being interviewed in a manner similar to that of a rockstar by an aspiring London-based Russian journalist told him that there were those who liked what he'd done and that he'd gained some kind of status. But, the fact that the heist was to become the catalyst for a growing movement, he had no idea. TV in Chiang Mai was never high on the agenda and he and Col were somewhat isolated from everyday news. However, they weren't naive either. They knew that simply telling anyone who they were put them at risk. People talk. Tarnasay, smartly interpreted the interview as a warning, as a reminder that he was not at all off the radar, that he should keep moving. And his recent reunion with Col at this point had proved timely. Mai Pen Rai would deliver their next move. Their next disappearing act. And no-one but them was to know where.

As the beers and beats flowed at Archie Spears, Tarnsay asked Nicolas and Rudy once again whether they believed the groups and small organisations truly had the same motivations as him. A simple pursuit of hedonism, a chance to experience materialistic luxuries usually off limits to someone like him – or whether they were simply bored anarchists or just outright criminals using it as a guise to steal. They said they didn't know much about the true motivations of other organisations but they were emphatic that the largest and fastest growing of them, The Pleasure Recycling Co, was not in it for purely financial gain. Rudy then said something that left Tarnasay speechless. He said it was his understanding that the company wasn't so much inspired by him, but rather his Uncle Lou.

Time stopped for Tarnasay. The good-looking, fresh, smiling faces of both Rudy and Nicolas hung before him like a snap shot. Uncle Lou. His beloved Uncle Lou was the real inspiration behind The Pleasure Recycling Co. He was stunned. Part of him wanted to rejoice at the thought of it right then, but another part wanted to know more. Rudy removed the scotch from Tarnasay's hand and replaced it with water. Tarnasay kept staring at the two young Germans, lost in time.

"Tarnasay, take a sip of water," said Nicolas. They knew such information, a revelation such as this would leave him spinning.

Ever since they'd mentioned TPR Co not long after he arrived Tarnasay had been nagging them to tell him more. But they had resisted for a time becoming vague whenever it was mentioned. Tarnasay however, despite being mostly distracted by living in his ancient castle and particularly after discovering the lost Picasso wasn't about to let something like this go. You don't just ignore the fact that someone has built a prominent successful young company on the back of something you've said. Of course, Nicolas and Rudy knew as much. They would never have mentioned it shortly after his arrival if they didn't want him to know about it. They would've let him discover its existence in his own time. But there were things they wanted to tell him about it, about its motivations, even if such information was only being offered to him as the observations of knowledgeable outsiders. They had big plans for TPR Co and they weren't about to tell Tarnasay that they, the two of them, were actually it. In time they would, but not now. Meanwhile, they just wanted to provide enough information to instil his faith in the organisation. They knew it was almost unfathomable that Tarnasay would ever accept on face value anything negative and misleading the international media had to say about them – but they wanted to be sure. They wanted to put the idea in his head that TPR Co was indeed worthy of his Uncle Lou.

What Rudy and Nicolas told Tarnasay about TPR Co worked. Tarnasay was secretly exalted by the positive information. In the meantime, now with his focus not so distracted by the mysterious organisation, he set about organising *The Lost Picasso Exhibition* with gusto. There was plenty of time to think about the company's operations and those behind it when he was done, meanwhile he needed to wrap up the final exercise in his epic adventure.

CHANNEL TARNASAY

Sitting in the hotel room, Tarnasay sipped his scotch heavily. Usually, he was careful not to allow his actions to affect others even when they had consented to the risk but this time he'd failed badly. He attempted to control it as much as possible, because he knew that at the core of all this, it was a selfish endeavour he'd embarked upon. Even if others didn't see it – or if they did – they must have only indulged it on the strength of his charm. That this adventure was really his. That it was about him. Him having fun. At almost any cost. And those such as Col who decided to accompany him on his adventures were doing so at their own risk. He wasn't responsible. Clearly. The fact that he decided to leave behind one of his signature notes at the Burg Katz was proof of that. Unfortunately for Ralph, Tarnasay's selfishness became apparent when he went from pretending to be Lord Evermore of the Burg Katz to actually becoming him. Ralph's pleas for him to enjoy the castle anonymously and discreetly had been ignored. More than ignored, it was as though his request had been lampooned, ridiculed. Anonymous became *Archie Spears*. Discreet, *The Lost Picasso Exhibition*. And now, as Ralph sat in a hotel room not unlike Tarnasay's but thousands of kilometres away with the rest of The Venkmann Equation frozen still before lines of cocaine, he listened to a TV report announce the "mysterious Lost Picasso Exhibition at the Burg Katz" and the "missing castle guardian Ralph Lehmann." Then came the bizarre appearance of his weeping father. He'd never seen his father cry let alone weep.

Meanwhile, as a means of distracting himself from thinking about the extremely difficult situation he placed Ralph in, and to allow himself a little space to breath and think about a possible solution, Tarnasay switched on his TV. Initially, he watched with some amusement as he caught a media report that seemed to be rehashing his criminal history back in Australia. A still shot from the past of the irate shock jock when he saw his missing Ferrari upon its return made Tarnasay laugh. 'Damn, that was a fun one,' thought Tarnasay. But then as he flicked through news station after news station he discovered the extent of the media frenzy around his latest antic. He then used his hotel room's complimentary PC and did a search of his name and discovered he was even trending on twitter, *#Tarnasay, #Cheerstarnasay!* were the two streams dedicated to him. Immediately, he noticed the mixed response to his actions, the positive, the negative and the impartially amused. He scrolled through the seemingly endless list of commentary until another news report on the TV distracted him. It was about The Burg Katz, *The Lost Picasso Exhibition* and the castle's missing guardian. 'Oh shit,' thought Tarnasay. "Fuck me, fuck me, fuck me," muttered Ralph to himself repeatedly as he rocked back and forth in his chair like an autistic child.

It seemed that the media had finally figured out how to categorise his actions. Initially, when he first came to their attention for taking someone's Ferrari before returning it unharmed (albeit re-painted) they described the act as an "antic." And even much later, when he took Ubetcha the media still had a tendency to refer to his actions in milder terms, but adding words like "audacious antics" or "crazy antics." But there were no in-depth reports about him because there were no in-depth details about him. The reports on US and English stations were almost jocular in nature, delivered by Newsreaders with a wry grin about an Australian "prankster of sorts" who had sailed across the Pacific with a chimp. Ironically, the reports were what was known in the industry as 'the dancing monkey,' throw away pieces at the end of major news bulletins alongside short 'good feeling pieces' or quirky news stories from abroad that would cap the news with the intention of leaving the viewer mildly amused. Tarnasay was mildly amused. His antics had rarely gained the attention of the international media until he'd taken Maxie B's yacht. From that point on they were on high alert for any stories regarding the "Daring Australian prankster." And although for some time the world media had, at large, considered his "stunts" innocuous and somewhat amusing, the copycat "pranksters" who idolised Tarnasay in a more aggressive and radical nature began to draw more serious attention of authorities. In turn, the media began to treat the mysterious Australian with more disdain and began calling him a "ringleader of dangerous anarchistic pranksters." Tarnasay now watched with some concern the increasing reports about groups and organisations that he supposedly had ties to. Some of whom were quite clearly not inspired by whatever philosophy he was supposed to have created but by their own motivations. Destructive, dangerous motivations. Nonetheless, Tarnasay couldn't help but laugh when barely a month had passed before reports of trouble from yet another organisation apparently inspired by him had appeared, 'The Anarchist Pranksters.'

All this attention now meant that international authorities were on the hunt for him. The problem was they had no idea who they were hunting for. And the craziest thing of all for Tarnasay, was that they were still on the lookout for Ubetcha long after she'd been re-birthed by a shady Hong Kong billionaire and he and Col were sailing the North Atlantic aboard Mai Pen Rai. In their defence though, he realised that thinking someone would, or even could, sell a superyacht was quite a remote angle and almost unthinkable. But that's exactly why he did it. He liked the unthinkable, the unlikely and the off-chance. That's where he'd been hanging out for years. It was always a powerful element within his criminal activities. And along with Franz and his wealth of contacts, sharp mind and a honed sense of intuition which these days bordered on the psychic, he figured they could pull off the almost unfathomable. It was 'almost' that was the key. Movies he'd watched over the years like Oceans Eleven explored such things through fantasy, but for Tarnasay he'd made it a reality. And only if those on the hunt for him began to expect the unexpected would they increase their chance of catching him. In the 'almost' he found trickery and the closest he ever came to a kind of magic. Authorities didn't know what he looked like, they didn't even have a computer composite of what they believed he may look like. All they knew was that he was Australian and had an unusual Christian name. So unusual that many people believed his penchant for signing off his 'borrowings' with his name may be his undoing. Certainly his name would have figured in their search for him but those engaged in determining exactly who he was never expected for a moment that it would be as simple as using his name to identify him. Experience and commonsense told them it would almost definitely be an alias. But it wasn't. Tarnasay was his real name and those who may have hoped to gain some kind of lead due to the rarity of his name would be disappointed. For the simple reason that when he wrote his name down he spelt it phonetically for the benefit of English speakers, but the exact spelling as recorded on all his personal records such as his passport, licence and medical records bore no resemblance. Many tabloids running pieces on him determined that on the basis of his Christian name alone we could be quite sure he was either of African, Asian or Spanish origin. Really narrowing things down. Such acute insight helped no one but Tarnasay who was nothing more than a heavily tanned version of white.

~

"You're fucking kidding me," said Ralph incredulous.

Tarnasay didn't think it was the best plan he'd ever had but he was never going to admit that to Ralph. What was important was that it worked. And it would work. It was just going to be "a bit of a hassle" as he explained to Ralph. Ralph tried to ignore the knowledge that for many Australians this type of comment often represented the greatest of understatements. Tarnasay's solution was to bring life to the theory that Ralph had been kidnapped. And seeing he'd left behind one of his famous notes inside the castle, the German Police would believe it was him. In fact, it wasn't a note. It was a large canvass he'd painted upon in beautiful cursive writing, *Cheers! Lord Tarnasay* it read, and he'd hung it in the grand bedroom which had been his for the six months he reigned there. Tarnasay explained to Ralph that once things around the Castle cooled down and Police presence there subsided, he needed to get into The Burg Katz, into one of the dungeons and remain there for a week before the Police would be tipped off regarding his cruel captivity in the bowels of the ancient structure. Ralph laughed loudly down the phone when he heard this.

"Sie sind verrückt, es gibt keine fucking so, wie ich bin, den zu tun," he said to Tarnasay sternly in German before realising and then repeating it in English. "You are insane. There is no fucking way I am doing that." It sounded no less disapproving in English.

"Look I'm sorry about the situation I've got you in Ralph. I fucked up. I got carried away when I found that Picasso. All I can do now is solve this with as little impact on you as possible. This is the solution. They already think I've kidnapped you, they think you're held captive somewhere, why not in the bowels of the Burg. They'll think I've just left you there." Tarnasay whipped his persuasiveness into full stride, like a galloping horse ridden into a battle once held at the ancient place he spoke of. "The alternative is you just wait out the next couple of weeks in the US, until you're eighteen, and then make a miraculous TV appearance telling your father to go and get fucked, he can deal with it, and explain why you've been living a lie for the last six months. Bear in mind, by doing this you may also risk blowing your cover in The Venkmann Equation, everyone will be asking questions, far more than the ones I've thought to cover if you head home. They'd ask about me too, why was I there, if you know me. It'd get messy."

"Jesus christ," said Ralph.

Tarnasay couldn't believe he had made such a bad misjudgment. He felt bad that he had betrayed Ralph's trust but nothing would've stopped him from opening up that beautiful ancient lump of sandstone history to the world. To allow more than a handful of privileged people to enjoy it. Nothing would've stopped him from opening one of the coolest night clubs in the Rhineland-Palatinate in *Archie Spears* at the top of it. And absolutely nothing would have stopped Tarnasay from hanging and then selling the lost Picasso and Mondrian. Even Ralph knew that. But what he should have done was stop himself writing that note, or rather, painting it. This was his miscalculation. This was why he now needed Ralph to do this and why it was time to call it quits. To head home, stop borrowing, stop pushing his luck and to end this epic adventure.

~

The next time Tarnasay heard Ralph's voice it came from the TV screen in the corner of his lounge room back home in Sydney. With the help of some friends including Nicolas and Rudy no less, Ralph had been successfully smuggled into the bowels of the Burg Katz. He knew many secret entrances to the old castle and which areas were not monitored by surveillance or security sensors. It was an uncomfortable week he spent there with little more than blankets, water, a secret stash of books, an ipod and what seemed a lifetime supply of energy bars. But it had to be convincing, Tarnasay had stressed to him, "otherwise don't bother."

"Today I turned eighteen," said Ralph Lehmann to a throng of media while shivering beneath a blanket and looking as malnourished as he ever did, "And I'm just lucky to be alive," he lied for Tarnasay.

THE ART OF BORROWING

It was Tarnasay's girlfriend of some years back, Mia, the talented graphic designer and artist, who once commented that he'd turned his borrowing compulsion into "kind of an art form." That he'd actually perfected this unusual skill to such a degree that people couldn't help but admire it. She certainly did, and that's why she went to some effort to create the tome, *The Art of Borrowing* with the idea of selling it as a quirky, cultish, uber-cool coffee table book. But Tarnasay acting as her first submission editor rejected it immediately. He played down the likelihood of there being a market for it which at the time he knew was wrong. The media had gone mad illuminating his "history of borrowing" and she would probably have made a considerable amount of money selling such a beautifully crafted book on the back of such a national frenzy. And it was a national frenzy at the time he made his most outlandish acquisition, that of a prominent radio shock-jock's purple Ferrari and it was indeed, a beautifully crafted book. Tarnasay's problem was that he simply didn't want his actions catalogued in such an obvious way. Better to let the investigators compile their own he figured. He had never been caught because – apart from his one indulgence for leaving behind handwritten notes – he wasn't too audacious, too cocky or rash. Besides, he hadn't finished yet. There was far more he wanted to borrow.

There really wasn't much Tarnasay had not borrowed. And the idea of borrowing someone's girlfriend was simply dangerous if not least sporting a "chauvinistic trait similar to that of many a trophy man" as Franz would later put it in his sometimes cryptic, poetic manner. In truth, at this point in his burgeoning career of borrowing it had less to do with borrowing per-se and more to do with his young ego and testing the limits of what he could get away with. And although it does indeed sound sinister, chauvinistic, and not to mention a little creepy, to state that, "He once borrowed someone's girlfriend," as many a person began retelling their version of this particular tale once in circulation; for Tarnasay, apart from maybe his ego at work on a subconscious level, the motivation was far more innocent.

At the time he was at University and living in a large apartment block with Franz and had noticed an attractive brunette lived a couple of floors above him. He may never have known she lived in the same apartment block had it not been that every Wednesday evening the young woman could be seen waiting outside the building dressed in fine clothes that looked destined to grace an equally fine restaurant. Tarnasay and Franz would regularly drink the early evening away from the comfort of their spacious verandah and it was here that the ever observant Tarnasay began to notice that increasingly, her boyfriend failed to pick her up.

"She gets stood up a lot," said the equally observant Franz when he noticed Tarnasay looking down to the street below where she stood waiting, staring at her shoes like a bored schoolgirl. "It's Tom Stolz she's seeing. Fuck knows why. You know that dude who briefly railroaded me into his basketball team because I helped him a bit with a fucking history essay. He came here a couple of times y'know to pick me up for training."

"Yes, I remember. Fuck knows why you were seeing him too," joked Tarnasay.

"Shut up wanker I wasn't *seeing* him. It was just unfortunate that he felt the need to repay me somehow for helping him and that came in the form of playing basketball. I fucking hate basketball."

"You hate all sport Franz. But you went along anyway so maybe you were attracted to him," said Tarnasay stirring.

"Shut the fuck up Tarnasay. I went because I'd thought it'd be rude not to. The guy's an obnoxious, over-confident, over-muscled boofhead, not my type at all."

"You can't deny he's good-looking."

"So the fuck what! Seriously - shut the fuck up now Tarnasay or I'll whip my cock out now and shove it in *your* mouth."

Tarnasay winced and fell quiet. They both sat there sipping their beers and puffing away on cheap smokes and watched as the girl checked her watch again and again, and eventually walked back into the building.

"That's pretty shit," said Franz.

The following Wednesday Tarnasay appeared on the balcony of their unit dressed dashingly in a tuxedo.

"Whoaa," said Franz. "Check it out! So where are you off to bro?"

Tarnasay just smiled and nodded his head towards the girl who again stood waiting for her again absent boyfriend Tom Stoltz.

"What the fuck?..." said Franz looking down to the street at the girl but before he could say or pry anymore Tarnasay vanished.

He then sat watching, waiting for Tarnasay to suddenly appear before the girl but instead he watched as a gleaming black, stretch limousine pulled up before her. "You're kidding..." muttered Franz from his birdlike vantage point. He watched as the passenger window slowly wound down and the girl went to it and began talking. She stood there for a while chatting and laughing. 'Ah yes, the Tarnasay charm at work,' thought Franz. Occasionally she would stand up and look around and then tilt her head over as though making the world's most difficult decision. Then Tarnasay appeared from the drivers side of the limousine smiling broadly like the lead in a toothpaste commercial and opened the twin doors of the limousine. The girl now smiling, delighted, hopped in and away they went. "Incredible," said Franz quietly as he watched the gleaming, black limousine drive away and he took a long, deep drag of his cheap cigarette.

That evening the two of them enjoyed dinner at a restaurant which at the time was beyond Tarnasay's student budget. To his surprise Tarnasay enjoyed the dinner far more than expected and he had an inkling that his impromptu date did too. Their conversation flowed and the two of them laughed easily. They connected. 'What is she doing with Tom Stolz?' he was thinking, 'She's way too smart and savvy to put up with shit like that.' Little did he know at the time she was thinking the very same thing, 'What am I doing with Tom?' she asked herself. At more than one point during the night Tarnasay felt a tad ashamed for the way he had scammed her into a date. He even considered revealing the truth at one stage but knew that this would probably just result in her dumping the remainder of her salted caramel apple cheesecake upon his head. Besides, he'd decided, attempting to appease his own sense of guilt for duping her, that as long as she was enjoying herself and wasn't spending another Wednesday night waiting on the street for no-show Tom, where was the harm.

"And entering stage right we have… wait for it… yes! Cunt No. 2!" said Franz as Tarnasay entered the flat. He was beyond pissed. Even in the early days Franz more than anyone, would get beyond pissed. He believed it briefly gave him greater clarity. The truth was it just allowed him to say what he usually never had the guts to. And Franz had the guts to say anything. Nonetheless, it was the only way he decided that he could tell his parents he was gay. To get completely obliterated one night and rock up home at 3.00am enter his parent's bedroom stumbling and bellow, "Mum and Dad – especially you Dad, guess what? I'm a poofter! Fucking deal with it." When told the next day what he'd done, he jokingly wondered for a moment whether he could just deny it and pretend they'd merely had a dream or more so, a nightmare. A shared one.

When Tarnasay heard that comment as he walked through the door he knew immediately that Franz had spent more than a few hours, and well more than a few drinks dwelling on the subject. It was also clear he'd come to the conclusion that his actions were lousy. Franz was not about to let him off as easily as he had himself and this became more evident by his next comment.

"I suppose you think you did her a favour. Whatever fucking story you made up to get her to go with you. I bet you didn't tell her the truth in the end hey Cunt No. 2?" Tarnasay didn't respond. There was no point. Franz was ruthless in this state of mind and besides in just a couple of sentences he already had him thinking again that what he'd done was indeed pretty shitty. Deceitful.

"I'm going to bed Franz," was all he said.

"Oh run-away then fucking hot shot! Mr fucking champion borrower! So you're even borrowing girlfriends now? What the fuck is all this borrowing shit about anyway?! Go on then Cuntanova! Get your beauty sleep!"

'Cuntanova, that's a new one,' thought Tarnasay. Although he'd never admit it to anyone, Franz was the only one who could cut him down, to get to him. To break his actions down to such small pieces that he couldn't put them back together again so easily. To let him know that he wasn't some kind of god.

It was Franz who'd once told him on a separate occasion that his gift, his charm, his borderline magic which "Fuck knows why – enables you to get away with what you do – but don't think for a moment just because it's endearing, fascinating and very, very amusing that it's also… special. Special cures cancer. Special is selflessness which is the polar opposite to the hedonistic fantasy you engage in golden boy. So don't fuck people over as you go about your weird business Tarnasay. Remember that. Or I'll be sure to see that you get fucked over well and truly yourself."

Franz had genuinely scared Tarnasay on the night he delivered that particular spiel. Many people make the mistake of thinking that poets and writers are always measured in manner, calm and thoughtful, too caught up in their intellectual pursuit to ever be aggressive, foul mouthed and dangerous. Franz was the talented living proof that this isn't necessarily the case. And Tarnasay had known him long enough already to know that alcohol wasn't the instigator, it certainly exacerbated it, but it wasn't the force behind his venomous, dangerous streak. He had that as a kid; a skinny little kid who even the bullies left alone. But on this particular occasion, on this particular night, Tarnasay felt a total unease with the outburst. It certainly wasn't the first time he'd taken a lashing from Franz's tongue but it was the sudden shift in mood on this occasion that worried him.

On that occasion Tarnasay remembers that only moments earlier the two of them had been laughing, dumbfounded by what they were watching on a commercial television station. The evening news that night ended featuring a montage of all his recent borrowings throughout the country. It was an impressive montage put to some good music that made the whole thing, his antics, his behaviour look cool, repetitive close-ups of his notes and police and "victims" frowning. It was like a fresh music clip for a hot new band. And the next day the network was heavily criticised for glorifying his actions but it was too late, it was already being simultaneously double clicked on YouTube by millions around the country. The two of them had been laughing at this together and when it ended Tarnasay shook his head in disbelief and looked over at Franz. It was then he saw Franz's face suddenly narrow, becoming more narrow than you would think his already narrow face would allow. It appeared almost birdlike to Tarnasay. Then the outburst came and the way he said it and the way he suddenly appeared to Tarnasay; the way his head made sharp, violent, jolting movements towards him when he spoke made it look as though he was actually trying to peck him. To puncture him with his words. If what Franz had said hadn't been so earnest in its threat, so definite, he probably would've laughed. Tarnasay was never to forget that rant which he smartly interpreted as advice.

Now on this night as he lay in bed thinking about the date, and the fact that he knew the girl had genuinely enjoyed herself and they'd made tentative plans to do it again, he founds those words coming back to him, dampening his enthusiasm and questioning the wisdom of meeting her again. Yet, what he may have lost in the form of romance at the time, he gained in the way of honing and perfecting his art. To use the skills he developed for outrageous fun, but also ever so careful not to "fuck people over" as Franz had warned.

~

Tarnasay would be the first to admit that the skills he has acquired to make his 'borrowings' are not particularly special and certainly not unique to him. It was more about patience and gall than anything else. The patience to wait, assess and plan to avoid things going wrong and the gall to block thoughts suggesting it will. He has never forgotten a trick his Uncle Lou once showed him in his early teens. He had been explaining to Tarnasay how easily people can be distracted, how little most of them pay attention and how unsure they are about how to react to something unexpected. Uncle Lou called the trick, his deception, 'The Laughing Man.'

Tarnasay remembers standing outside a cafe when his Uncle Lou explained that he was about to show him how he can obtain a free coffee merely be distracting the person serving him. Tarnasay watched as his Uncle Lou entered the cafe and immediately took on a brash, very loud, joking persona. He was acting. He was being a clown, telling jokes loudly to other customers and engaging the staff with witty banter. The material wasn't too bad Tarnasay remembers. He'd heard many of the jokes over the years when Uncle Lou came to visit, so although they weren't fresh to his ears, they still managed to make him smile. This was also why many people hearing them for the first time were now laughing out loud.

Tarnasay watched as Uncle Lou finished telling one last joke before he launched into exuberant, uproarious laughter as he was handed his coffee and continued to laugh loudly, infectiously. He took some steps backwards and the staff member who'd just served him was laughing along with him and other customers. And then Uncle Lou turned and casually headed out of the cafe all the time laughing loudly.

It was impressive. Tarnasay saw first hand the point he was trying to make. How easily people can be distracted and lose track of what they're presently doing. That is, most of the time. Unfortunately this one time, when he decided to share with Tarnasay his clever, very simple trick of deception, it backfired. Tarnasay had no doubt that the trick had worked a thousand shots of coffee before but sadly for his Uncle Lou on this occasion it didn't. Just as he walked up to Tarnasay with his boisterous laughter trailing off to a self-satisfied smile he got a shove in the back. "Hey!" said the petite but clearly feisty redhead girl who had served him in the cafe, "You didn't pay for your coffee funny man." Uncle Lou chuckled good naturedly and smile warmly at her before saying "I beg your pardon." But the slap that came next across Uncle Lou's fleshy left cheek indicated that there was to be no discussion entered into and clumsy with embarrassment he fished some gold coins from his pockets to pay the girl.

Despite Tarnasay's insistence that he understood what he was getting at, that he "got it" despite the slap, Uncle Lou set about showing Tarnasay cafe after cafe, coffee after coffee that this particular incident was extremely rare. Tarnasay doubts his Uncle felt the need to sleep for at least a week after that day. He also explained to Tarnasay later in a jittery manner, undermining somewhat the importance of what he was trying to say – which was, that such a "skill" or a "deception" should never be abused. He always paid for his coffee he said. He wasn't a shyster or a grifter. He seemed to pause at this point as if wondering himself what it was he was trying to teach him, as was Tarnasay. Sure, he simply wanted to show how people, more often than not, do not pay that much attention to what's happening around them. But why was he teaching him this and why did he think it mattered? To this day Tarnasay is still not sure of what his eccentric Uncle Lou was really trying to teach him, what the point of it was. But nonetheless he did learn a couple of things that day which although he had no idea about at the time, would one day be put to use when he began borrowing things.

It was the common vagueness of man as he goes about his business which Tarnasay came to believe his Uncle's esoteric lesson hinted at. The distraction to the slight of hand and mind. Before Tarnasay had ever borrowed an item of some note and value, he had read more than one book on infamous conmen. From a young age Tarnasay had always been a keen reader and when his Uncle Lou passed away, it was he who his Uncle decided should receive his book collection. Amongst the impressive collection of books which consisted mostly of fiction and reference materials, there was a small group of books about various successful conmen (well for a time at least) from around the world. Men who were like chameleons of society. On one level there were conmen whose sole aim was to dupe people for financial gain but on another level there were those who appeared to be doing so for an added motivation. Even when it was apparent that they had secured considerable gains from previous schemes, they would rarely pause before embarking on another. It seemed that the motivation for their actions had as much to do with personal gain as it did with reaching a certain apex of thrill. The thrill of acting, charading and convincing someone that you're someone you're not. They treated it like a game. In instances such as this, where it wasn't so clear that the motivation was purely monetary, many of the books speculated, discussed and concluded that such behaviour was the result of a sociopath's mind at work. That these individuals lacked empathy, that they held no regard for the consequences of their actions and felt equally rewarded by the buzz they received from duping victims as they did from seeing their bank account grow. It some cases the author speculated that certain individuals were a dangerous, conniving combination of narcissism and sociopathology. Their cleverness of a kind feeding what is essentially the narcissist's fragile ego, enabling them to nurture their delusions of grandeur, to attract much needed attention whilst having not the slightest feeling of remorse or responsibility for those they fooled.

Tarnasay was at once impressed and disgusted by the conmen he read about. Impressed by their creativity and ability to apply their minds to synthesis in realising their schemes but repulsed by their complete absence of conscience. He was glad he was able to see the distinction, where his fascination with their clever schemes and nimble thinking parted ways when he found himself thinking about the victims. It meant that, while he could admire their strategies on one hand, he could dismiss them as callous and self-serving on the other. It meant that, while sometime in the future he would draw upon some of the same techniques and attributes he read about, he would not do so without conscience or a thought for his victim. It meant he wasn't a sociopath. Nor was he a narcissist. There would be a crossover in his behaviour that would lead specialists within government bodies appointed to pursue him to profile him as a conman, a sociopath. But they would be wrong. Many of them allowing their preference for profiling to lead them down a path well away from where he would actually tread. Unbeknownst to them, this would prove to be their greatest challenge in their attempt to identify Tarnasay and apprehend him.

He was neither a narcissist nor a sociopath, his delusions, his impulses, his complicated messy ruses would not eventually see him unravel and exposed. He was simply a middle class guy who was prepared to take big risks to obtain and experience things that were otherwise out of his reach. They would have no idea that they were dealing with someone who, while possessing similar traits to that of the clever conman – the audacity, the recklessness – wouldn't eventually become visible purely because he cannot control his greediness, his power obsession, his need for a cruel form of excitement. It would never happen. He was not one of them. He would be doing it for something far more harmless and almost absurd. Something juvenile. He would be doing it simply for the fun of it, for curiosity's sake and to fuck with those he saw as greedy, wasteful and universally obnoxious. He would be doing it because he wasn't afraid to, because he knew how. If there was one negative mind-set behind the reason and motivation for his future behaviour it would be that he was disillusioned. Disillusioned with the way he saw the world operate on the privileged scale. The way the vast number of privileged people behaved at the expense of those not so, many of whom were quite possibly narcissists and sociopaths themselves. But it wasn't just the callousness of the privileged that brought forth his disillusionment, it was where he saw us heading as a whole. The competition. The race towards the mercurial material and the more. The More. He saw The More as a place. A place that wouldn't have been out of place in a Dr. Seuss book, *'The More is a place to which everyone strives but never arrives - because when they do, they say - Toota loo! - Having never known they were actually there.'*

And as far as he was concerned, almost everyone in the world, himself included, had arrived at The More and had kept going. It would only be to identify this disillusionment that may bring an investigator closer to establishing a profile, a mind-set, a personality which may in turn lead them closer to his movements and the type of places he may frequent and those he may socialise with. Otherwise, as long as he was always patient and well-planned, they would never catch him. He was *'A Master at the Art of Borrowing'* and they simply had no idea that's all he ever was.

Sam's Neverending Day Off (Part 5)

Sam sits on a surprisingly comfortable rock a third of the way down the hill from where she and Hasta had enjoyed their afternoon picnic. She's given up hope of Hasta waiting for her to descend so she is content to take her time, take in the view and just watch the train of tourist buses snake their way up past her. She watches as the last bus in the line slowly drives past and focuses on the illuminated digital signage broadcasting its final destination. She's some distance away but from where she sits she could swear it says: *Unauthorised clearance*. Sam finds herself reliving the moment that proved to be the ultimate catalyst for her recent life changing decision.

~

'Unauthorised clearance,' blinked rudely at her face from the computer screen. Her access had been denied. Her 'classified' security clearance had been retracted. A hand may well have come out and slapped her. It was over. She had failed. It made her almost nauseous to think that the last five years of her work, which also amounted to her life, was so immediately rendered futile. Redundant. In an instant she was made to feel that the whole thing, 'the whole bloody investigation' was in vain. It'd been a long time since she'd last experienced that feeling. Working on a case for a considerable amount of time only to see it closed by her superiors for reasons that weren't always clear. And that was when she was working within the AFP proper as an investigator and not once removed as she was now working for a private firm contracted by them. It'd been a long time because she'd been successful ever since, whether working alone or as part of a team engaged by the CACT. Luck had nothing to do with it either, it was due to instinct, talent and some serious hard work. Hours upon fluorescent lit hours stretching into normal peoples breakfast routines, morning runs and dog walks is what it'd taken. That's what it took to have an investigative record she knew was the envy of her colleagues, that and more than a few seriously damaged friendships. But now, she was experiencing it once more. And the 'Unauthorised clearance' flashing before her eyes told her far more than the immediate message it stated alarmingly. Sam recalled the sage advice one of her earliest mentors once gave her. He was a very successful, highly-respected investigator who not only taught her the many aspects of good investigation, but also how they sometimes applied to the internal mechanisms and habits of the workplace; "Good investigators always know when a case is being closed before it happens – because if you haven't seen it coming, you haven't been digging," he said. Digging around the Department of Foreign Affairs' database and getting slapped in the face was one sure sign. Sam now felt yet again – albeit many years apart, how it feels to have something that you've invested so much time and energy in suddenly taken from you. More than five years of dedicated investigative work which she now felt quite certain was about to end, and if she was right, it would end quickly. All the frowns that crowded the faces of those in charge when she'd spoken earlier of Tarnasay's escapades as possibly nothing more than "shenanigans" now seemed like a false memory. She knew that with the announcement the investigation was to cease, so too would any importance they previously had for it.

It felt absurd. She may well have spent the entire time at her desk trying to get her head around a complicated cross stitch pattern rather than trying to decipher the one that was Tarnasay. 'They really are a bunch of arseholes,' she thought. Pompous, arrogant men who were in truth, pissweak and gutless. Her seniors, her commanders, those who hold the power to make decisions with only career advancement in mind rather than the advancement of a difficult case. It seemed to her, that more and more, they based their decisions on little more than public interest. Not unlike TV executives deciding whether to cut a show based on ratings. It wouldn't matter whether there was a serial killer at large, for many of them, if the public wasn't concerned they wouldn't be either.

She had observed this increasingly. It was fast becoming more about statistics, public opinion and resource allocation than solving crimes. She'd remembered back when she actually had time to spend with a friend and they'd become addicted to *The Wire*, a television series which she had loved, her friend had asked – somewhat incredulous and doubting – whether an episode that dealt with the issue of policing by statistics to appease political pressure was in any way true. She had said no. But she'd lied a little. It wasn't as if she felt it was as ingrained within the AFP as the show implied it was within American police forces, but she knew that it was there all the same. That politics too often came into play regarding the investigative life of any one high profile case. She also wouldn't tell her friend that despite the show being nearly a decade old, it was as close to the mark as any cop show she'd ever watched, and that on more than one occasion she could've sworn she was in an episode. And just as such matters were explored in the show, she knew more often than not that the pressure which had come from those above her regarding a case, had in turn come from those above them. Senior police followed by their Commissioners often came under pressure from powerful politicians and rarely had the courage to stand up to them. There were exceptions of course, people such as her immediate boss Clayton who she knew, should he ever find himself in the position to do so, would have the conviction and the strength to stand up to the pressure they'd inevitably apply. But despite his talent in managing teams that actually solved cases, and the fact that it was always his name that appeared above the teams of successful investigations, he'd never risen to a higher rank in over a decade. It was as though he was perpetually suspended in mid-air, dangling from the mountain of career advancement in an abseiler's harness. Neither falling nor rising, but arms and legs flailing in a desperate attempt to grasp something firm and strong. Something to support his weight and allow him to ascend further. And it seemed obvious to Sam, none of his seniors would become that firm, secure hold. Most likely that's how they wanted it too. That they'd identified some time ago, he was someone who would push back when they never would, that he was "One of those guys" who'd stand firm for what he truly felt despite the consequences and this worried them. So his career had stalled, it was stagnant. And only recently had Sam noticed that it was finally beginning to wear on him. His easy going disposition, sunny even, had waned. He appeared hollow. The good cops marrow sucked clean dry. The nature of the work gets to some, Sam knew, but it was the system that was getting to him.

Sam's thoughts now returned again to her, 'I'd like to refresh your memory of my record,' email. Thinking about it made her cringe and shrink a little. She knew it had been a rash, unorthodox, desperate thing to do and wasn't surprised that her request was met with silence. She also found herself thinking again about Clayton and his final advice, "Time to move on" and how she'd agreed with him in the privacy of her mind but not in the way in which he meant it. She would move on. Move on out of the CACT and the AFP but before she did, she wanted to know if she got it right. If she had indeed uncovered the identity of Tarnasay. If her hunch about his name and its unusual spelling was correct. That Tom had finally come good for her despite him having not the slightest idea that he'd done so. So before taking what was to become her neverending day off Sam fired off an email to a close friend at the Department of Foreign Affairs who she knew would have clearance to the database to which she'd been denied. She asked her to conduct the search on the name. It wouldn't take long. She knew if she got his name, his real identity, this one thread could be pulled and picked to eventually unravel everything. She would have caught him. And when her friend delivered the information she knew would be right, it didn't matter to her whether she was there to receive the credit and patronising nods of approval from her seniors or not. She would have been proven right. That she was the best investigator they'd ever had. That they'd made a mistake, that they'd underestimated her.

Despite this major event in her life having only recently transpired, still fresh in her mind, Sam feels that she can already look upon it as something distant. Something that will always remain important but which – whether you like it or not – becomes lessened by time and by space, losing its stinging potency like a death in the family. She finds she can now look through her hefty notes, over half a decades worth of work, her life, purely as an observer. She didn't have to be analysing every detail, looking for a crucial piece of information that she may have overlooked. There was no doubt the case had fascinated her, more to the point, Tarnasay fascinated her. Now she finds she can allow herself to be entirely titillated, entertained even, by his antics without being hindered by some deeper feeling of guilt. That somehow she was being corrupted because, more than anything, she found his 'crimes' amusing. She also understood now that this was the reason behind her embarrassing habit of referring to his actions as "antics" rather than "crimes" much to the chagrin of her seniors. Unlike the many other criminals she'd investigated over the years, whether they be serial bank robbers, organised crimes bosses, conmen or insider traders, she'd never felt, or more importantly – had identified through professional analysis – that this man was just another narcissist. Sure, he stole valuable things and used them for his own enjoyment which to many people would be seen as narcissistic behaviour – an argument she acknowledged would be difficult to defend – but there was something about his behaviour that seemed to lessen the weight of his actions. Even when taking a superyacht or selling missing masterpieces. And this was reflected in the public too. For every person that identified him as a criminal there was one who saw him as an anti-hero.

Sam's instinct about the motivation for Tarnasay's behaviour, his "crimes" being more about personal thrill and high-end larrikinism than anything more sinister and self-serving was later supported by the discovery of two separate, very enlightening items on the internet. The first major discovery brought to her attention by an investigative journalist was the frenzy surrounding the sudden appearance of a bizarre posting on YouTube. It was the *Cruella – 'Man Slapping' Series* posted by someone calling themselves *Captain Swift* no less. Sam had clicked on the clip with more than a little scepticism. She had already been scouring the internet for some time. It was the mixed media reaction to his behaviour that had led her to pour through article after article about his activities, both online and in print. From mainstream media publications worldwide with their mostly hysterical reactions, to lesser known alternative media outlets that had a tendency to champion his actions. She'd even engaged the services of a media monitoring firm through her taskforce for a time. So desperate was she to find even the tiniest piece of information that revealed something about him which she may be unaware, something providing a new angle for investigation, a genuine lead. Sam went to great lengths to read anything that referenced Tarnasay. There was much to read. It seemed almost everyone had something to say about the man; whether it was a senior journalist writing for a national broadsheet in Slovenia; some bored kid in the backwaters of Ohio, America with a scrapbook blog dedicated to everything 'Tarnasay'; or a gun-toting, extreme right wing religious zealot on Twitter obsessing about shooting him on site like a hunted animal before decapitating him and posting a photo of it via the convenience of Twitpic. Whether she realised it or not, and with regard to Sam's sharp analytical mind she most likely did, everything she read went some way to forming her own opinion about him. Which in essence, almost always came down to any one person speculating about his behaviour and reaching a conclusion as to whether they thought he was good or evil. As though each person's decision on this matter was apparently a lone voice of reason amongst all the hysteria and obsessiveness, as though unlike everyone else, what they had to say about this matter came with greater clarity and clearheadedness. It was exhausting reading for Sam. If there was one thing she now found herself wishing to say to the masses as she moved through this cyber world it was: Stop it.

Eventually, after trolling through almost every means of communication for the written word, when she was close to quitting or otherwise joining a narcissistic cult herself due to her mind being warped, Sam was given the information about the YouTube posting. The media monitors had somehow missed it but the highly sensitive antennae of an investigative journalist hadn't. Sam watched the video and saw a series of different people at different locations in Asia getting slapped by a small, aggressive chimpanzee. Amongst the American, British and European accents, two Australian voices were clearly heard to cut through laughing and talking. One of them was the cameraman. She then noticed that featured throughout the montage of monkey abuse was one man in particular. He was repeatedly slapped and chased, and appeared to be a malnourished Asian man. Sam also noticed, and it was this that snared her attention and brought her investigative mind into focus, that much of the footage featuring the malnourished looking Asian man was on a large Superyacht. It wasn't Ubetcha, but it was comparable in size.

Sam showed her senior colleagues the footage. And the office erupted into furious laughter. Sam wasn't laughing with them. It annoyed her. Clearly, they were too busy being entertained to realise that what she'd expressed to them was right; that the man behind all this was not the sinister criminal mastermind they envisaged – apart from what could possibly be the mistreatment of a malnourished Asian man – there was no neo-anarchistic political threat going on here. No uber-criminal. It was just a couple of stupid Australian larrikins who got lucky.

The other revealing item Sam stumbled across later was an obscure online Poetry 'zine' compiled by a Russian exchange student living in London. It was all of twenty pages but within its small offering was literary gold. Well, for Sam anyway. *'A Master at the Art of Borrowing'* read the title of the interview which resided halfway into the zine nestled amongst what appeared at a glance to be the existentialist poetry moanings of an apparent lost generation. Initially, Sam read the interview with a disinterested mental air. She'd endured so much mindless bullshit recently she now acquired an internal editor who could identify the smell of it immediately sparing her further mental anguish.

But there was something about the tone of the interview and the supposed famous interviewee's answers that sounded right for Sam. There was a plainness married with a thoughtfulness to the respondent's answers. The questions weren't hyperbolic and nor were the answers. Sam found herself flicking back to the pages with poetry and read them more closely. They were actually quite good she realised. This wasn't the untalented attempt at fledgling poetry empire, if there exists such a thing, thought Sam. It was a genuine, humble online publication simply dedicated to sharing poetry of some substance. Suddenly Tom Stoltz's voice echoed disconcertingly in her mind, *"I can tell you now it wouldn't be this guy. No fuckin' way. He was just a joker. A party dude. A dumb arse dreamer with a weird–arse–gypsy–wog–name whose only motivation in life was to get fucked up. His mate, who I played basketball with, said they were 'journey agents.' Idiot. I was trying to save his sorry arse from the pains of poetry through playin' some ball,"* the real idiot had said. Sam's body stung from adrenalin for a fraction of a second. She went back to the interview and continued reading. The more she read, the more she realised it was genuine. The question about the man's motivations, or if there really were any, was the most intelligent speculation about the whole thing she'd come across in over two months worth of reading. From any source. Academics, criminologists and psychologists. It seemed every single person had decided there must be a major motivation behind his antics. That there was just no possibility that – more than anything else – he was just doing this for the hell of it. Just for fun. But yet here it was, in this tiny publication buried deep within the cyberworld, hidden in the shadows of far more important publications espousing the answers to everything Tarnasay, a question, which within its framing hinted at another plausible truth or at least asked for it. So what's the reason you do what you do? Are you trying to make some kind of statement as most suggest, or is it just for fun? "A bit of both," came the answer, "But definitely more of one than the other." Sam felt she knew which one. And that answer revealed more about Tarnasay than anything she'd come across in the past five years.

It didn't hint at a physical destination to head towards, but definitely a psychological one.

Sam realises that she too, had seen him as an anti-hero and she understood the reasons why completely. She is far younger than her peers, and the subversive behaviour that the younger generation in particular identified with was the result of many feeling disillusioned with the world. Their witness to the ever growing imbalance between rich and poor. The corruption of big business and governments. The gap, now a chasm, between the greedy and the giving. The philanthropist and the narcissist. And the stench of hypocrisy that reeked from within it all. She understood the attraction he held to the armchair observer watching the nightly news. That he may appear to some, particularly in Australia, as a kind of off-beat, modern day Ned Kelly type. Whether they thought his agenda was ultimately for his own benefit or represented something bigger, a man prepared to take huge risks in the face of authorities, to rebel against, to pinch society's symbols of success – the big boys' toys, as a way to lampoon them and to highlight what he sees as their misguided obsessions and shortcomings didn't really matter. To them it was just exciting to watch. Not unlike those who find themselves quietly cheering for the bank robber provided no-one got shot. "Fuck the banks," they say, "They're insured anyway." Sam could understand this way of thinking, it didn't rankle her like it did most her peers. But she also understood that you can't just have people running amok and carrying out crimes like this everywhere, undermining the law for which its sole purpose – whether it always succeeds or not – is to see society function fairly if not harmoniously. And for everyone, banks included. The reality is, Sam knew, that fear deters all but a few, and mostly the desperate, to don a balaclava and terrorise tellers for a sack full of cash. It was a rarer form of crime. And Tarnasay's crimes were even more rare again. His penchant for returning many of the luxury items he initially stole in perfect working order was unprecedented. It also helped to soften his actions in the mind of the public. For awhile at least. It was the commandeering of Ubetcha that changed things. Until this point, his international profile had been small but the successful heist of the famous superyacht brought focus upon him at an instant. He appeared outrageous. He appeared and disappeared, a criminal magician who caught the world's attention with his signature act, *The Disappearing Superyacht*. He became an overnight phenomenon that saw groups the world over, gangs of youths initially and organised crime groups later, begin to mirror his actions. But even at this point, Sam understood far better than her peers why many within society still viewed his behaviour with some amusement. She understood, particularly in parts of Europe where the youth felt entirely disempowered, how easy it was for them to embrace what some suggested he stood for – an almighty 'Fuck you' to the rich, the greedy and the corrupt. She got the argument that questioned and then dismissed unequivocally that he was the most dangerous of all criminals, of all persons on the planet: an evil man whose behaviour was "Tearing at the moral fibre of society and promoting worldwide anarchy" as cliché prone right wing CNN opinion puppets would rant and rave at the height of the 'Heistgeist.' She understood the misplaced hysteria, the hype, the need to sell news as entertainment and the need for governments worldwide to set in place strategies using propaganda to raise the level of fear so high within society at large that everyone is made to feel like a target. A target for the millions of Tarnasays now raping and pillaging the planet. The Tarnasay Army and the Revolution of Anarchy that will be marching into your garage at any moment and taking all your precious, idle shit. But despite all this, despite her understanding, and her empathy towards those falling short of criminal activity who secretly admired his antics, and even her own private amusement regarding them, Sam was always going to nail his arse if she got the right information. That was never in doubt.

Sam continues to make her way down the hill. She can see Hasta at the bottom racing around at speed across the parkland grass. The big dog marauding through upset picnickers who attempt to shoo him away but when he turns to face them they quickly turn and run away screaming. She chuckles to herself. She then found herself suddenly thinking about his owner. She now hopes to have him home before they arrived but had no way of knowing. They'd sure be missing him by now if they are. Earlier though, Sam hadn't thought that way. Then the irony of the situation suddenly occurred to her. That her first day off in years after investigating an organisation inspired by a man who supposedly 'borrowed' things and she had in fact done the very same thing. She had borrowed someone's dog. What's more, she had taken him in the exact same manner as he did. But he took things in two opposing manners, she remembers. Although his far more common trait or manner was indeed to 'borrow', the other telling manner was the opposite, it was simply to 'steal.' To take something indefinitely. Of course, no-one but Sam knew this information. And certainly not his targets. Sam now tries to recall in exactly which manner she had taken Hasta. How she had, at the spur of the moment, mimicked his trait. And why? She remembers being annoyed when she'd entered the courtyard and had seen both his water and food bowls upside down and his agitated state. She felt he'd been neglected. She felt angry at the time. The dog was clearly distressed by the neverending party at a neighbouring block of flats and most likely hungry too. Three days straight he'd been barking continually at the smashing of beer bottles in the laneway that bordered his courtyard wall. Three days straight no one had settled him down. 'Where was the owner?,' she wondered. "People like this shouldn't have dogs," she muttered to herself as she searched the courtyard for a leash. Eventually she had found one hanging in the courtyard. Its colour was faded, a washed out orange and its weave had begun to fray beneath a heavy coating of sticky spider webs. 'Jesus,' thought Sam shaking the thing clean, 'Does the poor fella not go for walks.' Later in the day, however, when she was feeling more relaxed on the picnic and witnessed his endless energy and watched his healthy, clean coat shimmying about his bulk as he ran, she saw just how fine a specimen he really was; that he was indeed well–looked after and had probably never gone hungry a day before in his life. 'So in exactly which manner had I copied this man, Tarnasay's actions?' Sam wonders, 'What decision did I make when I borrowed this dog? What was the subtle but telling difference which perhaps only I know, in the message of the note I left behind?' She can't remember. But she remembers Tarnasay had made god-like decisions. He had been – however frivolous or larrikin-like his actions may have seemed to some – making a judgement call on people. After everything that she's learnt about this man and his behaviour, earlier through professional assessment and later through personal musings, his decisions regarding people's possessions, his unbeknownst but powerful influence on others, she is now fascinated to know how had he influenced her – in exactly what manner did she decide to borrow someone's dog?

Hasta's barking brings Sam deep from within her thoughts. She can see him below at the base of the hill, he is sitting down but barking up at her, telling her to hurry up. Still clutching his bundle over her shoulder Sam finally reunites with him at the bottom of the hill. He now waits obediently for her, panting happily and lets her attach the leash again. For the first time all day, Sam notices that his energy levels are dropping ever so slightly, the relentless pull of the leash on her arm is now tolerable as they head closer to home. But there's still one detour on the way home which Hasta demands be met, and her efforts to rein him and redirect him are futile. Hasta leads Sam to the Salvation Army's recycled goods store.

Sam heaves the blanket onto the counter and proceeds to explain to the young purple and red haired girl behind it that Hasta found all this stuff and it was actually he who has brought her here. The girl doesn't even glance at Hasta, she simply looks at the bundle and Sam, and smiles politely if not a tad sympathetically.

As they leave the store, Sam notices a couple of tables with cardboard boxes full of books and decides to look through them. One catches her eye. The book is large and its spine is beautiful and on it are the curious words, *The Art of Borrowing*. Naturally, Sam is a little more than intrigued at its title and opens the impressive looking tome.

On the inside cover of the book Sam sees a personal handwritten note. Personal notes on the inside of second hands books have always fascinated her. Something about reading someone else's personal note inside a book hinted to her an entirely separate story to the one the book contained. It got her imagination going.

Apart from the dates, Sam can't decipher the terrible handwriting with the exception of one short sentence which appears before her eyes as though magnified.

'Happy Birthday Thairnearzie,' it reads.

THE COLLISION

There was a loud bang and then carnage in my bedroom. I heard men yelling aggressively, and then a hand grip the back of my neck and force my head deep into the mattress. Followed by more hands on my legs and back. Many hands. My arms were then wrenched back hard and I felt the pinch of handcuffs snap to my wrists like I was magnetised. Perhaps I am. Perhaps this was always heading my way. I was then flipped over like a rag doll. All the time there was yelling. Men yelling. Men yelling right into my face. I heard my name, "Collin Barrington! Collin Barrington!" I saw guns. Guns pointed inches away from my tired, bloodshot eyeballs. Guns that saw my pupils as targets. What a way to wake up. What a way for all the fucking fun to end.

There was little defence to be offered. I was to be given a 20 year non-parole period. If there was one good thing to come from my mother's's dementia it's that when they mentioned "Captain Swift aka Collin Barrington..." on News reports that's all she heard. She didn't hear that I'd finally been caught. That I'd stolen a famous, cocaine-laden superyacht. And sold it all. That I was the famous Tarnasay's accomplice. That I was big news in big trouble. She just smiled and clapped and laughed at the good memories that monicker represented. "The good times," as they say.

Tarnasay got away of course. Disappearing again like the fucking magic trick he is. He even sends me postcards from Germany and elsewhere in Europe. *'Cheers! Tarnasay'* they say, nothing else. Once he sent flowers. The mother fucker.

But it kind of makes sense. I was always in over my head. I was not Tarnasay. I hadn't made a career of borrowing. I was never going to be a successful career criminal like him. I wasn't careful enough or clever enough for that. Obviously. But the thing is, I still don't know how they got me in the end, I really don't. I'd learnt much from Tarnasay and I'd been so fucking careful, I just don't understand how. Even though they caught me, I'll always be more anonymous than him. My name will eventually fade in here, but his will go on forever. And to think that it's his real fucking name too. Yet I'm the one they caught. Fucking crazy shit really. They've told me nothing of course because they're still chasing him. Even my very expensive lawyer couldn't reveal what really went down. Anyway it means nothing now, it won't change anything, it's done. I'm done. Some of my sailing mates visit me here. And Franz. I see Franz quite a bit. He always brings me flowers for some reason. There are days where I wish things had been different, that I'd simply got fit and gone back to big wave surfing; if it was indeed risk and adventure that I still craved, if that was in fact the only hole in my head that needed filling. Instead, I allowed the charm and persuasiveness of Tarnasay to fill it. Allowed him to borrow my frustration and refashion it into a crazy misplaced form of daring. For me anyhow. Perhaps I'll write a memoir about it in the next 20 years. "Cheers. Stupid Cunt," I might call it.

Neatly folded little notes

Even now Tarnasay doesn't regret a thing. If in order to bring Hasta back he now had to change something of his past he wouldn't, he couldn't. It is who he is. An unorthodox adventurer, an anarchist, a prankster, a magician, a larrikin, a provocateur, a criminal, a borrower. A pleasure recycler. He is all those things.

Tarnasay pours himself a beer and looks around his large, leafy courtyard. The silence heightened by Hasta's absence. Usually, the big dog would be sitting at his feet murmuring away in dog talk trying to convince him to give him a snack, scratch his bulbous belly or take him for a walk. He has been hoping to see signs of an intruder, something that would at least allude to the reason his dog is missing, but nothing is out of order. The only thing that had been slightly askew in his neat garden courtyard was Hasta's upturned water bowl and food dish, and strangely, a small pebble placed in the middle of his BBQ table. Now the water bowl sits there full to the brim accompanied by a large, fresh bone straddling the food dish awkwardly, awaiting his return.

Tarnasay looks at the pebble in front of him and glances around the courtyard again. He then notices a small square piece of paper whipped up by a light breeze which dances in front of him before landing next to Hasta's dish. He reaches over and picks up the neatly folded piece of paper.

To the Owner.

Tarnasay stares at the words. They form a simple sentence but on this occasion appear sinister. He delays opening it. He knows all about neatly folded little notes and the kind of messages they contain. He doesn't want to read it. Something that exposes him, brings him undone. Something that serves as retribution for his antics and adventures.

Something that cuts to the core of his being, his happiness; revealing there are those who now know who he is and what truly matters to him. Something that confirms his friends' speculative notions about karma or more simply, the pushing of one's luck. A message that explains why none of his material possessions are missing but his beloved companion is. And he is so close now, so close to having everything wrapped up before heading abroad. His apartment is sold and by Monday, he and Hasta will be gone, on their way to Germany. Ralph, Nicolas and Rudy will be expecting them. Until now, he believed there was no obvious heat on him but it had been Franz who suggested he leave. To go abroad and disappear. And it was Franz who he'd engaged to investigate whether he was still under investigation long after he gone underground. Through his sources, Franz told Tarnasay that the investigation into finding him was fast closing but until then Samantha Alston, a reputable investigator with a flawless record would be stubbornly picking away at his case. "It would be best if you left for some time," Franz told Tarnasay, "To get away with it, you have to make sure you truly do," he added a little cryptically. But Tarnasay understood.

So for the next two weeks, Tarnasay had busied himself with preparations to relocate for a time to Germany. He'd arranged for Col who had also been advised to head abroad shortly afterwards to look after Hasta while he was gone. Initially, he had arranged for Col to mind Hasta for a week before deciding to extend his stay on the south coast of New South Wales where he was finalising leasing matters for a small holiday house he'd inherited from dear old Uncle Lou. The man who never ceased to surprise him. Uncle Lou had spent much time down the south coast trekking and fishing with friends particularly in the later stages of his life, but Tarnasay knew nothing of his little holiday house. He always had a penchant for surprise and the unexpected. The three Swiss bank accounts he'd set-up for Tarnasay and his siblings one Christmas was proof of that. However, the greatest surprise was the bequeathing of his secret south coast hideaway to Tarnasay who was nothing less than the son he never had. He'll never forget the day he was contacted by the solicitor handling Uncle Lou's will and testimony and given the key. He entered the humble coastal shack that had been lovingly renovated and wandered through it before arriving at the kitchen where the faintest smell of his Uncle's pipe still lingered. He remembers it was spotlessly clean and his attention was immediately drawn to small note on the kitchen table. He walked over to the spindly, 1970's linoleum covered table and looked down at the note. The letters were large and written with a thick marker pen as if to ensure they would – which they indeed have – become forever imprinted in the recipient's mind. *Cheers! Uncle Lou,* it had read. He'd never cried like that as a man before, weeping uncontrollably like an inconsolable, over-tired child. It hurt too much. That this patient, generous man who had become his father figure, who lovingly allowed Tarnasay to *borrow him* as a father, caring for him as he entered adulthood and shaping him in so many ways (and many others as it has turned out) had truly gone. The supposedly non-handy man who went on to become a great one, simply because he hated the sight of things going to waste. The man who was happy to be seen tearing around the streets on a bike three times too small for him chased by a group of euphorically screaming kids. The man who fixed things for free simply because he liked to see them put back to purpose. The man who gave so much more than he ever took. The man who was to never know that he was the true inspiration behind the phenomenon that was to become the hugely successful and now highly-respected, philanthropically–minded international conglomerate, *The Pleasure Recycling Co.*

Tarnasay had never spoken of his high profile antics to his Uncle which had taken place while he and Franz shared an apartment together when at University. His Uncle Lou only ever playfully probed him once about it too, "Not often you hear your name – in fact, I think you're the only person I know with that name. Perhaps when visiting your father in Wales I met someone...anyway, he's quite the trickster *this* Tarnasay isn't he? I notice it's spelt differently to you but the pronunciation is practically identical. Well, the way it's pronounced here anyway." "Yeah, I know. I was bit stunned too," was all Tarnasay said in response. He never elaborated because although he was happy enough for his Uncle to surmise it was him, he just didn't want to involve him. He didn't want to discuss it. He visited him often and he simply didn't want this matter to always be the focus of discussion, the main topic. Which he knew it would be. Because while his Uncle may have privately delighted in his daring antics he would also have worried about him getting caught, and if he discussed it openly with him, involved him, the worry would only grow. It was easier if he just kept it as his thing. So having noted the matter wasn't up for discussion, Uncle Lou simply took to a loosely cloaked way of imparting his wisdom and concerns regarding the "Cheeky Tarnasay" in the news as he called him, with the other one that visited him as his devoted nephew.

Tarnasay had rung Col and told him he would be staying on for a few more days. It had proven far easier to sell his own home than it was to leave his Uncle Lou's coastal retreat. But shortly afterwards and unbeknownst to Tarnasay, Col was involved in a boating accident that saw him hospitalised. Col had also made plans for his own farewell and had been fishing and waterskiing with a group of old friends from his yacht club when their speed boat collided with another. Two women within the group had been hospitalised with serious fractures and Col had suffered heavy concussion. For four days he was under observation and treatment. For four days he was in and out of consciousness, in oblivion. For four days Hasta was on his own. Hungry and increasingly agitated by the revellers smashing bottles against his courtyard wall, his barking perpetuated the situation and the passersby would stir him up some more. When Tarnasay arrived home and noticed that Hasta wasn't there he wasn't concerned, he simply assumed that he was with Col. The marathon party which had continued intermittently for the past four days getting louder and more raucous at night had all but ended and the neighbourhood was almost back to its usual quiet self. Now the only music to be heard is the muted beat of deep house music emanating from the previously full-on party house. His courtyard is the same tranquil sanctuary it's always been. He is oblivious to the revelry that had been and also the smashed beer bottles lining the opposite side of his courtyard wall like remains from a hail storm. It was only earlier when he'd noticed that Hasta's large water bowl was very low and piled full of leaves and his leash that is never used was missing, that he'd grown a little concerned. Hasta is so well trained and extremely obedient that Tarnasay hadn't used that leash since he was a pup. He knew too, that Col who'd looked after Hasta numerous times, and even taken the big dog out with him fishing on occasions had never used the leash either. At first, he'd wondered if he was just being paranoid following Franz's assessment, but there was something about the bowl, the leash and one other telling thing. The leaf build up in his courtyard. Col would never allow that to happen. He was a neat freak. Tarnasay can recall on more than one occasion when Col was coming around for a BBQ or a few drinks and arrived before he was home, he'd find the big bloke hard at it sweeping up his courtyard. He just couldn't help himself.

Tarnasay now looks at his courtyard that is partially umbrellared by massive plane trees which line the laneway outside and it looks like an oversized compost. He knows only too well how long it takes for leaves to build up like that at this time of year. Col hasn't been here for days, he concludes.

Tarnasay takes a deep breath and opens the note.

I borrowed your dog.
  Cheers! Sam.

The Pleasure of Recycling Co.